ENGINEERING HOME

A. AMERICAN

Engineering Home

Copyright © 2022 by Angery American Enterprises Inc. All rights reserved. First Edition: March, 2022.

All rights reserved. Except as permitted under the U.S. Copyright Act of 1976, no part of this publication may be reproduced, distributed or transmitted in any form or by any means, or stored in a database or retrieval system, without prior written permission of Angery American Enterprises Inc.

This is a work of fiction. Names, characters, places, and incidents either are the product of the author's imagination or are used fictitiously, and any resemblance to locales, events, business establishments, or actual persons—living or dead—is entirely coincidental.

Cover Design by Brad Harris.

Formatting by Disgruntled Dystopian Publications.

ACKNOWLEDGMENTS

I know this book has been a long time in coming. Four years is a long time, and I'm so happy it's finally complete! I promise there won't be such delays any longer. More books will be out this year.

I want to give a special thank you to Kim Piner for supporting the projects I'm working on. Kim is a great person and her husband, Audie, from what Kim has told me, was a great man.

In memory of Audie Piner May 15, 1963—June 12, 2018

I also want to thank some other folks—the Frazier boys of Starks, Louisiana. Johnsy, thank you for letting us intrude into your piece of heaven on the river. I cannot thank you all enough. Blaine, Shane, Hank, and Bean, you guys are generous to a fault and a hell of a lot of fun to hang out with; thank you.

Lastly, I want to thank Big Kev and Bridgit. It was a phone call between me and you that opened the door for us to come out to Starks in the first place; thank you, my friend. You two are dear to our hearts, as are all our Louisiana family

CHAPTER 1

Mom and Dad's arrival at the house wasn't the only one. There was another arrival that we all were thankful to see finally. It's funny the things you begin to notice when you're paying attention. Our world slowing down forced everyone to slow down as well. It wasn't a bad change, quite the opposite; it was a much-needed change. And it was because of this forced leisurely pace I noticed the dry crispness of the air. Fall was coming.

Several things were pointing to it. First, the grass was slowing its growth. In the Before, this was always my best cue. Second, I knew the season was changing when I could go from mowing the yard every weekend to once or twice a month. Finally, the days begin to feel a little different, the humidity finally releases its soggy grasp, and it can be downright pleasant outside. The temperature may still be in the high eighties, but relief is on its way.

And the change came at the right time. With Mom and Dad here now and the power restored to the community, there was a lot of work to do. We had to find Mom and Dad a house, and we had to work on the places with power issues. The power coming back on had brought to light a myriad of problems, air-conditioning systems among the leaders.

But that could all wait. There was time. Right now, I was focusing on Mom and Dad. They slept in Taylor's room the first night. She happily offered up her bed for them. The following day, they slept in, and I left them to get some rest. I was up early as usual and padded around the house barefoot to not make much noise. I enjoyed my mornings to myself. It was quiet, and I could think. It was the best part of my day. The rest was pretty much like a firehose to the face.

I carried my morning glass of tea out to the porch and sat down. The porch light was on, and I looked up at it for a long time. We all had power again but had no idea how long it would last. But I would enjoy it while it did. I was about to do something I hadn't done in a long time. I was going to take a hot shower. Just the thought of it brought a smile to my face. I scratched Meathead's back once more with my foot before getting up and heading for the bathroom.

Heaven, the hot water pouring over my head was pure heaven. With my eyes closed, I let it cascade over me, just taking it all in and soaking up the hot water literally. But while the water ran over me, I couldn't help but think of everything that needed to be done. How many wells worked? How many pumps would we have to pull and replace? Could we even find the pumps? What other unforeseen problems awaited us? And that's just here. Folks in town were sure to need help as well.

There was always something to be done. I smiled as I ran my hand through my hair at the thought of *free time.* Free time was a figment of the developed world's imagination we'd once lived. Now you had to work, literally, for every bite of food and drink of water, for fuel to cook and clean. The list was endless. So, I turned the water off, very reluctantly, and got out and dressed. I wasn't in a hurry and put on a pair of shorts and a t-shirt.

Wandering back out to the kitchen, I poured another glass of tea. I was about to go out of the backdoor when I heard a knock at the front. Looking at my watch, I moaned; it wasn't even seven AM yet. Opening the door, Sarge stared back at me.

He looked me up and down and asked, "You go out in public like that?"

Taking a sip of tea before answering, I replied, "You're standing on my porch, and I'm in my house."

"Oh, yeah, well, dress like a grown-up and come with me."

"Why? What's up?"

"Why are you still standing there? Get some damn clothes on."

With a grunt, I shut the door in his face and headed for the bedroom. Mel stirred as I came in and asked, "What's going on?"

"I don't know. The old man's at the door." I replied as I pulled a pair of pants on.

"What time is it?" She asked from under the blanket.

"It's early. Go back to sleep."

"Where are you going?"

Sitting down to pull my boots on, I replied, "I have no idea. Probably just going to follow a senile old fart around." And reached back and patted her ass.

"Be careful," she replied as she pulled the blanket up a little further over her head. I pulled it back down, and she squinted against the faint light coming into the room as I leaned over and kissed her cheek.

When I opened the door, Sarge looked at his watch. "Hurry up; the whole world is waiting on you."

With my plate carrier in one hand and my rifle in the other, I closed the door behind me and asked, "What the hell is up?"

"Dalton found something you need to see."

That got my attention. As I pulled the rig over my head, I asked, "What?"

"Stop beating your gums, and I'll show you."

I held my hand out with the body armor on for him to lead the way. As we walked, Sarge began talking. "He saw them last night when they came in but decided not to do anything. He wanted to see what they were up to."

As we headed towards the bunker, I asked, "Wait, what? There were people in here last night?"

Sarge nodded. "Two."

"Why the hell didn't we grab them?"

"Calm down, keep yer britches on. Gulliver kept an eye on them to see what the hell they were up to."

Irritated, I asked, "And? What the hell were they doing?"

"They were monkeying around with the fuel tanker. But they didn't get any fuel or anything."

As we talked, I saw Dalton step out into the road. He was standing at the intersection where the bunker sat. He didn't look very concerned, and it confused me.

"Top of the morning, lads!" Dalton greeted us.

"What's up? The old man here says you saw a couple of people poking around and didn't stop them?" I asked.

He nodded with no indication of concern whatsoever. "Indeed. Follow me," he said as he spun on his heels.

We followed him over to the tanker. He stopped a little short and stood staring at the ground. Sarge and I stood to either side of him, following his eyes to where he was looking. Two sets of footprints were apparent in the sand of the road.

"What the hell did they do?" I asked as I looked at the tanker, looking for signs of tampering.

"They just looked at it. Poked around for a minute. Then they whispered to one another and left," Dalton replied.

"How did they get in here?" I asked.

Sarge pointed down the road. "Tracks run that way." Then he looked at Dalton and asked, "Did you follow them out?"

Dalton nodded. "I did. They go out to the south here, onto the ranch."

What we called the ranch was a forty-acre parcel that once had been a hayfield. The owners took good care of the field, cutting and rolling it up to sell. "Then they turn east and go into the reserve. They used the reserve to go around to the north-west where they got on motorcycles."

"You tracked them already?" I asked.

"I followed them out." His reply troubled me, and he saw it. "Don't worry; they didn't see me. I kept my distance."

"Ok. So, these guys came in, looked around, took nothing, and left."

"They took something," Sarge replied, "knowledge. They know we have a nearly full fuel tank here. You remember that little incident down on nineteen at forty?"

I slowly nodded. "Yeah, Mike crushed the bike."

Sarge nodded. "And they have a truck, a truck that runs on diesel."

"So, you think they're after the fuel?" I asked, more thinking out loud to myself than anything else.

"Ya fucking think, Einstein?"

Rolling my eyes, I replied, "It was a rhetorical question." Then it was my turn to be a dick. "That's a big word; you need a dictionary?"

"I know it's hard for you, but, for just a minute, can you put your stupid away, so we can talk like adults?" Sarge replied.

Dalton laughed. "Ha! You two? Adults?" With his hand on his belly, he laughed uproariously.

Cutting his eyes at Dalton, Sarge replied, "That'll be enough out of you, Gulliver."

"So, what do you think? They coming back?" I asked.

"I doubt it. I think they came in here looking for the fuel. Of course, now they know it's here, and they'll probably try and make a play for it," Sarge said.

"That's what I'm afraid of. What bothers me even more is that they aren't stupid. Taking that long circuitous route means they have some tactical common sense," I replied.

"We should double the guard at night for a while," Dalton replied.

"I think we should put everyone on alert, to a degree. We don't know how many people they have," I replied. "They're pretty smart.; took the longest possible route to get in here. They think they got in and out without being seen."

"We can use that to our advantage," Dalton said.

"We could lay up an ambush out there where they cut through the reserve; try and catch them coming back in," I replied.

"If they come that way. While they did try and be sneaky about it, they came in and out on the same track. They're not that smart," Dalton replied.

The old man rubbed his chin. "True. I wouldn't, would you?" He asked, looking at Dalton, who shook his head. "I think they'll have to come back with the truck. They'll need a way to haul the fuel. Trying to come tear assing in here on motorcycles to try and steal fuel isn't a very good plan. I think if they come, they'll come in force and try to fight their way in."

"Or," I interrupted, "they could just ask for some."

Sarge scoffed, "Get yer head outta yer ass."

"Think about it. They got in here and know we have the fuel. They know who we are and what we have. Would you want to try and kick the door in on this place? I wouldn't. Not at first, at least. I'd roll up and knock on it, see if anyone answers. Ask to trade for it. If that didn't work, then move to desperate measures."

Sarge took his hat off and scratched at his gray head. "That makes sense," cutting his eyes at me, and he added, "as much as it pains me to admit it. Let's double the guard for now. I'll tell Wallner, and he'll handle it. Let's have everyone keep a shootin' iron handy for the time being too."

"Good," I replied. "Now that that's settled, Miss Kay got any breakfast on?"

"Of course, she does!" Sarge barked. "Unlike some people around here, she does her job!"

I pointed at Dalton, "He's talking about you, you know."

Dalton slapped his belly, "Either way, I gotta eat. I'm starving."

We walked down to Danny's house. Sarge said he'd get with Wallner later to discuss the changes to the guard. As we passed under the shade of the trees hanging over the road, I commented, "You guys feel that? The change in the air?"

Sarge looked up. All he could see was the canopy of the oaks above us and replied, "Yep. About damn time too. It's been hotter than the Devil's nut sack for far too long."

"I'm looking forward to having a fire in the fireplace," I replied.

"Hold yer horses there dipshit, let's just enjoy some cooler weather before we go getting into fireplace cold," Sarge replied.

"Old people don't like cold weather," Dalton added.

Sarge cut his gaze onto the big man, giving him the stink eye. Dalton shrugged, "Just sayin' is all."

"Yeah, well, you best be sayin' it about someone else, Gulliver."

"Just an observation," Dalton replied as he opened his stride, putting a little distance between him and the old man. "Makes 'em grumpy."

Surprisingly Sarge didn't go after him. He just grunted, "You just hope you look this good when you're my age."

The house was crowded when we got there. Dad was sitting on the porch with a cup of coffee. Sarge called out, "How's the coffee, Butch?"

"Best I've ever had. But then, every cup I've had since I got here has been the best."

"That's what I think of every cup, too," Sarge replied with a smile.

Dalton nodded as he bolted up the steps, "There any grub left?"

Dad stabbed a thumb over his shoulder, "There's more food in there than I've seen in one place for a very long time."

I dropped into a chair beside him as Dalton and Sarge went into the house. It was quiet out, and we sat looking at the yard for a long time. Dad finally broke the silence. "This is amazing. I have to admit, I wasn't sure about coming here. But this," he held his hands up in a general gesture, "this is really hard even to believe."

"I chalk it up to dumb luck. A lot of things happened that all led us here."

He shook his head. "You walked all the way here from Tallahassee?"

I nodded. "Yeah. Took about a month. It sucked. I damn sure don't ever want to do it again."

"Hell, I guess not!"

"But I'm thrilled you two are here now," I replied. Then I looked over at Dad, "I should have got there sooner. And I'm sorry."

Dad visibly jolted. He leaned back in his chair and replied with complete sincerity, "You don't owe me or anyone else a damn apology! You had to take care of Mel and the girls. Hell, what you did to get back to them was a feat in itself. Then what you've done here, all these people. It's beyond imagination."

"I appreciate it. Means a lot to me."

"What you've accomplished, what you have here, people would kill to have. I know it's been a lot of arduous work, but it really is something."

I shuffled my feet, uncomfortable at the thought of those that had tried to kill for it. "You're right about that. Plenty of people have died for this. And, sadly, the killing isn't done. We had some people sneaked in here last night."

Dad looked surprised. "How'd you know?"

"Dalton, that giant that just walked by, he saw them last night. He watched them and tracked them back to where they came in from."

"Why didn't he do something?"

"We had that very conversation just a minute ago. He said they didn't do anything; just monkeyed around the fuel truck a bit. So we figure they're looking for fuel for a truck. We ran into this little group once; they have an old deuce and half."

Sipping from his cup, Dad replied, "That would be a good reason to be looking for fuel."

"It's damn sure a rare commodity today."

Dad looked down the road in the direction of where the tanker sat. "How'd you guys get that tanker of fuel?"

"We took a trip up to Eglin Air Force Base. The old man, Linus, has connections there and they supplied us. We brought back all kinds of supplies, medicine, clothes, and all kinds of stuff. The fuel was part of that."

Dad sat shaking his head in thought for a long moment. "So, the Army is out helping? We never saw any help."

"I wouldn't say they're out helping. We went to them for assistance. Linus was made a Colonel," looking at him, I smiled, "that really pissed him off."

"He seems like the kinda fella that would get pissed by something like that. I had a First Sargent in Vietnam like him."

"He's a pain in the ass, but I like him. Once you get used to his way, he's actually fun to have around. And there's no one I'd rather have beside me in a fight than him. Well, him and some of the others here. Everyone here can handle a weapon. This place would be a hard nut to crack. Hell, we've taken down harder places."

We sat quietly for a little while, just enjoying the cool morning air. Then Dad asked, "What's on the agenda for today?"

"Well, I guess we need to find you guys a house to live in."

"What about that one on the other side of you?" Dad asked, pointing in the general direction.

"That could work. Let's walk over there and look at it."

Before the power was turned on anywhere, we would go around to each structure and turn off the main breakers. You never know what could happen, what may have been left on or running in a house, so it only made sense to make sure everything was off. Dad and I went through the house. I'd been in it several times before, but this time we weren't just looking for stuff we could use, but at the overall condition of the place.

"It's a big place. We don't' really need this much space," Dad said.

"It is big. But, what the hell. Not like you have to worry about a big power bill," I replied with a smile.

"I reckon not," Dad replied as he looked around. "It's kind of weird, though. Being in someone else's house."

"It ain't someone else's house. It's yours now."

"I guess so. Let's go get mom and see what she thinks of it." Dad replied.

"Let's make sure the power works first," I said as I headed back towards the laundry room where the panel was mounted.

Much to our relief, the power flicked on when I clicked the breaker. We went through the house testing things to ensure all was well and found that the AC wasn't working. Cooling wasn't an issue now, but the heat soon would be. The only other thing we found was that the fridge didn't work either. That was a disgusting event because I pulled the door open without thinking and was hit in the face with a putrid smell that seemed to have a physical presence. It felt as though it settled on my skin, and I couldn't wipe it away.

Coughing and gagging, as Dad laughed at me, I said, "What the fuck. Why'd I do that?"

Still laughing, Dad asked, "Why in the world did you open that thing? After this long, what did you think would be inside it."

"From the momentary glimpse I got, it appears to be a really fucked up science experiment. How can a fridge with no food grow shit like that?"

"We don't need a fridge anyway. You guys all eat together over at Danny's, right?" I nodded in reply, and Dad added, "Then we'll just haul that thing out of here. We don't have anything to put in it anyway."

"Good idea," I managed as I gagged again. "I'll look at the AC and see if I can sort out what's going on with that."

"No rush. We don't need it right now," Dad replied as he stepped into the bathroom off the hallway. I heard the toilet flush, and he came back out smiling, "That'll make the Momma happy."

"A flushing shitter is a wonderful thing."

"It's what separates us from the savages," Dad replied.

We walked back over to Danny's place so he could bring Mom over to show her their new home. I stopped on the porch, where several people stood gathered up, and asked what was going on.

"We're just going to take a ride," Ian replied as he secured his plate carrier.

I looked around. Ian was there with Jamie, Jess, Doc, Perez, and Lee Ann. "Just bored, or out flying the flag?"

"Both," Jess replied from where she sat on the porch beside Doc.

"What are you guys taking?"

"The old man's Hummer," Doc replied.

"That's gonna be crowded," I said.

"We'll manage," Jess said as she pressed in close to Doc.

It made me smile to see them. Their relationship had been slow in the making and was still taking time to mature, which was good. Because if it did turn into something, I knew it would last. Just the thought of anyone finding happiness in the current situation was a reason to be celebrated.

I looked at Lee Ann and asked, "You tell your mom what you're up to?"

She nodded, "Yeah. She knows."

I looked at the Hummer sitting in the driveway. A SAW jutted out the turret. "Looks like your guys have it under control. You have radios?" Both Jamie and Perez held one up, and I nodded. "Y'all be careful." I needed some breakfast.

As was the norm, the house was full of people. Danny had a fire going in the fireplace, probably not needed, but it did make the place feel cozy even if it was a little warm. Mel spotted me as soon as I came in and asked, "You hungry?"

"You know this! Man!"

"Well, take a seat, and we'll get you fixed up," Kay said.

I slid into a stool at the kitchen bar, and Mel pushed a bowl in front of me. "Hot damn!" I said, "biscuits and gravy!"

"And it's so good too!" Little Bit shouted from the table where she sat with her bowl.

Dad managed to get Mom to leave the kitchen as I ate, which was no small feat. I guess being back in a functional kitchen with running water and the like excited her. But then, I would imagine she was probably more excited about the working toilets than anything. As they went out the door, I heard the Hummer startup.

"You know Lee Ann is with them?" I asked Mel, gesturing with my head in the direction of the truck.

"Yeah. She said she wanted to go. She's getting bored."

Sarge came in from the back porch with Jace and Edie, clinging to a leg. He held his coffee cup over his head as he made exaggerated strides with the little kids hanging on and squealing. Taylor intercepted them in the dining room, reached down, and grabbed Edie under her arms.

"Alright. That's enough, you two monsters. Let's go." She said as she tried to pull the little girl away.

She held on for dear life, and it wasn't until Sarge reached down and ruffled her hair and said, "Alright, you two. That's enough for now. Old men can only take so much playing," that she relented.

Taylor finally got the kids' attention directed somewhere else, and Sarge could refill his cup. When he turned to the counter where I was sitting, I asked, "You have a radio on you?"

Taking a sip of coffee, he reached behind his back and pulled one out. Then, holding it up, he replied, "Right here. Where's yours?"

"I'll go get it. I didn't know anyone was going to town today."

"You do now. What's your next excuse?"

Pretending to be deep in thought for a moment, I said, "Probably that I broke my radio over some old asshole's head."

"You shouldn't talk about your Daddy like that." Although you gotta admit, the old bastard was quick.

Finishing my breakfast, I carried the bowl to the sink and rinsed it out. Mel asked, "What are you doing today?"

"We're going to take mom over to see the house on the other side of us. I think it'll be good for them. We've already checked it out, and it's in pretty good condition."

"That'd be nice, having them right next door."

"That's what I thought," I replied.

"Hey, momma!" Dad called out. He'd referred to her as momma for as long as I could remember. When I was little, I remember being in an Oshman's sporting goods store in a mall. You know, back in the day when you could still go to the mall and buy a gun. Anyway, we looked for her and my sister and couldn't find them. So he stood in the middle of the store and shouted, *momma! Momma!* She came running, embarrassed at the display. But it worked.

It was second nature to her now, and she simply looked up when he called. "Come on, want to show you our new house," he said.

As we walked over to the house, she commented on how things worked around our little community.

"I can't believe you have so much. Running water, more food than I could've imagined. Kay is a sweetheart."

"It's been a lot of work, and a lot of things have happened to allow this to be," I replied.

"Where did you find Kay?" She asked.

"She was in a FEMA camp that we took down. So her and a couple of the other women and even one of the DHS guards came here."

Dad looked at me with utter shock. "You took down a FEMA camp?"

"Yeah. It wasn't what they were advertised to be. It's not like we wanted to. It just had to be done, and there was no one else to do it."

"What happened to all the people?" Mom asked.

"Some of them are probably still there. It was a very nice camp; they were just doing some horrible stuff there. The guards that survived the assault were sent to a detention center in Frostproof. But they never made it. Someone ambushed the convoy, and some soldiers were killed."

"Where'd they go?" Dad asked.

I shrugged, "No idea. We haven't seen them."

"Hard to imagine you overthrew a camp like that," mom said.

Now I laughed, "We've done a hell of a lot more than that. We took out a DHS base and a Russian forward deployment point. Granted, we had some help from the Air Force on that one."

"The Air Force?" Dad asked.

"Oh yeah. The chair force is still around. Just operating in a minimal capacity." He seemed to dwell on the answer.

"This is a huge house," Mom said as we walked up onto the porch.

"It is," I admitted. "But it'd be nice to have you guys next door, and the place is in pretty good shape."

Opening the door, I stepped inside. Mom followed me in and took a long look around. Then, after a long minute, she asked,

"Dave and his wife. They were older and didn't have any kids at home. They went to the camp but weren't there when we changed management."

Dad snorted, "Changed management. That's one way to put it."

Mom wandered into the kitchen and tried the faucet. It coughed and spat, and in a moment, water began to flow, and she shut it off.

"Toilets work too," Dad offered.

"That's all I care about, honestly. If I don't ever have to use a five-gallon bucket again, I'll be just fine."

She reached for the door to the fridge, and I nearly broke my legs trying to get to her as I shouted, "No, no, no, don't open that!"

"We'll have to get rid of that. It doesn't work," Dad said.

Mom wrinkled her nose, understanding the implication. "We don't need it anyway."

"What do you think?" I asked.

She took a long look around the house before replying. "It's nice. But it feels weird being in someone else's home."

"It's not someone else's. It's yours if you want it. We can take out anything you don't want."

She walked across the living room and into the master bedroom. After inspecting both the bedroom and the bathroom, she came back out. "I need to do some cleaning. Wash the linens and things, but I think it'll work. I just can't get over the feeling of being in someone else's house. There's still clothes in the closet."

"At this point, I seriously doubt they're coming back," I replied.

Mom looked a little uncomfortable. She held her arms close to her side as she looked around the place. "It still feels a little strange."

"Look at this way. Some of the clothes might fit. And we sure don't have much right now," Dad replied.

I hadn't thought of that. They didn't bring much with them. I looked down at dad's feet and saw his shoes had holes in them. Mom's looked a little better, but they were pretty worn as well.

"I think that's a good idea," I chimed in. "Go through the clothes and stuff and see if you can use any of it. We have more as well." Then, looking at Dad, I said, "We also have a huge pile of boots."

He cocked his head and asked, "Where'd you get them?"

I shrugged, "Some are worn, some are new. I'm sure we have a new pair that will fit you."

He caught onto my deflection and said, "I'd like a new pair of boots. Didn't think I'd see anything like it in my lifetime."

"What about cleaning stuff?" Mom asked.

"That, we will have to get a little creative about. But we do have some stuff. For example, we make soap and also vinegar."

"Better than nothing," she replied and then looked around and asked, more to herself than to either Dad or I, "Wonder if this place has a vacuum?"

I knew then she'd be alright and said, "Come over to Danny's when you need the cleaning stuff. I'll leave you two to get things sorted out here."

Dad nodded, "We've got plenty to do for now."

Perez sat in the web seat of the Hummer's turret, smoking, of course. Jamie drove; poor Ian would probably never see the steering wheel of another vehicle and rode shotgun. Jess, Doc, and Lee Ann all crammed into the back. They'd left the market in Altoona where there was little more than the usual trade going on and were headed into Umatilla to check on things there. As they passed a two-story brick house just outside of town, a rifle shot cracked close overhead.

Perez nearly choked on his cigarette as he ducked the round, and Jamie jerked the wheel. Getting back up into the turret, another shot cracked close by, and Perez saw movement by the house. He swung the SAW towards the house and opened fire in long, tearing bursts. Several people scrambled around the brick two-story as the bullets ripped into it, sending chips of brick, wood, and glass raining down on them.

Doc was sitting on the driver's side in the back and had to lean across the two girls to see the house. What he saw shocked him, and he started beating on Perez's leg and yelling, "Ceasefire! Ceasefire!" Then he hit the back of Jamie's seat and shouted for her to stop. Perez let up as the truck skidded to a stop in the middle of the road. Doc was immediately out and running towards the house.

Another shot rang out, and Doc held his hands up, screaming, "Cease fire!" As loud as he could. The scene went quiet, except for a woman screaming. Doc ran towards the house and slid on his knees to a woman sitting on the ground cradling a small boy in her arms. His face was ashen, and he was breathing in quick short gulps, his mouth working unnaturally as his lungs searched for air. He stared straight into the bright morning sky, unblinking.

Doc quickly cut the boy's blood-soaked shirt off. The wind was sucked out of him when he saw the hole on the left side of the little boy's chest. For his size, the wound was enormous, and part of a lung protruded from it. Doc found the entry wound behind his left arm. He watched as the boy took one more gulp of air and gave a final crackling, bubbling exhale. His chest ceased moving, and the woman began to wail even louder.

The sound of Jamie screaming brought him out of his stupor, and he looked up to see her red, tear-covered face standing over him, pointing her rifle towards the house. Jumping up, Doc looked around. Everyone was out of the truck, weapons trained on the side of the house. He held his hands up and shouted, "Stop! This is all wrong! Just stop!"

"That fucker killed Perez!" Jamie screamed through sobs.

Stunned, Doc looked back at the truck to see Perez's body slumped over in the turret. His immediate instinct was to run to his fallen comrade. But the rivulet of blood pouring from the open door told him it would be a wasted effort and instead turned to see who they were pointing their weapons at.

In the heat of the moment, Doc hadn't noticed the small, dark-skinned man clutching the rifle wide-eyed to his chest. Or the fact he was talking a hundred miles an hour in Spanish. The woman at his feet was also going on in Spanish, and Doc couldn't understand a word of it. But he put himself between the man and his distraught friends. Then, holding his trembling hands up and speaking softly, he said, "This has been a terrible mistake. Lower your guns."

Jamie, now openly crying, replied, "He killed Perez, and I'm going to kill the bastard!"

Doc took a step towards her, "Jamie, he shot Perez after Perez shot his son. Perez was still alive when I got out of the truck. The last shot killed him. I don't think this guy was shooting at us." He slowly and deliberately reached out and put a hand on the muzzle of her weapon. Any resolve she had to kill the man evaporated, and she collapsed on the ground, bawling. Ian dropped to her side and whispered gentle words into her ear in a futile attempt to console her. Janie stiff-armed him, and Ian fell on his ass.

Doc turned to face the man, still gibbering, and held his hands up. He motioned to the rifle and for the man to put it down. He spoke slowly, saying the same as he did. The man looked at the old bolt gun, then at Doc, then at the group of people gathered in his yard and leaned the rifle against the house. Then, swallowing hard, he quickly went to the woman's side and dropped to his knees. They spoke to one another in Spanish, and he began to cry along with her.

Doc looked over his shoulder at Jess and Lee Ann, who looked on in shock. "Either of you speaks Spanish?" Both shook their heads slowly, and Doc walked towards the Hummer. As he passed Jess, he quietly said,

"Very slowly, walk over there and get that rifle. Don't clear it or anything. Just secure it."

He stood momentarily looking into the truck and the pool of blood on the ground beside it. Then, hesitantly he reached in and grabbed the inside of Perez's thigh. Then, after a moment, he gripped the other. His head dropped and shook slowly from side to side. Then, pulling the radio from his vest, he took a deep breath and pushed the PTT button.

CHAPTER 2

There was total confusion over the radio when I turned it on. I was standing in the bedroom and had just picked it up. The truck had just left. What the hell could possibly happen that quick? The old man was screaming about QRF and wanting confirmation from people.

"What the hell's going on?" I asked over the radio.

"The truck has had contact. There's casualties!" Sarge shouted back.

My knees got weak, and I asked, "Who?"

"He's not saying. I just said we need to get down there. I'm coming in the War Wagon," the old man replied, and I could hear the diesel engine of the small vehicle through his radio.

"I'll be in the road," I replied as I ran for the door.

Almost immediately, the old man was there with Dalton, Mike, and Ted. I crammed myself into the backseat and held on as he sped off.

"What the hell is going on?" I asked.

Ted shrugged, "Don't know much. Ronnie said they took contact, and there's casualties."

"Ours or theirs?" I asked as a lump rose in my throat. He just shrugged.

We didn't have to wait long to find out. Pulling up, we saw a uniformed figure lying on the ground beside the truck. My heart sank as I thought of who had left in the truck. But I knew immediately when I saw Jamie knelt on the ground with Ian standing behind her.

"Oh shit, it's Perez," I moaned as we walked over.

"What the hell happened?" Sarge asked as he looked down at Perez's body.

Doc ran a blood-stained hand through his hair. "It's a fucked-up mess."

"Spit it out, Doc," Sarge snapped back.

Doc looked toward a house on the side of the road. "Someone out there, past that house, took a couple of shots at us. Perez saw movement and just started shooting. I saw the kid—" Doc's voice broke, "but it was too late. I yelled at Perez to stop shooting. Jamie stopped the truck, and I got out. Then there was another shot. The kid's father over there shot Perez."

Sarge didn't say anything for a long minute, then looked at Dalton, "You speak Spanish?"

Dalton nodded, "Enough."

Pointing, Sarge said, "Go over there and talk to them. Get their side."

Dalton walked towards the stricken parents as I knelt beside Perez. He was covered in blood and was hard to see. The bullet had hit him in his right cheek, under the eye. It was apparent he died instantly. I took his hand and held it for a moment as the weight of what just happened sank in.

"Well, old friend. Have a smoke for me in Valhalla," I said quietly as I gently placed his hand on his chest.

Jamie sat holding his other hand, and I looked up at Ian. His face was grim, and he shook his head. Then, reaching out, I gripped Jamie's shoulder.

"I'm so sorry, Jamie. We're all going to miss him," I said.

She wiped her nose with her free hand and replied, "It's all fucked up. It's just so fucked up. Perez didn't need to die."

"He thought he was protecting you guys. You're right. It is all fucked up and shouldn't have happened." Squeezing her shoulder, I stood up.

Ted came up with a body bag, something else we'd picked up at Eglin, and he and Mike started to lay it out. Mike was uncharacteristically quiet as he unzipped the bag and laid it beside Perez. Leaving them to their somber task, I walked over to Sarge and Dalton talking to two people. Dalton talked to them in Spanish as I approached, and I stopped beside Sarge and asked, "Well, what the fuck?"

Taking his hat off, Sarge wiped his face. "It's a fucking mess. Someone took a couple of shots at the truck. We still don't know who did that. But Perez opened up on these folks and killed the boy," he finished by pointing at the body of a very young boy lying in the lap of his mother.

"Who the hell shot Perez?"

"The kid's dad there did. Not that it means shit now. It's not his fault; he just saw his son killed. I can't say I blame him, honestly. It's just a damn mess."

"That's pretty much what Doc said," I replied as I looked around.

ENGINEERING HOME

"Go get a body bag for the boy," Sarge said. I nodded and walked back over to the war wagon.

As I passed Jamie, I glanced at her and felt like shit. My head was swimming, this whole thing was such a cluster fuck, and I was trying to figure out how it all happened. With everything we have to deal with, incidents like this were not on my radar. The thought that we could have something like this happen was just unimaginable.

Doc helped me load the boy into it when I returned with the bag. But unfortunately, his mother didn't want to let him go, and her husband had to pull her away so we could complete the unpleasant job.

"Dalton, ask him if he wants us to help him dig a grave for the boy," Sarge asked.

Dalton spoke in Spanish briefly, but even I could tell from the man's movements what the answer was. "No, he just wants us to go the fuck away."

"That's what I thought," I replied.

Sarge spun on his heels and headed towards the truck. He went into the back, pulled out two MRE cases, and carried them back. Then, setting them down by the man's feet, he looked at Dalton and said, "Tell him we're very sorry and that all this was an accident." Dalton sputtered, and the man looked at the cases, then up at Sarge. Again, he stuttered, and Dalton translated.

"He asked if we think a little food makes up for killing his son."

"No, it doesn't. It was a terrible accident. We're very sorry, but this is all we can do for now," Sarge replied.

Then the man looked at me and started speaking again. I didn't know what he was saying, but I did understand one word, policia. I looked at Dalton for the translation.

"He asked if you're the police. He said you should do something about this. That this is wrong, and someone should be punished."

"Someone was," I replied and pointed back to Perez's body. "You killed the man that killed your son. Your son's death was wrong, and one of our men paid for that mistake with his life." Then, looking at Dalton, I said, "Tell him."

Dalton translated what I said, and the man stood for a moment, saying nothing. Then, he looked over at the body bag lying in the road by the truck. Then, after a pause, he shrugged and wiped tears from his face and said, "Lo Siento."

"Sorry," Dalton said.

"So are we," I said and reached out and took the man's hand. "How do you say very sorry?" I asked Dalton.

"Lo sentimos mucho," Dalton replied.

Gently shaking the man's hand, I said, "Lo sentimos mucho."

The man nodded his head and released my hand, and that was it. We were done dealing with his problem. Now we had to deal with ours. Not that two cases of MREs were going to make these people whole, but there was little else we could do right now. So I decided then that I would make an effort to help these people if they would take it. And I wouldn't blame them if they didn't. How could I blame them if they told me to fuck off and die? But I would try so that maybe, just maybe, Perez's death wouldn't be in vain. Though I wish I didn't have to. That none of this happened. But you can't bend reality to your desires. You have to accept it and deal with it as it is, and sometimes it isn't pleasant.

Quietly and calmly, we loaded Perez into the truck. We handled him gently and with reverence. It was the least we could do for our friend. Once Perez was in the truck, Jess walked up and held out a rifle. "What do you want me to do with this?"

Mike took the rifle and opened the action. It was an old Winchester model 70. When he opened the action, a spent case rattled to the ground. He then worked the action, spilling bullets onto the ground. Then, looking up, he said, "Mags full. He only fired the one shot."

"It all adds up," I said. "This is just horrible." Then, shaking my head, I picked the bullets up from the ground and took the rifle from Mike.

"What are you going to do with it?" Jess asked.

Looking at the old rifle, I said, "Give it back to him," and carried it back over to the man. I handed him the rifle and dropped the bullets into his hand. Then, without saying anything, I turned and walked back to the truck. Jamie, Ian, and Jess were in the war wagon. Lee Ann was standing by the back of the Hummer, and I stopped.

"You ok, kiddo?" I asked.

She was looking at the ground where Perez's blood stained the road a dark crimson as it congealed. "There's so much blood."

I put my arm around her shoulder and said, "Yeah," and turned her away from the sight. "Get in with those guys, and we'll bring the truck back." Without replying, she nodded and moved towards the buggy.

Walking around the truck, I looked inside. The rear passenger seat was full of blood as well as the floor. Sarge came up behind me and put his hand on my shoulder. "Why don't you ride back with them. No one needs to sit in that."

Doing some quick math, I replied, "We don't have enough seats here."

Dalton clapped me on the back from behind, "Come on. We'll sit in the bed on the back of that thing."

Sarge nodded, "That'll work."

Dalton and I walked over to the war wagon as Ian started it up. Jamie was in no mood to drive, and we climbed in the back. Ian looked over his shoulder to make sure we were in and headed back towards home. While it was a short ride, it was a very long trip as our thoughts consumed each of us.

When we pulled up to Danny's house, the porch was packed with people. It appeared that everyone knew something was going on. Thad was the first one off the porch when he saw us coming. We pulled the buggy up so Sarge could get the Hummer closer to the house proper. People slowly began filing into the yard with expectant looks on their faces. When Mel saw Lee Ann, she rushed over to her and wrapped her in a hug. Then, uncharacteristically, she returned her mother's embrace.

Everyone gathered around the Hummer. Miss Kay held a hand over her mouth as she did a headcount like everyone was doing. Then, we opened the back of the Hummer and lifted Perez out, and laid him on the ground.

"What happened?" Thad asked.

Sarge took a minute to collect himself before clearing his throat. "Everyone, listen up. I'm only going to tell this once." Once the group closed around him, he relayed the story of what happened. There were several gasps and more tears. When he wrapped it up, several people began asking questions. Having heard enough about it before we even returned, I walked away and sat down in a rocker on the porch. Dad soon joined me.

We sat rocking in silence for some time before Dad spoke up. "That's a hell of a thing. You were right earlier when you said the killing wasn't done. I didn't think it would happen this soon, though."

"Me either. I was really hoping we wouldn't see anything like this."

"That's a hell of an accident. Horrible for everyone."

I thought about that for a moment. "It is. I feel for the kid's parents. Their little boy is dead for no reason. The father killed the man that did it, but that doesn't bring his son back. And we lost a good man."

"I didn't really get to know him yet, unfortunately," Dad replied.

A slight smile cut my face, "He was something else, that's for sure. He smoked like a damn chimney."

"Smoked?" Dad asked. "Where the hell did he get cigarettes?"

"From Eglin, to start with. Then he loaded up big time after we hit the Russians. Apparently, those guys smoke like damn demons. He had a pack stuffed with them."

"Well shit. Russian smokes. Wonder what they're like."

"You thinking of starting again?" I asked.

Dad laughed, "No, just curious." He paused and looked over. "So, now what?"

With my gaze fixed on the body bag lying in the yard, I replied, "Now, we dig another grave. There's been too many already."

"I've dug my share since all this shit started. We lost a lot of people back in our neighborhood. You know, there were a lot of old folks there. Most of them died off pretty quick. Some of it was hard to watch because a few suffered so bad."

"Believe me, I can relate."

Ian walked Jamie into the house as we sat talking on the porch. She wasn't crying now; she just looked beat. She looked blank almost, and it worried me. I watched them go inside and said, "I'm worried about her."

"Were they close?" Dad asked.

"Real close," Thad replied. He'd walked up as they went into the house and stood on the porch looking into the door.

"How are you doing?" I asked him.

Thad was quiet for a minute before replying. "I'm ok." He paused for a long moment, then added, "Just sick of this. Especially this sort of thing. There was no reason for this today." He shook his head. "Senseless, just senseless."

I stood up and patted him on the back. "I know, buddy. I know."

Still looking into the house, Thad said, "I'll get the tractor."

"I'll meet you out back," I replied.

Dad stood up and added, "I'll help. I didn't know him yet, but I'll help put him to rest."

Dad and I walked towards one of the sheds to get shovels. As we passed by the truck, I heard Sarge talking to Ted.

"...figure out who they are," Sarge was saying.

"Figure out who who is?" I asked.

"The sum bitch that took the shots at them today. It wasn't that old man, but someone damn sure shot at them."

"How the hell are we going to do that?" I asked.

"Me and Mikey will go to town and poke around a little," Ted replied.

"Take some people with you," I said. "We should make sure we're moving in force for a bit."

Sarge nodded, "I was already thinking that good call."

"We'll grab a couple of Wallner's people," Mike said.

"We have a grave to dig," I said. "We'll have the service for him this evening."

"We won't be long. I'll make sure to be back in time for it," Ted said.

Dad and I stood by the pond, waiting for Thad. Danny came out as well, and then Mary. She looked solemn and wasn't talking. I was sure Jamie was feeling whatever Thad was feeling. The two of them were very close, and I knew that when he suffered, she did as well.

"You Ok, Mary?" I asked.

She nodded. "Yes. It's just sad."

I put an arm around her shoulder. "It is. But we have to keep going, ya know? All we can do is all we can do."

She wiped her eyes and nodded. "I know. I just hate seeing this." As she spoke, Thad rode up on the tractor. I still had my arm around her, and he smiled when he saw it. I winked at him, and he tipped his head in acknowledgment. It's just what family does.

"Where are we going to put him?" Thad asked.

Danny looked around at the other graves already there. He pointed to a spot between two cypress trees, and Thad nodded and eased the tractor towards the site and began to scoop out the soft ground.

Dad snorted, "Damn. Nice to have a tractor."

"Yeah, it is," I replied. "We've had to do this a little too much."

We didn't talk much while Thad dug out what he could. Once he'd made the grave as deep as the tractor could manage, Danny and I jumped in and began to shape it with the shovels. Dad and Thad chatted with Mary as we finished the job, which didn't take long. Once it was ready, we left the shovels and walked back to the house.

Dad said he was going to his place to check on Mom and parted ways with us as I stepped up on the porch. Sarge was sitting with Miss Kay and Jess, and I asked if they'd seen Mel.

"She went to the house with the girls," Sarge replied.

"She's coming back over here, and we're going to walk down and check on Fred. I've fixed her some lunch. She needs to eat to feed that baby," Kay added.

"How's she doing?" I asked.

Kay smiled, "Her belly is growing. That baby is getting big."

Mel and Little Bit came from the direction of our house, and Little Bit rushed over and hugged my legs. I tussled her hair, and she giggled. Kids are amazing creatures, the pure innocence they have, and the fact that they are blessed with being ignorant of many things adults have to deal with. She made me smile.

"You going with mommy to see Fred?" I asked her.

She clapped her hands, "Yes!" Then, smiling devilishly, she added, "I want to feel the baby kick."

Mel patted her head and said, "We'll see, baby. If Fred says, you can."

"She'll let me! She always does!"

Kay rose to her feet and looked at Sarge, "Linus, we'll be back in a while." She picked up a basket, its contents covered by a dishtowel, and looked at Little Bit, "You ready, sweetie?"

"Can I carry the basket? Please?"

Kay smiled and handed it to her. "Be careful with it."

"I will!" She replied as she bounded down the steps into the yard.

"You alright?" Mel asked.

I smiled, "Yeah, I'm fine. But, you guys, be careful." I looked down to ensure she had her pistol on and was happy to see she did. I gave her a quick kiss and patted her ass as she walked after Kay and Little Bit.

Sarge stood up and called out to Little Bit, "You keep these two out of trouble now, you hear?"

She smiled and laughed, "They're not trouble! And I'm just a kid!"

Sarge smiled and picked up his coffee cup. "Alright then. You ladies, be careful. I need to refill my cup."

"I could use some too," I said as I followed him into the house.

Sarge filled his cup, and I slid one in front of him for myself. He poured it about half full, and I reached over and tipped the pot, "Keep going."

After topping off my cup, he looked up, "You know how precious this shit is?"

I laughed, "You drink it like there's no end in sight."

Putting the pot back on the burner, he replied, "Well, there is an end to it."

"How much is there?" I asked, now concerned.

He smiled, "We have plenty, just pulling your leg."

Taking a sip, I replied, "Good. Dad just got here, and I want him to be able to enjoy it for a while."

Taking a sip from his cup, he replied, "Then you should stop drinking it and save it for your daddy."

"What? I hardly ever drink this shit!"

"Stop yer bellyaching. I told you I was just pulling yer leg."

Walking back out to the porch, I sat down in a rocker, more complicated than you think when wearing a plate carrier. Thad and Mary were in the garden. They were getting some winter crops ready. He continued to surprise me every day. Thad had taken sole responsibility for our gardening efforts. Of course, we all chipped in with weeding and taking care of the plants, but it was Thad that oversaw all these efforts. He started all our plants from seeds we'd collected from all over. Unfortunately, some of these were useless. In several cases, there was complete failure to germinate. Thad was always undeterred though, and would simply move forward with different seeds. Because of his efforts, we were kept in a reasonably steady supply of vegetables and some fruits. We even managed to can some of the produce, so prolific was his efforts.

Thad's efforts had additional benefits. For him, it was cathartic. Thad would go to the garden and piddle around whenever he was a little stressed. Sometimes he'd pull weeds; sometimes, he'd go over the tomato plants and remove hornworms, a never-ending battle in which we all participated. Finally, the worms were dropped into a cup and delivered to the waiting and eager chickens who made short work of them.

This same therapy was available to all, and every evening there would be someone in the garden. I even found myself in there from time to time. I liked the early mornings in the garden when the soil was still moist and cool. You could go in there and forget about everything for a bit. You were losing yourself in the sights and sounds of the small jungle. And there was always something to do there, so it wasn't wasted effort.

"I like seeing him out there," I said as I watched Thad and Mary moving in the garden.

"I keep an eye on him. When he's out there, I know he's alright. When he's not out there, I start worrying," Sarge replied.

"I think he goes there for therapy."

Nodding, Sarge replied, "I think you're right. It's a good place to go to clear your mind."

"Guess that's why I never see you out there then," I replied with a grin.

"That's right. Don't need to clear my mind."

"Cause there's nothing there to clear," I replied.

Sarge's face twisted, "Ain't you got someone else to annoy?"

"I could, but you're so much fun."

"Kicking you to sleep would be fun too."

I shook my head. "Violence is never the answer."

Sarge laughed, "It has been my professional experience that violence is always the answer. It just has to be applied with speed and force."

"Hey, since we're talking about violence, what the hell are we going to do with Ivan?"

"Eglin is sending a Blackhawk down to pick him up."

"Soon, I hope," I replied.

"Shouldn't be much longer. I know you want rid of him."

"He's just taking up space, and we have to feed him and his little toady. Yeah, I'm ready for them to go."

As we talked, Thad walked up. "Morgan, we need to go over and look at the harvester. Cecil needs that corn picked, or we're going to lose most of it. I know we have to take care of Perez tonight, but we also have to get this done."

"We'll get together and go over there in the morning," I replied. "What I'm more worried about is who was taking shots at our truck. I want to find that son of a bitch."

"Shit," Sarge snorted. "That could have been anyone. Hell, it could've been a kid just taking a pot shot, not intending to hurt anyone. But, unfortunately, we'll probably never find him."

"I want to try," I replied.

Sarge gripped my shoulder. "Look, Morgan, I get it. You want revenge. But I've seen this many times. You'll never find him unless he decides to try it again. Then you'll get your chance. But don't think you'll just go out and find this guy. Ain't going to happen. The only reason I sent the boys out was so that everyone would feel like something was being done."

"Don't spill that basket," Kay admonished Little Bit as she swung it back and forth as she walked.

The little girl giggled, "I won't."

Kay glanced over at Mel and asked, "You alright? You look like you're thinking hard about something."

"I'm just thinking about Perez."

Kay sighed, "It's so sad. He was such a quiet man." Then her face became very animated, "And he smoked like a chimney! Lord, that man likes to smoke."

Mel smiled, "He did. It always made me smile when I saw him because he always had a cigarette in his mouth. It's funny considering where we are now. No one has cigarettes, and yet Perez was always smoking." Mel was nearly laughing when she finished talking.

"Smoking is bad!" Little Bit shouted over her shoulder.

It brought a smile to Kay's face. "Little ears are always listening."

"And she doesn't miss a thing, ever," Mel replied with a smile.

Aric and Fred were sitting on the porch when the ladies walked up. Aric smiled and quickly rose to his feet to greet them. It took Fred a moment longer to get to her feet with Aric's help.

"You stay sitting down!" Kay called out. "No need to get up."

"It's good for me to stand up," Fred replied.

Little Bit ran up and handed the basket to Aric. "Here's your lunch and some stuff for Fred," she announced as she handed it over. He tussled her hair and thanked her. Then, she ran over to Fred, who was standing on the porch talking to Mel, and grabbed her hand. "Fred, can I listen to the baby? Is she awake?"

Aric returned from the house after putting the basket away. "How do you know it's a girl?"

Little Bit gave a devilish smile. "I know it's a girl. I can tell."

Fred eased herself back into her chair and said, "Come here, Ashley, she's kicking right now. You can feel her."

"How are you feeling?" Mel asked as Little Bit rested her head on Fred's belly.

"Better. I'm not sick anymore, so that's a plus."

"It's not so bad from now on then," Mel replied.

"Can you feel the baby?" Kay asked Little Bit.

A huge smile spread across her face, and she nodded her head. "She's wiggling around. I can feel her."

"Him," Aric added.

"It's a girl!" Little Bit called back.

Mel glanced over at Aric, "Have you heard the news?" Kay's face fell, and she started to tear up.

"What happened?" Fred quickly asked.

Aric leaned against a porch column and asked, "What happened?"

Mel glanced at Little Bit and whispered, "Perez was killed this morning."

Aric bolted from the column, "What? What happened?"

Mel motioned with her head, and the two walked off the porch. She told him the story as she knew it and answered Aric's questions as best she could.

"So, we don't know who did it?"

"No. Morgan wants to go get them."

"Me too," Aric replied as he disappeared into the house and quickly returned with his rifle and kit. He leaned over and kissed Fred on the head and said he'd be back, then disappeared around the house. The sound of an ATV roaring to life followed shortly after, and Aric came racing around the house and down the road.

Fred sat watching as he rounded the corner. "What's he think he's going to do? They don't even know who it was or where they were, for that matter."

Kay patted her leg. "Don't worry about him, hun. Just boys being boys. Linus said the same thing you did; they have no way of knowing who it was or if it was even on purpose."

"How's Jamie taking it?" Fred asked.

"Not well," Mel replied. "We're going to bury him this evening, and I think that will hit her."

"I'm coming too," Fred said.

"Now you're in no condition to go all the way over there," Kay protested.

"I'm fine, Kay. There's nothing wrong with me. I can ride on the four-wheeler to Danny's house."

Kay fidgeted with her hands for a moment, then said, "I just worry about you, is all."

"I know you do," Fred replied as she leaned over and patted the older woman's hand.

CHAPTER 3

As Mike and Ted lowered Perez's body into the ground, we stood in silence. They performed the task delicately, not allowing him to bump or tumble into the hole. Once he was in the grave, they pulled the ropes out and looked to Sarge, who stood with Kay holding onto his arm. Because of the nature of his death, we kept the bag zipped. I, for one, wanted to remember him how he lived. Not how he died.

"Hell, of a way to go, old buddy," Sarge said. "Even for a Mezcan," he added with a smile. "I'll miss you, my friend."

The old man leaned down, grabbed a handful of the soft dirt piled beside the grave, and tossed it in. "Farewell."

We all slowly filed by the grave, performing the same ritual. We were dropping in a handful of dirt and saying the kinds of words one is expected to speak at such times. Little Bit was holding Mel's hand and watched her mother's tear-streaked face as she took her turn. Then the little girl took up a tiny fist of dirt and dropped it in as well. She held a small stuffed rabbit that had recently become her constant companion. She held the plush toy out and looked at it for a moment.

"Baby bunny," she started, "you keep mister Perez company, so he's not lonely," and dropped the plush rabbit in the grave.

It was already an emotional moment for everyone, but seeing Little Bit perform this small act hit everyone hard. Jamie was waiting, I imagined she wanted to go last, and when she witnessed the act, she broke down again into sobs. Little Bit ran over to her and wrapped her arms around Jamie's legs.

"Sorry, Jamie, I just didn't want him to be lonely."

Trying to smile through the tears, Jamie knelt and replied, "I'm not upset with you, sweetheart, not at all. On the contrary, I think it's a very nice thing you did, and I'm happy he won't be alone. Baby Bunny will be there to keep him company, and that makes me happy."

Little Bit smiled and wrapped her arms around Jamie's neck, kissing her on the cheek. Then she leaned in close and whispered in her ear, "Don't worry. It gets easier."

Jamie leaned back and stared at the child in confusion, unsure of the meaning behind the simple statement. Before she could ask, Little Bit ran back over to her mother and took her hand once again. I'd watched all this and waited as everyone made their pass. Dalton stopped at the grave and stared down into it.

In a booming voice I couldn't understand, not that I understood most of what the giant did. He held his arms held up to the sky and began to bellow,

"Lo, þar gerekr sjá minn faðir.
lo, þar gerekr sjá minn móðir,
minn systirokr minn bróðira.
lo, þar gerekr sjá linerinn ór minn fólk,
aptr til beginningrinn.
lo, þeir gerkallar til mik,
þeir bid mik takminnr staðr among þau
inn hallanórr valhalla,
hvere braveinn munu live forever,
hvere thine enemies hafmuniðr vanquished,
né munu vér mourn en rejoice,
fyrir þau hverr hafdejumkr
gloriouandeathr"

Then he pounded his chest with his right hand, knelt and scooped up a double handful of dirt, held it up to the sky, shouted something else I didn't understand and dropped it in the grave. Then, rising to his feet, he turned and walked away without looking back.

Ted then stepped up to the grave. He stood staring down into the dark hole, so dark he could no longer see the form lying in the bottom in the fading light of the setting sun. I watched as he rubbed his eyes and heard him sniffle. Then, clearing his throat, he began to speak, his voice trembling as he fought to control himself.

"Pater noster, qui es in caelis,
sanctificetur nomen tuum.
Adveniat regnum tuum.
Fiat voluntas tua,
sicut in caelo, et in terra.

Panem nostrum quotidianum da nobis hodie,
et dimitte nobis debita nostra,
sicut et nos dimittimus debitoribus nostris.
Et ne nos inducas in tentationem,
sed libera nos a malo.
Amen."

Finished, he turned and started towards me, "What the hell was that?" I asked.

"It was the Lord's prayer in Latin," Dalton's voice boomed over my shoulder. I looked back to see Dalton give Ted a nod as he passed me and asked, "What the hell was that gibberish you said?"

"It's a Viking poem for warriors," Dalton replied. He put his arm over Ted's shoulder, and the two men disappeared into the night.

Once everyone had passed by the grave, Jamie stepped up with Ian at her side. She held a carton of Russian cigarettes clutched tight to her chest. She looked down into the infinitely black hole for a long time.

Shaking her head, she finally said, "You dumb old man. Why'd you have to go with us? Why'd you have to have your fat head sticking up out of the truck?" She started to sob again and dropped to her knees. Ian followed her but didn't touch her. Just making sure she knew he was there. "Why'd you have to go and get yourself shot? And for what?" She pounded the ground with her fist and sobbed some more. Finally, getting herself under control, she wiped her face, took a deep breath, and cleared her throat. "I'm going to miss you, Poppie. I brought you these," she held the carton out over the hole and looked at them. "Yeah, I know there's more, but this is all you get. You need to quit anyway. I'm keeping the rest, and every night we'll have a smoke together." With that, she gently tossed the carton into the grave.

Ian gave her a couple of minutes before he rose to his feet and gripped her shoulders. "Come on, babe."

Jamie reached up and squeezed his hand, and nodded. Then, getting to her feet, she took one last look at the grave before turning and letting Ian lead her away from it. Once they were out of earshot, I stepped up to the grave and looked down.

"Sorry it went like this, amigo," a smile cracked my face as I thought about him. "Guess we have an opening for the laziest SOB around." Kneeling, I took a handful of dirt and tossed it back and forth between my hands. "I'm getting tired of doing this. Especially for my friends, and you were certainly among friends." Then, tossing the dirt into the hole, I added, "I'll see you in Valhalla."

Thad suddenly appeared at my side, his approach utterly silent. But he didn't startle me. On the contrary, something about Thad always brought comfort and ease. Even if you didn't know the big man was there. And for a man his size, it was amazing how quietly he could move.

"I'll take care of him from here, Morgan."

I leaned against his bugling shoulder and replied, "No, we'll do it together."

We both took up shovels and began filling in the grave without saying anything. We used the tractor to dig graves but never to fill them. At least not for our friends and family. It just didn't seem right to be running over them with the big machine. Raiders and the like, I didn't give a shit either way. Hell, I was fine with letting the buzzards deal with them.

Dad found his way out to us as we leveled the patch of fresh dirt out. He stood by and watched for a few minutes before saying, "Looks like he isn't the first."

"Sadly no," I replied.

"Let's just hope he's the last for a long while," Thad added.

"Why don't you two go up there and wash up. Kay has some supper ready, and I'm sure you are hungry," Dad said.

"I don't have much of an appetite tonight," I replied.

"I imagine not," Dad replied with a knowing nod. He'd seen his share of friends die, both in Vietnam and since The Day.

Tossing the shovels over our shoulders, we headed for the house that was unusually quiet for this time of day. Generally, supper time was when everyone got together to talk and carry on. But, instead, there were only whispers this evening. The light even seemed dimmer tonight.

I joined the others, more picking at my food than anything. When supper was finished, people started to wander off. Kay carried a small parcel over to Sarge and said, "Here's some food for the prisoners."

More out of general irritation than anything else, I barked, "How much longer are we going to have to keep that asshole here?"

Sarge cut me a sideways look. "What's up yer ass?"

"If DOD wants him, when are they coming to get him? Why do we have to keep feeding him and dealing with his ass?"

"It'll happen. Why you bitchin' anyway? You don't have to deal with him. When was the last time you were even over there?"

The old man was right. I didn't have any interaction with Ivan. Primarily because I didn't want to, nor did I need to. Wallner's people guarded him, and Kay cooked for them. It was simple frustration at having just buried Perez. As I walked back towards the house, I couldn't stop thinking about him. He was probably the laziest man I'd ever met. You could always count on Perez to do the absolute minimum. Maybe he'd spent too much time in the Army.

But I still liked him. He was funny and always good for a laugh. And while he was lazy, there was no denying that you could count on him when you needed him. Never once did Perez waver when the chips were down, or there was something important to do. You just had to convince him it was important to *him*, or it probably wasn't going to happen.

As I was about to step up onto the porch, a noise caught my attention. Looking over towards mom and dad's place, I saw mom standing on the porch beating a rug hung over the rail with a broom. I smiled and walked over.

"You getting thing's settled?" I asked.

She looked up, brushed some hair from her face, and replied, "The place was dirty. I didn't realize it until I started cleaning up."

"It sat empty for a long time."

She looked back at the house. "Well, whoever was here before sure wasn't much of a housekeeper."

It made me smile. "Tomorrow me and Mel will come over and help."

She dismissed the offer with a wave. "Her and the girls were here earlier, and we already did it. I was just finishing this up. The place is really clean now."

"Well, I want to see what it's like then."

I followed mom inside, and the place did look a lot different. All the photos of the previous occupants were gone, along with most of the brick-a-brack people collected over the years. The furniture of the living room had been rearranged with the fireplace as the focal point. The large TV that had occupied one wall was gone as well.

"Wow. You guys didn't waste any time in here."

Mom stood at the door with her hands on her hips as she surveyed the house. "I figured if we were going to live here, we might as well make it home."

I smiled, looking at her. I'd seen that same pose and expression so many times in my life. It warmed me, and I forgot about Perez for a minute. "Where's Dad?" I asked.

"He's still over at Danny's. Thought he'd be with you."

"I slipped out," I replied. "Days like today take a toll on me."

With a mother's knowing glance, she replied, "I bet they do."

"If you're good. I'm gonna go to the house and take a long hot shower. That's about the only thing that makes me feel better."

As I went to pass her in the door, she stopped me and hugged me. "You've done more than anyone person could be expected to do. Everything that happens isn't your fault."

I hugged her back. "I know. It just really sucks to lose friends." Then, giving her one more squeeze, I went out the door.

Mel and the girls were back at the house when I returned. Lee Ann was sitting on the porch when I walked up. Stopping on the steps, I asked, "You doing ok?"

She nodded, "Yeah. It's just so sad. Everything happened so fast."

"These kinds of things do happen fast, and it is sad. Mistakes, terrible mistakes like today, come with terrible consequences. And that's all we're left with."

"Yeah. Jamie is pretty messed up. She had a strange love for Perez. They were always messing with each other. She could say things to him that would start a fight if anyone else tried it."

I smiled, "They were certainly the odd couple. Ian will take care of her, though."

"Yeah."

"I'm gonna go take a hot shower. Having one of life's true luxuries back is something I'm not going to miss out on. What are you going to do?"

She looked out across the long shadows in the yard and replied, "I'm going to sit here for a while."

Stepping up on the porch, I patted her head, "This wasn't your fault either, kiddo. So, don't let it eat you up inside. Perez made a terrible mistake, and it cost him his life. There's no one else to blame."

"I know."

She worried me. I remembered the incident from out on the river when Thad stopped her from doing something terrible. People have a habit of looking for permanent solutions to temporary problems. Maybe tomorrow I'll ask him to talk to her. He always has a way of talking to people so that they don't know that's what he's doing. He is a remarkable man.

Mel was crossing the living room with a sleeping Little Bit in her arms and a young Ruckus, the squirrel, scurrying around on her back. She smiled at me as I came in, and I smiled back at the sight. Taylor was sitting on the couch reading a book. Even though the power was back on and movies could be watched, the kids generally preferred to read a book or do a puzzle which was the latest craze sweeping our little community.

I remember when Jess brought one back from the market. It'd been a big deal at Danny's house. Someone set up a folding card table in the living room, and people would gather around for hours working on it. Anyone who passed by would always stop and see if they could work a piece in. The frustration emerged on the second day when someone realized there were two different puzzles in the same box, and neither was complete!

That realization had set off another round of scavenging the neighborhood for puzzles, of which there were many. A real honey hole was found in one house where one of the occupants must have had a thing for them because over a dozen were found in one closet. There was much debate about how they would be allocated, who would get which one, and the like. Finally, it was decided to do them one at a time and leave them at Danny's. That way, they could be a group effort. And so there was always a puzzle working in the corner of his living room.

Mel was sitting on the bed with the limb rat when I came out of the shower. The little rodent was running around the bed, under the sheet, over the sheet, on the curtains.

Drying my hair, I asked, "What the hell are you feeding that thing? Meth?"

The squirrel ran past, and she grabbed it. Then, holding it up in front of her face, she spoke directly to it. "We're starting to eat real food now, aren't we?"

"You talking to me or the rat?"

Scowling at me, she replied, "Ruckus is not a rat. She is a squirrel."

"Ok, it's a bushy-tailed rat," I replied with a smile.

Getting up from the bed, she headed for the door, replying, "She's not a rat. But it is time for her to go to bed."

By going to bed, Mel meant it was time for the rat to go in its cage. She'd had me scouring the neighborhood for a big cage for a week before I got lucky at the market in Umatilla. Talking with an older lady there as I perused the usual offerings, she asked me what I was looking for. As a joke, I said, *a big ass cage.*

Her face lit up, and she nearly shouted, "I have one at home! It was Maurice's old cage. He died three or four months ago. He was old, though. I'd had him for nearly fifty years, and he wasn't a chick when I got him."

I thought she'd go on forever, and to save myself some time, I asked the inevitable question, "Who's Maurice?"

"Oh, he was my parrot—such a gentle creature. I really miss him. But it would be hard to feed him nowadays."

"So, it's a big parrot cage?"

She nodded, "Yes, it is.

"That's exactly what I need!"

We ended up working a deal for some flour, sugar, and salt. It's incredible what people need when it comes down to it. And those commodities are the most valuable around. We are fortunate to have the stores we do since all that was handed out after our last trip to Eglin has surely been consumed by now. For a short time, it was seen as currency and traded in very small quantities in very lopsided trades, so valuable were these staples that we'd taken for granted just a year before.

When I began my prepping, it was in response to hurricanes, so most of my plans were very short-term in nature. Generators and fuel were at the top of the list to keep some power on after a storm moved through. That evolved over time as I became aware of just how fragile our world was, and it was only getting frailer as time progressed. Technology allowed humans to make remarkable advances in the quality of life, medicine, information sharing, and the like. But it had an Achilles heel that was as delicate as a Dandelion seed head. Even the slightest movement can destroy it, and we are now living that reality.

My migration towards more self-reliance is what is making the difference today. Unfortunately, we are not genuinely self-reliant, and nearly everyone who claims to be is not. All we can do is try and move farther in that direction, which I did, thankfully. Storing seeds and keeping a garden for all those years is paying off now by keeping my small community fed. All those buckets and bags of food are long gone, and I never planned on providing for nearly the number of people our community has grown to. Renewable methods are best. Gardens, livestock (which comes with its own set of challenges), and foraging are what matter. Not the number of buckets you have. Sure, they will help initially, but you better have a plan for the long-term.

I lay in the bed staring up at the ceiling fan. Even though we have a small solar system, it just wasn't enough to run everything, so we had to decide what was necessary. Then, of course, on sweltering nights, we'd run fans. But to be able to lie in bed and watch those blades spin was like looking back into the past.

Mel returned and closed the door. "Now, I'm going to take a hot shower."

"A what? You never liked hot showers. What you consider hot, I consider room temperature at best."

"Distance makes the heart grow fonder. And I've been a long way from a hot shower for a long time. So, I'm going to take as hot a shower as I can stand."

I propped myself up on an elbow and gave her a devilish grin. "Need any help?"

She stepped into the bathroom without answering, and I heard the water come on. I was about to lie back down when her bra flew out the door onto the bed. "You could wash my back if you want." But, of course, I ended up washing a lot more than that. I had to make sure to keep this hot water thing going for sure.

I woke up early as usual. Lying in bed, I looked up at the fan. It wasn't moving. Getting out of bed, I slipped into a pair of shorts and pulled a t-shirt on, and headed for the living room. Seeing into the kitchen, the clock on the oven was off, and the power was out. "Damn, already? That didn't last long," I muttered as I went outside. Turing the main breaker off, I reconnected the solar. Stepping over the dogs who didn't even bother taking notice, I went back inside and opened the fridge. My tea was still cool, not cold, but not room temp either. The power had been off for several hours. After pouring myself a glass of tea, I slipped on shoes, slung my rifle across my back, and headed out the door. This time the dogs were interested in what I was doing and followed me.

It was a brisk morning, and the chill in the air gave my legs goosebumps, but I didn't care. It felt good after the long hot summer. I always enjoyed the mornings. It was quiet; in reality, the world was more peaceful in general now. As I walked down the road, the only sound I heard was the calls of birds beginning their day, some squirrels barking back and forth like old women, and the jingling of the dog's tags, a relic leftover from Before.

Three Guardsmen were on duty at the bunker and came out in the road to meet me. One of them was a young kid with the last name Billingsley on his name tape. He was a friendly kid, probably twenty-two, and always looking to help out. But there was one thing about him that had me nervous. I'd noticed Taylor hanging around him, or him her, lately. It was only natural that two young people would gravitate to one another. But, in my mind, she was too young.

"Morning, Sheriff," he greeted me with a sly grin.

"Knock that shit off, already told you," I replied good-naturedly. "What's up, anything?"

He shook his head. "No. We saw the power go out last night a little after one AM. But that's been it.

"Yeah, I noticed it when I got up. Heading over to the old man's to see if he knows anything."

"Ok. Shift change will be hereafter breakfast. Been uneventful so far."

"Good," I replied and took a sip of tea. "I like uneventful."

After exchanging a few words with the other two, I headed down the road towards the old man's place. The garage door was open, and I saw the guard posted to watch Ivan and his lackey sitting on a stool in the opening. Walking up, I asked, "He giving you any trouble?"

Looking over his shoulder, the man replied, "No. He's pretty much given up. He is pissed he hasn't been moved yet. Apparently, he thinks he's pretty important."

"That true, Ivan? You a big deal?" I asked.

Ivan leaned back on his hands and studied me for a minute. Then, in his typical thick Russian accent, he asked, "What's the matter, Sheriff? You don't like me here in your community?"

"No. I don't. You're a waste of resources. We have to feed your useless ass. Assign men to watch you. So, no, I don't like having you here."

With a smug look on his face, Ivan replied, "You could just let me go."

"Or, I could just kill you," I replied, and the smug look evaporated from his face. It made me smile.

"Come on now, Ivan. You're great Russia has never had a problem killing those that wouldn't go along with the program. So why should we be any different?"

"But you are different. You Americans believe you stand on some fairy tale moral high ground. That you are somehow superior to the rest of the world. And yet, Americans are responsible for more death in modern times than any other nation."

I laughed, "We are superior, at least to you people. As far as the killing, America will never catch up to just the number of Russians killed by your own government."

Now he smiled. "But you're doing a pretty good job of killing each other now." He paused as though he was thinking. "I would imagine more Americans have died since the beginning of this little event than Mother Russia has in all eternity."

He was trying to goad me into getting mad. "You're probably right about that. I imagine tens of millions of people have died. And yet, here you sit. We still destroyed your force and captured your worthless ass."

Before he could reply, Sarge stepped through the door to the house. Ivan looked over his shoulder and saw him. He motioned towards me and said, "Colonel, I do not like talking to this svin'ya. You, at least, are intelligent and can carry on a decent conversation."

Sarge looked at him. "You ought to be careful fucking with that man. He'll feed you to the pigs." Sarge looked at me and went on without pausing. "We got problems. The power is out, and I can't get in touch with Cecil. We need to ride to town and see what's up."

"That's why I'm here," I replied. As I did, I could hear the MRAP start up.

"Ted and Mikey are getting that beast running. Then, we're going to take it to town."

"I'm going to get a couple of people to go with us. But, first, we need to go by the ranch and look at that harvester. Then, it's time to get that corn cut," I replied.

"Get whoever you want, just hurry up. We're going to take the Hummer as well. I don't want any bullshit like the last trip to town."

"I'm going to borrow your ATV to speed this up," I said as I turned to leave.

First, I stopped at Dad's. No one came to the door, so I continued over to Danny's. At this hour of the morning, I should have known that's where everyone would be, and they were. The back porch was crowded with people having breakfast, and I made a general statement to them as soon as I came through the door.

"Power's out, as you know, and we can't get Cecil on the radio. So we're going to town to see what's up."

Thad looked up from his grits and said, "I'll go. I just want to be dropped off at the ranch so I can look at that harvester."

Danny quickly got to his feet, "I'll get my stuff. I want to see it too."

Dad didn't hesitate. "I don't know anything about power plants or corn harvesters, but I'll go and see where I can help."

As soon as I started talking, Ian and Jamie stood up and carried their dishes to the kitchen. As Jamie passed me, she said, "We'll get our gear."

"You sure?" I asked.

"I'm fine," she replied with a cold finality to her voice. I clearly understood our conversation was over.

We loaded into the MRAP and the Hummer. As we did so, I looked around at the people either in or waiting to get into a vehicle. I didn't see Aric, who I'd seen earlier, and I asked Sarge if he'd seen the man.

"He's staying here. I asked him to keep an eye on our security. I'm worried about those guys poking around the other day," Sarge replied.

Then I realized I hadn't seen Dalton either. "Where's the giant?" I asked.

"He's staying here too." Sarge paused and rubbed the back of his neck as he thought. "That man scares me," he said, looking me straight in the eye. "I've been all around the world, and I've met some bad men in my day. But there's something about that man." He paused again, "Even Ivan sees it. He fears Dalton, said we should too."

I was shocked at the statement. "I'm not afraid of him. He's never done anything to any of us. Hell, he's done nothing but help since he got here."

"I'm not afraid of him. When I said he scares me, I meant what he's capable of. That's a dangerous man and I am thankful as hell he's on our side, which is why he's staying here too. I don't think anyone will get past him."

"Where is he?" I asked.

The old man shrugged. "I don't know. Where is he most of the time? He's out getting his Sasquatch on, I guess."

I thought about that for a minute, and Sarge was right. Dalton was always disappearing and showing back up without a word about where he'd been or what he'd been up to. But it didn't bother me. I wasn't scared by the man, and it was quite the opposite. Whenever I was around him, there was a level of comfort. Kind of like Thad, but the feeling was different in a way I couldn't lay my finger on.

"I'm not afraid of him. But I know what you mean about him being a dangerous man. I feel that as well. But he's one of us, and I don't see that changing any time soon," I replied.

"He is one of us, and the fact that he's out there skulking around in the woods is why I'm not too worried about so many of us leaving. With Aric, Dalton, and Wallner's men, I think we're safe."

Squinting one eye, I said, "You know, Jess would probably split your sack open and run your leg through it for not thinking she is contributing to the defense here. Mel would probably be a little pissed too."

"Oh, bullshit!" Sarge shouted back. "I don't need to mention them because it'd be like saying you or I weren't doing our part! That's a given that those ladies are doing their part, carrying their share of the load."

"Calm down, you grumpy old fuck; I was just messing with you," I replied with a laugh.

As I replied, Doc stepped around the side of the MRAP. Sarge and I both looked at him. He looked at each of us, then spoke. "It's good you know the ladies do their part. They sure know it." He stopped for a beat, then continued. "So, I guess I don't need to tell them about this conversation then?"

I laughed, "Go ahead!"

Sarge's lip curled, "Ronnie, you little asshole, get in the fucking truck!"

Doc smiled and slapped the old man on the back, "Sure thing, boss."

"You're lucky I didn't slap the taste out of your mouth for that smartass shit," Sarge gruffed as Doc slammed the door shut. Then, looking at me, he said, "Ride with me in the Hummer. Your dad is there too. We're going to find Cecil. The rest are going to the ranch," Sarge said as we pulled out onto the road. "But we're stopping by the power plant first."

"Good," I said and leaned back in my seat.

We found Baker, Scott, and Terry inside the small control room of the turbine. A diesel generator could be heard running outside, and the instrument panels glowed with numerous small lights. I stopped at the door and looked around. Baker and Terry were bent over a control panel, and Scott had his head inside the open door of a long grey cabinet.

"What about now?" Scott called out.

"That's one, "Terry replied.

"Only one more," Baker said. "And I think we'll find it on the fuel skid."

Scott slammed the door shut, and Terry and Baker straightened up. They looked like shit. It was obvious they'd been up all night.

"Well?" Sarge asked.

Baker rubbed her forehead and pinched the bridge of her nose. "I think we've got it narrowed down. Shouldn't be much longer now, and it'll be ready to restart."

"What happened?" I asked.

Terry patted the console. "Old shit. Just old shit."

"There was a small overload here, blew some fuses and shit. So we had to find Cecil last night and get his help. That man is amazing. He knows where everything is in this rickety old place," Baker replied.

"If Cecil hadn't come to help, we'd still be scratching our asses," Scott said.

"That probably answers another question then," Sarge said. "We were worried about him, couldn't reach him on the radio."

"He's probably sleeping," Terry said. "We took him home a couple of hours ago."

Sarge nodded, "We'll stop by and check on him real quick."

"How long before you're done?" I asked.

"Another hour or so," Baker replied.

"We'll get the turbine back up and running. It'll take a little while longer to get the power back up. I had Eric go out and open some switches on the line. Once the plant is back up, I'll have him close those switches, and it'll be back on," Terry answered.

"Sounds like you have it all under control then," Sarge replied. "Is there anything we can do for you?"

"No, we're good. Soon as we get this up, we'll grab some sleep," Baker said.

"Alright then, we're going to check on Cecil, and then we'll head to the ranch. We've got a corn harvester to get running," Sarge replied.

We turned to head back to the truck. Dad was standing in the control room door, taking it all in. I paused to look at him. "What do you think?"

"How in the hell does this thing run?" He asked.

"We've wondered that ourselves. I don't know why, but there's still natural gas. The line, this one at least, has pressure. From what we've found here, the line comes from the west coast somewhere," I paused and looked back into the control room. "I don't know why, and I don't care. It works; that's all that matters."

Dad pointed at Baker and asked, "Who are they? Look military."

"That's Doc Baker. She's an Army engineer, and so are Terry and Scott there. We've got one more as well. We got lucky having them here."

Dad smiled and shook his head. "You know, since we got here, I haven't stopped being amazed. I'm standing here beside a damn power plant that operates, and I just can't believe it."

"You didn't think this shit would last forever, did you?" I asked with a grin.

"You know, I'd spent a lot of time thinking about that. I thought about mom and dad and growing up after World War Two and all they had to do. I thought about what this country went through during Vietnam. Then I thought about the state of the country when all this went down." He paused and looked at me. "And I guess I did think this would last forever. I figured we were done. I didn't think enough people could come together to get things going again. I see, thankfully, I was wrong, and there is hope, and I'm glad I can be a part of that."

I gripped his shoulder and squeezed it. "You damn sure are a part of it." Then I realized something. "I can't believe we haven't gotten you some weapons yet. So soon as we get home, we'll go into the armory and get you set up." Dad was looking at the Colt slung on his hip. "I know you have that, but we have way more. You need a rifle."

Dad lifted his tattered shoe, "And that pair of boots."

It made me laugh, "And that pair of boots, for sure."

As we rolled down the road, Dad asked, "Where are we headed?"

"I met some folks with a ranch just outside of town. They still have a couple hundred head of cattle, and we're working with them. Dave's a good guy, and I like him. He's got some good folks there."

"Cattle? How in the hell do they still have cattle?"

"Ole Dave has the manpower to secure it. But they're generous," Sarge replied. "He's donated beeves to the town to feed wounded and such. We traded fuel to him for a couple pregnant heifers."

Dad's head cocked to the side, "You have cattle?"

I nodded. "A couple." Dad laughed, shaking his head.

We pulled up to the gate and stopped. Almost immediately, a man on horseback appeared out of the woods. The horse wandered slowly over as we waited. Once I could make out who was on it, I stepped out and approached the gate.

Travis halted the horse, and I climbed up on the gate and reached for his hand. "Hey man, good to see you."

"You too," he replied. "Your other people are already up at the house." He dismounted and unlocked the gate.

"Good deal. How're things going here?" I asked.

"Good. No one bothers us."

"The best way to have it," I replied. "I'll take that any day."

Sarge pulled through the gate, and I closed and locked it. Then, giving Travis a wave, I said, "I'll catch you later, buddy."

He waved and turned his horse back towards the woods he'd been sitting in when we arrived. Sarge headed for the house, where we found Dave and Janet sitting on the porch. I was surprised not to see Mike and Ted up there. We got out and climbed up onto the porch and introduced Dad to them. We chatted for a couple of minutes, and I asked where the guys were.

"They're over there at the harvester with a couple of our guys," Janet replied.

I looked at Dad and said, "Let's head over and see what we can do."

Dad held his hand out, "Good to meet you, Dave, Janet." With that, we headed off towards the old barn where the machine sat.

Old barns, ranches, and farms were always interesting to me. They were littered with old machines, tools, and livestock handling equipment. Some of it I could figure out what it did. Some of it was a complete mystery. But more than that, I always wondered about the man that set it in its resting place. The last man that sat in the seat or walked behind the mysterious piece of machinery I happened to be looking over. It was an utterly unknowable mystery lost in the depths of time. Left to the weeds that grew up through it and the slow battle of the elements as rust made it unusable and at times unrecognizable. Even though there would never be an answer to these questions, they always popped into my head.

Dave's guys had hitched the machine to a tractor and pulled it out of the high weeds that were determined to consume it, out to an open area where it could be worked on. Danny was on his back under the machine, and Thad was standing over him, gone up to his shoulders as two of Dave's men worked at pulling and yanking on various parts. Mike and Ted stood slightly off to the side, and I walked over.

"Why aren't you two in there," I asked.

Ted rubbed his chin, "We're better at breaking shit than fixing it."

"Yeah," Mike chimed in. "We looked at it, but I couldn't find a barrel, trigger, or breech anywhere on the damn thing."

I laughed, "Yeah, I guess not. Why don't you two head up to the house? I think there's something up there you two can work on."

Ted smiled, "Well, we want to help out too."

I looked at the men working on the machine. "I don't see where you'd even get in there. Go on. We got this."

Mike wasn't as graceful with his thoughts. "Cool man, I think you're right. There is something up there I can work on."

Ted and Mike quickly disappeared, headed in the direction of the big house. I smiled as they walked away. It was good to see them interested in something, or rather, someone. Then, with the guys gone, I turned my attention back to the machine. One of Dave's men was going over how it operated.

"…and these flaps here pull the ears into this here, and it shells the corn. Takes it off the cob."

"Nice, so it picks the corn and shells it," Danny repeated.

Thad smiled, "This is going to be sweet. Whooooo!"

"If we can get it running," Dave's man replied.

Dad was leaned over the contraption looking at its inner workings. "I think we need to pull all these chains and get all the links moving again. It's pretty simple, really. But, first, let's drain the gearboxes and put fresh fluid in them. I don't think this will be too difficult."

The machine was pretty simple, as any good farm implement should be. It was PTO powered from a tractor via a driveshaft. This turned a gearbox that provided power to the various chain drives and screws that moved the shelled corn. It would be carried up a chute via a screw and collected in a crib that would be pulled behind it. What came out was finished whole corn ready to be ground or used for feed.

"What about the crib?" I asked.

Dave's man didn't look up from the gearbox he was working on. "We've got 'em. Not a problem. Just have to check out the doors and make sure they operate, is all."

When the man stood up, I asked, "What's your name?"

He wiped his hands on a rag and held one out, "Audie. Audie Piner."

"Good to meet you, Audie. Morgan." We shook, and I took a minute to introduce everyone.

"We didn't see you last time we were up here," I said.

He laughed. "I keep away from the house. My wife, Kim, and I have a little place in the barn. I prefer to be working on something."

"I imagine there's no shortage of that around here," Dad replied.

Audie laughed and shook his head. "No, no shortage of things to do around here. We're always trying to find a way to make do with something. Like this thing here," he motioned at the New Deal. "It'll be good to have a bunch of corn."

"Well," I replied, "let's see if we can get it running."

Audie slapped the top of the machine, "She'll run."

We worked lubricating chains and getting stuck links freed for most of the day. Like most farms and ranches, Dave had five-gallon jugs of gear oil, and Audie and Dad had the gearbox cleaned up and turning in no time. I was lying under the machine when I heard Janet's voice. "Dinner time. I'm sure you guys are all hungry."

I looked out to see her and Ted each carrying a large basket. Thad looked up and smiled. "You didn't have to do that."

Janet set her basket down. "Daddy always said, working men need to eat. You work, you eat. It's just that simple."

Janet proceeded to unload the basket on the hood of the hummer. Removing a dishcloth from a large bowl, she revealed fried chicken. Another bowl contained biscuits, and Ted set an insulated jug of coffee out.

"Is that fried chicken?" Dad asked.

Janet nodded with a smile. "Yes, it is. We butchered a bunch of birds the other day. We've got so many now we had to do something with them."

Dad reached in and took out a piece of chicken. Taking a bite from it, his eyes rolled back as grease dripped down his chin. Then, eyes still closed, he sat chewing. "Mmm, man, that's good. I never thought I'd taste anything like it again. What'd you fry it in?"

"We render beef lard down," Janet replied as she took a leg from the bowl.

I looked at a piece and replied, "So this is the heart surgeon special, huh?"

Janet laughed and replied, "You don't have to eat it."

Holding up a hand in protest, I replied, "No, no, I'll eat it. Let's not get carried away."

"That's what I thought," Janet replied as she took a bite of the leg.

We enjoyed the chicken and biscuits along with the coffee. It was a good lunch. The kind eaten by hard-working men and women for decades in this country, decades ago. We all sat around while we ate, chatting. Janet asked about our progress, and we filled her in on what we were doing.

"So, you think you'll get it running?" She asked.

"I think we will," Dad replied as he drained his cup.

"I know we will!" Audie replied. I was starting to like this guy.

We thanked Janet for lunch, and she and Ted collected the remains and headed back to the house, leaving us to finish our work. We'd been at it for a couple of hours when Sarge walked up with Mike and Ted.

"We're going to ride into town to check on Cecil," Sarge said.

"Ok," I replied. "We still have work here to do."

"We'll be back," Sarge replied as he climbed into the driver's seat.

As Mike and Ted passed, I asked, "The old man ruin your fun?"

Mike didn't look too pleased. "Like he needs us to ride to town. He just doesn't like seeing anyone happy. Hell, the old fuck could take Ian and Jamie, but no, it has to be us," he replied in disgust.

"No one goes alone, Mikey, you know that," Ted replied as he opened the door.

"Quit your bitchin' and get yer ass in here!" Sarge barked.

"Yep," Dad said with a laugh, "he's a lot like a First Sargent I had in Vietnam."

The Hummer rumbled to life and was soon headed towards the gate. We went back to our work and finally managed to get the last chain off the machine. Then, we worked on freeing up the links using hammers and whatever kind of oil we could find. As I was working one side of a link while Dad held the other, Danny walked up.

"We need to replace some of those rubber flaps that move the corn into the shucker. I'm going to see if I can find some old tires or something."

Without looking up, I replied, "Ok, cool."

"I have an idea, Danny," Audie said and waved for Danny to follow him.

The two men walked into the old barn and reemerged with a sizeable black roll on their shoulders. Returning to where we were working, Audie looked over his shoulder at Danny and asked, "You ready?" Danny nodded, and they tossed the load from their shoulders.

"This will work better than tires," Audie said as he cut a piece of cord holding the roll together. Unrolling it, he explained, "This is an old conveyor belt. It's perfect for what we need."

Looking over at it, I asked, "Is there anything Dave doesn't have around here?"

Folding his knife up, Audie replied, "Well. I'm not sure. I haven't been here that long."

"You're not part of this group here?" Thad asked.

"We are now. But we've only been here a couple of weeks. Kim, my wife, was getting pretty weak. I ran into one of Dave's men, Travis, and he talked with Dave and agreed to meet us. After we talked for a bit, he invited us to stay here. So these are good folks here."

"Dave seems like a good man," I replied.

"How much corn do you have?" Audie asked.

"It's about forty acres. Cecile planted it, and we're hoping to get it all picked with the help of this thing," I replied.

"Well then," Audie replied with a smile, "let's get her put back together."

Mike sat sulking in the sling seat of the Hummer. It seemed every time he tried to spend some time with Crystal, something came up. And that something was Linus Mitchel. Eustis was quiet as it had been since the day of the attack by the Russians. The pockmarked streets and burned buildings still told the tale of that day. Gone now were all the bodies. Most of them had been buried in a mass grave dug between Grove and Bay Streets where the old hospital once stood.

Sarge steered the old truck slowly down the small town's streets that were still littered with debris from the attack. Cecil lived in a small, neatly cared-for house on North Hawley Street. Pulling into the yard, Sarge grunted to himself. Stepping out of the truck, he looked down at the recently cut grass and chuckled. Mike and Ted quickly got out. They either didn't notice the grass or didn't comment.

Sarge walked up to the house door and rapped on it with his knuckles. After a moment, the door swung open. Cecil stepped back as it did, and Sarge noticed the old revolver in his hand.

"Afternoon Cecil." Sarge offered as a greeting.

Cecil smiled that broad toothy smile. "Afternoon, Linus. What brings you out here?"

"We just came to check on you. I couldn't get you on the radio and got worried."

Waving Sarge in, Cecil replied, "I was up at the plant till the wee hours. A damn breaker tripped and caused some other issues. It took a while to get it all sorted out."

"I stopped by the plant. Baker told me you were there all night."

"You want some water or something?" Cecil asked. 'There ain't much, but I got some water."

"Naw," Sarge replied as he looked out the door. "Matter of fact, I got something for you." Then, leaning out, Sarge shouted, "Hey Ted, bring that stuff in here!"

Ted came through the door with a small bundle of cloth and handed it to Sarge. "Hey Cecil, good to see you," Ted said with a nod before disappearing.

Sarge handed Cecil the bundle, "Here's you some dinner."

"What's this?" Cecil asked as he unwrapped it. His eyes widened in wonder, "Is that fried chicken?"

"Yes, sir. That Janet makes some fine fried chicken."

"Well, be sure and thank her for me," Cecil replied as he carefully wrapped it back up. "I'll save this for supper time."

"Morgan and the boys are working on that picker. I think they'll have it running today, maybe."

"That would be great. I'm anxious to get that corn picked. I don't want to lose any of it. It's good and dry. Ready to be picked."

"Why don't you get your tractor and follow us over to the ranch. They'll probably have the thing ready by the time we get back," Sarge said, motioning to the tractor.

"Might as well. I'm up now," Cecil replied with a smile.

It didn't take Cecil long to get things in order, and he was sitting on the old tractor in no time. Sarge pulled out onto the street, and Cecil followed behind, shifting the tractor to get it up to speed. The trip to the ranch only took a little longer than the ride to Cecil's place. One of Dave's men met us at the gate and quickly let us through. Cecil smiled and waved at the man on horseback as he trundled through the gate, and the man replied with a nod.

At the barn, Cecil shut the tractor off and sat in the seat, looking at the little machine that was going to save so much time and labor.

"What'cha think? She gonna run?" Cecil asked.

Audie looked up from where he was leaned over into the top of the contraption and replied, "Why hell yeah, she'll run!"

Cecil smiled and walked over with his hands on his hips in the way of old men. He looked the harvester over and smiled with satisfaction. I took a moment to introduce Audie to him. Audie was climbing down from the machine, wiping his hands on a rag. Then, getting them clean enough, he held his hand out, and the two men shook.

"Good to meet you, Cecil," Audie offered.

"You as well," Cecil replied. "Any man that can get me one of these is a man I want as a friend."

"I hear you got a field of corn about ready to pick."

Cecil nodded, "I do indeed, and this is going to make it so much easier."

Audie nodded at a large wagon with four rubber tires and high sides. It had a long hitch coming off its front, and the front wheels articulated to make turning easier. "That grain trailer is in good shape and should do the job just fine."

Cecil looked over, and a smile spread across his face. Then, shaking his head, he replied, "This is just something else. I honestly thought we were going to have to pick all that corn by hand."

"Not now," Audie replied with a smile. "Things are as good as we are going to get them. We've got all the chains tightened up and greased the entire thing. If you want, back over here and hook up to it. We'll put her in gear and see how she runs."

Cecil wasted no time getting up into his tractor and backing it over. The PTO driveshaft was connected, and the New Deal harvester was connected to the tractor. This took a few minutes as the barn was scoured for the correct size pins to complete the task, but like all barns, you can usually find what you need if you look hard enough.

Audie stepped back and pushed his ball cap up on his head. He looked around and said, "Well, here goes nothing." And waved at Cecil.

Cecil engaged the PTO and let the clutch out. The harvester bucked and lurched as the sprockets began to turn, and the chains tightened up. In a moment, the old piece of equipment was whirling away.

Audie smiled and shouted, "Hot damn!"

Cecil's toothy smile was spread across his face as well. He disengaged the PTO, and the machine stopped. Climbing down, he asked Audie, "You think we could get another tractor to pull that grain truck? It'll make it easier than me having to unhook everything and run a load to town."

"Dave's got this tractor," Audie replied, pointing to the one they'd pulled the New Deal out of the weeds with, "I don't see why he wouldn't let us use it."

"This corn is for everyone. You folks will get your share of it as well," Cecil replied.

"Let me run up to the house and talk to Dave, I'm sure he won't care, but it's his tractor."

"You two hop into the truck," Sarge said, motioning to the Hummer, "I'll drive you up there."

Mike slapped Ted on the arm and shouted, "We'll go with you!"

Before Sarge could complain, both men were already in with Mike sitting in the turret. Sarge grumbled under his breath as he climbed into the driver's seat.

Dad and I watched them drive away. When the Hummer disappeared, Dad looked at the harvester. "This is something else." He studied the machine for a few minutes, then added, "how are you going to grind the corn?"

"We found a couple of grist stones that we're engineering back to their old purpose up at Renninger's. Still trying to figure out how we'll make that work."

"Being able to grind that corn will be a game-changer. There's a lot of food in that field." He thought for a minute, then asked, "Where are the stones?"

"They're in town somewhere. Cecil knows where they are."

"I can surely help with trying to sort out a way to turn them."

I laughed, "You always were good at Rube Goldberg engineering."

"Story of my life. When you ain't got nothing, you gotta make do with what you can."

Danny and Thad walked over to the MRAP where Jamie and Ian had been keeping out of the way. Thad pulled the water keg we kept inside to the edge of the back door and filled a plastic bottle. As he drained it, Danny did likewise. I motioned at it, and Dad and I walked over to get ourselves a drink as well.

Thad offered up his bottle, and as Dad filled it, I asked him, "You feel better now that the corn will be picked in time?"

Thad smiled, "I feel better that it will be picked, shucked, and hulled and we don't have to spend days and days doing it."

"Not to mention sparing a lot of blisters," Dad offered.

"We just need to get those grist wheels set up somehow," Danny replied.

"I was thinking about that," I replied, "I think we should take them to the orange juice plant. There's all kinds of machinery in there, we should be able to come up with something."

"That's a good idea," Thad said with a nod. "I was trying to figure out how we were going to turn them." Then, he smiled and laughed, "I forgot all about the power and was working on how we could use the cows to do it."

Dad snorted water out of his nose. "I'd like to see you convince a cow to walk in a circle turning a grist wheel!"

Thad nodded, "As I said, I was working on it. I didn't know how I was going to get a cow to do it either!" He said with a laugh.

The Hummer returned, and Cecil and Audie hopped out. They were talking between themselves and gesturing. Audie quickly mounted his tractor and pulled it over to the grain wagon. Cecil was there waiting on him, and the two had the trailer hooked to the tractor in a flash. Cecil walked back towards his tractor with a smile.

"We're going to go get started right now," he said as he stepped up onto the machine.

I nodded, "We'll ride over with you," I called back.

Knowing what was happening, Jamie was already in the MRAP. The engine rumbled to life, and I heard the air brakes release. Looking at the guys, I said, "Guess that's our cue."

We climbed into the enormous armored truck, and Jamie was moving before the back door was even shut. We made for an odd procession down Highway 44, two tractors, one with the harvester and one with a grain trailer attached. The Hummer and the MRAP bringing up the rear. The mental image this conjured as we rolled down the road was a perfect statement about our current situation. The two things that seemed to matter most in our new world were food and weapons.

In the Before, there was a never-ending discussion on gun control. There were arguments over the improperly used term *assault weapons* and magazine capacities. These were issues with hot passions on either side. But, to me, it was never a question. Our Constitution clearly recognized our right to bear arms. These rights weren't granted to us in that historical document but recognized. Something most people failed to realize.

And it was surreal that guns were the only issue where society at large was held accountable for the individual actions of others. Whenever some psychopath committed a heinous crime with a firearm, every gun owner in the country was convicted in the media court. Because some people were crazy, the rest of us were supposed to surrender our weapons, thereby relinquishing our means of self-defense. And yet these same people would go to an extreme to not draw the same conclusions when presented against the *chosen* classes of the day.

I had to admit, that was one good thing that came out of what happened. All those inane, useless arguments were moot. No one was arguing over whether or not you needed a gun today. Hell, the only people alive were those with guns. That thought made me laugh, the fact that we now live in a nation of universal gun ownership. I wonder what those politicians that spent their lives trying to strip our rights away thought of that. If they even considered it. Or if they were even alive.

I leaned back against the truck with a smile. Dad sat across from me and cocked his head to the side, questioning. I gave him a thumbs up with a little shake of my head. He nodded and relaxed. The rest of the ride passed quickly as I ruminated on the politics of the past that meant absolutely nothing today.

Jamie followed the tractors towards the cornfield, rolling off-road and parked near the old oak tree where Cecil often sought relief while out working. We all climbed out and watched as Cecil and Audie discussed their plan.

"Odds on this working out?" Mike asked.

"You jinx us, and I'll choke you till yer dead, swear to the Almighty!" Sarge barked back.

"It'll work," Thad offered.

"It has to," Danny added.

We watched as they lined the tractors up on the first two rows. They were at the far end of the field from us, intending to work back in our direction. Cecil set up on the first two rows and waited as Audie lined the grain wagon with the discharge chute. Then, with a nod from Audie, Cecil put the harvester in gear, and the tractor moved into the corn. We all fell silent in anticipation of what would come next.

I watched the chute, trying to will the corn out of it. We could see the stalks wobble and fall to the big machine, and in a moment, corn began to spray out of the discharge chute and into the grain wagon. As people started to clap, hoot, and holler, a cheer erupted. There were several high fives and back slapping as well. As the tractor moved down the row, we watched in awe as it closer with each falling stalk. When he was within shouting distance, Cecil took off his hat and waved it at us.

Standing up on the tractor, he shouted, "Now that's how you harvest corn!" he looked back at the discharge chute and the spray of corn pouring out of it. "Look at it all! Looks like gold! Better than gold!"

As he completed the row, he watched the chute, and when it stopped spitting out corn, he nodded to Audie, who pulled his tractor away to allow Cecil to turn around. They performed the same choreography on the other end of the field, and corn was soon pouring into the grain trailer again.

"Well, I'll be damned," Dad said.

I looked over and asked, "What?"

Dad was shaking his head and smiling. "It's just amazing. I mean, we're watching corn being mechanically harvested. I thought the days of technology were over. I figured the world now operated on manpower alone."

"Well, there isn't much, I guess. But we're working on bringing some of it back." I looked over at him for added emphasis, "Not all of it, just some of it."

Dad grunted, "Yeah, there's a lot of shit from then we don't need back."

CHAPTER 4

With the process now well underway, we had a new problem. I voiced it to Dad and Sarge. "What are we going to do with all this corn now? Where are we going to put it?"

"I been thinking on that, and honestly, I haven't come up with a solution yet," Sarge replied.

"There any silos around?" Dad asked.

"There are, just not where we can keep an eye on it," I replied.

We tossed a couple of ideas around, with Thad and Danny offering their thoughts as well. Eventually, it was decided to simply take it to the orange juice plant and dump it there. The plant was large enough to drive the tractor and wagon into it and then dump it on the floor. Also, the grain wagon was a belly dump style so emptying it wouldn't be difficult. Plus, there was the added benefit of full-time security there since the power plant was located there.

"I'm going to ride down to the plant and take a look at it, " I said.

"I'll go with you," Dad said, and Thad said he would as well.

"Get it figured out," Sarge replied. "It won't be long, and that wagon will be full."

We took the Hummer down to the plant to take a look. Then, going inside the cavernous building, we used the manual bypass, a chain hanging beside the door, to open the large roll-up door on one end. There was all manner of processing equipment inside, but there was more than enough room on the south end of the building to pull the tractor in and dump the corn.

As we stood looking it over, Thad said, "We need to get some shovels in here. He'll have to pull in here and dump as he turns around. It'll take a little shoveling to keep it all together."

"Yeah, some of those big ones would be good," I replied.

"You're going to have a problem with rats in here," Dad said. "You'll need to figure something out to keep them away."

"Yeah, I was thinking about that. There's just no way to contain it all. I think there's going to be more of this than we think," I replied.

Thad laughed, "Yeah, I'm thinking we're about to have a damn mountain of corn."

Looking at Thad, I asked, "You want to hang out here, and we'll ride back and tell them where to come to? Then, you can point them to the right spot when they get here."

Thad nodded, "Sure. I'll keep an eye out for them."

As we walked back to the truck, I looked at Dad and asked, "You want to drive?"

Surprised, he asked, "Huh?"

Pointing at the Hummer, I said, "You want to drive? I figure it's been a while since you drove anything."

It obviously wasn't something he'd considered. After a moment, he replied, "Sure, why the hell not."

He got in the driver's side and looked around for a minute. I pointed out where the starter switch was, and he fired it up and pulled out of the plant onto nineteen. As he drove back towards the field, he laughed out loud. It made me smile, and I asked, "What's so funny?"

He was still laughing and shaking his head. "All this, everything. I mean, a couple of weeks ago, I figured I'd never see any more of the world than what I could walk to. Damn sure never thought I'd be driving down the damn road in a Hummer, no less! Not to mention having to figure out what to do with forty acres of damn corn!"

I slapped him on the shoulder. "Well, I'm glad you're here with me, driving down the road, in a Hummer no less!"

He looked over smiling, then broke out into a laugh. His laughing got me to laughing, and we laughed all the way back. Where we would turn off the road into the field, we saw a man standing. He had something significant with him, and I sat up in my seat, the laughter gone.

"What's this about?" Dad asked.

I checked the chamber of my rifle and replied, "I don't know. Slow down and stop a little away from him."

Dad nodded, and the truck rolled slowly as we approached. Finally, about twenty feet away, we came to a stop. The large object turned out to be a bicycle with a trailer attached. He was a pretty big man, which struck me because of most people's diet today. He stood, leaned against his bike, watching the work in the field. He looked over with one eye squinted, smiled, and waved when we got closer.

I stepped out of the truck with my rifle hanging from its sling. I nodded and waved as I stepped in front of the immense desert tan machine. The man waved again and called out, "Hello!"

"How's it going?" I asked as I stepped towards him.

He gestured to the field and replied, "Just watching the show." Then, he looked back towards where the two tractors were working and said, "Haven't seen anything like that in a long time." He looked at me and continued, "I've been around quite a bit, and this is the first time I've seen tractors out working a field like this. No one has fuel, ya know."

I nodded. "Yeah, we got lucky."

He looked back at the field and said, "What'cha going to do with all that corn?"

"We've got a lot of people to feed."

He nodded, "That's good. Lots of hungry folks these days." Then he squinted, looking at me. "Is that a badge?"

I nodded, "It is."

He turned to face me. "You a Sheriff?"

"Of sorts. For this area anyway."

He looked around as though searching for something. "What is this place?"

"You're between Eustis and Umatilla," I replied.

The man shook his head. "Not what I meant. I mean," he gestured to the field again, "there's equipment out there picking corn," then he pointed back to me, "and there's a damn Sheriff standing right here in front of me. I haven't seen anything like this since before things went to shit!"

"We're trying to get things back together. To improve people's lives."

"Are there a lot of people here?"

"A fair amount."

He seemed to be thinking. Then, after a moment, he asked, "Where'd you get the Hummer?"

"From the National Guard."

He shaded his eyes with a hand and pointed into the field, "What about that MRAP out there? Where'd it come from?"

I looked out across the field at the big truck sitting under the tree. "We uh, acquired it."

The man looked back, one eye squinted again, "From the DHS?" The question made me a little uncomfortable, and I just shrugged in reply. "I don't know if you've had any dealings with them yet," he paused and looked me in the eye, "but you don't want any."

"You run into them?" I asked.

The man nodded. "Yeah, and you're about to." He replied.

I gripped my rifle, and the man held up his hands. "What do you mean by that?" I asked.

"Not from me, but they're on their way this direction. So that's why I'm on the road, trying to stay away from them."

"What do you mean they're on their way here?" I asked.

"I was over in Davenport, and they rolled through. People thought they were coming to help. Turned out that wasn't the case. They've got MRAPs and a couple of Hummers. There's a bunch of people with them, and they're not all DHS. They've got some real scumbags with them as well. Gang members and shit."

"How do you know they're coming this way?"

He gestured at me with a hand, "You and some old grumpy Army guy tangle with them up at a camp or something?" I nodded. "Shit," he muttered.

"Why's that a problem? And how do you know about it?"

"Because they said they're coming here, specifically."

I tensed at the statement and felt my stomach fall out from under me. "They said they're coming here? Mentioned Eustis specifically?"

"Oh yeah, they're pissed. They didn't mention any town names, just two people," he pointed at me, wagging his finger, "and I'm guessing you're the guy they're pissed at. Well, one of them. They mentioned that older guy, the Army guy."

"And they just told you all this?"

He laughed, "Hell no! I didn't spend a lot of time with them. I stayed out of sight for the most part but heard enough to piece it all together." He pointed at the field again, "they're going to love this." He shook his head, "you guys are fucked."

I walked over to him and asked, "What's your name?"

Turning to face me, he replied, "Aaron Metcalf."

I looked down at the pistol in a holster on his hip. It was a Glock of some variant. "Can I trust you to leave that shooter in its holster?"

He looked down at it, "Oh yeah. I'm not going to bother you none."

"Would you mind taking a ride out into that field with me? I've got some other folks I'd like you to tell your story to."

Aaron looked at his bike, "I don't want to leave this here. Don't want anyone to take it, ya know. You can't leave shit just sitting around."

"It'll be perfectly safe here, I promise you. No one is going to mess with it."

He shrugged, "Okay then."

We walked over to the Hummer, and I opened the passenger door, saying, "Sit up front here." Aaron climbed in without comment as I got into the back seat. Dad looked back, and I nodded, and he put the truck in gear and started into the field.

Aaron looked back over the seat, "This is really cool! I haven't been in any kind of vehicle in forever!"

Dad rolled to a stop, and Sarge turned to look back. Then, seeing another person, he started towards us. He looked at Aaron when I got out, then at me, awaiting an explanation. I began by introducing Aaron to Sarge.

The old man nodded, "Good to meet you, Aaron. What can I do for you?"

"Aaron, tell him what you told me," I said.

A curious look spread across Sarge's face. It didn't last long as Aaron started into his tale. As he retold it, people began to drift over, and before long, he was standing in the center of the group. Eyes darted back and forth as they listened, and people began to fidget. It was unsettling news at best. When Aaron finished, it was quiet for a long moment.

Sarge was the first to speak. "Aaron, you're certain of this? You heard them say they were coming here?"

Aaron nodded, "Oh yeah, they were pretty clear about it. Chuck and that Japanese guy were really pissed about that whole camp thing."

Sarge and I looked at one another, then I asked, "Japanese guy?"

"Yeah, had a weird name, began with an N."

"Niigata," I said flatly.

Aaron snapped his fingers, "Yeah! That's it. You know him?"

"Know of him," I replied.

Aaron looked at the group gathered around him. "So, you're the guys they're so pissed at. What did you guys do?"

"An incomplete job from the sound of it," Sarge replied. "How many people do they have with them?"

Aaron shrugged, "I don't really know. But there's a bunch of them. They have a lot of guns. Bunch of trucks."

"You said they have MRAPs?" Sarge asked. Aaron nodded. "Anything else?"

"They have a couple of Hummers and some other diesel trucks, like old Army trucks. They pull a big tank of diesel around with them. They have MREs and all kinds of stuff."

"You didn't answer my question. How many people do they have? Ballpark," Sarge reiterated.

Aaron thought about it for a minute. "Fifty, sixty maybe. I mean, I didn't count them. I tried to stay out of the way. They weren't very friendly."

"Shit," Ted muttered.

"Did you see any heavy weapons? Big machineguns, anything like that?" Sarge asked.

"Oh, they have machineguns, belt feds mounted to the trucks. I saw one fifty cal on one of the MRAPs."

Sarge thought the reply over. "Well, they have some light armor and machineguns. I can't say if they have any heavy weapons at all, but I'm betting they don't. They're DHS, and they wouldn't have had that shit to start with and really aren't going to come up with it now."

"That's a hell of an assumption," Ted said.

Looking at Aaron, I asked, "Where are you headed to?"

"Nowhere, really. I was just trying to stay out of their way. Guess I screwed up and came to the very place they're looking for."

"Well, I appreciate you bringing this to our attention. With that said, you can't leave." He looked at me, shock on his face. "I don't mean forever, just for a little while. You have to see it from our side; we don't know that you're not here doing recon for them."

"Look, I don't want no trouble," Aaron replied. "I'm just passing through; I'd like to just be on my way."

"Morgan is right, Aaron; you're going to have to stick around for a bit. But we're not going to do anything to you, and you can keep your pistol and any other weapons you have. The only thing we're going to do is offer you a place to stay and feed you."

Aaron perked up at the last part of the statement. "I have a tent; I don't need a place to stay. Did you say feed me?"

"Yeah, we'll keep you fed while you're here. As I said, you're not going to be a prisoner, but you're not free to leave either. Not yet, at least," I replied.

Aaron looked at the people standing around him. His eyes lingered over the collection of weapons clearly visible. "Like I said, I don't want any trouble. If you want me to hang out, I'll hang out. I mean, you said I could keep my pistol, so you can't be that bad."

"We're letting you keep your pistol because you've done nothing to threaten us. And we're not bad people, you'll see," Sarge said. "If you want to stay in your tent, we'll give you a spot to pitch it. You can get a shower and some hot food this evening."

"A shower?" Aaron asked.

"Yeah, a hot one," Thad replied.

Aaron smiled, "Hell, this is getting better all the time."

"Just hang out here for a while. We'll be headed home later, and you can set up your tent and whatnot, and we'll get you fed," Sarge replied.

Aaron looked out towards the road, and I said, "It ain't going anywhere, promise you that." He relaxed after that and asked if we had any water.

"There's some in the MRAP," Thad replied, pointing at the truck.

"This is going to be a problem," Sarge announced grimly.

"No shit, if they have that many people, they're going to be a for-real no shit problem," Ted replied.

"Nah," Mike voiced. "We have the Bradley. It'll smoke those MRAPs they have without breaking a sweat. Might as well be driving in here in cardboard."

"That's true." Sarge shot back, "but with that many of them, we'll have to catch them all at once, or we'll have a hell of a fight on our hands."

"At least they don't know we know they're coming. That's something," I said.

Sarge grunted. "A big something too. Try and find out from that guy where they were and see if you can figure out how long it's going to take them to get here."

Sarge and the guys wandered off to talk things over. I looked at Dad and said, "Why don't you go with them. You've got some experience in this sort of thing."

Dad shrugged, "Unless you've got a Loach with an M-60, there isn't much I have to offer."

"We ain't got a Loach, but you've seen enough of this kind of shit. More than most of us here."

He nodded. "I see what you mean," and walked over to where the guys were.

I looked at Aaron and asked, "You hungry?"

"Who isn't these days?"

I walked towards the MRAP and motioned for him to follow me. I pulled an open case of MREs to the back door and pointed at it. "Grab what you want. That water keg is full too."

Aaron didn't hesitate. It struck me that he didn't even look at the menu and just tore open the bag. In moments the ground was littered with bags and boxes from the meal. As Aaron quickly ate, I reached in and took the cup we kept for the water keg and filled it, handing it to him. "Here, wash some of that down before you choke."

He took the cup and started to chug it. He stopped almost immediately, grimacing. He looked at the cup and announced, "Holy shit, that's cold!"

"Oh yeah, there's ice in the keg."

"Ice? Where the hell did you get ice?"

I smiled, "I told you, we're trying to get things fixed around here."

Aaron looked at the cup, then the MRE, then the truck. "Damn, I wish I could stay here. This is amazing."

"You're welcome here. We've got plenty of places you can stay. We can always use another good man."

"I don't know what good a former car salesman can be."

"Everyone has skills, buddy. You've made it this long." I pointed back towards the road, "You came up with that bike and trailer. You've probably got more skills than you think."

He shrugged, "You know. You just keep going. Do what you gotta do."

I pointed at him, "It's that attitude that I'm talking about. You came to us with a lot of info that you gathered. That's a skill in itself."

Between bites, he replied, "I like to talk to people. But, you know, being in sales it was just a thing. I talked to a lot of people where those guys were staying. It was kind of funny how they operate." He took another bite. "From what I got, when they first come into town, they sort of throw their weight around, take what they want, who they want," he looked at me, "know what I mean, women."

I nodded. "Sadly, we have personal experience with that."

"Well, after they make sure everyone knows they're in charge, they kind of ease up. If they tell you to do something and you do it, they leave you alone. If you don't, well, anything is possible."

"And they're not working for the government?"

Aaron snorted, "Uh, no. They made it pretty clear that first, there wasn't a government and that they were the ones protecting people."

"Sounds like they're doing a fine job of protecting people."

With his mouth full, he nodded, "Yeah, and they are scared shitless of the Army. That was always a thing with them. I guess they think the Army is the only one that can stop them. But they haven't seen any of them in a while."

"Yeah, DOD is pretty busy dealing with the Cubans and Russians. I think they took care of the Chinese at this point."

He pointed at me with his spoon and nodded. "Yeah, those Russians are a real pain in the ass. I guess these guys have run into them before too. But they kind of worked with them or at least decided to leave one another alone. Unfortunately, I didn't really get the full story on that."

I mulled that over, more to let him eat in peace than anything. I watched as the two tractors worked the field together. It looked like a perfectly choreographed dance between the two machines. Corn spewed out of the chute and into the trailer that Audie was pulling. As I watched, I noticed the nuance of what was going on. Audie watched the corn as it piled into the trailer and adjusted where it fell to make sure the entire trailer was filled.

When the mound rose above the side of the trailer to the point I could see it from where I stood, I saw Audie call out to Cecil. Cecil halted his tractor, and Audie pulled up beside him. They spoke for a minute, and Audie pulled away and headed towards where we were gathered. Then, pulling up, he shut the tractor down. I walked over to him as he wiped his forehead with a handkerchief.

"She's full," Audie announced.

"Ready to dump her?" I asked.

"I reckon so. Got to empty this so we can get the rest of it."

"Good idea. We're going to have to find something to put this in," I said as I looked at the trailer and thought about the amount of corn it contained.

"I've got some ideas on that too," Audie replied.

Looking back out at the field, I said, "Damn, there's gonna be a lot of corn."

Audie smiled, "Looks like we'll be eating a lot of grits."

"Let me get the guys to escort you back," I said, looking over where Sarge and Dad were talking with Mike and Ted.

"I don't think we'll need that," Audie replied.

"Yeah, who'd want a trailer fill of corn? No one would try and take that."

Audie laughed, "I guess you're right."

I walked over and interrupted the conversation. "Ted, can you and Mike escort Audie back to the plant so he can dump this load?"

"Sure thing," Ted replied and nodded at Mike and the two-headed for the Hummer.

"So, what are you guys thinking?" I asked.

Sarge looked down at the ground before replying. "Well, we've got a serious problem on our hands for damn sure."

"What are you thinking?" I reiterated.

"We're going to have to get them into town," he nodded in the direction of Eustis. "We'll need them all on Bay Street and use the buildings to prevent their movement."

"Make it a kill zone," Dad added.

"How are you going to manage that?" I asked.

"We're going to have to take a look at that. I have some ideas," Sarge replied.

"We're going to need more people," I said.

Sarge nodded. "We're going to have to use everyone we have, that's for sure."

Dad stepped around us and looked at the cornfield. Cecil walked up as he surveyed the field.

"You got a long way to go," Dad said.

Cecil spun around to look the field over. "Sure enough. I don't think we'll get it all today. Probably take tomorrow to get her all done."

"There's gonna be corn coming out of our ears," Dad replied.

"We got plenty of mouths to fill with it," Sarge added.

"Y'all sorted out the grist mill yet?" Cecil asked.

"Dad, Audie, and them boys at the ranch are going to work on it," I replied.

"Audie seems like a pretty smart feller," Dad said.

"Glad to have him. We need folks that can sort things out," Sarge said. "We've got to get a plan on how we're going to deal with these assholes that are headed this way."

"Again," I said.

Thad and Danny sat on the old spool, talking quietly to one another. Finally, Thad spoke up, "We have to finish it this time. We can't leave a single one of them. This can't happen again."

I was surprised at the statement. Thad was always very level, predictable. He was a kind man with a big heart, and it surprised me to hear him talk about leaving no survivors. To kill every person that showed up with this gang. I knew he was right, of course. We'd let them go once, tried to apply the law and punishments from the before. But the law didn't get this new world we lived in. The only punishment that fits today was of the permanent variety. And death was the only thing permanent in this world.

"You're right, Thad," Sarge replied. "We can't allow a single living soul to escape, or we'll be doing this all over again."

"What's up?" Cecil asked.

We gave him the elevator version of what Aaron told us. As he listened, he looked Aaron over. Aaron didn't engage in the discussion. Instead, he continued to work his way through the open case of MREs like it was a job or compulsion. After Cecil had been filled in, he asked Aaron, "When was the last time you ate?"

Dropping an empty retort pouch onto the ground, he replied, "You know how it is. You eat when there is food to be eaten."

"Around here, we do things a little different," Sarge said.

"We eat regularly. You don't have to stuff yourself," I replied.

Aaron looked at those gathered around him. "Look, you look like nice folks here." He looked at the MRAP he was sitting on and added, "And you've got a little hardware. But what's coming, what's headed this way? I don't think you guys understand just what it is. I've seen these people do some horrible shit."

"Well, Aaron, there's more to us than meets the eye. We've already dealt with these shitheads once. We took down a FEMA camp they were running. We have a few tricks up our sleeves as well."

Aaron didn't look convinced and shrugged the comment off. "That's all well and good. But I wish you would just let me be on my way."

"Sorry, friend. You're here until this is done," I replied.

"When the guys get back," Sarge started, "we're going to head home. We've got work to do." Then, looking at Thad and Danny, he asked, "Can you two stay here with Ian and Jamie to keep an eye on this?"

"We'll be here," Danny replied.

"We'll take the MRAP back and leave you the Hummer," Sarge replied. "We've got a lot of work to do."

"We need to get with Dave and his people. We're going to need them," I replied.

Sarge nodded. "We will. But I want to go through the armory and get an idea of how many people we can field. We're going to need every trigger puller we can find."

"I think you need to get on the horn with Eglin. Get Ivan's ass out of here, and since they're coming, they can bring some party favors," I said.

"Way ahead of you, Junior. Leave the big ideas to me," Sarge replied.

The tractor and Hummer came rolling into the field with the truck heading our direction and Audie steering the tractor back to the unfinished rows. Seeing him, Cecil gave us a nod and headed back to his tractor. Sarge told the guys to load into the MRAP and get it started, and we piled in.

"Thad," I pointed towards the road, "there's a bike and a trailer out there. Can you load that up and bring it back to the house?" He gave me a thumbs up in reply.

"I'd rather take it with us now," Aaron quickly said.

"It won't fit in here," I said, pointing to the door of the big ass truck.

"But, I will get it back?"

I clapped him on the shoulder. "I promise you." Aaron nodded and climbed into the truck.

Dad nodded at me as he started to step up into the truck, and I grabbed his arm. "I'm sorry you're here now for this."

He smiled at me. "It's been a long time since I've seen combat." Then, he leaned in close and whispered, "I'm looking forward to this."

When he leaned back, there was a hard grin on his face and a glint in his eye I'd never seen before. Then, gripping the sides of the door, he pulled himself up into the truck. I climbed in as Ted started it up. We rode in silence for a while. Mike was studying Dad, and after a while, he asked, "You're ready for this, aren't you?"

Rocking in his seat, Dad's face remained stoic. "There was a time I sought out combat. I loved it. It was my element. I thrived in it."

Mike smiled, "Nothing makes you feel more alive, does it?"

"Or more terrified."

Mike's smile broadened, "Even more alive."

Dad's head cocked to the side, "How much combat have you seen?"

Mike shrugged, "I've had three deployments. One in Iraq and two in Afghanistan."

"I spent two years in Vietnam. I flew combat missions every single day. Some days several. There was no going home for a few months and coming back. Combat was every day and almost all day. Our firebase was under rocket and mortar attack if I wasn't being shot at while flying. But to answer your question," he nodded his head slowly, "nothing makes you feel more alive."

Mike's smile was gone now. Instead, a stern look now painted on his face. He leaned out with a fist extended in front of him. He bounced slightly in his seat. After a moment, Dad leaned forward and bumped his. Then they both leaned back into their seats, saying nothing more for the rest of the ride home.

Ted stopped by the bunker, and we all piled out. Sarge looked at the men manning the bunker and shouted, "Find Wallner and tell him to get his ass to my house! Mikey, get a count on the Russian hardware. I want to know exactly what we have. Morgan, go to Danny's and do the same. I'm not interested in anything that isn't an AR or AK."

"Come on, Dad, let's go. You need a rifle," I said.

"And some boots," he replied.

"And some boots," I replied as I put my arm around him. He really wanted those boots!

We made our way down the road towards Danny's in what was a pleasant afternoon sky. After a while, Dad asked, "Is it always like this? How often does this kind of shit happen?"

"Too often. It's kind of difficult, really. Every time we think we're getting somewhere, the shit hits the fan. It just never ends. Tiring, really."

"We didn't have these kinds of issues back on the river. Our biggest issue was keeping people fed. Finding open ground to bury the day's dead. Every day there were dead. It seemed like it would never end." He walked in silence for a moment, then added, "I kind of prefer it this way."

"It does make it easier when you can at least affect the outcome, whatever it may be," I replied.

"If I gotta go, I'd rather it be in a pile of brass up to my ass! I don't want to die quietly in the night."

"Well, that may be the way it works out," I glanced over at him and added, "someday. But not this time. I've yet even to start fucking with you. I have a lot of shit-giving to make up for. It's been a while since we had the chance to hang out. So, you'll just have to wait on that pile of brass."

Dad Laughed, "I didn't mean tomorrow or anything. We've got shit to do yet."

At Danny's, I went into the spare room; it was Miss Kay's room now, but the closet was huge in the room, and it's where we kept all the captured guns. Opening the door, I stepped back as I flipped the light on. Dad let out a whistle.

"Damn, that's a lot of guns," he said.

"Yeah, a lot of them are government issues, too," I replied with a smile. Then, pointing into the closet, I added, "Pick out what you want. We need to get a count on all this."

Dad stepped into the small space and picked up a nearly new-looking AR with an ACOG. Then, turning, he pointed it out of the closet at the other side of the room. "I like this scope," he said.

"ACOG is a good optic. It's fixed magnification, and you can't adjust it. But it's only three and a half power, so it's not bad at close range and gives you some magnification at longer ranges."

Dad nodded as he looked the rifle over. He pulled the charging handle back and looked into the chamber. "I like this one. Been a long time since I've shot one. But I still remember how it works."

"We've got plenty of ammo. We'll get you out on the range with it. Pick out some web gear too. You'll need that as well. Then fill it with mags. The boots are in another closet. We also have clothes, tactical shit, if you want some of that."

Dad went to work looking through the various kinds of load-bearing gear we'd collected. He eventually settled on a plate carrier with ceramic plates. It was already set up with mag pouches that all had mags in them and a blowout kit. There was a Camel Bak connected to the back of the carrier as well.

As he was digging around, I looked through the rifles. We had a load of guns in the closet, and I was already dreading counting them. Then, standing up and running a hand through my hair as I let out a long sigh, I saw a clipboard hanging from a nail and picked it up. It was an inventory of the guns, type, caliber, how many mags we had for each, and even how much ammo was in the closet. I laughed as I looked at it. Danny simply could not stand the idea of things not being done correctly. I knew he'd made the list.

Holding the carrier out, Dad said, "Let's find some boots."

I held the list out, "This just made things easier. Danny probably inventoried all this. Now we have our counts."

I led him to the closet where all the boots were. He waded into them and pulled out a brand-new pair in his size. I reached up onto a shelf and pulled down several pairs of mil-spec socks, and handed them to him. "You'll want these too."

Dad took the socks and looked at them and the boots. He slowly shook his head as he turned the boots over in his hands. "I thought I'd never see another new pair of boots in my lifetime. Let alone new damn socks!"

"There's more, come on," I said as I closed the door to the closet.

We went upstairs and into another bedroom. There was a closet with a crawl space. As I opened the closet door, I asked dad what size pants he wore. "Thirty's now," he replied.

I nodded and dropped to my knees, and crawled back into the small cubby. A keyless light fixture was mounted in the small space, and I pulled the chain, turning on the light. There were piles of pants, t-shirts, and both BDU tops and combat shirts. All folded in piles. We had a lot in black and some in MultiCam. I didn't care for the black myself. It's what the Feds wore, and I damn sure didn't want to look like them. I found two pairs of pants and tossed them out, "Try those on." I found a couple of shirts I thought would fit as well and grabbed a few t-shirts for him. Turning off the light, I crawled out. Dad had a pair of the pants on, and I tossed him one of the shirts. "Try this on too."

"These fit pretty good," he said, looking at the pants. He pulled the shirt on and buttoned it up, "This is a good fit too," he said as he ran his hand over his chest, smoothing out wrinkles.

It was a stark image. Seeing Dad in uniform. He'd worn another, long ago, and managed to survive that. I was nervous at the thought of him being involved in this shit. But he knows what he's doing and can handle a gun, that I know. Reaching out, I patted his shoulder, "Looks good."

He looked at all the new gear he'd just collected and said, "I'm going over to the house and change. I'll come find you when I'm done."

Giving him a nod, I headed downstairs. Miss Kay was in the kitchen when I hit the bottom of the stairs. She came up, wiping her hands on a dishtowel. "What's going on, Morgan? And don't try and lie to me. I can tell something is happening."

She was correct, of course, and I smiled weakly at her. There was no way I could lie to her or try and hide the truth. "Some old friends are coming back for a visit. We're going to have to deal with them again."

"Who?"

"Tabor and some of his people."

Kay gasped as her hand went to her mouth. "No, not them. I thought we took care of them. I thought they were gone."

"They were, we sent them away to prison, but they never made it there. The bus was found, ambushed. Now they've gathered additional people and are basically terrorizing the country. And they're coming here."

"They're coming for us, aren't they?" Kay said as her eyes teared up.

"They're coming, yes. But they are the ones in for a surprise. We know they're coming, and they don't know we know it. So, we will ambush them, and there will be no survivors this time. We'll kill them all." Kay looked terrified, and she started to sniff. I stepped over to her and wrapped an arm around her. "It'll be ok, trust me."

She pushed away and looked up at me, "Does Linus know about this?"

"Of course. We're going to start getting things ready. We have a couple of days yet. I'll tell Sarge you want to see him."

She nodded. "Thank you."

I left the house and went home to check on Mel and the girls. They were in the living room when I walked in. Little Bit was sitting on the couch holding her little squirrel. She looked up and smiled at me, "Both of her eyes are open all the way now."

I rubbed her head, "They are. She'll make a good buddy."

She held the little rodent up and kissed it on the nose. "She is my buddy."

Taylor looked up from a book she was reading. "Hey, Dad."

"What's up, kiddo?"

She stretched, "Nothing. Just being lazy."

Mel was sitting on the couch, and I held my hand out, "Come with me. We need to have a chat."

"About what?"

"Come on," I replied, nodding towards the bedroom.

She got up, and we started towards the door. Lee Ann was sitting at the dining room table; her H&K disassembled before her as she cleaned it. I stopped beside her and asked, "You good?"

She nodded. "Yeah, just making sure it's clean."

I patted her head, "That's good. A clean weapon is important." The thought of what was coming was vivid in my mind as I pictured her firing the little submachinegun.

Mel was sitting on the bed when I came into the room. "What's up?" She asked as I fell onto the bed beside her. She leaned back on her elbow and looked at me expectantly.

I let out a long breath before telling her what was going on. She sat quietly and listened. When I finished, she was quiet for a long moment, staring up at the ceiling. "So, there's another fight." She said flatly.

"It looks that way."

She laid back on the bed. "Well, is there anything we can do to avoid it?"

"No. They're coming for us. It's personal this time."

She sat back up on her elbow. "I'm in this time. If it's personal and they're coming for us, then I'm going to help kill them." I reached up and ran my hand through her hair. She pushed it away, "I'm serious."

"I wasn't going to try and stop you. We'll need everyone we can get. You'll get your belly full this time." I paused to pass my fingers through her blonde hair again. "I just wish you didn't have to. That I didn't have to, but we'll do it together this time."

She sat staring into my eyes for the longest time before replying. "If these are the same people that ran that camp and they're coming back for us, us personally, I want to make sure they're all dead, for real this time. Like they can't come back, ever. And if that means I have to pick up a rifle and kill them myself, I'm going to do that."

Rolling onto my back, I stared at the ceiling. "You aren't going to pick up a rifle. I have another idea for you."

She bolted up in the bed. "Don't even think about trying to keep me out of this. I'm not going to be sitting somewhere safe while everyone else is out there risking their lives."

Grabbing her arm, I pulled her back down to the bed. "Babe, that's not what I'm thinking, trust me. I have a plan for you, you, and Erin, I'm thinking. It'll be dangerous as hell. But important. Like I said, when this is over, you'll have your fill of killing."

She laid beside me silently for a long time. "I'll do my part. Whatever it is. I just want to make sure the girls are protected. That's all that's important."

"And they will be. I have a plan for that as well." I sat up and looked back at her. "I gotta go. I need to meet with the old man and the others to get this sorted out."

Rolling over and propping her head on her hand, she replied, "I'll see you at supper."

Giving her a quick smile, I left the room. Lee Ann looked up at me as I came out the door. She slid the bolt into her weapon and asked, "When is it going to happen?"

"Soon, kiddo. Soon."

She nodded, looked down at the weapon, and continued assembling it without comment. I looked at her sisters; both focused on what they were doing. Taylor was reading her book, and Little Bit cooed at her little limb rat. I hoped that I would be able to stand here and see the same sight in the near future. This, this simple little image is all that matters, and I would do anything to preserve it.

Collecting my rifle and kit, I started for the door. "Be careful, Daddy," Little Bit said. I looked over my shoulder to see her nuzzling the squirrel. She wasn't even looking at me.

"I will, baby girl," I replied and turned and left the house.

Walking down the drive, Meathead and Drake decided they were interested in what I was doing and fell in behind me. When I stepped out onto the road, I saw Dad coming out of the gate to his place. He waited in the road for me, and I took in the sight of him. He was decked out in full camo, boots, and armor with a rifle slung over his shoulder. It was at once both impressive and frightening, foreign yet natural.

Dad spent his time in combat. Though I imagine he would give as much as I would for a Little Bird for him to ride door gunner in. He knows combat. He's tasted it before, and here he stands now, decades later, looking much like that eighteen-year-old kid he was the first time. But this time, he already knows the elephant.

"You look like a real pipe hitter dressed like that," I said as I walked up to him.

He looked down at himself before replying. "Didn't think I looked much like a plumber."

I laughed, "Has a different meaning these days. Well, it did, back when the unending war on terror was a thing."

"Well, either way, let's go see what the plan is." He looked at the dogs and asked, "Who is this?"

"Oh, this is Meathead," I said, pointing at him. "And this one is Drake. Drake came to us through, how should I say, difficult circumstances."

As we started walking, he asked, "And just what were they?"

"Some crazy bastard grabbed Little Bit one day. It took us a few hours to find them, but we did."

Dad looked at the ground and asked, "And?"

"He was properly dealt with."

"These men, they helped you, I assume."

I nodded. "We're lucky to have them with us. It's the strangest thing really, looking back at how we all came together. Each a single small event that brought us all here, now."

"It's funny how things work out," Dad replied. "What was it about a butterfly flapping its wings? Some crap about that, I don't remember."

"Yeah, I heard it. I don't know about a butterfly, but shit happens."

We found several people gathered at Sarge's place. The front yard was full of people. The garage was open, and I saw Ivan sitting on the floor, leaning back on his hands and smiling as he watched the hustle and bustle going on in the yard. I stood watching him for a moment. I hated the man. To me, the thought of foreign invaders in our country was far more repugnant than anything that had happened to the nation to date. And here sat the very physical manifestation of that afront.

"Morgan, get your ass over here!" Sarge barked.

Breaking my eyes away from Ivan, I walked over to the old man. Before he could say a word, I asked, "Why the hell is he still here? When is he going to be packed off?"

"Tomorrow," Sarge barked back. "But that's not what this is about. We've got to get some shit sorted out. We've got some hard men coming this way, and we have to prepare them a little reception."

I was more struck by the statement that Ivan was leaving tomorrow than anything else that could come. "When did you get that sorted out? I haven't heard anything about it."

"You just did! Are you not listening? Now get yer head out of yer ass! We've got work to do."

Holding my hands out to my side in plain annoyance, I asked, "Well, what are we going to do?"

Sarge looked at Dad and nodded, "You look good, Butch."

Dad looked himself over and replied, "It's been a while since I've been in this sort of, well, uniform."

"A warrior is a warrior no matter what they wear. I can tell a warrior when I see one." Sarge studied Dad for a moment, then added, "I can tell a man that's killed in combat. It shows, and you've got the look."

Dad stiffened a bit. "It's been a long time. But I still remember how."

Sarge nodded, then began. "There's a helo coming in tomorrow. They're picking up Ivan the asshole over there and dropping off some party favors for our friends that are on their way. We need to get with Dave's people and get them armed up properly and set our plans to work. We've got a lot to do and not a lot of time to do it, so we need to step to it."

"What do you need?" Ted asked.

"Let's get a load of this Russian hardware loaded up and take it over to Dave's place. You and the boys need to put them through a crash course in running the weapons and some basic tactics. We're going to place their people in static positions. The rest of us will be the maneuvering force," Sarge paused and looked around, "where the hell is Gulliver?"

Everyone looked around, and I asked, "Anyone seen him since we got back?" There were shrugs all around. "He'll turn up. He always does."

Looking at Ted, I said, "When you go to Dave's, take Mel with you. Put her on a two-forty. Show her how to operate it and get her up to speed."

"That's a lot of weapon for a woman her size," Ted replied.

"She'll have support too," I replied. "Erin, the nurse over at Dave's place."

"What are you intending them to do?" Sarge asked curiously.

"We're going to put them on a rooftop somewhere. Somewhere she can fire on the bastards but be safe enough out of the way. I can't keep her out of this one."

Sarge stared at me for a minute, then nodded. "That's good because we're going to need every single body we can get. Let's get everyone together at Danny's place to discuss what's to be done. It's late, and we're not getting anything more done today."

"First thing in the morning, we'll load up the commie hardware and get it over to Dave's," Ted said.

"Let's get everyone rounded up," Sarge replied with a nod.

CHAPTER 5

After a quick supper, we all gathered on the back porch of Danny's house. Though it was crowded, it was quiet. The mood was somber at best. I sat with my family, all of them for once, and whispered. If not for what lies ahead of us, it would be a fine evening. Little Bit sat in Dad's lap, the two of them playing with Ruckus. Ruckus was now Little Bit's constant companion. I'd made a small harness of paracord for the little rodent, and at the moment, it was scampering around the table, sampling everyone's plate. It was funny how something so small, a rodent really, could bring so much joy to everyone.

Ruckus sat on Dad's arm. He held her up to look at her as she ate a piece of potato. He smiled, "Look at her. I remember having one when I was little. Only he wasn't quite as friendly as this one."

"She's a good squirrel," Little Bit said as she stuffed a piece of biscuit in her mouth.

Thad and Mary came through the screen door on the porch. I looked up, and he had a broad smile on his face. He stopped and looked around the porch as everyone looked back at him in expectation of what he was about to say.

Sarge sat drumming his fingers on the table. Then, after a moment, he blurted out, "Spit it out, Thad. If you don't, I think you'll explode."

If at all possible, his smile broadened. "We have a calf now!"

There was a round of cheers and shouts. "It's a little steer," Mary added with a smile. "It looks healthy and is suckling at its mother now."

"You mean it's a bull!" Sarge barked. "They ain't steers until they've been cut."

The kids immediately were on their feet, wanting to see the calf. Mel and Taylor quickly shushed them back into their seats. "You'll have to wait till tomorrow," Taylor chided them.

Kay jumped to her feet. "Do you know what this means?" She shouted.

"That we have an extra cow?" Mike asked. Sarge scowled at him, and Mike shrugged.

"Now that the calf has dropped, we can milk her. So we'll have butter, milk, and cream," Kay announced with joy.

Standing up, I said, "This is wonderful news!" Then, looking at Thad, I said, "We need to get a milking shed built. It'll be too hard to try and milk her tied to a post."

"You've got to have feed to lure her into the barn," Sarge said.

Looking over my shoulder, I replied, "We're harvesting corn right now. So we'll have enough to use as feed for the cow. It won't take much. Just enough to get her to come inside."

"We could use it to feed the hogs, too," Thad added.

"Things are starting to look up," Danny said.

Sarge slowly rose to his feet. "Let's not get ahead of ourselves. We still have a long night ahead of us, as it were." The statement sucked what little joy had found its way into the group out like a demon taking a breath. All fell silent again and looked at the old man. He looked at Ted and motioned.

Ted stood up, went to a corner, and retrieved a large roll of paper. Using tacks, he hung it on the wall of the porch. It was a map, an actual map, of Eustis. Sarge picked up a small silver pencil-shaped object and extended the old radio antenna. Then, using it as a pointer, he started to speak.

"We've got some real desperados headed our way, and they are not going to go easily. While we have no numbers on just how many are coming, we can be certain it is far more numerous than the small group we have." The old man paused to let that sink in for a minute.

"The fight we face will certainly be larger than what we have in numbers. But we are going to even the odds with a little skullduggery. If you're fighting fair, you ain't fighting correctly. There is no such thing as a fair fight, and we're not about to offer these bastards one. So instead, we are going to use every underhanded dirty-ass trick at our disposal."

"You have a plan then?" I asked.

"Pay attention. I'm only going to go over this once," Sarge replied and turned to the map with his pointer.

We sat silently as the old man laid out the plan. As I listened, I was at the same time impressed, terrified and emboldened. As he ran his pointer down Grove Street and explained how we would block the road, thereby forcing the enemy onto Bay Street, I began to understand his intentions.

He knew we couldn't take them on in a head-to-head fight. And he had no intention of doing so.

When he finished laying out his plan, the old man snapped the antenna closed, "Any questions?"

Mike raised his hand before anyone could. "Uh, that's a lot of explosives you're talking about. We have a little C4, but not that much—"

Sarge cut him off, "There's more coming. The bird is coming in for Ivan the Pathetic is bringing in more. A lot more. We have the Bradley, the Goose, and plenty of weapons. Our only hope is that things go exactly as planned here. We have to funnel them onto Bay Street," for emphasis, he snapped the antenna open and slapped it against the map.

"How long do we have?" Jess asked.

Sarge sat down on the end of a picnic table and scratched at his head. "Well, there's the real problem. We just don't know."

"We need to find out," Ted interjected.

Sarge smiled and pointed at Ted, "That's what I like about you, Ted. You have a masterful grasp of the obvious. Thank you for that. With that said, no shit Sherlock. That's why we're going to have to do a little recon."

"We need to get that fella Aaron and find out where he saw them last," I offered.

Sarge nodded. "We do. Go talk with him. See where they were and get an idea of how long we have."

"I offered him to stay in one of the houses, but he wanted to sleep in his own shelter," I replied. "He set up in the yard at my place. I'll go talk to him."

"Tomorrow, Ted, Mike, and Gulliver, if he ever comes back, will head out to find where these assholes are," Sarge said.

With the seasons changing, the days grew shorter, getting dark earlier. As we sat on the porch, it was already that short period of twilight where you couldn't say it was light out, yet not dark either. The little light from the bulbs on the porch didn't reach far into the dark past the screen. So, everyone jumped when Dalton's voice came from the inky black, "I'm ready to go when you are."

Startled, everyone turned to look in the direction of the voice. Dalton stepped forward into the dim light. "I'm ready when you boys are. Don't worry about me."

Sarge rose to his feet, "Where the hell have you been?"

Dalton shifted the AK slung across his chest. "I need alone time." He looked at everyone gathered on the porch and continued, "You may have noticed I'm not much of a people person. In fact, I'm much better at killing people than I am at dealing with them. I don't much like people, really. People equal problems." He paused, and everyone stared back at him. He rocked his head from side to side, emitting an audible pop as he did, then continued, "But I like you people. I've never had much of a family till I came here. Now I have one; you are my family. So, don't worry about me when I wander off. I'm never far, and I'll always be here, whether you know it or not."

No one said a word in reply, and just as fast as he appeared, he disappeared. Stepping deftly out of the dim light and fading from our view. Sarge stepped up to the screen and called out, "Where the hell are you going?"

"I've got some work to do before we start this party. I'll see you in the morning," Dalton's deep voice called back.

Thad stood by the screen door, still. Finally, he shivered and said, "That man scares the hell out of me."

Sarge reached up and put a hand on the big man's shoulder. "You're not the only one old friend. That's one dangerous son of a bitch right there."

Dad looked at me from across the table and asked, "You trust him?"

I'd never turned at the sound of Dalton's voice. I don't know why exactly, but he never unnerved me. Sure, he could scare the shit out of you when he snuck up. But I never felt anything bad or out of sorts when in his company—quite the opposite, for me at least. Instead, there was an odd familiarity I couldn't quite put my finger on.

"Totally," I replied flatly.

"That makes one of us," Sarge replied, still looking out the screen.

I stood up and clapped him on the back. Then, with a smile, I replied, "If you're scared, say you're scared."

Still looking out into the darkness, the old man replied, "I ain't scared of shit! Just wondering how many rounds it would take to kill that bull."

"Linus!" Kay snapped, "There are children here."

Her mouth full of biscuit, Little Bit replied, "It's ok, I've hears him say it before."

The porch erupted into laughter. Edie and Jace both laughed so hard they nearly choked. At first, Little Bit didn't understand why everyone was laughing. But the reaction of the other two kids quickly infected her, and she was soon shaking with laughter as well.

I stood up and walked past her, rubbing her head as I did. Mel caught my arm and asked where I was going. "To get Aaron. I told him to come for dinner, be he never showed. We need to talk to him."

She smiled and released my arm. As I approached the door, the bulk that is Thad blocked it. He was still smiling and looked genuinely happy. "What are you so giddy about?" I asked.

"That little calf. It's so cute. Just seeing a baby anything is wonderful."

"I guess you're right," I replied and nodded at Fred and Aric. They sat together on the Chase lounge at the end of the porch. Aric's hand was on Fred's enormous belly.

Thad smiled and asked, "You know, that's an awful big belly. You think there's more than one in there?"

I was dumbstruck. I'd never even considered the possibility. Now, I stared slack-jawed at the two of them. Then I looked at Thad, who busted into laughter at my expression. Finally, spinning on my heels, I headed back to where Mel sat at the table. Leaning over her shoulder, I asked quietly, "Is it possible Fred has twins on board?"

"Of course, it's possible," she replied without looking back.

Grabbing her head with both hands, I slowly turned her head. Mom's gaze followed. "I know it's possible. That's not what I mean. But, you know, look at her, is it *possible?*"

Mel stared at her for a moment, and then Mom spoke up. "I'd say probable. She's awfully big."

Mel looked back at Mom, and now she was stunned. "We never even thought of that," then turned her attention back to Fred.

Little Bit pushed her plate away and wiped her mouth with the back of her hand. Then, smacking her lips, she said, "I told Fred there's two. She doesn't believe me, but I felt two, and I can hear them when I put my head on her belly."

All eyes at the table were on the little girl, then almost in unison, we all turned back to Fred. "If that's true, we need to talk to Doc," I replied.

"It's true," Little Bit replied as she stood up, grabbing Jace and Edie's hands and pulling at them, "Come on, let's go play tag!" The kids were quickly up and scrambling for the screen door, which Thad held open as the riot of children passed through it and into the yard accompanied by a chorus of shrieks and giggles.

"I'll go talk to her," Mel said as she rose from the table.

"Me too," Mom added as she also got up.

Dad looked at me and said, "Guess I'll go with you."

I shrugged and jerked my head in the direction of the door. As I passed Thad, I paused, looking him in the eyes. "You better be wrong," I said in a less than enthusiastic voice.

"Ain't my fault," he replied with a laugh. "Aric did it to her!"

From the other end of the porch, Aric looked up just in time to see Mel and Mom closing in. "Did what?" He asked, genuine concern and confusion in his voice as the two women approached.

Dad and I left the porch and started towards the house. As we rounded the corner, Dad said, "That would be something, twins."

"Yeah, something really iffy," I replied. "One baby is bad enough, but two?"

Dad slapped me on the back, "It'll happen either way. Babies don't need hospitals. Hell, I saw 'em born in rice paddies in Vietnam."

We found Aaron sitting on the ground in front of a small one-man tent. He had a headlamp on and was fiddling with something. Hearing our approach, he looked up. "Everything alright?" He asked nervously as he tucked something down between his legs.

His body language bothered me, but I didn't say anything about it. "Nothing, man," I replied as I squatted down in front of him. "Just wanted to know where you saw those guys last."

Aaron leaned back on his hands, stretching his legs out and crossing his ankles as he did. I caught a brief glimpse of a handheld radio lying on the ground. "I first saw them up around Davenport. They'd taken over the stores right there at I-4. Their people didn't bother me none, asked me some questions, and pretty much let me be. But there's like two groups of them, and there seems to like an inner and an outer group."

"You mean like clicks?" I asked.

"Well, yeah, that, but also physically. There's an outer ring of like newer people. They all kind of answer to this dude they call Chief. He's a Seminole Indian, and there's a bunch of other Seminoles there too. They're nice guys, and I kind of hung out with them a little. Chief sort of interviews people, and you can be invited to stay with them."

"Did they ask you to stay?" I asked.

Shaking his head, he replied, "No. I told them I was leaving, that I kind of liked it on my own. They said there was strength in numbers, and I'd be safer with them. But I don't really like being in a big group, especially one as big as theirs."

"How many people would you say they have?" I asked.

He shrugged at the question, "I, I don't know, no more than a hundred maybe."

"How the hell are they feeding that many people?" Dad asked.

"They've raided a lot of places, I guess; they have trucks full of stuff. All kinds of trucks and trailers. They have this system for pumping fuel out of the underground tanks of truck stops to keep all their trucks running. They fill the tanker and take it with them everywhere."

I thought for a few minutes, rubbing my chin. "So, they have a hundred or so people and lots of trucks with plenty of supplies on them. Is that what you're saying?" He nodded in reply.

"Of those hundred," Dad asked, "how many are armed? What's the size is their fighting force?"

"That's a lot smaller. Their security unit, that's what they call them, is only a small part of the overall group. Chief runs his people, and they're responsible for keeping the civilians in line. Inside that ring is the actual DHS people and the ones they've taken on with them."

"Do they all move at the same time?" I asked. "You said they were coming here. Is this hoard just going to descend upon our small town?"

Aaron shook his head. "No, the DHS crew, they still call themselves that even though they make up a small number of the actual group, go out ahead and find a place to move to. Then the rest of the group packs up and moves to their location."

"So, they have radio communications?" I asked.

He quickly nodded his head. "Yeah, they do, but it's not like some super-duper radio system. A lot of the time, they have to have people in the middle to relay calls."

"So, they have VHF radios then," I said out loud, looking out over Aaron's shoulder. Then I looked down at him and pointed down at his legs, "Like the one you're sitting on? Can I see it?"

The statement visibly shook him, and he started to stammer. "I uh, um…."

I stopped him, "I saw it when we walked up. And it's not a big deal, depending on what you're doing with it." My eyes drifted down to the pistol on his hip as I spoke.

He noticed and looked down at the pistol himself. I held out my hand and asked, "Can I have the radio?"

Aaron slowly reached between his legs and handed me the radio. "You probably won't believe anything I say."

Taking the radio, I looked at it. A simple Motorola walkie talkie. Pulling the battery, I looked at the back of the radio. I saw I was wrong. It was in the UHF bands, which meant it had limited range and low power. Putting the battery back on, I turned it on, and it was dead. Looking back up at Aaron, I asked, "So, why do you have it?"

Letting out a breath he'd been holding, his shoulders slumped as he began to speak. "I stole it from one of Chief's guys." He looked up suddenly, his eyes nearly pleading, "If they catch me, I'm a dead man." He motioned at the radio, adding, "I don't even know why I took it. I used it for a couple of days, staying close to the group, but far enough away they couldn't find me and just listened to it. That's all. The group scared me, and I wanted to know what they were doing. It's how I found out they were coming here. I heard it on the radio."

"Then why in the hell did you come here of all places?" Dad asked.

"I didn't know they were coming here, to Eustis. I only figured it out when I saw his badge," he replied, pointing at me. "They've got a serious hard-on for you, you an that old Army guy." Aaron looked up at dad and asked, "You the Army guy?"

"No, I'm not the one they're looking for. Just another grumpy old vet they'll have to deal with when they show up."

"You get any idea where they were headed when they left Davenport?" I asked.

He nodded quickly, "They were headed into Clermont. So when I left them, I rode down I-4 to the 429 and rode up here on that. I thought that was the way they'd go. So I was surprised and relieved when I heard they were headed towards Clermont. I figured I'd never see them again."

"So, you're not here to try and get intel? To set us up for them or to report back to them?" I asked.

He was eager to impress upon us how that was not the case in the least. "No, no, no, I was just trying to get away from those guys. I was only looking at the radio because I was thinking of how I would get rid of it. If they catch me with it, they'd kill me."

"Aaron, in light of this new information, I hate to do this, but I'm going to ask you to give me that pistol for now. Then, if everything turns out like you said, I'll give it back to you. No harm, no foul."

Nervously, he looked back and forth between Dad and me. "But you'll give it back to me?"

Nodding, I replied, "I promise. But with you suddenly having a radio that belongs to the group that's coming to attack us, you see why I'm a little nervous, don't you?"

"I mean, I'm not going to cause you any trouble."

"And you very well may not. However, I don't know you, and you don't know me. You won't be treated any differently. You're still invited to our meals. We eat together for most of our meals, and we'd like you to eat with us. You'll be welcome here as long as everything you've told me is true."

"Everything is true," he replied childlike.

"Then you've got nothing to worry about, Aaron," I replied as I held my hand.

Hesitantly, his hand started to move towards the holstered pistol. As it did, I flagged a finger at him, "Move very slowly, Aaron. I don't want there to be any accidents here."

He immediately held his left hand up as his right slowly withdrew the pistol from its holster, keeping it pointed at the ground, and held it out in front of himself. I politely took the proffered weapon with one hand and patted him on the leg with the other.

"Thanks, Aaron. The only people around here that know what you just told me are you, me, and Dad. So long as everything remains cool, no one else needs to know. You're free to move around and, like I said, join us for meals. We eat pretty good around here, better than average, I would guess, so please join us."

"I appreciate that, and I won't be any trouble, I promise." He paused for a moment, then looked up at me and asked, "I guess this means I can't leave any time soon then?"

"No, you're here until this is taken care of."

"Well, if I'm here, I'm here to help in any way I can."

As I tucked his pistol into my back pocket, I replied, "You already are."

Fred sat looking at her belly, gently rubbing a hand back and forth over it. Aric watched her hand going back and forth, his lips slowly working, but no sound could be heard. Kay sat in a chair just opposite the two. The smile on her face would be nearly impossible to remove.

Looking up, Fred asked, "You really think it's twins?"

Mel cocked her head to the side, "You're big. I wouldn't be surprised at all."

"Doc has never said anything about twins. He listens with a stethoscope, and he's never said he's heard two heartbeats," Aric replied.

"It could be hard to hear that with just a stethoscope," Mel replied. "It usually takes a sonogram, and I don't think we'll be having one of those any time soon."

"What's it mean then? If she has twins?" Aric asked.

"That you'll have two babies, silly," Kay replied, delighted with herself.

Giving Kay as much of a disapproving stare as he dared, Aric asked, "No, I mean, what's it mean for Fred? Is this going to be dangerous for her?" He spoke the last part as he looked at Fred, who looked back up at him with concern in her eyes.

"Babies are born all the time without hospitals," Mel replied. "It's actually the way most of the world does it. But, to be on the safe side, I'll get Erin. She's the nurse over at the ranch. I'm sure she can help out with this."

Fred looked up at Mel and smiled. "I'm going to have twins." Then looking at Aric, she added, "We're going to have two babies."

All of Aric's nervousness faded as he looked down at his glowing wife. The excitement in her eyes was more than he could stand. Grabbing her hands, he clasped them in his own and kissed them. "Yes, we are, and you're going to be an incredible mother."

She leaned her head over on his arm, "And you're going to be a terrific father."

Aric smiled as he ran his hand through her hair. Though he was smiling, inside, he was terrified, and a million questions and concerns were pounding through his mind. He'd been excited about the thought of having a son; naturally, it would be a boy, but the idea of two babies doubled the threat to Fred. While Aric was well acquainted with the notion that there was a danger to Fred during childbirth, he'd mitigated that in his mind by saying just what Mel said, *babies are born all the time without hospitals.* But how often were twins born this way with no complications? That was what now weighed on his mind.

Mel and Kay spent some time assuring Fred she'd be fine and Mel saying she'd bring the nurse from the ranch over the next day to take a look at her made everyone feel better. Fred and Aric both asked several more questions before the two women said their goodbyes. It took Mel a bit of effort to get Little Bit pulled away from Fred's belly as she continued to want to *hear the babies just one more time.* However, the little girl brought some levity to the situation that took the anxiety of things down a notch.

As Mel and Kay walked back towards the house, Little Bit stayed out in front of them without a care in the world. Mel smiled as she watched the little girl skipping along the dirt road.

"It must be nice," Kay interrupted.

"What's that?"

Kay nodded at the little girl. "To be so happy all the time."

Mel laughed, "Well if we didn't have a care in the world, we'd be skipping down the road too."

Now Kay laughed, "You might, my dear." She patted her thighs and added, "But these old hips skipping days are long past."

"You know what I mean, Kay," Mel replied with a friendly nudge.

"Yes, dear, I know what you mean. I spend a lot of time watching these children, and they seem so happy all the time. And you know I worked in a school cafeteria, so I've spent a lot of time with children." She pointed at Little Bit and continued. "But these kids seem to be far happier than any of those kids I saw in the lunch line."

Mel nodded her agreement into the darkness. "I know what you mean. I think these simpler days make for less stress and naturally better mental health."

"And not just the children either," Kay added, "us too. I don't know about you, but aside from those early days that were pretty hard, I haven't been this happy in years."

"I know what you mean. It's been nice having Morgan home so much. I like everyone gathering in the evening for dinner. It's little things like that that really mean something to me."

"Well, I'm not too worried for Fred," Kay said. "I think she'll be fine. I've seen my share of babies born and even helped in a couple." She nudged Mel with an elbow, "And you've done it once or twice yourself."

Mel laughed, causing Little Bit to pause and look back over her shoulder. Then, seeing everything was alright, she continued skipping down the road. "That's true, Kay. But all three of mine were in the hospital, and I wasn't much help at the time."

As they approached Danny's house, they could see lights suddenly come on and voices shouting. "What's all that about?" Kay asked.

"I don't know; let's go see."

As they came through the gate, the Hummer sat idling in the driveway as men rushed about in the beams of the headlights. Then, finally, Thad tore out of the driveway on a four-wheeler, smiling as he did, and headed up the road.

"Well, it can't be too bad," Mel replied. "Thad was smiling."

Smiling herself, Kay replied, "He's always smiling."

Getting close to the house, Mel saw Ian and asked what was going on.

"There's a bird on its way to get Ivan and deliver supplies," he replied.

"In the dark?" Mel asked.

"What kind of supplies?" Kay asked.

Ian shrugged, "I think most of it is ordinance of some kind or another. And, yeah, Mel, in the dark. These guys don't work banker's hours."

"No food?" Kay lamented.

He shrugged, "Maybe, I don't really know. I just know the old man asked for a pretty serious load of shit that goes boom." Ian caught himself and added, "Sorry Kay, stuff, stuff that goes boom."

Mel stopped and crossed her arms over her chest. "What? I don't count?"

A wave of confused fear washed over his face, "I uh, what I mean is, um—"

Mel cut him off with a laugh, "Don't worry about it, Ian. You do remember who I'm married to, right?"

Ian smiled, "Oh yeah. I gotta run, ladies. I've got work to do."

As Ian continued whatever mission he was on, Kay spotted Sarge, and the two women walked over to him. "What's happening, Linus?" Kay asked.

"The helo should be here shortly. We're headed out to meet it."

"They taking those two men?"

"Yeah, Morgan can finally stop bitching. They'll be gone."

"You can't blame him," Mel replied. "Those people hurt some people he loved. Killed one, if you remember." Mel added with more than a bit of snark.

Bobby was Mel's aunt, her mother's sister. So, her loss really hurt Mel, leaving a scar that would last for years. While she did her best to remain stoic, Mel was far less prone to emotional outbursts than Morgan. Yet, the pain was still there. She was the balance that kept him level. Without Mel, surely, he would tip over into the abyss.

You can say what you want about the military. But it has been my personal experience that they are professionals that can accomplish nearly anything. It may not always be the right thing, but they will get the job done. For example, I watched in awe as the process of the big twin-rotor CH-47 Chinook helicopter came in for a landing.

Sarge stood in the open door of the Hummer talking to the pilots on the radio. We'd brought everything with wheels out to the field across the road from our little compound. We'd long ago cut the fence, so it was a simple matter of driving the big two-and-a-half-ton truck out there along with the Hummer, Thad's little truck, and even the old Suburban. The trucks were lined up with the headlights on high to light the field up. We could hear the thudding of the rotors as the massive machine beat the air into submission as the damn thing simply shouldn't be able to fly!

"Mikey!" Sarge shouted, "Lasso!" Mike stood out in the field and held his rifle up, working the muzzle around in a circle.

"What's he doing?" Mel asked.

We were leaning on the fender of the Suburban, and I had my arm around her. "He's using the laser to show the pilots where we are."

"I don't see anything."

"It's infrared. They can see it with their night vision."

"Oh, that's cool."

"It is," I replied as I pulled my PVS-14 out of the pouch on the plate carrier. Then, turning it on, I checked it was working and could see Mike's laser. "Here."

Mel took it and looked out over the field. "Oh, that's cool!"

"On final!" Sarge shouted, and Mike started to move towards the trucks. He turned on an IR strobe mounted to his helmet as he did.

The blades of the giant bird thudded into the air, and it was obvious they were close. I tapped Mel on the shoulder and pointed, "Look over there."

As she turned, she asked, "What am I looking for?" Before I could reply, she saw it. "Oh, wow, what is that?" She dropped the optic to look with the naked eye before quickly returning it. "That is so cool."

"The rotors create like a static charge you can see with these."

Handing me the device back, she pressed in a little tighter. "That's really neat. Thank you."

"I guess it's not often you get to see one of these come in for a night landing all blacked out."

Even in the dark, you could see the behemoth as it came in. After that, it was simply a patch of even darker sky, A void in the darkness without stars. Then, as it began dropping down, I said, "You better turn around. This is going to kick up a lot of stuff in the air." She turned her back to the field and pulled the collar of her coat up to shield her face.

I turned a shoulder into the breeze and saw Ted taking Ivan and his lackey out of the Hummer. Ivan didn't look quite so defiant now. I guess these were probably his good ole days, and he was in for far worse when they got him to Eglin. I smiled, watching him look around nervously. Then the big machine was overhead and slowly dropping towards the ground as the ramp lowered. As soon as the big helicopter was on the ground, Sarge shouted for everyone to move, and we all ran in a crouch towards the ramp.

The interior of the bird illuminated red light that spilled out on the ramp and ground at the rear. When I got to the open ramp, I saw the bird packed with what looked like an insanely long row of pallets. "Holy shit! That's going to take forever to unload!"

Then someone grabbed my shoulder and pulled. I staggered to the side as one of the oversized pallets began to roll towards the ramp. Then the engines surged as the pilot lifted the nose off the ground, and the ship started to creep forward. When the pallet hit the ground, he kept the power to it, and in a flash, the pallet was on the ground with another one coming right behind it.

As strange as the big machine looked in the air, it was even more ungainly on the ground as it slowly moved forward, spilling its cargo onto behind it. I could see the crew chief inside as he released the pallets one at a time. In minutes, the entire load was on the ground, and the pilot set the machine back down. Two men in flight suits and helmets quickly jumped from the ramp and trotted towards Sarge.

One of them nodded at Ivan and asked, "This our man?"

Sarge nodded, "Both of them. They're all yours."

Ivan's hands were bound in front of him with zip ties. It was all we had that was kind of convenient. One of the men pulled a pair of EMT sheers out and cut the ties while the other sorted out a mess of small silver chains. I watched as Ivan was cuffed and a waist chain wrapped around him. Then his feet were shackled as well, and he looked like any prisoner headed to a corrections transport. As his subordinate was being chained, he looked over at me with a big smile on his face and gave me a little wave from the waist where his hands were bound. In return, I shot him the bird. I hoped the crew threw him off the ramp. His head rocked back, and he laughed a deep guttural laugh I could hear over the twin rotors and screaming turbines.

He was quickly hustled towards the back ramp and disappeared inside. Then, just as fast as the big machine had appeared, it vanished in a cloud of dust and debris. After a few moments, the rotors faded into the night, and it was quiet. Well, it would have been except for the old man screaming and shouting.

"Move your asses, people! Let's get this shit loaded onto the trucks. It's nearly bedtime!"

Mike, Doc, Ted, and Dalton were already there, unstrapping the load. Dad hopped into the big truck and backed it over to the pallets, and we formed a chain of people and began passing the material up. Sarge moved from pallet to pallet, pointing out what was to be loaded when. It took about an hour to get it all, and I was shocked at the weight of some of the ammo cans, crates, and odd containers we hefted up.

"Damn," I said, "I haven't had a workout like this in a long time!"

"Welcome to the Army," Mike said with a grunt as he passed along ammo can up to Dad and Ted in the bed.

"What is all this?" I asked.

"Ammo!" Sarge barked, adding, "dip shit!" I just shook my head. But he wasn't done yet. "Just get it on the truck. You can look at your presents tomorrow morning."

I laughed, "Tactical Santa?"

Sarge didn't reply. Instead, he just slammed a fifty-cal ammo can into my chest. "Less beating of the lips and more working!"

Once it was all loaded, we headed back across the road. All the trucks were at Sarge's place, and there was a large gathering of people as we inspected some of the material sent to us, and there was a lot. Doc and Jess were taking boxes, crates, and cases from the back of the Hummer. There was all manner of medical supplies and even some equipment. Seeing several silver tanks, I walked over.

"Is that oxygen?" I asked.

Doc nodded, "Yeah. We didn't have any, and we've been lucky we didn't need it before now."

Jess cut him off, "I found it, Ronnie!"

She was holding a plastic bag with medical supplies in it. "What is it?" I asked.

"A birthing kit for Fred," Doc replied, then looked at Jess and asked, "Are there two?" She smiled as she held up the other one.

"That's awesome you thought of that, man," I replied.

"Obstetrics isn't my favorite, but we gotta take care of Fred. I think she'll do fine, though."

As we were talking, Sarge interrupted everyone. "Alright folks, that's good for tonight. We've got a lot to do tomorrow, and it's gonna be a big day. So I suggest that everyone go home and get some sleep. Tomorrow is range day."

Everyone was pretty spun up about the arrival of so much material, and we talked about it as a group as we walked back towards the house. Dad was the first one to speak.

"Damn, that's a lot of ordinance."

"It wasn't all ammo," Mel replied.

"Did you see something else?" I asked.

"I saw an obstetrics kit that Ronnie ordered for Fred. Two, actually."

"Did anyone see any food or anything like that?"

"There's a bunch of MREs," Danny replied.

"What is tomorrow going to be like?" Mel asked.

"It's going to be a long day. First, we need to make sure everyone has hearing protection. Then, I imagine it's going to be pretty loud," I replied.

CHAPTER 6

Mike jerked awake when the old man kicked his bed. "On yer feet, Mikey! And for the love of God, put some damn close on!"

Lying face down, he sat up on one elbow and rubbed his eyes. "What's up?"

"We got shit to do, now let's go!"

"I need some coffee."

"Get yer lazy ass up and get a cup!"

Rolling onto his side, Mike propped his head up on an elbow. "Why don't you run along and get me a cup?" He said, barely able to contain his laughter as he posed, hoping to piss the old man off.

Sarge shook his head. "How old will you be when you finally grow up? I mean, what the hell is wrong with you anyway?"

With a shrug, Mike looked down at himself, raising one leg on bent knee, "Looks pretty grown-up to me."

"Oh, for fuck sake," Sarge replied, throwing his hands up and walking out of the room.

Mike smiled to himself as he got up and pulled on his pants. Then, after dressing, he wandered out to the kitchen, following his nose in a hazy sleep stupor to the source of the aroma. Ted was sitting at the small table, a cup in one hand a newspaper in the other.

"Where the hell did you find that?" Mike asked as he poured his cup.

"In the garage in the recycling bin."

Mike asked, taking a seat at the table, "How old is it?"

Without looking up, Ted replied, "Little over a year."

"Why the hell are you reading a year-old newspaper?"

"Can't find a more recent one. Besides, it's just something to do. It's actually kind of funny to read. To see the things everyone was worried about a year ago. Shit, that has zero bearing on what matters." He flipped through the pages in an exaggerated fashion, "There's not a single article in here on gardening, food preservation, or even how one can wash their clothes when the power is out."

"Is there a sports section?"

Ted tossed it to him, "Now that is some useless shit. Even in the Before, all that was good for was wrapping fish."

"Just because you weren't an athlete doesn't mean it's useless."

"Let me know what you learn from it that will help in our current world. Bunch of overpaid crybabies that play with balls for a living."

Mike looked over the top of the sports section, "You're in the Army. Playing with balls is part of the job."

Sarge came into the kitchen from the garage and threw a case of MREs on the table. "Get yourself some breakfast. We ain't got time to go down to the big house."

Mike pulled the case open, "What's the plan?"

"I want to get two or three of each of the commie weapons to take over to Dave's. First, we need to get everyone trained up on their operation and get them competent with them."

"That's going to take a lot of ammo," Ted replied.

"Ammo ain't a problem. We got more than we could ever shoot."

"We did haul a shit load of it out of the auction," Mike added.

"That reminds me, I found something in those piles of crates when I was going through them this morning," Sarge said. Both men looked at him expectantly. Sarge stood leaning on the counter, looking back at them over the top of his cup.

"What?" Ted asked.

"Three Kornet launchers and several cases of rockets."

Mike nearly choked on his coffee. "Really? Holy shit, that'll make this a cakewalk!"

"Calm down, dip shit. Yes, they will help, but we've got to have operators that can fire the damn things, and I don't want to waste rockets teaching people to do so. Not to mention, we'll be in tight with these assholes, so getting a shot with one will be a lot harder."

"Minimum distance on them is one hundred meters," Ted said. "It could be done."

"Could be yes. If we had trained people to fire them," Sarge replied.

"The three of us know how to fire them. You, me, and Mikey all on one to initiate the ambush, then we can push out. Taking out three of their MRAPs in short order would probably take the fight out of them."

"We're going to figure out where to use them. We can train someone to fire the Goose. That's pretty easy. It's not like these damn wire-guided things. So, four vehicles knocked out in the first few seconds of an ambush would stack the odds in our favor. Not to mention the mines."

"What mines?"

"We got some M19s and M16s."

"Holy shit!" Mike shouted. "Anti-tank mines? And Bouncing Bettys? With all this shit, those assholes don't stand a chance."

Sarge cocked his head to the side. "Have you learned nothing in all these years? No plan survives first contact. We are still outnumbered. A hundred assholes with Kalashes will be a bad day no matter what."

"True, but if they don't survive the trip into town then it doesn't matter how many assholes with Aks they have. They'll come in mounted, and we'll kill them before they dismount."

"That would be nice but, we've got to plan for them not to walk in all cooperative to our ambush. The good thing is, they don't know we know. Or at least we don't think they do. So that's on our side."

Ted drained his cup and folded the paper, setting it on the table. "I guess it's time to get the party favors out."

I want to stop by Gina and Dillon's on the way out today," I said to Mel as she scrambled some eggs. I was busy rolling balls of Masa for the tortilla press.

"That'd be nice. I haven't seen Gina in a while."

"I'm going to ask Dillion to come out to Dave's and get trained on weapons."

"I think everyone should," she replied, looking at me sideways.

"Don't worry," I replied as I smoothed out the plastic wrap lining the press. "You're gonna get plenty of training."

"Oh, I know. I'm tired of all this sitting around crap while you guys all run around playing commando."

"We don't play commando."

"You know what I mean."

"I do, and I'm sorry I haven't involved you more in this kind of thing." I pressed the handle down over a ball of dough. "It's not as fun as you think, and you probably will get all you want with this. It sucks." Taking the tortilla out of the press, I said, "Running out of this sucks even worse, though."

Mel looked at the empty Masa bag sitting on the counter. "That the last of it?"

"All gone."

"It's not like we need it. Kay does an outstanding job with what we have."

"We're not going to have burritos anymore?" Taylor asked as she walked into the kitchen.

"These are the last one's kiddo," I replied.

"That's a bummer. I really like it when you guys make them. Kind of like how things used to be."

I wrapped my arm around her shoulder, "I know. I'll miss it too. But! There is an upside."

"What upside? How is there an upside to not having breakfast burritos anymore?"

"Well, we're harvesting the corn right now. So soon we'll be able to have fried mush again!"

Little Bit came running into the kitchen and slammed into my leg. "I love fried mush! But we need bacon. You gotta cook it in the bacon oil! It's so good like that!"

"That was good," Taylor replied. "Where did you come with that from?"

"That's an old thing poor people in the country have eaten for decades. I found it on one of those websites I trolled around on. There are lots of things like that that people simply no longer know about."

"Alright, girls, it's ready!" Mel announced as she slid a plate piled with burritos onto the table. "We even have a little treat to go with them this morning."

"Treat, what treat?" I asked.

Mel took a small jar from a cabinet. "Mary made some salsa. It's delicious too."

The salsa was a huge hit, and we killed the little jar. We tried to have breakfast a couple of times a week at home. While it was nice to eat with everyone, it was important to us to make sure we maintained our family, and having meals with just us was one way we could do that.

After I finished my second burrito, I rose from the table. "Well, there's lots to do today, and we're all going so, you girls get ready to go. Make sure both of you have your guns."

"When do I get a gun?" Little Bit asked.

I palmed the top of her head and turned it to look at me. "You're too little, baby. Your day will come."

She slumped in her chair. "It's unfair. I'm a better shot than Taylor!"

"No, you're not!" Her older sister shot back.

"Am so!"

I turned Little Bit's head back to her plate, "Enough of that. Hurry up and eat, or I'll eat it for you! While you ladies get ready, I'm gonna walk over to Mom and Dad's."

They were sitting on the porch when I cut through the fence. Dad had a coffee cup in his hand as I came up onto the porch. "You get some coffee?"

He nodded as he took a sip. "Sure did. Found a thermos in here, took it over, and filled it up. Damn, it's nice to have coffee again!"

"It sure is," Mom replied as she lifted her cup.

"When did you start drinking coffee?" I asked.

"This morning," she replied as she took a drink.

"You drink coffee," Dad replied.

"Not in a long time."

I sat down with them. "Well, I'm just glad you guys can have it."

"So am I, little buddy, so am I."

"Going to be a lot going on today. First, we're going to load up a bunch of weapons and go over to Dave's ranch to get everyone trained up."

"Sounds like a good time," Dad replied.

"You all have fun with that," Mom replied as she rose to her feet.

"You're going too," I replied.

Mom stopped and looked back, "What?"

"It's a different world, Ma, and you need to know how to use this hardware just as much as anyone else around here. The girls are going too. They have their own weapons and know how to use them."

"Ashley has a gun?" Mom asked.

"No, not her. I mean, she does have her rifle, but she doesn't carry it around and isn't expected to be in anything dangerous. But in this world, everyone needs to know how to run a gun."

Mary scratched the old heifer's nose. "The calf is so cute."

Thad ran his hand over the cow's back. "He is. These are pretty good cows too. They'll let you handle them."

"Of course they do. They're cows," Mary replied with a laugh.

Thad raised an eyebrow, "You must not have much experience with cows."

"Well, no. But, I mean, Aren't they all friendly?"

Thad laughed, "No, not at all!"

"Oh. I've never been around a real cow. You know, not at a petting zoo or something like that."

"I need to find some lumber to build a milking shed. If we start milking her, she'll stay in milk for a long time."

"Kay is excited about the milk. She's already talking about making cheese and all kinds of stuff."

"You know what I'm really excited for?" Thad asked.

Mary was kneeling looking at the calf and asked, "What?"

"Ice cream."

Mary bolted up, "Ice cream? How are we going to do that?"

Thad's face lit up. "Oh, it's easy. Momma used to make it all the time in the summer. We never had store-bought ice cream. She'd always make it, and it was so good."

"The kids will love that!"

"Everyone will love it! Come on, let's go over to Danny's. There's a lot to do today."

Mary stood staring at the calf. "What are we going to name him?"

Thad stepped over and put a hand on her shoulder. "Probably shouldn't name it." Mary looked up, her eyes wide. "We are going to eat him, aren't we?"

"We will. It's different when you actually see where your meat comes from, isn't it?"

Mary looked at the little animal. "It is. He's so cute. So small."

"You don't have to eat it if you don't want to. I mean, it's gonna be a while before that comes, but you don't have to."

"Oh, I'll eat him," Mary laughed. "I look at food a lot different now. Before, it was just food. You went to the store and bought it. It came in packages, even the meat, and you didn't have to think about it." She looked up, "But I like this better. It's like, taking responsibility for yourself. We know where pretty much everything we eat comes from. It's better this way. I think it's how it was meant to be."

Thad wrapped her in a hug from behind, "I think the same way." He leaned down and kissed the top of her head. "I love you, Mary."

She spun to face him, wrapping her arms around his thick waist. "I love you too, Thad," she replied and raised herself up on her toes and kissed him. She took his big hand in hers, and they walked to Danny's.

Danny's had the feel of a Chinese fire drill. People were moving around all over as engines idled. People were coming and going putting their gear into one of the trucks. The water keg was filled, and we made sure we had enough MREs with us if someone wanted to eat. Once everything was loaded and ready, Sarge called out, "Alright folks, let's go! We're burning daylight!"

I was taking the old Suburban today. Most everyone was going to the ranch, and we needed the space. Plus, we were going to stop by Gina and Dillon's and see if we could enlist Dillon's help. So the girls were piled into the back, and Mel and Mom sat in the backseat as we bounced out onto the county road. The girls thought it was big fun to actually be driving. Little Bit seldom got a ride anymore, and as a result, she was particularly animated.

"We're going to stop by some friends real quick. See if Dillon will help us out with this," I said to Dad as we turned onto the short road to their house.

"I think we could use all the help we can get," Dad replied.

I left the truck running as I got out. Dillon was already standing at the open door, and a smile smeared across his face. "Hey Morgan, how the hell have you been?"

"Good ole buddy, how are you and Gina?"

Stepping out and letting the screen door slam behind him, Dillon replied, "We're good. Gina's been doing real good lately. What are you guys up to?"

I took a minute to introduce Dad and Dillon and explain what was going on. Dillon listened to what I had to say, concern clouding his eyes as I spoke. "You're damn right I'll help," his reply was immediate and solid.

Gina had wandered over from her greenhouse while we talked. She was as pleasant as always, offering smiles and hugs as she always did. Dillon caught her up real quick, and she immediately volunteered.

I tried to be gentle in my reply, "Thank you, Gina, but I'd rather you not get involved in this. We have no idea what is going to happen when this starts, and we may move fast."

She cocked her hip to the side and crossed her arms over her chest. "I can still help. I'm incapable."

"I never said you were. And there's plenty you can do. Just not on a rifle in the ambush."

"As long as I can help, I'm fine."

"We're headed over right now to get everyone up to speed on the weapons and to go over the plan we're developing."

"Let me grab my rifle," Dillon said as he disappeared back into the house.

"I'll put some shoes on," Gina said as she followed him inside.

I walked back to the truck and leaned on Mel's window. "Why don't you get upfront, sit in the middle so that they can sit back here with Mom."

As I pulled out onto the county road, I said, "We're going to go by and check on the corn harvesting."

"That's right," Dillon replied. "I was wondering what was going on with that. I figured we'd be out there trying to pick that by now. So how come you didn't come to get me?"

I looked at him in the mirror, "You're good, Dillon. It's being picked as we speak."

"Who's picking it?" Gina asked.

Audie and Cecil."

"Only two people?" Dillon nearly shouted. "It'll take them forever! It'll rot before they finish."

"You don't know, do you?" I asked.

"Know what?"

"We got a small harvester. They're picking it with tractors right now."

"Is that what that big helicopter brought yesterday?" Gina asked.

"No, Dave had it at his place. We had to get running again, but we did. So we'll have plenty of corn soon."

"Wait a minute, a minute ago you said Audie was picking it, and now you're talking about Dave. Who are they?"

"You're about to meet them. Dave owns a big ranch on forty-four. Audie works for Dave."

"We got the cows from Dave," Mel told Gina.

With a humorously dismissive wave, Gina replied, "I guess we need to get out more," getting a laugh from Mel.

The tractors were continuing their choreographed dance in the field when we arrived. It was amazing to see so many rows of stubble sticking out of the field where there were whole stalks yesterday. The two men had made serious progress, and the area was about half done.

"Damn, they're making some serious time," Dad said.

"Oh, wow," Gina said as she craned her neck to see out the window.

I drove across the field and pulled up alongside Audie. "Looking good, Audie!"

He had a huge smile spread across his face and pulled his hat off to wave at me with it. "It's beautiful, and We're going a hell of a lot faster than I thought we would!"

Cecil leaned back in his seat waved.

"Y'all need anything?" I asked.

Audie shook his head, "Nah, we're good. So you headed to the ranch?"

"Oh yeah. Shit's about to get western!"

"Well, I'm gonna miss the training, but I know how to run a gun."

"There'll be plenty to do, buddy, don't worry about that."

I didn't talk for the rest of the ride to the ranch. Too much to think about. But, I could hear Mom talking to Gina and Dillon. Looking at her in the mirror, I had to smile. She never did meet a stranger and was always up to ratchet jaw for a minute. It made me feel so good to have them here. The girls giggled and talked in the back. It was hard to believe we were on our way to get all these people trained on the operation of

Soviet-made weapons to ambush the remnants of DHS personnel and kill them. All of them. The day seemed more like a family outing to the springs or the beach, anything but the true nature of the ride.

Pulling up the gate, I waited as the rider came out of the woods and to the gate. Then, having been around enough to know everyone's face at least and be known by them all, I got out and waited by the entrance. Once the rider was close enough, he tossed me the key to the gate.

"Hey Morgan, how's it going?" He asked as I inserted the key.

"Good man, how's things around here?" I asked as I tossed the key back.

"Nothing ever happens around here. This place is quiet as a graveyard."

I laughed, "You're lucky. It won't be for long. There's going to be plenty of action for everyone here soon."

"I'd like some action," he replied as I started to get back in the truck.

Pausing, I replied, "Be careful what you wish for."

I pulled through the gate, and Dad jumped out and closed it, making sure the lock was secure. I drove up towards the house and saw the MRAP and Duce sitting in the open pasture behind it. I went around the house and to where everyone was gathered up. Sarge was barking orders, and all manner of weapons were laid out on a tarp on the ground. Some were on bipods, and two powerful Russian DsHK 12.7-millimeter machineguns were on tripods. These are the equivalent of the US Browning .50 cal., a lethal weapon.

And there were other weapons I wasn't quite sure what they were. And there were several faces I didn't recognize. Some of these poor souls looked pitiful. Their clothes were rags, and two men didn't have shoes. The small group of eight or so stood off to the side, watching and whispering to one another.

"Who are they?" I asked Sarge.

He looked over at those assembled. "I picked them up this morning on our way in. Some are from the market in Umatilla and some from Altoona. I asked for volunteers, told them what was coming, and they raised their hands."

"You going to train them up?"

"That's the idea."

"Look, I don't need to be trained on these weapons. I know how most of them work. Those men need some clothes, and a couple of them need shoes. We have all that back at the ranch. I'm going to get them sorted out."

"Good idea. We'll get everyone going on training. Dave's folks are providing dinner today. I told them we'd feed them as well, and I think that's what motivated them."

I looked back at the small cluster of men. They reminded me of looking at Depression-era photos or maybe pictures from the Dust Bowl. Raggedy beards and tattered clothes were a testament to the difficulties of today. There was no *new* anything. You had to keep what you had serviceable. No more running to Wal-Mart for a new pair of jeans or any of that. If your shoes wore out, you were barefoot.

I went over to Mel and told her what I was going to do. She agreed it was the right thing to do and gave me a quick kiss. Sarge was barking orders for everyone to get on line. As the men made their way to the firing line, I intercepted them and took a small Write in the Rain notepad from my pocket. I looked at the little spiral-bound book and thought about how I would probably never see another one.

"What size shoes do you wear?" I asked the first man as he approached.

"Tens. Why?"

Looking at the group, I said, "We have boots and some clothes. Write your names on here with your shoe size and your pants size. I'll see what I can do for you."

"Where the hell did you get *extra* boots and clothes?" One of them asked.

"We've been collecting them whenever we find them. Since you men are willing to help in the coming fight, we want to make sure you've got decent shoes and pants. You'll also be getting fed every day you're here for training."

"You have food?" Another man asked. I could clearly see the hunger on his gaunt face.

"We do. You'll also receive a ration of cornmeal as soon as we get it ground."

"We heard about a cornfield," one of the others said.

"We planted about forty acres, and it's being harvested right now. We found a couple of old grist stones at Renniger's and need to figure out how to get them into action. Still working on that."

"Where the hell did you guys get all this? Corn, boots, and clothes. You guys have trucks and more weapons than I've ever seen. Who the hell are you?"

"I'm just a regular guy that made some plans in the Before. Not that any of that really matters because everything I laid up is long since gone now. But we're trying to make a difference. We're trying to make life better for everyone around here, not just us."

"I saw you execute a man, *Sheriff,*" there was a heavy sarcastic edge to the last word.

"What? You didn't agree with it? Which one?" I asked.

"Which one?" The man nearly shouted back. "How many men have you killed?"

"Killed or executed?" I asked, looking him straight in the eye. "I don't see much difference in the two."

"Morgan!" Sarge shouted. "Some of us have shit to do today! You mind?"

The men finished jotting down their sizes and handed the notepad back. "What times lunch?" One asked.

"Don't worry. You'll get to eat. They do a pretty good job here," I replied.

"I could too if I had cattle," another commented.

"Then you should have got some," I replied as I pocketed the pad. "You better get over there and pay attention," I said as I looked over at Sarge. "He can be a mean old bastard."

Aaron was standing at the back of the group as Sarge launched a dissertation on firearm safety. I put a hand on his shoulder and said, "Why don't you find somewhere and get comfortable. You're not going to be in on this." He looked at me, a questioning look on his face, and I added, "For obvious reasons."

Aaron nodded, made his way over to the Hummer, climbed up on the hood, and sat down. I jumped back in the Suburban and headed out. Jim Gifford was on horseback let me through the gate. I told him what I was doing, and I would be back soon. He nodded and headed back to the tree line as I pulled out onto the road. I had an idea and decided to stop by the plant as I drove.

CHAPTER 7

I found the engineers in the small control room of the plant. Like typical engineers, they were hard at work with their feet propped up on consoles drinking coffee.

"How the hell are you guys getting coffee out of the old man?" I asked as I stepped in, the air in the small room thick with the aroma of the black elixir.

Terry held his cup up, "It's a fair trade, don't ya think? Little coffee for some power?"

"Shit, I'd give it all to you!"

Baker laughed, "I'll tell him you offered to give us all his coffee to keep the lights on."

"You do that," I laughed, "let me know how it turns out."

"This just a social visit?" Terry asked.

"No, I need a couple of buckets or something."

Scott got to his feet, "Come on, I know where there's a stack."

I followed him out and into the plant. As we walked, he asked, "What have you guys got going on?"

"Getting folks up to speed on all those Commie weapons we have. We're probably going to need all the help we can get."

"We told the old man we'd help, but he said he didn't want us exposed like that." Then, he looked at me with an exaggerated look, *"we're too valuable,"* he scoffed.

"I'd have to agree with him, honestly. Anyone can pull a trigger. You guys know how this plant operates, and we really need it."

"Yeah, we're going into town here in a bit to try and get the power on to one of the streets where a lot of people live."

"How's that going?"

"Pretty good. The biggest issue is going around and making sure that the main breaker is turned off to all the houses before we heat it. We had an AC unit catch fire on one the other day. I killed the power to the house, and we got it out pretty quick."

"Well, you guys just keep doing what you're doing. It's helping everyone."

"Here are the buckets," Scott said as we rounded a corner in the plant. "What do you need them for?"

"I need to load up some corn to take back to the ranch. We're going to start messing with those grist wheels and see if we can get the corn ground."

"Who's doing that?"

"We're all kind of working on it."

Scott leaned back against the wall. "You know, I just happen to know a couple of engineers that could figure this out pretty quick."

I felt like a complete idiot. "Why in the hell didn't we think of that?" I laughed.

"Just bring them here, and we'll sort it out. There's a ton of motors and linkage and all manner of shit here. We'll have that working in no time."

"I'll drop them off on my way back. Thanks, man. I don't know why we didn't consider that."

I grabbed four buckets and went to the end of the plant, where the corn was being unloaded. As I approached, I could hear a scraping sound. It was the unmistakable sound of a shovel on concrete. I was surprised to see Alex, the Canadian guy I'd encountered weeks before.

"Hey Alex, what's up?"

He paused from his labor and looked up. "Hey, Morgan. Just shoveling this corn up, so there's room for the next load."

"How'd you get involved in this?"

"Cecil asked me. I kind of hung out with him, and he said they needed help, and I didn't have anything else to do. These engineers you have here are some good people."

I looked at the massive mound of corn. "Damn, that's a lot of corn."

Alex scooped up another spade full and tossed it up onto the pile. "Sure is. That's a lot of food. But, it's funny, corn was not something I considered food. Even though it used to be in everything."

"It's damn sure food now!" I laughed.

He scooped up a handful. "It sure as hell is." Then, with a smile, he tossed several kernels in his mouth.

I laughed at the sight. "You eating that shit raw?"

"I just suck on them. Eventually, they get soft, and I chew them up. It's more something to do."

Hearing him talk about it got me thinking about a dip. I hadn't had one in; I don't remember how long. "I used to have a habit like that. But it wasn't corn."

He nodded at the pile, "Try it."

I scooped up a small handful and tossed them into my mouth. "What the hell," I said with a smile. Alex shoveled my buckets full for me and helped me carry them out to the truck. After closing the tailgate, I asked, "You need anything?"

Smiling back, he replied, "No. I'm right as rain. Thank you." I waved bye to him and got in the truck headed to the ranch.

Sarge had everyone on line as Mike and Ted handed out weapons. "When you're handed a weapon, don't finger fuck it! Just hang onto it until your given further instructions! This is not a game, ladies and gentlemen! This is deadly serious shit, and you will treat it accordingly!"

Mike and Ted questioned Dave's folks and the new group as they handed out the weapons. Of course, the answers dictated what weapon they were handed. As they went about this, Sarge continued, "We're all adults here, and I don't give a shit about your feelings! There are only three feelings on the range, hot, cold, and recoil!" He colorfully explained firearms safety and the fundamental rules of weapons handling.

Mel stood in line, waiting for the guys to get to her. She wore her pistol belt and had her AR slung over her back. Ted was a couple of people down from her talking with one of the townspeople. "What's your name?" Ted asked.

"Call me Bubba, Bubba West."

"Alright, Bubba, you got any prior service?"

"No, sir. But I've been a shooter my whole life."

Ted looked him up and down. "You don't have any guns now?"

Bubba reached around to the small of his back and revealed a Glock 19. "This is all I have now. Well, all I have that has bullets anyway, and I don't even have a full mag of these."

Ted pulled a Glock mag from his plate carrier, "Here. It's a seventeen mag."

Bubba took the mag, looking at it. "You serious?"

"I'd rather there be more guns in the fight than me having ammo, and you not, ya know?"

Bubba quickly and smoothly changed out the mag in the pistol for the new one before returning to its holster. "Thank you. I wasn't sure about this, honestly. But you all are making me feel better about this by the minute."

Ted looked Bubba up and down. Finally, he stepped over and picked up and PK machinegun. "You think you could handle this?"

Bubba took the weapon from Ted. Then, in a smooth motion, he pulled the bolt to the rear and opened the feed tray cover, wiping a hand over the feed tray and checking the mechanism quickly. "I think I can sort it out."

Ted smiled. "You've seen one of these before, haven't you?"

"I went to Knob Creek a couple of times, and both times I made sure to shoot this. I used to watch YouTube videos of the war in Syria, and those idiots were always hip shooting these things. So I figured if it could take the abuse those morons dished out to it, it must be a pretty good weapon. I like it," he finished with a smile.

Ted patted his shoulder, "Me and you are gonna get along just fine." He looked over his shoulder at Mike, "Just keep an eye on that squirrelly little fucker."

Bubba smiled, "I recognize jackassery when I see it."

Mike stood in front of Dad. "You good with that M4 Butch?"

"I'd prefer an M-60."

Mike smiled. "Well, we don't have one of those, but!" He held up a finger, walked over to the pile of weapons, and picked one up. Then, holding out the PK machinegun, he asked, "Would this work? Basically, the Russian version of the sixty."

A look washed over Dad's face. "Yeah, I know what it is. A gook with one of these shot me down once. Damn, I hate green tracers."

"You want it?" Mike asked, uncertain.

"Why hell yes!"

Ted finally made it to Mel. She smiled excitedly, waiting to see what weapon Ted would give her. "Hey Mel."

"Hey Ted," she replied and looked past him at the pile of weapons.

"There are special instructions for you," he replied.

"What do you mean? What kind of special instructions? If you men think I'm not going to be involved in this fight, you're out of your damn mind!"

Ted held his hands up and took a step back. "Hey, don't yell at me. I'm just the messenger."

"This is bullshit!" Mel shouted.

"What the hell is going on over there?" Sarge barked.

Mel stepped out of the line and walked straight to him, holding an accusatory finger up in his face. "If you and Morgan think you're going to put me someplace *safe*," she nearly spat the last word, "you're out of your damn mind!"

"Oh, calm down, woman!" Sarge barked back.

"Don't tell me to calm down!" She scowled back at him.

Her response startled the old man, and he flinched. "Now hold on, Mel, just hold on. You're not being treated special, and you'll be in the thick of it, I promise. Morgan just wanted you to have a particular weapon."

"Oh, what?" She glared as she crossed her arms over her chest.

Sarge walked over to the MRAP and took out his Minimi. "Here, you're going to run this. Is it enough gun for you?"

"What is it?" She asked as she took the little machinegun.

"It's pure hate, Mel. It's one badass little machinegun. You just hang onto this, and we'll educate you on its operation. Happy now?"

Still looking at the weapon, she absentmindedly replied, "Yeah."

Sarge shook his head and gave her a wink as he walked up to the front of those assembled. "Alright. If you have a rifle, go over there with Mikey. If you have a belt-fed weapon, come over here with Ted and me."

When I came through the door, Miss Kay was in the kitchen, as she generally was. Jace and Edie sat at a picnic table on the back porch, drawing or coloring.

"Hey, Miss kay," I said as I came through the door.

She looked up concern on her face, "Oh, hey, Morgan. Is everything alright?" She asked as she wiped her hands on a dishtowel.

"Oh yeah. We just got some people from the town who will help out, and I need some boots. There are eight of them. You got anything I could take them to eat? Janet will fix them dinner, but these folks look like they're starving to death."

She looked at the counter, "We have about a dozen biscuits leftover."

"Can you wrap them up for me? Then, I'll get the boots and all for them."

"Sure thing."

I went upstairs into the closet and started picking through the boots. One of the names caught my eye, Sky, size seven. It made me wonder how old this kid was. I'd need to check on that. It didn't take long to pick out a pair for all of them, and most were even new. Next, I grabbed two pairs of socks for each of them and went to look at the pants.

Since we had so much black, I decided to give them those. It was unlikely that the DHS was still in black, and I was only giving them pants. With everything I needed finally located, I pulled an old duffle bag from the closet and piled it all in. Going downstairs, Kay had the biscuits wrapped up and ready to go.

"Thank you. They'll surely appreciate it." I said as I picked up the bundle.

ENGINEERING HOME

"You're very welcome. How's it going over there?"

"Sarge is doing his thing. I gotta run. If you need us, just call on the radio."

"I'll be fine."

"Say, have you seen Dalton?"

"Not since breakfast. Why?"

"No reason, just need to talk to him real quick."

I loaded the stuff in the truck and headed to the bunker. Wallner was there with a couple of his men and Dalton. Pulling up, I called to Dalton, "Hey, jump in."

"What's up?" he asked as he walked over.

"Hey Morgan, everything ok?" Wallner asked.

"Oh yeah. We're good. How about you guys? Need anything?"

"Nah, we're good. I have two men in the burned-out MRAP out front and a couple outback as well. Dalton built them one hell of a hide. So if anyone tries to get in here, we'll know about it."

Dalton got in the truck, and I waved bye to Wallner. Then, as I pulled away, I asked Dalton, "Where's your still?"

"In the same place, why?"

With a conspiratorial grin, I replied, "Got you something."

Dalton didn't ask what and, in a minute, we were pulling up to the house. I pulled around behind it; driving on the lawn wasn't an issue now-a-day. Then, getting out, I walked around back and opened the tailgate. "This should be enough to get you started."

Dalton looked at the corn, and a smile spread across his face. "That's just beautiful."

"Is it enough for a run?"

It's a small still. If I can do this and it works, I'm going to build a bigger one."

"You need to get with those engineers. Let them build you one. That orange juice plant has a ton of equipment. I know we could build a hell of a still over there."

"Not a bad idea. Then I can keep this one, you know, for medicinal purposes."

I nodded, "Yeah, medicinal. You need anything else?"

"Nope, I just needed the corn."

"I'll leave you to your work then."

I left Dalton to his chemistry experiment and headed towards Eustis. I'd started thinking about it on the drive. I needed to see Shane and Sean as they were the police for Eustis. If anyone needed to know what was happening, it was them. I passed Baker and her engineers in the old bucket truck they'd managed to get running on my way. They were headed into Umatilla. Maybe some more folks in town will have lights on this evening.

Shane and Sean were standing in the parking lot with three other men when I pulled up. They were standing around a cool-looking old Jeep with a small trailer. The Jeep looked like something you'd see at an overland event. There was a rack on the roof and a swing-away tire carrier with Jerry cans on the back. The small trailer had a canvas top, and the whole rig looked really nice.

"Hey Morgan," Shane greeted me.

"Shane, Sean, how are you boys doing?" I asked.

"We're good. S.O.S., you know."

"Is that thing diesel?" One of the other men asked.

"Sure is. Has a Cummins in it."

"That's really cool. This old Jeep here," he pointed at the olive drab rig, "is diesel too."

"No shit? I didn't know Jeep ever did that. What year is it?"

"It's a 1964 CJ5."

"Factory?" I asked.

"Oh yeah. I've had this baby for years. It was just something to tinker with and take out on the weekend."

"Now it's our saving grace." One of the others replied. He was tall with dark hair, taller than the man I talked with. The third man was shorter than the other two.

"Where you guys from?" I asked.

"We move around a lot," the third man replied. "We all lived in Kentucky but have been moving around since things went to shit."

"You a Sheriff's deputy?" The first one asked.

"Kind of," I replied with a little chuckle.

"That's an understatement," Shane said, "he's the Sheriff."

"I was kind of appointed, not something I went looking for." I held my hand out, "Morgan Carter."

The first man gripped mine, "Karl Erickson."

"Imri Morganstern," the taller of the other two offered.

"Imri? Where's that from?" I asked.

"Israel."

The third man thrust his hand out, "Ignore the heeb. He's not housebroken. Chad Hulsizer."

"Good to meet you guys."

"Is there a reason for you dropping by?" Shane asked.

"Unfortunately, yes," I replied, thinking about these three newcomers as I did. "You remember that load of Feds we sent to Frostproof?"

"Yeah, they didn't make it there, did they?" Sean asked.

"No, they didn't. And they're on their way back."

"What?" Shane asked.

"We've got some intel that there's a large force moving this way. Apparently, those assholes got away and came up with some new equipment and have been collecting human garbage to fill the ranks."

"What are you talking about? Feds? Frostproof?" Karl asked.

"We kind of kicked them out of town. They were being transported to a DOD detention facility in Frostproof."

"You've done a hell of a lot more than that," Sean said.

"DOD has a prison around here?" Chad asked.

"There was. But I think they shut it down. When the Russians showed up, there were far more of them than DOD had around here."

"Russians are assholes," Imri snapped.

"Yeah, we made dead out of a shit load of them," I replied.

"How the hell did you do that?" Karl asked. "I mean, that's a pretty badass Suburban, but we've seen the Russians and all the equipment they managed to get over here."

"They had a little help from the Air Force," Sean replied.

Karl laughed. "The Air Force, DOD! Who are you guys?" He pointed at Shane and Sean, saying, "We have police," then at me, "and a Sheriff!"

"We're just normal folks trying to get by," I replied.

"So, you say those assholes are coming back?" Shane asked.

"Someone came into town and told us about them. They were over in Davenport at the time but were headed to Clermont. Old Chuck is pretty pissed, and they're coming here for some get back."

"How many of them are there?" Sean asked.

"A hundred. Ish. Heavy on the ish."

"Holy shit!"

"We don't believe they have any heavy weapons. Done right, we can probably take them. The old man thinks so."

"Wait," Karl interrupted. "How many people do you guys have?"

"Not sure how many we're going to be able to field," I replied. "We've got a bunch training right now."

Karl and the other two shared looks between themselves. After a moment, Imri asked, "You want to help them out?"

"I think we should," Chad quickly replied. "I'm fucking bored and ain't killed no one in," he looked at Imri and asked, "how long's it been?"

"If you gotta ask, it's been too long," Imri replied.

"Hey guys, I appreciate you wanting to help us. And I don't' mean any offense, but we don't know you guys at all. I'm having to plan on dealing with a bunch of real shitheads that are on their way here, and you guys roll into town. Do you see how that makes me a little uneasy?"

"oh, yeah, I totally get it," Karl replied. "You don't know us, but you can trust us, and we'll show you that you can."

"He's not telling you, but Karl is a retired Sargent Major from Fifth Special Forces Group," Chad offered.

"Chad was a sniper in the Army," Imri added.

"And he's Israeli SF!" Karl barked.

"Do you have any prior service people here?" Karl asked.

"Uh, yeah," I replied with a laugh.

"You should take them to meet the old man," Sean said.

I looked at the Jeep they were driving. "How are you keeping fuel in that thing?"

"We have a pump system we use to get fuel from underground tanks. It works pretty well, and there's usually fuel in the tanks we check. Gas is tough to find, but diesel is usually there."

"We have folks being trained right now. So if you guys want to follow me, I'll take you over there and introduce you to Sarge."

"Sarge?" Karl asked.

"He was a First Sargent in the 101st Airborne," I replied.

"What's his name?"

"Linus Mitchell."

Karl doubled over in laughter. "You mean Blanket? You guys have Blanket here with you?"

"You know him?"

"Oh yeah, I know him. He's a damn good soldier, and we worked with them often."

"We have a couple of other guys as well, Rangers."

"Well, I gotta see Blanket!"

Shaking my head, I replied, "You may not want to call him that. He gets pretty pissed about it."

"Oh, I'm calling him Blanket!" Karl laughed.

We left Shane and Sean and headed back to the ranch. I watched them in the rearview mirror as we passed the cornfield. I could see them pointing and craning their necks to look. Pulling up the gate, we waited for the security to come open the gate. I watched as the horse came out of the woods and headed towards us. Getting out of the truck, I waited at the gate for the rider.

As we waited, the sound of heavy gunfire echoed through the air. "What the hell is all that?" Chad shouted.

"Training!" I called back.

Karl stepped out of the Jeep. "How much ammo do you guys have?"

"More than we'll ever shoot!"

"How the hell did you do that?"

"We took it off the Russians!"

Karl laughed, shaking his head as he climbed back into the old Jeep, muttering, "More than they'll ever shoot."

"Hey Morgan," Jim said as he tossed me the key.

"Hey, Jim. How's tricks?"

He laughed. "Same old shit, buddy. Give me the key, you guys, just head on back, and I'll lock up."

Tossing the key back, I replied, "Thanks, man."

He looked at the Jeep behind me. "Who's this?"

"Some guys I found in town. It sounds like one of them might know Sarge. Going to find out. Catch you later."

We drove across the ranch and towards the sound of numerous weapons hammering away. There were lulls in the fire, and it would cease for a few seconds before taking off again. I pulled up beside the Hummer and parked. Mike, Ted, and Doc were moving up and down the line working with individuals that were having trouble. Sarge was working with the smaller group with belt-fed weapons.

"You guys have armor too?" Imri asked.

"Where the hell did you get these from?" Karl asked.

"Kind of a long story," I replied. "Hang out here, and I'll get the old man."

I walked over to Sarge and interrupted his instruction. "Hey, I want you to meet these guys."

He was clearly annoyed. "I'm a little busy right now."

"One of the guys is Fifth Group, says he knows you."

Sarge looked at the three men standing in front of the Hummer. "Which one?"

"On the left."

Sarge squinted and started walking towards them. He called out, "Mikey!" When Mike looked over, he waved for him. Mike came at a trot.

"What's up, boss?"

"Take over for me for a minute."

"Roger that."

As we got closer, Karl started to smile. I looked at Sarge, and he was smiling ear to ear. "Bangin' Bravo!" Sarge called out.

"Well, if it isn't First Sargent Linus Blanket Mitchell!" Karl replied as he started to walk towards the old man.

The two men shook hands enthusiastically and quickly embraced in a hug. "Holy shit!" Karl shouted. "How many years has it been?"

"Too many!"

The two stepped back and looked one another up and down. "You still it?" Karl asked.

"Hell no!" Sarge barked back. "I'm retired."

"Me too!"

"He's not retired," I interrupted. "Are you, Colonel?"

Karl looked surprised. "Colonel?"

"Ignore him. Like most kids, he doesn't understand he's supposed to be seen and not heard."

"Doesn't change anything. You were retired; you're not now."

Sarge took a minute to give the Cliff Notes version of what we'd be through. First, sharing the current state of the conflict between the Feds and DOD and our relationship with the military.

Sarge pulled a handkerchief from his pocket and wiped his forehead, "So, that's our story. What the hell have you boys been up to?"

"That's a hell of a story. I've had no contact with DOD," Karl replied. "We've just been moving around trying to find a good place to live, honestly. We've worked security for a couple of people in exchange for food and such."

"Yeah, but that didn't work out most of the time," Chad added.

"At least we got to kill some scumbags," Imri chimed in.

"Funny how so many people sink lower than a politician's IQ when things go to shit," Sarge said.

"That they do," I replied. "We've dealt with a few like that as well." Imri nodded as I spoke.

"So, what's all this?" Karl asked, nodding at the line of trainees.

Sarge turned to look at them. "Well, we need trigger pullers to deal with these assholes headed this way. Some of these are our folks, some are with this ranch here, and some are from town. We're going to need all the help we can get."

Imri nodded at the pile of guns lying on a tarp, "You have enough fucking weapons, for sure."

"We've got guns and ammo. Bodies are harder to come by," I replied.

"Well, Top, I mean Colonel," Karl smiled when he said it, "we're here if you need us. Just tell me what to do."

"Knock that shit off, Karl. And I would appreciate your help." Sarge pointed at Chad and Imri, "If these boys are anything like you, you'd certainly be a huge help."

"These chipmunks?" Karl said as he looked at Imri. "This one is Israeli SF. Chad here was a sniper in Iraq. I think we can help you guys out."

"Would you be willing to take over this training for me? I've got other shit to do."

"Yeah," I interjected, "we need to do a recon and find these assholes."

"No shit, Sherlock," Sarge snapped back.

Karl laughed, "Good to see you haven't changed, Linus."

"So, it's true?" I asked Karl.

"What's true?"

"He's always been an asshole?"

"I'm gonna shove my boot up your asshole," Sarge barked. "Morgan, go tell Mike and Ted to come over here. Give them a break."

I went to the truck and got Miss Kay's biscuits and the duffle bag before getting with Mike and Ted. The trainees were told to clear their weapons before leaving the line, and as they came off, I went to the group from town.

"Here's some biscuits for you guys to hold you until dinner," I said as I handed the bundle to one of them. "And this has boots, socks, and some pants for all of you."

The biscuits were quickly unwrapped and passed around. It was shocking to see how fast some of them ate. "Slow down, guys. You'll get more to eat."

"If you guys have so much food, clothes, and boots, weapons, why haven't you handed it all out?" One of them asked, and I was shocked to see a woman.

"It's not my job to do that. And we do give it out, all the damn time. We're doing it now, and you're eating our food right now."

"Yeah, but if you have so much, why aren't you helping people?"

"What's your name?"

"Sky Sommerfeldt."

"It's like this, Sky," I made sure to look all of them in the eye, "we have been helping. We've defended town several times. We deal with the criminal element here. We've brought food into town multiple times and kicked the DHS out of Lake County. We destroyed a Russian forward operating base and provided medical care for people hurt or wounded. We're doing a lot; you think the power coming back to town is magic?"

"Power?" Bubba asked.

"Yeah, power. We got the turbine at the juice plant running. We've been getting the power back on in the Umatilla area and will be bringing it to Eustis shortly."

"No shit?" Bubba replied as he chewed his biscuit.

"No shit," I replied. "Here, you guys get this sorted out. Get your boots on," I looked down at the bare feet of two of the men, "seeing you guys barefoot just kills me."

"Thank you, Morgan," Bubba replied.

Sarge introduced the three muskee queers to the new group. As military personnel will do, they were quickly joking and laughing. As the new members were getting to know our people, everyone took the time to get a drink of water or whatever necessaries they needed at the moment.

Mel was sitting with the girls when Erin walked over to her.

"This is crazy, these guns," Erin said.

"It is a lot to take in all at once."

Erin smiled and looked back at the firing line where Mel's Minimi was lying. "You get a big enough gun?"

Mel laughed, "I wanted something that would make a difference. It's way easier to shoot than I thought."

As the two women talked, Doc and Jess walked over. "Hey Erin," Doc said.

"Hey, Ronnie, right?"

"Ronnie, Doc, whatever you want to call me. Say, you're a nurse, right?"

"I was a surgical nurse."

"You still are. We want you to get trained on these weapons, but you're not going to be in the ambush. You have a skill set we can't afford to risk."

"What? You don't think I can do it?"

"That's not it at all. You have a high degree of medical training and experience. That is far more valuable than having you on a trigger. I'll get with you later."

"Okay," Erin replied.

"Bye," Jess said with a little wave and smile.

"Bye," Mel and Erin both replied.

Erin watched the two walk away. Then, looking at Mel, she said, "Oh, thank God. I was so scared of this. Aren't you scared?"

"Terrified," Mel replied. "But I want to make sure these guys will never be a problem again, and if I have to pick up a rifle to make certain of that, then that's what I'm going to do."

"I'm scared to death of this. I'm not one of these people that thinks they can kill people. I don't know if I could do it."

"Now, you don't have to worry about it. By the way, could you come back with me this afternoon and check on Fred for us?"

"She's pregnant, right?"

"She is, and Doc thinks she may have twins."

Erin's eyes went wide. "What? Really?"

"She does have two babies!" Little Bit shouted.

Erin looked at her sideways, "How do you know that?"

"I can hear them. There are two heartbeats when I listen to her belly. No one believes me, though."

"I believe you," Erin said. Then, looking back at Mel, she added, "I'd love to come over. Going anywhere right now would be a treat!"

Mel laughed, "Tell me about it. But I must say, I kind of like this slow pace. It's nice to have everyone around all the time."

"If we were at home, I'd agree with you. It's nice here, but there's a lot of people here, and we don't have our own place."

"You should have Travis come with you. There's a lot of houses in our neighborhood that are sitting empty. You could pick one and move into it."

Erin stared across the open pasture to where Travis was knelt down, working the action on an AK. "That would be nice. I'll talk to him. But we don't have any food or anything. We kind of trade food and shelter for work."

"It'd be the same over there. We all eat together, Miss Kay does a great job with meal planning, and several of us pitch in to help."

"I'll talk to him."

Sarge called for everyone to get back on line, and people started making their way back to their places. I walked over to Thad and Mary as they slung their AKs. "What do you think, Mary?"

"This is kind of scary. I've never shot one of these before."

Thad smiled as he adjusted the sling around his thick neck. "You can't say that anymore. You have been shooting it all morning."

She gave him a playful slap on the arm. "You know what I mean."

I smiled at her, "It's a good look for you."

"Thank you, Morgan," she replied with a broad smile.

"Alright! Listen up, people!" Sarge barked.

He took a few minutes to introduce the group's new members and let them know that these men would be their instructors moving forward. I was surprised he didn't give the bona fides of them. But I guess his time in the Army instilled in him the possession of unquestioned authority. In other words, it is what it is because he said so.

When he was done with his introduction, he turned things over to Karl. Next, Chad and Imri paired us with Mike and Ted, Imri going with Mike and Chad with Ted. The training changed slightly in that the shooting stopped, and the men took time to get with each individual to set up their web gear. We'd collected this from both the DHS and the Russians.

They went down the line assisting in adjusting straps and showing each person how to put their mags in the pouches and a quick inspection of the items already on there. This ended up being a good thing because they recovered more than a dozen hand grenades, smoke grenades, and other items these people weren't trained on yet.

The grenades ended up piled in the back of the Hummer. Mike was walking towards it with several in his hands when I stopped him. "Give me a couple of those."

He handed over a couple, and I slipped them into a pouch on my plate carrier. "These might come in handy," I said.

"I love grenades!"

"You love anything that goes boom," I replied with a laugh.

"The bigger the boom, the better," he replied with a maniacal laugh.

"Find anything else cool?"

"Just some smokes. Got a couple of forty-millimeter rounds as well."

"Nice. Do we have any more of them?"

"We have a couple hundred, I think, and we have five tubes for them."

"I want one."

"I'll set one up for you."

Looking at my carbine, I asked, "Can you put it on here?"

"You don't want that."

"Yes, I do! I want more firepower."

"I mean, you don't want it mounted to your carbine. We have a couple of 320s. So that's what you want."

"Ok, I want one of those then," I replied with a laugh.

He winked, "I'll hook you up. Tomorrow we'll bring a couple, and I'll train you on it."

Dalton carried two of the buckets of corn over to Danny's. Setting them down near the shop, he grabbed a small dust broom and cleaned out the large mortar Thad, and I made for the Kudzu. After getting it cleaned up, he dumped in some corn, picked up the large pestle, and started pounding the corn.

As he pounded, he started to hum, and before long, he was singing quietly to himself. "What are you up to?" Aric asked as he approached, interrupting the song.

"Just pounding some corn," Dalton replied cheerily.

"Making grits? Cornmeal?"

"Naw, just cracking the corn."

"Why?"

"Whole corn doesn't do so well when making liquor. Cracking it produces the best results."

Aric's eyes went wide. "You're making liquor?" He looked down into the hollowed-out stump.

"Yes, sir!"

Looking around, Aric asked, "Where's the still?"

"It's at another house up the street. I just need to crack this corn. I've got a couple of plastic drums I'll make the mash in. Plastic isn't the best thing to use, but I don't have anything else."

"How long will it take?"

"Couple of weeks."

"Weeks? Are you serious?"

"You have to ferment the mash. That takes time. I've never made liquor down here before, so I don't know how long it will take."

"Where have you made it before?"

Raising and dropping the big pestle rhythmically, Dalton replied, "Up in the mountains where I'm from, Appalachistan."

"Appalachistan? Where the hell is that?"

"It's an area that runs through north Georgia, North Carolina, and Virginia. It's like Afghanistan with trees. I know them, boys, up there are doing just fine."

"Huh, wondered where you were from."

"I never told you?" Dalton asked curiously.

"Shit, no one knows anything about you. I remember when you first showed up. Everyone thought Morgan was crazy inviting you in, You just walked up out of the night, and he invited you to the house."

"Morgan is a good man. I'm not a people person, and I like him."

"He is something else. Yet, somehow he keeps all this shit moving."

"Don't sell yourself short. Everyone here helps keep this going. He's just one cog in the machine you guys have here."

"Yeah, well, if it weren't for him none of us would be here."

I was sitting on the hood of the Hummer watching the training. Aaron walked over and climbed up beside me. "Who are these guys?"

"One of them knows Sarge. They're all prior service, Green Beret, Army sniper, and that tall one is Israeli SF."

"You just met them?" He asked, and I nodded in reply. "And you're letting them help you guys out?"

"I see where you're going," I replied and looked over at him. "The difference is, they didn't have a radio from Team Asshole. Plus, we're keeping an eye on them."

"I'm more than willing to help out."

"I know you are, and your time will come."

"Morgan!" Sarge barked. I looked over at him, and he waved for me to come over.

"He looks like he's got something on his mind. Let me go see," I said to Aaron as I slid off the truck.

Sarge walked over to the back of the MRAP and got a drink of water. He hung the cup up as I approached.

"What's up?"

He leaned back on the step to the backdoor of the truck. "We need to get some eyes on this shit show headed our way."

"I was thinking the same thing, honestly. But, unfortunately, we're kind of in the dark right now."

"We need the guys here to keep this going for a while. These people not only need weapons training, but they also need small unit tactics as well. I need to know how many days we have before trouble shows up. I hope we have enough time to get these people up to speed."

"So, what are you thinking?"

"You, me, and Dalton. That giant seems pretty good at sneaking and peaking."

"I was thinking the same thing. You know, if we find them, we could let him go in and see what sort of dirt he can dig up."

The old man rubbed his chin, "I don't like the idea of that, honestly. But it would be great if he could."

"I think he could handle himself pretty good."

He looked over at me, "Let's talk to him this evening when we get back. I want to go do this tomorrow."

About then, a clanging racket started up. I looked over and saw Dave holding a large metal triangle, beating its inside with a piece of rebar. "Dinner is ready y'all!"

"Alright, Teddy! Shut it down for dinner!"

We all hiked up to the house. Dave's large porch was set up with tables and chairs, but there wasn't enough for everyone. We had a large group here today. The eight from town stood in line together, craning their necks to look at the large steaming pot sitting on a picnic table.

Seeing their curiosity, I asked, "Hey Grandpa, what's for dinner?"

Dave looked up, a ladle in one hand and bowl in the other, "Chicken and dumplings!"

"Chicken and fucking dumplings?" One of the townspeople muttered.

"Well, it's more dumplings than chicken, but there's some in there," Dave added.

Eric closed the door to the panel and started across the yard to the next house. He hated this part of the process, turning off mains to all the homes on the following line they wanted to energize. So instead, the team worked one block at a time. They would do each block, starting at both ends working toward one another to meet in the middle. Then they could be confident that nothing would catch on fire, the most significant risk they faced.

"Come on, Eric, smile!" Terry shouted from a yard over.

Eric looked over and gave him an exaggerated toothy smile. "Happy?"

Terry gave him a thumbs up, "That's better!"

Eric rounded the corner of the next house, and for an instant thought, he heard voices. As he walked up the side of the house, the sound grew louder, but it wasn't talking he was hearing. Instead, it sounded like someone crying, sobbing, or maybe lifting something heavy, grunting at the effort.

As he came to an open window, he froze in his tracks. A young girl was lying on the bed. A man mounted on top of her. He held her wrists down on the mattress as he thrust himself into her very forcefully. The girl's head was to the side, and Eric could see right into the brilliant green eyes set into her tear-streaked face.

"Help me," she mouthed. Not daring to say the words aloud.

The man's head snapped to the side and a growl emitted from the thick beard covering his face. "What the fuck!" He shouted as he reached for a pistol lying on the bed.

Seeing the gun, Eric was roused from his trance and spun on his heels, and started to run. He could hear the man cussing in the house and the sound of furniture crashing. As he ran, Eric began to scream.

"Terry! Terry!"

The back door of the house burst open, and the man bounded out, losing his balance and rolling in the yard. The pistol he gripped in his right hand went off during the fall. Eric let out a shriek as he thought he was being shot at. The man got to his feet and started to run again. He was shirtless and wore tattered blue jeans with a large oval buckle hanging from a thick leather belt. The buckle made a clinking sound as the man moved.

Then he heard Terry, "Drop the gun motherfucker! Drop the fucking gun, or I'll kill you where you stand!"

Eric stopped and looked back at the man. His eyes darted back and forth from Eric to Terry. In a moment, other people were yelling as well.

"Eric, get your damn rifle up!" Baker called out as Terry continued to yell for the man to drop the pistol.

"Just drop the gunman," Baker said. "We're here to get the power back on, that's all."

The man's attitude quickly changed, and he raised his hands, "Hey, sorry about this. I was just surprised when I saw someone looking in my window."

Now looking down his rifle at the man, Eric shouted, "Who's the girl! How old is she!"

Confused, Terry asked, "What girl?"

Eric pointed at the house, "There's a young girl in there!"

The man gave a dismissive wave. "Oh, you ain't got to worry about her."

"What are you talking about, Eric?" Baker asked.

"He was fucking a young girl, really young! I saw him, holding her down."

"Hold on, hold on. It's not what you think," the man protested.

"You either drop that pistol, or I'm gonna drop the hammer on this rifle!" Terry shouted.

The man looked at the handgun for a moment before letting it fall from his grip. "Satisfied?" The man asked.

"Take a couple of steps towards me!" Terry shouted, and he complied. "That's far enough!"

"Look, I don't want no trouble. I didn't know you guys were working on the power." He smiled, trying to lighten the situation. "Hell, I mean, power? Really?"

"Who's the girl?" Baker asked, "Where is she?"

"That's just my girlfriend. She's in the house."

"Call her out here!" Baker ordered.

"No. I don't have to explain shit to you people!" His anger was returning.

"The fuck you don't, asshole! Do you see this rifle? It says you have to explain shit to us!"

Suddenly the back door of the house opened, and Scott appeared, leading a very young girl outside, wrapped in a blanket. All the shouting stopped, and everyone stared at them. Scott was stone-faced and staring a hole through the shirtless man. His only words were, "You better call Morgan over here."

"What the hell is going on?" Baker asked, confused.

"Eric's right. She's thirteen."

As Sarge and I discussed some of the particulars of our upcoming mission, my radio suddenly crackled to life.

Morgan!

Sarge and I both looked down at the radio. "Who the hell is that?" I asked.

Sarge shrugged and pulled the radio out. "Go ahead."

This is Baker. We need you to come to town, now.

"What's up?"

We have a, uh, a situation. Bring some people with you.

"On my way, where are you?" I asked, then looked around. "Thad, Ian, Jamie, let's go!"

We're on Wisteria Ave. You'll see us.

"It can't be too bad, whatever it is," Sarge said.

"We'll see," I said as I climbed into the driver's seat of the Hummer. Jamie ran up and gave me a look that could kill for driving. "Just get in!"

"What's going on?" Thad asked as he opened the passenger door.

"I don't know. Baker just called and said we needed to get to town and to bring some people with me."

When everyone was loaded up, they headed for the gate. As we drove, I started to honk the horn. As I hoped, Jim came galloping out of the woods on his horse, headed for the gate. He got there in plenty of time to open it, and I never slowed as we passed through it. Jim stood at the gate, unsure what the hell was going on.

There wasn't much talking as I drove, pushing the truck as hard as it would go. The ranch is close to town, and we were there in less than fifteen minutes. Stopping in the street and leaving it running, everyone quickly hopped out.

Not seeing anything that looked particularly troublesome, I asked, "What's up?"

Scott walked over with a young girl wrapped in a blanket. He went to Jamie and asked, "Can you take care of her for a minute?"

"Sure," she replied. Then, she smiled at the girl, "Come over here with me."

Scott came back to me and said, "This is a problem."

"Please enlighten me?" I said as I glanced over at Thad. He had his Ak to his shoulder, looking around.

"That little girl is his stepdaughter. Her mom's dead, and she's been living with this asshole."

I looked at the man sitting in the tall grass of the yard. "So?"

"He's been molesting her."

"What?" I asked as I looked at the man again.

"For years. Since before the Day. When her mom died, it only got worse."

"Sick fuck," I said, already thinking about how we would execute him.

"What do you want to do with him?" Scott asked.

I looked over at Jamie and the girl. "I guess I need to go talk to her."

"Hey, you're the Sheriff, right?" The man asked.

"I am."

"So, what are these supposed Army assholes doing harassing me? They go no authority here."

"If what they say is true, they have every right."

"You can't believe that little bitch. She's been lying about me for years."

"I saw it!" Eric screeched. "I fucking saw you!"

The man rose to his feet, "Look," his words were cut off by a rifle splitting the quiet. And just like that photo of General Nguyen executing a Vietcong in the streets of Saigon is an image most people have seen and recognize, the image of the side of that man's head exploding will forever be burned into my mind's eye.

"What the hell!" I shouted, looking around.

Jamie was advancing towards the man's body, her rifle at her shoulder. Rage masked her face. As she moved, she fired again. Through gritted teeth, she muttered, "Die motherfucker. Die."

"Whoa, whoa!" I shouted and started to move to intercept her. She fired again before I was close enough to her to grab her rifle. "What the hell are you doing?"

She stopped, staring at the body. She said, "You were going to do it anyway. I did you a favor."

"We don't know what the hell is going on here."

Jamie lowered her rifle. "Yes, you do." She turned and pointed to the young girl. "Look at her. Do you think she's lying? You think Eric is lying? She told me everything. She's just a little girl."

"No, I don't think they are. Hell, I don't know, actually. What the hell is going on here?"

"You know exactly what is going on," Jamie replied. She looked at the body again, then spit on it. "Fuck him."

As she turned to walk away, I grabbed her arm. "We can't do shit this way."

"Why not?"

I nodded towards the end of the block, where several people were gathered. "Because it doesn't look right. If this is all true, he needed put down. But it should have been done in public with an explanation. We can't appear to be dishing out vengeance when justice is what's called for."

"I see what you're trying to say. But one person's vengeance is another's justice. So it works both ways."

While gunfire didn't draw the sort of attention it once did, shooting in town would naturally attract attention. The shouting and shooting had drawn a few curious residents to the end of the block where they stood talking. I turned and looked back at the body. We had to move it. We couldn't just leave it here.

Jamie was leaning on the door of the truck, smoking a cigarette. I walked over to her. "Listen, we can't leave the body lying here. You killed him so you can load him into the truck."

"What about her?" Jamie asked, nodding at the girl.

Taking my hat off, I ran my hand through my hair. "That's a harder problem to solve. Does she know anyone in town?"

"I haven't asked her."

"What's her name?"

"Tammy."

I walked around to the passenger side, where the girl was sitting, dangling her bare feet out the door. As I came around, I looked at her. She was so small, looked so young, and the thought of what she was just going through made me sick. The bottoms of her feet were black, and it looked like she hadn't had a bath in some time.

"Hey Tammy, I'm Morgan."

She looked up, squinting against the mid-day sun. "I know who you are, Sheriff. Everyone does." The statement surprised me. I hadn't thought about the star all that often.

"I'm really sorry for all this. What you went through."

She shrugged, "It's just life. Just the way it is."

"It'll be different now," I assured her.

She let out a long breath. "It'll just be someone else. That's all I am. Something to fuck."

It saddened me to my core to hear such a young girl say that. "I promise you. It will never happen again." She looked up and shrugged. "Do you know anyone here?"

She scoffed. "Yeah, I know the people he traded me to for food or booze or whatever."

"You mean, there are other people as well?"

"You know, for a Sheriff, you sure are out of touch. Do you not know what's going on around here?"

"We've been a little busy with some bad folks. Sorry, we didn't find out sooner." As I spoke, she sat there swinging her legs back and forth. "Do you have any family or friends here in town?"

"No." She replied and looked up, "I'll be fine."

"We're not leaving you here."

She shrugged again. "I don't have anywhere to go."

"Yes, you do," I replied. "Go inside and get some clothes and whatever you want to take. I'm taking you out of here."

"Where to?"

"Somewhere safe. Go on, get your things."

Tammy hopped out of the truck, adjusted her blanket, and started towards the house. She walked slowly towards the man's body lying in the yard and stopped, looking down at it. In a flash, she was screaming and kicking the body. I started to go to her, but Jamie stopped me, saying, "Let her. She deserves to."

"I guess she does."

We loaded the body while Tammy was inside. Thad, Ian, and I hefted the body into the back. It would be a little cramped in the truck, but we were only going to the house.

"This is one hell of a mess," Thad said as he closed the truck.

"To say the least," I replied.

"Maybe killin' someone will cheer Jamie up a little," Thad said with half a smile.

Rolling my eyes to the side towards him, I replied, "Too soon."

He simply nodded. "What are you going to do with her?"

"Only thing I know to do is to take her home. We'll figure out what to do with her."

He stared at the house. "Might be good for her to be around your girls for a while, ya know?"

"We don't know how damaged this kid is and that worries me."

"Well, she'll be better off with us than what's she's been living with."

Tammy came out carrying a backpack over one shoulder. She'd dressed in clothes far too large for her and wore a pair of flip flops. She walked straight to the truck and climbed in without saying a word.

Looking at Jamie, I said, "You drive. I'll sit in back with the body."

It was a pretty short ride back to the house. Jamie parked in front of Danny's, and we all got as Miss Kay came out onto the porch. She smiled when she saw us, but a look of confusion spread over her face when she saw Tammy.

"Hey Miss Kay, this is Tammy," I said as a quick introduction.

Still unsure what was going on, Kay smiled and held out a hand. "Very nice to meet you, Tammy. Come on up here, let's get you something to eat, honey. You like hungry."

Tammy looked back at Jamie, "Go on, I'll be right there," Jamie told her.

Without any sign of care in the world, the girl walked up onto the porch, where Kay quickly wrapped an arm around her and ushered her into the house.

"Jamie," I said, "can you Ian stay here with her? I know Kay will take care of her, but she might need some help."

Jamie looked at the house. "She'll be fine. But we'll stay here with her."

"We'll be back later."

Thad drove back to the ranch. I was staring at the passing country when he interrupted my trance. "How many people do you think she was talking about?"

"I was trying not to think about that."

"If it's happening to other kids, we need to do something about it."

"I know. That's why I don't want to think about it," I looked at him. "Like there isn't enough crazy shit going on right now? Isn't Life hard enough? People still have to do shit like this?"

"There may be fewer of them now, but there are still sick people in the world."

"True. And they'll have to be dealt with. But we've more important shit to do right now."

Jim was still at the gate when Thad pulled up. This time he dismounted and unlocked the gate. I climbed out as he was doing so.

"What the hell was that all about earlier," he asked.

"We had some trouble in town. It's been dealt with."

"Oh, ok then," he said as Thad pulled through.

He stopped, and I jumped in, and we were back on the range in a couple of minutes. The trainees were in the middle of an evolution of fire when we pulled up. Seeing us, Sarge quickly walked over.

"Well? What was it?" He asked. Thad and I took a minute to give him a rundown on what had happened.

"Sounds like it's taken care of then."

"Not really," Thad said.

"What do you mean?"

"The girl said he was basically pimping her out. So there's others," I said.

"We got more important shit to do right now."

Thad smiled, "That's what Morgan said."

"For once, Thad ole buddy, he's right."

"See Thad. That's what I'm talking about."

"What's that?" Sarge asked.

"That's what I like about you," I replied. "You always have something positive to say."

Turning around and giving me a wave, Sarge said, "Come on dip shit, we're about done for the day."

"How are these folks from town getting back?" I asked.

"We'll carry them up there in the Duce."

The group from town was gathered together, and I walked over to them. "Well, Bubba, Sky, what do you guys think?"

"This is a lot more complicated than I thought it would be," Sky replied.

"Yeah, I figured they'd just give us a rifle, and that'd be it," Bubba added.

"You guys haven't even gotten started yet. You're learning the weapons, but the SUT will be a lot more difficult."

"SUT?" Sky asked.

"Small unit tactics. Shooting and moving and working as a unit. Movement is life in a gunfight. A stationary target is just that, a target."

"We'll be back tomorrow for sure. The whole day was worth the lunch alone," Bubba said. "I ain't had nothing like that in a damn year."

"We'll try and get you guys some food to take home with you tomorrow. We should have planned on this from the start."

Mike was walking with Crystal, holding her hand. I was surprised to see such an open display from them. But then, what does it matter? No one today begrudges anyone who can find some happiness in this world. Earlier in the day, I'd seen Mike *instructing* Crystal. He was helping her with a proper cheek weld on her rifle, standing behind her with his arms around her. It made me laugh, like watching kids in junior high.

And Mike wasn't the only one. Ted was standing with Janet at the back of the MRAP, standing very close. He took a drink of water from the keg, and Janet took the cup from him and finished it. The girls were running around in an impromptu game of tag, and Little Bit was *it*, apparently. It felt good that even in a time of preparing for the horror that awaits us, we can all still have fun.

After putting her Minimi in the MRAP, Mel walked up and put her arm around me. Then, she asked, "What was that about earlier?"

"Yeah, we need to talk about that." She looked at me, concerned, I continued. "We have a young girl back at Danny's with Kay right now. The engineers were turning off main breakers to houses they were going to bring power back to when Eric, remember him, the young engineer? Anyway, he saw a man raping the girl."

"Are you serious?"

"I wish I wasn't."

"You brought her back to our place?" I nodded, and she asked, "What about the man?"

"He's not an issue."

"Morgan!" Sarge shouted. "What the fuck is this!"

"Oops, maybe he is an issue."

"What do you mean?"

"I forgot his body is in the back of the Hummer," I replied as Sarge continued to shout unpleasantness in my direction. Then, I walked over to the Hummer, where a crowd was gathering.

"Yeah, sorry, forgot about that," I said, pushing my way through the people.

"We should have done something with him," Thad added.

"You're damn right you should've!" Sarge hollered. "What a fucking mess. You're cleaning my truck out when we get back!"

"What are you going to do with him?" Danny asked.

"You better bury his ass!" Sarge barked.

I hadn't thought about what to do with the body until now. Burial would be the obvious choice, but I suddenly had another idea. "We'll get rid of it on the way home. Sarge, you drive the Suburban back. Thad, you and Danny come with me, and we'll get rid of it."

Sarge was still bitching when everyone loaded up. I was waiting for them to get moving before we headed out. As Janet and Crystal waved by the guys, I walked up to Janet. "Hey, you got any rope we could get?"

"Sure. How long a piece do you need?"

"Fifty feet or so should do it. You mind if I poke around in the barn for a minute?"

"Sure. If you go in there, you'll find a couple of bundles of rope hanging on the right wall."

I thanked her and got in the truck. "What's the plan?" Thad asked.

"We're going to hang him up at the Circle K in Umatilla with a sign. I want everyone to know what's going to happen to pedophile rapists when we catch them."

"I like it," Danny said. "It's a pretty clear statement."

We found a hank of rope in the barn that would work for us, and I looked around for material to make the sign out of. A half sheet of 3/8ths plywood and a can of spray paint took care of the sign. We took a couple of minutes to discuss how to word it, and Danny painted the words on the wood. Then, loading the rope and sign up, we headed to the store.

It was late in the day, and the plywood tables were empty. The traders were gone. They'd get a hell of a surprise in the morning. There weren't many options for where to hang him from. The store had no big sign out front, and we settled on the large concrete pole that held the traffic lights up. Two jibs were sticking off the pole holding street signs. I backed the Hummer up to the pole, and Thad tossed the rope up.

It took him three tries to get the rope over the jib. It was a high toss for a half-inch rope. I wrapped the rope around the ankles and secured it. Then all three of us heaved to get the body up. I wanted it as high as we could get it, and we pulled until the feet were touching the jib. It took Thad and me holding the rope while Danny tied it off to the bottom of the pole. We had to have a little slack in it for Danny to get the knot done, and when we let off, the body dropped about two feet. But it was still plenty high enough. We leaned the sign against the pole.

Leaning on the hood of the truck, Danny said, "That should send a pretty damn clear message."

The sign read:

Rapists and pedophiles will be executed.

CHAPTER 8

Dalton, Sarge, and I discussed our upcoming recon mission over dinner. We decided we would take the Suburban to keep a lower profile. In addition, we would wear civilian clothes. We planned to head up towards Clearmont, going through Howie in the Hills.

"We should stop by the Sheriff's office on our way," I said.

"I don't know," Sarge replied, studying the map.

"Why not?" Dalton asked.

"We don't know their situation right now. But, they could very easily want to confiscate our truck, weapons, whatever," Sarge replied.

"I didn't think of that. I guess we haven't talked to any of them in a long time," I replied.

"Let's see what it looks like as we go. I don't want to waste time checking on them."

"We could leave the truck and move in on foot at night. Use the NVGs to poke around," Dalton offered.

Sarge nodded, "I like that idea. As a matter of fact, let's do all our movement at night. Load a camo net into the truck. We'll cover it up during the day and drive at night."

"We need an equipment list," I said. "We need some Jerry cans of fuel, water, food, weapons, and ammo," I said.

"I'll get Doc to put together an aid bag for us as well. A couple of cases of MREs should cover food. So pack your personal kit, and let's get the rest of the gear together. Let's plan on leaving tomorrow evening, at sunset."

Dalton got up from the table and carried his plate into the kitchen. "Miss Kay, do you have any yeast?"

"We sure do!" She replied cheerily and opened a cabinet. It was stacked nearly full of packs of yeast.

"Damn, where'd all that come from?"

"It came in some of that stuff from the Army. How much do you need?"

"Just one pack should be enough."

She plucked one from the shelf and handed it to him. "What do you need it for?"

"Oh, little chemistry experiment."

From where I sat on the porch, I could hear the conversation. I looked over at Dalton and caught his eye, and winked at him. He smiled in return, tossed the yeast brick in the air, and caught it.

"Thank you, Miss Kay. I really appreciate it," he replied before disappearing into the night once again.

"I got some shit to do," Sarge said as he got up.

I also got up from my table and went to sit by Mel. The girls were seated at a table with Tammy and the kids. They were laughing and talking, like typical teenage girls. Tammy looked as though nothing was wrong.

"Did you talk to the girls?" I asked as I sat down.

"I did. I talked with Tammy a little bit as well."

"How is she?"

Mel studied the girl for a moment before replying. "She seems normal. I didn't ask about specifics, but she's obviously been through some shit. But she's so young, I guess to her, it's her reality."

"I'm kind of worried about her, ya know. Like she's damaged or broken."

"I'll keep an eye on her. I think being with the girls will help her. Being here, eating regularly, being somewhere safe, I think it will all help her."

Just then, Little Bit ran over. "Can Tammy stay the night with us? Please?" She bounced as she asked, her excitement just too much to contain.

I looked over at the table with the girls. Ruckus, the limb rat, was scampering around the table, picking from the kid's plates, and they all laughed and giggled at the antics of the rodent. Tammy put out her hand, and Ruckus climbed onto it. She brought her hand close to her face, and the little squirrel stood up in her palm, putting a paw on her nose. All the kids laughed, and Tammy was beaming.

"Of course, she can," Mel replied. "We'll just fix her a place on the couch."

"No, she can sleep with me!"

"We'll figure it out," I said, and that satisfied her, and she ran back to the table.

I looked over at Mel, "Did she get a bath?"

"She took a really long shower. We found some new clothes for her too."

"Good. Look, tomorrow night, me, Dalton, and the old man are going to go and see if we can find these assholes. First, we need an idea of where they are and when they might be here."

"Is everyone else going to continue training?"

I nodded and looked over at a table where Karl, Chad, and Imri sat. "Be right back."

As I got up, I heard Mel ask Erin if she would take a look at Fred. "Sure. You know, we eat pretty well over at Dave's. But this is way better. You think we could move over here if there's an empty house?"

"I'm sure we can work something out," I heard Mel reply as she and Erin made their way towards Fred and Aric.

Walking over, I sat down on the end of the bench. "Did you find a place for you guys to crash?"

"Hey, Morgan!" Karl replied. "We're good. We have our own camp. We set it up over in front of that house that burned."

"You sure you don't want to use one of the houses?"

"No, we like our camp," Chad replied, "it's comfortable."

"Whatever you guys want. You guys can get a shower if you want."

"We do, and we will," Imri replied. "At least, I will," he added with a smile.

"I appreciate your help. Tomorrow we're headed out on a recon to find out how long we have before trouble shows up."

"We'll keep training. But ya know, with all the hardware you guys have, a hundred men with rifles isn't really a problem for you," Karl said.

"You guys have a fucking Bradley!" Chad shouted.

Imri leaned over the table, "How did you guys come up with all this? We haven't seen anyone that has nearly what you guys do." He picked up his plate; he hadn't finished it yet. "Look at the food you have! Weapons, armor, you're harvesting corn, for fuck sake!" He looked around the table before continuing. "How? How in the hell did you manage this?"

"It's complicated," I replied.

Imri looked around and said, "Doesn't look like there's much to do. We got the time."

"Where to start?" I asked myself. I spent several minutes giving them the high points of how we all came together. The three men sat and listened without interrupting. When I was done, the three men sat looking at one another for a moment.

"That's a hell of a story," Karl said.

"Let me get this straight," Chad said. "The military and the DHS are fighting one another?"

I nodded. "I guess someone in DOD had a conscience and decided the shit they were doing wasn't right. We ended up getting connected with the Army through the old man. He was retired, and they essentially reactivated him and made him a Colonel. We have radios, and he can contact them. They see what we're trying to do here and are aiding us our efforts."

"Have you been anywhere? Outside of this community?" Imri asked.

"Not really."

"Then you don't know what it's like out there. How bad it's been for people," Chad added.

"We've seen it," Imri added.

Karl leaned forward on the table, "It's worse than the movies Hollywood dreamed up about it. People were not prepared for this. They simply didn't know how to live without all the trappings of society. They didn't possess even the simplest of skills. We've seen cities--," Imri cut him off.

"We smelled them long before we saw them."

"Right," Karl continued, pointing at Imri. "They're disease-infested wastelands. We've seen slavers. Bands that travel around looking for women. Humans are once again a commodity. Then there's the warlords."

"We haven't seen anything like that here."

"You guys have everything you need to become *the* warlord," Imri said.

"Because word about this place is getting out, and the evil bastards of the world don't want to be anywhere near you guys," Karl added.

"Wait, people are talking about us here?"

Karl nodded. "Oh yeah. Don't worry, and the talk isn't that this is a place to run to for safety and food. What's more, the bad guys don't want anything to do with you guys. So, they stay away. So, you've executed people?"

"Those that deserved it."

"What'd they do?" Chad asked.

"Rape, murder, that kind of thing. For theft, we use public humiliation, hard labor, that kind of thing."

Karl pointed at me. "And that's why you're not a warlord. I can tell you guys aren't. With everything you have and have access to, you could take over this state probably."

"We just want to try and get a semblance of normal life. Not really what we used to have, more of a liberty-based ideal. Where you're free to live your life as you see fit so long as it doesn't interfere with the liberty of others. Well, that's my idea. It's not like we have a plan or anything."

As we talked, I was watching the girls and Tammy. She and Taylor were whispering and looking at me. Taylor was on her feet and making her way to me in a moment. "Dad, can we go home and watch a movie on the iPad?"

"Of course, you can."

"Can the kids come with us?" Tammy asked.

"Sure. You just have to bring them back when you're done."

"We will!" She responded as she spun on her heels and all the kids crashed through the screen door, and the rowdy rabble disappeared around the side of the house.

"You're girls?" Chad asked.

"They are, except the one with long blonde hair. I'm not sure where she's going to end up."

"She the one you rescued today?" Imri asked.

"I don't know if rescue is the right word or not."

"What do you mean?" Karl asked.

"What do you think the age of consent should be?" I asked.

Karl shrugged, "Eighteen, I suppose."

"Why?"

"Because you're an adult at that age?" Karl questioned.

"Says who?" I asked.

He thought about it for a minute before replying. "I guess because it's the way it's always been. I see where you're going, though. Was she with him voluntarily?"

"No. He needed to be killed, and he was. But it does create some difficult questions, doesn't it?"

"I guess it all comes down to, as it always has, consent. If two people are willingly together, then that is their choice to make."

"Exactly. However, at what age should someone be able to make that decision?"

"In many parts of the world, it's puberty," Imri said.

"That's what we need to sort out, I guess."

"It's a hard topic to figure out," I replied. "I'm going to call it a night. We're going to have a long day tomorrow."

"You guys want any help?" Chad asked.

"We need you guys to train these people, if you will. We just don't have the time right now."

"We'll do whatever we can to help," Karl replied with a smile.

"I have a question," Imri said as he sat back in his chair. "Do you guys eat like this every night?"

"Depends, really. You know, we're dependent on what we can grow and when we can grow it. That and what we get from the DOD. They do provide some food and other stuff when they can. We distribute a lot of it to people in town."

"Well, this is the best we've eaten in," Imri looked at Chad, who shrugged and continued. "I don't know when."

"Hey, we eat pretty well," Karl said.

Chad rolled his eyes. "We *eat*. We do not eat well."

"It's called survival for a reason, Chadster."

"Yeah, well, I prefer this kind of survival," Chad replied, pointing at his empty, nearly clean plate.

"It was excellent," Imri added.

Standing up, I said, "See you guys later."

Mel was sitting with Mom and Dad, and I sat down with them. "What'd you think of the training today?" I asked Dad.

Dad had changed his clothes before supper. He leaned back on the bench, "It was an interesting day. I didn't realize how much I'd forgotten. It's kind of funny how you don't remember something until you start doing it, and it comes back to you like you never forgot."

"It's like that old riding a bike thing, ya know? It's still in there; your brain just stored it away," I replied.

Dad smiled, "It's fun, really."

I smiled, "Shooting is always fun."

"It's crazy we're shooting all this ammo just to train."

"We have a lot of ammo. I mean, an obscene amount. But, we can afford it."

"It's good you do. You guys have a pretty formidable force here. What with the weapons and people you have."

"We're just heavily armed hicks in the sticks. I just wish we could stop having to carry a gun every day."

Dad sipped his coffee. "You've always carried a gun. So what's different now?"

"Because before the Day, I carried one in case I needed it. Today, we carry them because we know there's a damn good chance you *will* need to use it. Plus, I didn't carry a rifle or have to wear plates."

Mel put her hand on my shoulder, "Hopefully, we won't have too much longer. After this is done, there's no one to worry about."

Her sentiment was nice, but the reality was different. "We'll always have to carry them, baby. For the rest of our lives, I would imagine."

"I don't mind carrying a gun. We did before, and we'll keep doing it," Mel replied.

"I'm headed to bed. Tomorrow is going to be a long day for me."

"You guys leaving out tomorrow?" Dad asked.

"Tomorrow night," I replied. "We're only going to move at night and use the day to lay up and observe."

"Good idea. Besides, you guys have night vision, don't you?" Dad asked.

"We do, and that's why we're going to move at night. No reason to run a risk we don't need to."

"I hope you guys are careful," Mom said.

"That's why we're doing it the way we are."

"Alright, babe, let's go," Mel said as she got to her feet."

"Goodnight," I said, standing up and taking her hand.

We walked back to the house holding hands. When we saw Aaron's tent glowing softly in the dark, she asked, "What's up with him?"

"I'm not totally sure. That's why I'm keeping him close."

"Are you worried about him?"

"Not at all, really. It just makes sense to keep an eye on the unknown. Does he bother you?"

She shook her head, "No. I haven't even talked to him. Just see him around."

"Well, if he does anything weird, let me know."

"If he does anything weird to the girls or me, I'll shoot him."

Putting an arm around her, I pulled her into me. "That's my girl."

"Oh, what did Erin say about Fred?" I asked.

"Definitely twins. She can hear the two heartbeats. Fred's blood pressure was good, and she seems to be doing really good overall."

"That's a relief. She and Travis staying at Danny's?"

"Yeah, they'll ride back to the ranch tomorrow."

The girls were all piled up in the living room on a mound of pillows and blankets. The iPad was propped up against the bottom of the couch. A cartoon of some sort or another was playing on the small screen. They were all snuggled up close together like girls will do, propped up on their elbows watching.

"Did you put Ruckus in her cage?" Mel asked.

"I did, Mom."

"Alright, you guys can hang out in here as long as you want. Tammy, do you need anything?"

"No, Taylor got me blankets and pillows."

"You're sleeping with me tonight!" Little Bit shouted.

"She can sleep wherever she wants to, Ashley," Taylor shot back.

"Alright, girls, enough. Work it out," Mel replied.

"Mel, the food was really good. Will we eat like that tomorrow night too?" Tammy asked.

The girls were looking at her, confused. Mel didn't miss a beat. "You'll get breakfast in the morning. We always eat over at Danny's, breakfast, lunch, and dinner."

"We don't always eat lunch, it just depends on what's going on that day," I added.

"Wow! Really? Every day?" Tammy asked.

"Every day, kiddo."

"You guys are so lucky," Tammy replied. Then she ran a hand down the t-shirt she was wearing, pinched it, and pulled it up to her nose, inhaling deeply. "I haven't had clean clothes in a long time. And I got a shower. A hot shower! Where do you get the soap?"

"We make it. We work hard around here to make all this as comfortable as possible. If you need anything, just ask. Okay?" I added.

I grabbed myself a glass of tea before heading to the bedroom. Mel was in the bathroom and asked, "So, what are you guys going to do?"

"We're going to find this group and see where they are and how long we have until they may arrive."

"You're not going to try and do anything to them, are you?"

"No, no. Just recon. I don't want them even to see us."

"Ok, good."

Pulling my shirt off, I said. "I'm gonna grab a shower."

"I'm going to change the sheets real quick."

Wadding up my shirt, I tossed it into the hamper. "Really? What's the special occasion?"

She had the flat sheet off and was rolling it up, "We have power and a washer. That's the special occasion."

"Figured it was something like that."

As was now becoming my habit, I took a long hot shower. In the Before, when people would talk about the end of the world, they would always ask what I would miss the most. My reply was always the same, hot showers and AC. While in the modern world, and I guess it still is for most of the planet, bathing daily was typical and expected. We were undoubtedly a cleaner society than in previous centuries. But that comes at a cost.

People and bacteria have a symbiotic relationship. They need us, and we need them. The race to always be as clean as possible led to us driving a wedge into that relationship. People got sick from bacteria that ordinarily wouldn't bother them in previous times. A little dirt never hurt anyone. With that said, I liked to stay clean, but I wasn't a Nazi about it or anything.

After my shower, I pulled on a pair of shorts and a t-shirt and helped Mel finish making up the bed. Clean sheets are always nice. When you first lay in them, the feel, the smell. It was something I hadn't even realized I missed. Just one of those unconscious things you take for granted. Not even noticing its absence until it returns.

"I'm tired," I moaned, falling onto the bed.

Mel laid down beside me, running her hand through my hair. "How long will you be gone?"

"I have no idea. But it shouldn't be very long."

"I hope so. Roll over."

I did, and she proceeded to give me a nice back rub. "That feels so good, babe," I nearly whispered.

"You can do it for me too."

"Tonight, we're going to call this a sixty-eight," I said.

"Sixty-eight?"

I turned my head to look at her, "Yeah, you do me, and I'll owe you one."

She laughed and pushed my face into the pillow. "You owe me alright," she added with a laugh.

I woke up to a quiet and dark house. Mel was sleeping softly beside and for a moment, I was disoriented. I had no idea what time it was and looked around. There was no light coming through the windows, so it must still be night. Getting up, I took a piss and went out into the living room. It's kind of crazy how dark nighttime is now. All the little LED lights and displays that used to provide a little light in the house were mostly gone now, and things were closer to how they should be.

The kids had decided to camp in the living room and made a pallet on the floor out of pillows and blankets. They'd pulled the dining room chairs over and positioned them around it, pulling a couple of sheets over them to make a fort. I clicked on my little flashlight, keeping it cupped in my hand to diffuse the light, and peaked in. Four girls were in there, all sleeping softly. I quietly lowered the sheet and went back to bed. Checking my watch, I saw it was just after two in the morning.

In the Before, I often stayed up until the wee hours. It was not uncommon for me to be up until two or three in the morning. That was another thing that stopped. Gone were all the distractions one could utilize to simply waste time—no videos, social media, TV, and movies. So now you went to bed relatively early. But, again, this is the more natural way of doing things, and it felt better.

Before, if I awoke at night, I would avoid looking at a clock. Doing so only to see my alarm going off in an hour or so always meant I wasn't going back to sleep. Now, it didn't matter, and I wouldn't hesitate to look at a clock. But, I also didn't live my life by one any longer, that or a calendar.

I went back to sleep for a few hours and wasn't in any hurry to get up. So instead of jumping up, I just rolled over and put my arm over Mel. She stirred but didn't wake, and I lay there feeling her warmth and smelling her hair. It was peaceful, quiet, and lying there; you would never guess what the world outside was like. But all good things must come to an end, and I finally got up.

The kids were still sleeping in their fort. I grabbed a glass of tea and headed to the porch. The dogs were lazing in their usual spot, and I had to step over them to get to a chair. The morning was crisp, giving me goosebumps as I stepped out.

"You lazy mutts," I whispered with a smile. "Maybe a dog's life ain't so bad?"

I sat and enjoyed my tea and the quiet as the dogs snored at my feet. But I had a lot to do, and I wanted to grab a nap later in the afternoon before we headed out. I was nervous about this little mission. We'd be away from home for an unknown length of time, hopefully not more than overnight. I needed to get my gear together and get with Dalton and Sarge to go over the concept; I wouldn't call it a plan of what we were going to do.

I'd sat quietly for a spell when I heard movement in the house and went inside. Not seeing anyone up, I shrugged, then the toilet flushed in the hall bathroom. Tammy came out, rubbing her eyes and yawning. I was headed to the kitchen and smiled at her. Seeing me, she followed me.

"It's so nice to use a flushing toilet again," she said.

"Yeah, a lot easier, huh?"

She nodded. "Toilet paper would be nice."

"I know, I miss it too," I laughed as I opened the fridge and poured myself another glass.

"Is that tea?" I nodded and held it up in a questioning manner. "Yes, please," she replied.

I took another glass from the cabinet and poured her some. She thanked me and took a drink. "Mmmm, that is so good. I love tea but haven't had it like, forever."

"I love the stuff. It's kind of a necessity. For me at least."

"It's delicious. Can I have some more?"

"Tammy, you're welcome here, and you can help yourself to anything like that you want."

I poured her glass full again, and she jumped up on the counter. Swinging her feet back and forth, she looked around the kitchen. "This feels so weird. Being in a house that has power, running water, and food. I mean, I just watched a movie! I didn't think I'd ever see another movie. It's really nice here, Sheriff."

"First," I filled my glass again, "don't call me Sheriff. I'm Morgan, and I'm glad you like it here. I'm sorry we didn't know what was going on sooner."

"It's alright. I'm used to it."

The statement bothered me. "You know it shouldn't be, right?"

She took a messy drink of tea and wiped her chin. "I know. But it's the way it is. I can either sit around feeling sorry for myself or find ways to deal with it."

"Was."

"Was what?" She asked.

"The way it *was.*"

She smiled. "That would be nice. But I know no one gets a free ride, ya know."

"The only thing you have to do here is be a kid."

She placed the glass on the counter, stretched her arms and legs, and yawned. "Morgan, you mind if I go back to bed? I haven't slept this good in a long time."

"Of course not. Go on. There's no reason to be up right now."

As she hopped off the counter, she asked, "Then why are you up."

I laughed. "There's nothing you have to do around here. There's plenty I have to."

"Can I help?"

"There will be ample opportunity for you to help around here. Just not with the stuff I do."

She looked at me. "You look different."

"How?" I asked, surprised.

"I've seen you in town. You're always in that bulletproof vest with guns all over you. You look intimidating."

I looked down at my shorts and worn t-shirt. "Not very intimidating now, am I?"

"No," she laughed, "you're not scary at all."

"Scary? Who says I'm scary!"

Her face changed, "People in town are scared of you, and those people you're always with, the soldiers. Some of them are really scared of you."

That struck me. I'd never considered myself anything but approachable. Maybe I needed to think about how I present myself. "The only people that need to be scared of me are people up to no good. I'm not going to bother anyone as long as they aren't bothering someone else."

"That's why they're scared," she said and yawned again on her way out of the kitchen.

As I watched her crawl back into the fort, I thought about what she said. If there were people around doing bad shit to others, we needed to figure out who and want was going on. The world may be different now, there may not be a government in the traditional sense, but actions still had consequences.

I went back into the bedroom and got dressed. I picked up my plate carrier and rifle on the way out the door. Mel never stirred, and I didn't wake her. I slipped through the living room and set the carrier and rifle outside before grabbing my boots. Some days I liked to try and sneak out of the house. Not because I didn't want to talk to them. I wanted them to sleep. It meant something to me to leave them sleeping, peaceful, and lovely.

I dropped my plate carrier over my head when I heard Dad's voice. "You're up early."

"Usually am," I responded as I slipped into the rifle sling.

He pointed at the plate carrier. "Is that standard every day?"

"Pretty much. You never know when some shit is going to kick off. Just easier to have it on." I winked at him, "If you stay ready, you ain't got to get ready."

"This is true," he replied and drained his cup. "I need some of Top's coffee."

A broad smile spread across my face, "That sounds like a fine idea. Let's go ruin his morning,"

Dad laughed and slapped me on the back as I came off the steps. I looked at Aaron's tent as we passed it. The outer surface was covered with tiny drops of water; he was still in there. Danny's house was warm and inviting when I opened the door. The warm air was rich with the mixed aroma of coffee, yeast, and cooking meat. The space was warmly lit, full of smiling faces and chatter, like an oasis of fellowship in an empty world. This is how I started my day every day. It did so much for me to step through that door every morning. I looked forward to it, and I needed it. I needed my tribe.

Sarge saluted us with his cup as we came in, "Mornin' Morgan, Butch,"

We both replied in kind and took a seat at the kitchen bar. Kay picked up the coffee pot and poured Dad's cup full, then set one out in front of me and filled it as well. I picked up my cup and tipped to her, "Thank you, Miss Kay."

"You're welcome. How is everyone this morning?"

We chatted the usual pleasant talk one usually does when sitting with friends. As we did, more people arrived. Jess was in the kitchen helping Kay with breakfast. There were never any assignments or anything in our little group. People just did what needed to be done when it needed doing. Seldom was there a shortage of help when there was work to be done.

Mel and the girls came through the door before I'd finished my coffee. Little Bit stormed through the house, running straight out the back door as Ruckus clung to her back. Jace and Edie were already sitting out there with Danny, and she joined them.

It immediately became a game of who was going to hold Ruckus. Or so they thought. It turned out to be a game of who did Ruckus want to try and hide on. This naturally led to howling laughter and squeals. Now the morning was complete.

I looked around but didn't see Mike or Ted and asked Sarge where they were. "They're with Karl and his crew going over the training for today."

"Ah," I nodded. "What time do you want to head out?"

"1700 hours."

"Just before dark, good idea."

"I figure we'll just move at night to reduce the chance of us seeing anyone." Sarge sipped his coffee. "You figure out the route?"

I pulled my notepad from my carrier and flipped through a couple of pages. "I did. I got it on here, and I have it highlighted on a map at the house. What about comms?"

"I've got that covered. One of Wallner's people will always be on the radio. I did a PACE plan, and they have a copy."

"Good, I've got the same for our route."

"Make a copy to leave here," Sarge replied, sipping his coffee.

"Already got one started."

Sarge looked around the house, "Anyone seen Gulliver this morning?"

"I's be here, boss," Dalton's voice boomed in a deep baritone from the porch as he walked around the corner into the light.

"You got your shit together?"

"Always boss."

Sarge spun on his stool and leaned back on the bar. He studied Dalton for a minute before getting to his feet. Then, he looked at me and jerked his head towards the porch. Dad looked at me and shrugged as I got up. Dad followed me out to the porch, and the four of us gathered in a dim corner of the porch.

Stuffing my hands into my pockets, I looked around, "This doesn't look suspicious."

The old man had a serious look on his face and got down to it, "Serious question, Gulliver."

"Shoot," Dalton prodded.

"You can say no, but I wanted to ask this. Would you feel comfortable trying to walk into their camp? Get in there and see what you can hear?"

"No problem," Dalton replied without a moment's hesitation.

Dalton's eager reply surprised me. Personally, I would have hesitated to answer that question. Not Dalton. It was as if the answer was preloaded and just waiting for the opportunity to lose it. I guess that's what makes Dalton, Dalton.

"It'd be the best chance for us to try and get some real intel. You need to really dress for this part. That wild ass hair and beard of yours will sure as hell help sell the idea that just a wanderer."

"Not a problem. Despite the fact that I'm taller than most people, I can blend in pretty much anywhere. I like that sort of thing, honestly."

"Good, good. I'm going to bring my M1A. We'll try and set up a hide somewhere so we can overwatch you if it's at all possible."

"Makes me nervous sending him in there alone," I said.

Dalton looked at me, his face devoid of emotion, "I'll be fine. Trust me."

If anyone could do it, he could. "If you say so, man."

"Concealed pistols, no plate carriers. We'll take them, just not wear them unless shit kicks off. Bring it all. Just be dressed for discretion. We want to blend in."

"Saying that reminds me," I interrupted. "Last night, Tammy said there were people in town that were scared of us because of shit they're doing. So we might need to start looking around."

"Scared how?" Sarge asked.

"She just there's people in town that see us as a threat because of something they're doing, and they try to avoid us."

Sarge smiled broadly, "Well if they're up to no good, that's your problem."

"We'll deal with it later. I just wanted to mention it. When we're done here, maybe I'll just go to town and hang out."

"You two can sort out your field trip later. We've far more important shit to do right now," Sarge huffed.

"Yeah, yeah, don't spill your Geritol," I fired back. "I'm going to go back to the house and finish getting my shit ready and loaded."

"Good idea. They're about to leave for the ranch here in a minute. Kay is gonna fix us some food to take with us, and we'll have some MREs."

Coming back into the house, Mike intercepted me. "Hey man, since you guys are leaving, I want to show you how to use that 320."

"Oh yeah, I want to take that with us for sure."

Jerking his head to the side, he said, "It's in the truck out front. I can show you how it works. It's easy."

We walked outside, and Mike took the little black weapon from the truck. Holding it, he went over its operation. How to flip open the sights and the range estimation marks and their use. He then covered loading and unloading it, a surprisingly simple weapon.

"Looks pretty easy to me," I said when he handed it over.

"It is," Mike replied as he took a belt of grenades out of the truck. "The ones with the black band are high explosive. Shoot anything with them. Good for cars, trucks, and especially people," he said with a sadistic grin. "The yellow are incendiary, self-explanatory?" He asked, and I gave him a *no-shit* look. "Alright, these green ones are HEDP, high explosive dual purpose. These will fragment and will also penetrate light armor. These are good on block structures as well. Questions?"

I dropped the belt over my shoulder, "Nope. Think I'm good. Thanks, man."

Mike headed back into the house and waved over his shoulder, "No prob, man!"

I went back into the house and found Mel. She was getting the girls ready to go. It was strange to see Taylor and Lee Ann with their weapons leaned close at hand. It was an odd juxtaposition to see teenage girls laughing together while at the same time armed to the teeth as though it was perfectly normal.

"You guys good?" I asked.

Mel turned, smiling, "We're good. You need anything?"

"No, I'm good, baby. You guys getting ready to leave?"

"Yep. I want to go shoot my machinegun!"

I chuckled, "You like that thing, huh?"

Her face beamed. "I love it! It's just so much fun. Not to mention the fact that it makes me feel like I can defend myself or make a difference. It's hard to explain."

I hugged her, "Oh, I know, baby."

"Will I be home before you leave?" She asked.

"I don't know, but don't plan on it."

She wrapped her arms around me and kissed me. "You guys, be careful. I'll see you tomorrow."

I smiled at her lie. We both knew there was no way to tell how long we'd be gone. "Tomorrow," I whispered and kissed her again.

Little Bit ran up and hugged my leg. "Bye, Daddy! See you tomorrow!"

Taylor and Lee Ann each hugged me on their way out the door as well. Tammy stopped on her way out and asked, "Where are you going?"

"Little sneaking and peaking is all," I smiled.

"Is it dangerous?"

"Hopefully not."

She considered the statement for a moment. "I hope not too, Sheriff," she replied as she walked out.

Mel looked at me with raised eyebrows. "That's interesting."

"Yeah. She was up last night when I woke up."

"You two talk?"

"A little. We had a cup of tea and chatted for a minute."

"And?"

"And nothing. She likes it here. She hasn't seen any of the comforts we have here in a long time. She seemed completely normal. She drank two and asked for more. I told her two that fast was plenty. She didn't argue or anything. She's done whatever I've asked to her without complaint as well."

"Maybe it'll rub off on our girls," Mel snorted.

We hugged again, and they went outside where the trucks sat idling. I watched from the porch as they loaded up. Little Bit waved from the door of the Hummer like kids will do as they went through the gate. I couldn't help but smile to myself. And like that, it was suddenly quiet.

I lingered on the porch for a few minutes. I could see the light blue smoke of diesel exhaust hanging in the cool morning air as the acrid odor assaulted my nose. I could still hear the truck engines rumbling down the road. The sound rose and fell in relationship to the shifting of gears. I considered how that sound was nearly completely invasive in the previous world for a minute—now reduced to an oddity.

With everyone gone, I decided to finish getting my gear sorted and returned to the house. The silence in the inside was deafening, and it felt strange. Going out the backdoor, I headed for the shop. Back in the Before, I had a mountain of rucksacks and other gear. But after abandoning the house and only taking what we could carry, I lost most of it. I really wanted a pack that didn't look military in any way.

The only thing I came up with was midsized ruck in Real Tree camo. However, that was common enough and not military in any way that it would work. So I swapped my gear from the tactical ruck I usually used to this one. I decided on Carhart dungarees for clothes, and I'd bring a denim jacket and a fleece.

With that sorted out, I went out to the Suburban. I hadn't driven the thing as far as we were sure to on this little trip in quite some time. I've always been one to go over any vehicle I was going to take a road trip in, and this was probably the one trip most fraught with danger for me. I needed to ensure we were as ready as we could possibly be.

There was already a Jerry can of water in the truck, so I added another. Next, I checked the jack and spare to ensure they were good, rolled another spare out from behind the shop, and loaded it. Then, tossing some cans into the back of the truck, I pulled over to the fuel tanker and filled them. Four full Jerry cans of fuel should be plenty.

Bringing the truck back to the house, I went over the engine, checked all the fluids, and gave the belts and hoses a look. Unfortunately, there were no spares for any of these, and it made me think about hitting an auto parts store and see if I could find any. But I had a feeling there wouldn't be time for such frivolities.

Audie and Cecil sat in the shade of the oak tree, having a drink of water. They looked out over a field of cornstalk stubble. The two tractors were cooling in the early morning air, and the wagon was nearly full to overflowing with bright yellow corn.

Cecil nodded at the field, "I'm thinking two more trips, and we'll have it, Audie."

"I think so too. Then I gotta get to work on that mill," Audie cocked his head to the side and looked at Cecil. "You familiar with that juice plant?"

"Oh yeah, I worked in there for years before I retired. There's plenty of machinery in there that we can scavenge to get something that will turn them stones."

One of Sarge's war wagons turned off nineteen and started in their direction as they talked. Wallner's people provided security for the field. While the corn grown in this field would be for everyone, we didn't want people coming out and stealing it before we could harvest it when we could impact the most people and prevent it from being wasted.

Red Atkins and Matt Walters climbed out of the buggy when it stopped. The men greeted one another and chatted as the other two Guardsmen collected their gear.

Red surveyed the field, "Looks like you about got it all."

"So, when's the whiskey gonna be ready?" Matt asked.

Audie squinted and looked at him, "I've heard rumors."

Surprised, Matt asked, "Really?"

"That's the rumor," Audie replied with a big smile.

The two being relieved, carried their rucks over and dropped them into the buggy. Barry Boulier dropped his ruck in, saying, "I don't know about you guys, but I'm ready for some whiskey!"

"I think we all are!" Matt shot back.

"I think you're right," Cecil replied, rubbing his chin. "I know I sure could stand a taste."

Audie clapped his hands, "I want more than a taste!"

The other Guardsmen being relieved, Heath, jumped in as well. "I'm not much of a moonshine drinker, but even I want some good ole corn whiskey."

Red leaned back on the buggy, "Hey, when you guys get back, Wallner wants to see you before you get some sleep."

Heath plucked the radio from his armor and waggled it, "I talked to him earlier."

"What's up?" Barry asked.

Red just shrugged, "Hell if I know. Just said to get with him."

Matt interjected, "Probably about the upcoming mission."

Heath hung the radio back on his armor and added, "That's all it is."

"That can't come soon enough," Barry quipped. Then, looking around, he added, "I'm getting bored. Coming out here is the most action we've seen in a long time."

"I know you young men are all full of piss and vinegar," Cecil admonished them, "just be careful what you ask for. From what I've heard from Linus, this ain't going to be no cakewalk."

"Oh, I know. But, believe me, I'm not wanting to run out and get shot at. I just want to see something. Do something. Anything!" Barry lamented.

Audie pushed his cap back on his head. "I know how you feel, buddy. I've been stuck on that ranch over there since I got there. Don't get me wrong; I'm happy as a dog with two peckers to be there. But it's way better than being out there on your own, scratching and clawing for every bite to eat. Not sleeping well because you're so worried someone is going to sneak up on you in the middle of the night and cut your throat." Pulling a worn handkerchief from his hip pocket, he mopped his brow. "With that said," he looked at those around him with a crafty grin and added, "But it does get kind of boring, and a little trouble can be a lot of fun."

Cecil snorted. "Seems all we have these days is trouble."

"Well, I'm not afraid to say it," Red cut in, "I'm ready to kill some motherfuckers. Things are getting quiet, and life is starting to improve, here at least, and these assholes want to come in here and start screwing with us? Fuck 'em. Kill 'em all."

Matt pointed at him, "Amen, brother."

Dalton watched as water poured from the hose he held. Then, shaking his head, he said, "It ain't mountain water. Let's see what this does."

He'd filled a large kettle sitting on a grate over an open fire. He had a candy thermometer clipped to the inside of the kettle. He stood back and rocked on his heels as he watched the mercury slowly rise. It's said a watched pot never boils, but Dalton has the patience of a Greek statue. When the temp reached 165 degrees, he pulled on a pair of welding gloves and pulled it off the flame.

He had a bathroom scale sitting on the concrete slab at his feet with a bucket resting on it. He poured corn into it until it read twenty-five pounds and repeated the step. Once the corn was in the water, he poured the two twenty-five pound bags of sugar in and stirred it a little before adding the yeast.

Stepping back, he admired his handy work. "Here goes nothing," he said as he placed the lid on the huge pot.

Imri laid on the ground beside Mel. She was lying behind the Minimi, stock to her shoulder. Under the weapon was a pile of spent brass and links. Imri reached over and pushed the pile off to the side. As he did, he said, "A good way to control your fire is to say, *die motherfucker die, die motherfucker die.* That will give you the burst you want. So give it a shot."

Mel cracked her neck and settled back behind the weapon. Then, she squeezed the trigger and mouthed the words. Using this method, she ran through several evolutions. Finally, when she stopped and looked at Imri, he said, "You don't have to actually say it out loud. You can say it to yourself."

"Was I really saying it?" Imri nodded. She laughed and added, "I had no idea."

The class was put through up drills consisting of holding their weapons at low ready and on the command, *up,* bring the weapon to their shoulder, and fire the instructed number of rounds. In addition, there were turning drills where muzzle awareness was the primary concern—learning to manipulate the weapon close to others without muzzle sweeping anyone. They practiced turning left, right and a complete 180 degree turn to engage targets.

Engagements were varied. Accuracy was drilled into the students, constantly focusing on the high A zone, the head where the focus was from the nose to the orbital sockets. There was a box drill where students engaged two targets, putting one round into the chest of the first target, one round into the chest of the second target plus one to the head of the second, and a final round to the head of the first. Failure to stop drills were also run, two to the chest and one to the same zone of the head.

"Alright, folks. Let's take a break and grab some water," Karl called out. "Remember, we're running a hot range. Only clear a weapon on the line. If your weapon is hot, treat it as such."

Mike walked off the line holding Crystal's hand. They kept some distance between themselves and the others. "Have you thought about it?" Mike asked.

Crystal looked at him, "I've been thinking about it. Why don't you just come here?"

"I need to stay over there with the guys. I know you want to stay around your family; I get it."

"That's not really it. Dave asked me to convince you to come here. He said we need to keep family close right now."

Mike pondered her words for a minute, then smiled at her. "I can see why he wants that. We'll just keep doing what we've been doing."

Crystal stepped in front of him, and Mike stopped. Wrapping her arms around his neck, she said, "I want to go with you. I want to be with you. Not just see each other occasionally." Then, with a demure look, she added, "I'd like to spend the night with you."

"I really want to spend more time with you, Crystal. I want to get to know you," he smiled devilishly at her, "and I want to spend the night with you as well."

"Don't you live with the guys? In the same house?"

"I do. But there are a bunch of empty houses in the neighborhood. We could just pick one and live in it."

"I've never even been over there."

Mike straightened up, exaggeratedly pointed at the ground, and said, "We'll fix that today! Why don't you come back with us? Spend the night," he looked through his eyebrows at her, "and stay with Miss Kay so that we can hang out some. You can see the neighborhood and all."

Crystal swiveled her shoulders back and forth, "I would love that."

While Mike and Crystal worked on their future, Mel and Erin sat under a large oak tree with the girls. The kids sat together as Ruckus scampered back and forth between them. Little Bit held onto the paracord leash I'd made for her, though it didn't appear the rodent had any intention of running off.

Erin held a small stick, poking it in the dirt, "This is really intense."

"It is a lot to take in," Mel replied.

Erin shoved the stick into the ground, pushing it until it snapped. "Mel, I've spent my life learning to save lives. To keep people alive," she looked at the AK lying on the ground beside her. "The idea of taking lives, I don't honestly know if I can." She looked down, covering her eyes.

Mel put a hand on hers. "Erin, I know. I don't know that I can either. I'm terrified of this. Scared shitless, to be honest. But I will tell you this much if someone is trying to kill me," Mel nodded at the girls sitting a few feet away, "or them. I'll kill anyone. I'll use anything at my disposal to make sure they don't hurt my family. Before, we didn't have much opportunity to impact what happened in our lives. Yeah, you could call the cops if there was trouble. But like Morgan always said, when seconds count, help is only minutes away. I am my own first responder. And so are you."

Erin looked at the machinegun lying on the ground beside Mel. "Is that why you got such a big gun?"

Mel looked down at the weapon, running a hand over it, careful to avoid the still very hot barrel. "It's genetics. Some are just bigger than others," Mel laughed and continued. "I love guns. Always have. We went to events in the past where I got to shoot guns like this. I loved it. Just feeling the power of the thing in your hands. I can't really describe it. It makes me feel formidable."

Erin started to rock her head back and forth. Then, in a sing-song voice, she began, "I like big guns, and I cannot lie!"

"Fuck yes!" Mel shouted and laughed.

"I'm just thrilled they said I'm going to be doing what I know how to do, what I can do and, not bragging, but what I'm really fucking good at."

"Bitch, please. Not bragging?"

Erin's eyes went wide. "Bitch? Really?"

"Look, I cuss. I don't care what anyone thinks of how I talk. I say what I want; call it how I see it. And for too long, I've been suppressing that about myself. I don't know why. I just did. Maybe it was the change. I think it kind of shocked me. You've heard of the fight or flight thing, haven't you?"

"Yeah, when something happens, you fight or run," Erin replied.

"Well, there's another part to it. Freeze. Most people will freeze. They'll just stand there and watch as whatever is coming at them just rolls over them. I think I froze for a while."

"You a frigid bitch," Erin's head rocked back, and she laughed.

"This frigid bitch is thawing!"

"The people here are kind of stuffy. They don't cuss much, and Dave is sort of the boss, and no one argues with him. They treat women like they did in the fucking fifties. Not bad, just like we're not as capable. They want to keep us in our place."

"Less bitchin', more kitchen kind of thing?"

Erin laughed, "Yeah, like that."

"Fuck that! There is no *boss,*" Mel practically spat the word, "with us. Morgan handles some things, Sarge other stuff. People look to them for advice and guidance. But they are not bosses, and I will, and have, told them both to screw off."

"It's not that way here. Don't get me wrong; it's not bad. We're safe, and it's pretty comfortable. It's just, I don't feel like an equal if that makes sense."

"I think this was such a profound thing that happened that it shocked people. We were set back in a way, and I think it was a natural response for men, some men, to see it as their responsibility to protect the weak women. But we're not weak. We're just as capable as the men. Moreso at times." Mel pointed at Jami, who sat on the hood of the Hummer smoking a cigarette. "Look at her. Does she look weak to you? Like she needs protecting?"

"No, that's a bad bitch right there."

"You have no idea. She shot a man in the fucking head yesterday. Morgan said he was talking to the guy, and suddenly his head exploded. She doesn't fuck around. She stabbed a DHS bitch to death once too." Mel looked Erin in the eyes, "We are not weak, Erin. We are a force to reckoned with, and we're going to show everyone that."

Erin was looking at Jamie with a look of shock, "That's a crazy bitch right there." She glanced over her shoulder in Tammy's direction. She kind of nodded her head at the young girl, "the thing with her?"

"Yeah," Mel replied, looking at Tammy. "Jamie just did what was going to happen anyway. He would have been executed one way or another."

"I've talked with Travis. He's open to us moving over there. Here, we're sharing a house. There, we could have our own. I just want to make sure we won't burden you guys. You know, more mouths to feed and all."

"You saw what dinner was like last night. That's pretty much how it is every day. We do breakfast and dinner every day, and we all eat together. It's nice, like a big family gathering. I would love it if you moved over there. Having you there would be a big relief for Fred as well."

As the two talked, Doc walked up. "Hey Erin, Mel." The ladies smiled and greeted him. "Erin, we're going to have to give an aid class to these people. Can you help me with that?"

"Of course. What do you want to do?"

"It'll be basic. Plugging holes, applying tourniquets, managing airways, that kind of thing. We'll have to make some tourniquets and prepare some bandages and all. We have some other medics that are going to help as well."

"What are we going to do with severe wounds? Do you have surgical capabilities?" Erin asked.

"That's where you come in," Doc replied. He pointed at Karl, "He's a Green Beret medic, as close to a surgeon as we'll get. Between the two of you, you're the surgical unit."

"Do we have instruments? We don't have alcohol or anything. So how are we going to sterilize things?"

"Karl will show you all that. But, right now, I just need your help to get ready for the aid class."

"What do you need me to do?"

CHAPTER 9

With the truck as ready as I could make it, I was sitting at the table looking through an atlas of Lake County. Highlighter in hand, I marked the route I intended to take towards Clearmont. I didn't start the highlighted route from our place but from town. If we lost the map, I didn't want anyone to be able to drive up to the door. The route covered several pages of the book, and I was getting annoyed with flipping the pages. Taking my knife from my pocket, I cut out the appropriate pages. After a bit of searching, I found a roll of clear packing tape and started attaching the pages together.

I had a rather large map that showed our place, the route, and the areas surrounding it when I finished. It was big and covered much of the table. I knew there was a particular way to fold a map, but I couldn't remember it. I was scratching my head, thinking about it, when there was a knock on the door. Looking over, I saw Dalton, "Come in!"

He came into the house and immediately saw the map. "This our route?" I nodded, and he stepped over and inspected it. "Bit of a ride."

"It will be. I mean, it's only about an hour drive in normal times."

"It'll take us a lot longer than that," he replied. Then, picking up the map, he started to fold it.

"I was trying to remember how to do that."

"I wish we had some acetate or something to protect it with."

I held up the packing tape, "We could cover it with this."

"We could, but it would make it stiff and kind of hard to deal with. The weather looks pretty good, so it shouldn't get wet or anything. I think we'll be alright."

Just then, the radio crackled. It was Wallner calling Sarge.

What's up? The old man asked.

We've got company out on the county road. They're asking to talk to whoever is in charge.

Morgan, you hearing this?

"Yeah, Dalton is here. We're on our way."

"Were we expecting company?" Dalton asked as I pulled the plate carrier over my head.

"No. Let's go see who it is," I replied as I picked up my rifle and headed for the door. "Let's take the truck."

When I pulled through the gate, Sarge was coming up the road in one of his buggies. Pulling out, I stopped and waited for him. "Any idea what this is?" I asked.

He looked towards the county road. "No idea. Let's go find out."

Four men were standing in the road in front of two motorcycles. The bikes were enduro-style, made for the street or the trail. Two of our Guardsmen stood ten feet away, casually gripping their weapons, muzzles pointed at the ground but ready to engage if needed.

I saw the men nod in our direction as we got out of the vehicles. Dalton moved off to the side of the road, taking a position that kept our people out of the line of fire if things got western. The vibe was casual as we approached the group. I nodded and said hello as we approached.

One of the men stepped forward. He was of average height with tattoos on his arms. Looking at the two of us, then at Sarge and asked, "You in charge around here?"

"We are," Sarge replied.

"And you are?" I asked.

"I'm Vincent. You met some of our people a while back."

"Nice way to put it," another of the group interjected.

"Destroyed my fucking bike," yet another added.

"Well, following us around is not the best idea," Sarge replied.

"I think we got off on the wrong foot," Vincent cut in. "We weren't trying to do anything to you guys, nothing nefarious."

"How about the night you guys snuck in here and poked around our fuel tanker?" I asked. The group of men shared nervous looks among themselves. "Yeah, we know you were here." I turned and pointed to Dalton, who stood with his weapon in low ready, his face impassive. "You're lucky he didn't kill your people."

"You didn't even see us," one of the group replied.

Sarge laughed. "We didn't, but he did, and he followed your people as you took your route out the back to the east before turning to the north."

I shifted my rifle and said, "We know you guys are staying up at

Juniper. We know you have that duce and were probably looking to get some fuel for it."

"We weren't looking to steal it. Just see what you guys had. You're pretty squared away here, and when we realized just who you guys were, we left and didn't fuck around," Vincent replied.

"Who do you think we are?" I asked.

Vincent pointed at me, "Well, you're obviously the Sheriff." Then he looked at Sarge, "We're not sure who you are." He then looked at Wallner's people and added, "they look like military to us. So if you guys are connected to the Army or something, then what are you doing? Why is the Army out here, and why aren't they doing more?"

"Well, here are," Sarge said. "What can we do for you?"

"You're not going to answer any of that?" One of Vincent's guys asked.

"No," Sarge replied flatly.

"Look," Vincent started, "you guys have a lot of stuff. Trucks, tanks, fuel, food, you have more than anyone around here. We hear you're getting the power back on. How?" He paused as though waiting for a response. When neither of us did, he stammered, "we want to know if we can get some help from you guys."

"We have a lot of people back at the spring," one of the others added. "Women and children."

"What are you looking for?" Sarge asked.

"We're doing pretty good on food. The spring is providing us a lot. But, we could use some fuel, both diesel, and gas. We also have some medical issues we could use some help with," Vincent said.

"Clothes too," another added.

"And shoes. I've got youngin's with no shoes, and it's gonna start getting cold," a tall man with a deep voice added.

Sarge looked at me, jerked his head in Dalton's direction, and started to move away. "Give us a minute," I said and followed him.

Sarge stopped beside Dalton and looked back at the group. "What they're asking for isn't unreasonable."

"Not at all. Remember when I talked about them knocking on the door before trying more desperate measures?" I asked.

"You were right about that," Sarge replied. "Honestly, I'm surprised. I thought they would take the hard way first."

That was as close to a compliment as I would probably get from the old man. "I don't want to have them come in here. It sounds like they have a lot of people out there, and it would probably be best for us to go out to them."

Sarge nodded, "That's what I was thinking. We could take Doc and that nurse from Dave's place with us."

"We have a lot of shit we could give them like I did the folks from town that are training."

"Alright. I don't know when we can do it, but let's get a list from them. We'll find what we can, and when we have time, we'll ride out there. Work for you?" Sarge asked.

I nodded. "Works for me."

We walked back over to the group. "We'll be happy to help you guys out. We can't do it today, though. We're kind of in the middle of something important at the moment. We need a list from you guys, shoe sizes, and the like." Sarge paused and looked at one of the soldiers with us. "Jump in the wagon and go get two cans of gas and bring them back." The man nodded and quickly departed. "We'll give you guys some gas today for your bikes. I'm sure you need it. We'll fill them up. Then, get your list together and bring it back, give it to the guard out here, and we'll get it together and come out to the spring. When we do, we'll have medics with us to take a look at your people."

"Make it a wish list," I added. "Doesn't mean you'll get it all, but we'll get you what we can. We don't have any kids' shoes. But there's a guy in town who makes shoes. I'll get with him and have him make what you need. So, get me measurements of their feet."

"How the hell is he making shoes?" Vincent asked.

"Carpet and tires," I replied.

"No shit? Huh, I never thought of that."

"Necessity is the mother of invention," Sarge offered.

The buggy pulled up, and the men filled the tanks on their bikes. When they finished, Vincent offered his hand, which Sarge and I both shook. "I really appreciate your offer to help. I'm sorry we got off on the wrong foot. But as you well know, it's hard to know who you can trust. People will steal anything you have."

"Most of the world's problems come down to either a lack of communication or poor communication," I replied. "Just talk. Be upfront, introduce yourself and talk."

Vincent smiled, "We know one another now; I hope we become friends."

"I do as well."

"You boys, get us a list together, and we'll do what we can," Sarge said, putting an end to the impromptu meeting.

We watched as the men mounted their bikes, wheeled around in the road, and headed back north on highway nineteen.

Dalton walked up beside us, watching as the motorcycles grew smaller and smaller. "That went better than I first thought it would. I was worried, but when I saw there were only four of them, I knew it wouldn't be a problem." He pulled the folded map out from under his armor and handed it to Sarge.

"You make this?" Sarge asked as he unfolded it.

"Naw, he did," Dalton replied, pointing at me.

"What'd you cut this out of?"

"An old atlas I had. Flipping through all the pages got on my nerves, so I cut them out and taped them up."

He studied the map for a minute. "This is good. I made one too. I'm going to take this and make some notes on it and the other one. I'll mark some phase lines and the like for radio checks, and we'll leave one here for the TOC. Let's talk about this route later."

"Well. I put some thought into this. I'm avoiding the bridge over Lake Harris. I remember Thad ran into some trouble there when he came this way. This is probably the safest route with the fewest chokepoints."

"I'll look it over; good work Morg."

"I went through the truck, checked all the fluids, hoses, belts and all. Added a couple of jerry cans of water and fuel. There's a case of MREs in there as well. Can you think of anything else we need?"

"I'll bring some stuff over later," Sarge replied. "Dalton, you got your shit together?"

"I'm the ready boss. If you stay ready, you ain't got to get ready."

"Yeah, yeah. You two should grab some sleep. Going to be a long night."

"That's my plan," I shot back.

"Let's meet at my place about 1500."

Giving him a wave as I headed for the truck, I replied, "See you then."

Dalton followed Sarge towards the buggy, "I'm going to go back with him."

I headed back to the house for a nap.

Audie and Cecil stood looking at the open field of stubble. Finally, Audie slapped Cecil on the back, saying, "We did it, Cecil."

"We sure did, ole buddy."

"You want to follow me down to the plant, and we'll look for something to turn those grist stones?"

"That's a good idea. We need to get to grinding soon. Let me get them boys over there. They can ride to the plant with us and radio their ride and let them know to pick them up there."

Looking back towards the tree the two men were resting under, he saw they were already walking in his direction. "Well, here they come."

"Looks like you boys got it all," Red said, surveying the field.

ENGINEERING HOME

"Went smooth too," Audie replied. "I was nervous that machine would go down before we finished." He patted the harvester connected to Cecil's tractor. "But she held together and actually got better as we went, in my opinion."

"All we need to do now is get ground up," Matt said.

"You two climb up there in that hopper. We're going to the plant to dump it and see what we can find to run those stones," Cecil told the two.

"Let us grab our rucks real quick," Red replied as he headed back to the oak tree.

Red and Matt climbed up into the hopper, hanging their legs over the side. Red ran his hand deep into the golden kernels. He lifted a handful as Cecil started the tractor and let them fall from his hand. Matt scooped up a small handful and dropped several kernels into his mouth, and started trying to crunch them up.

"Hmm," he grunted.

"How are they?"

"Be better with some salt and butter."

Red screwed his face up, "Good luck with that."

"Thankfully, we have salt."

"No butter, though," Red replied.

It didn't take long to get to the plant. Matt and Red jumped off the hopper as Audie operated the chain to open the big door. Then, ducking under the slowly rising door, they stepped into the cavernous building. Alex had been lying on a stack of pallets waiting for the next load and got up to meet the guys as they came it.

"Damn!" Matt exclaimed, "That's a hell of a pile of corn!"

Alex looked back at the pile was taller than he was. "There's a kernel or two over there for sure."

Red looked at the big scoop shovel Alex held. "You pule all of this by yourself?"

"Yep. Not as hard as you think, really. I just took my time."

Matt surveyed the pile, "Looks like a hell of a lot of work to me."

Cecil backed the hopper through the opening. The pile was extensive and covered so much of the floor that there was no longer room to drive in and turn around. Audie walked over and opened the belly gates, and the corn began to spill out.

"Damn!" Matt exclaimed. "Look at it all!"

Cecil watched the corn build up under the hopper and slowly pulled forward, creating a long golden mound. Alex shouldered his shovel and started towards it. "Looks like there's work to do."

"You have any more shovels?" Red asked. "We have time before we're picked up and can give you a hand."

"Yeah, we've got a couple more. I'll get 'em."

"Come on, Audie. Let's go look at this machinery and see what we can come up with," Cecil called out. The two left the other men to consolidate the corn and wandered off into the bowels of the plant. "What are you thinking of?"

"We need a motor and a gearbox or a reduction gear of some kind. Some linkage and other parts maybe," Audie replied.

The two men spent quite a bit of time going through the plant. Audie inspected each motor and gearbox they found. He identified three options for both of the major parts they needed. Audie looked over all the equipment they came to. The motors and gears and the conveyors, rollers, screw augers, and other machinery. His mind began to turn.

"You know Cecil," he said as he inspected the nameplate on a motor, "there's a lot of equipment here. We could do a lot with this."

"Whatcha mean?"

"Well, we were thinking rather primitive, just a motor to turn the runner. But we could make a pretty automated mill with elevators and screws to move the grain to the mill and to take the grist away."

"Runner?" Cecil asked.

"There's two stones. One moves, and one doesn't. The one that moves is the runner. There's a hole in the center where the drive shaft connects, and the grain also falls in. The wheels turn and grind the grain. The grooves cut into the stones slowly push the grain out the sides. There needs to be a container around them to catch it. From there, a screw auger could move the grist. The corn looks dry, but it still has moisture in it. The movement from the screw finishes drying it. We could even put in some screens to sift out debris and sort the grist by size."

"Sounds like a big job."

Audie shrugged, "You got something else to do?"

Cecil laughed. "Naw, guess not."

"We'll need some labor, but I think there's plenty of that around. I'm sure we could get some volunteers to come down here and work. Everything is here, and it wouldn't take too long to knock it out. I mean, it won't be easy. We have to try and repurpose everything that's here. There probably won't be any new material around."

"That's not true," Cecil interjected, "follow me."

Cecil led Audie through the plant. He was as familiar with the plant as he was with his own home. Coming to a door, Cecil pulled a ring of keys from his pocket, unlocked it, stepped inside, and flipped on a light switch. "This was the maintenance shop. As you can see, there's all manner of parts in here."

"Hot damn!" Audie exclaimed as he waded into the rows of shelves and racks. "This is perfect!"

The shop contained all manner of material from electrical components to spare bearings, gearboxes, conduit, pipe, hose. You name it there was at least some of it there. Audie's mind was racing with ideas. Solutions to problems he didn't even know about yet swirled in his mind.

"This is perfect," Audie said aloud.

"I thought you'd appreciate it."

Audie looked around, "I need a notepad."

Cecil stepped over to a desk and retrieved a yellow legal pad. "Here you go."

"Alright, I've got work to do. I'm going to start sketching this thing out."

Karl stood in front of the assembled students. "I know you guys have had a lot of crap thrown at you in the last couple of days, but you've done a great job. Everything we do will continue to build on what we've already done. You'll keep using those skills while adding to them. Tomorrow we're going to get into shooting and moving as fire teams. It'll be a little more stressful, but we'll only move as fast as you guys can get the skills down. Any questions?" No one asked anything, probably because they all just wanted to be done for the day. "Okay then, see you guys tomorrow."

The group broke up and started to drift off towards the vehicles. Mel walked with the girls as they all chatted about the day's events. Taylor looked at Mel, "Mom."

Mel looked at her and saw she looked stressed. "What, baby?"

Taylor looked at the ground. "I'm scared, Mom."

Mel stepped over and put her arm around her oldest daughter. "What are you scared of?"

She looked at the rifle slung over her shoulder with disdain. "This, I don't want to do this. I'm scared of what's going to happen. I hear people talking about it," she pointed at Mel's Minimi, "that thing is so loud. There's going to be explosions, and there's a tank! I'm really scared."

"Baby, look, you're not going to go into this fight. You're not here to learn this so you can go into this fight. You're just here to learn so that if you need to defend yourself, you can. That's all."

"You sure?"

Mel cocked her head to the side, "I'm your mother. You don't do anything unless I say so. And I'm not about to," she lifted Taylor's chin and smiled, "okay?"

"That makes me feel a lot better," she smiled back.

"Awe isn't this sweet," Erin said as she walked up.

Mel squeezed Taylor tighter. "Yes, it is."

"I know it's kind of a weird time, but I convinced Travis to come over tonight and look at your place. You think anyone will mind?" Erin asked.

"Of course not. It'll be fun."

Mel and the girls climbed up into the MRAP and found Mom and Dad sitting in there. Little Bit ran to them, attempting to wrap her arms around them both while she shouted, "Grandma! Poppie!" Ruckus jumped off her and onto Mom, who immediately freaked out.

"No, no, no, get this thing off me!" She shouted.

Mel started to laugh, and Dad reached over and scooped the little critter up. "Oh, calm down. She ain't gonna hurt you," Dad said with a smile as he lifted the rodent to his face, "are you, honey?"

"You don't like squirrels, Grandma?" Lee Ann asked.

"I don't like them on me," she replied and looked at Dad. "Rocky, the flying squirrel broke me of that. No way, nope."

"Who's Rocky?" Little Bit asked.

"What happened?" Taylor asked as Jamie started the huge truck.

"Rocky was a flying squirrel I had when your dad was little," Dad replied to her.

"Yeah," Mom interrupted, "he flew across the living room one night and landed on my head and bit me!"

"A flying squirrel?" Little Bit asked, "I want one!"

"He didn't bite you," Dad objected. "He might have scratched you."

"No, he bit me. I know he bit me."

"What happened to it?" Mel asked.

"I let it go. Didn't have him real long," Dad replied.

The chaotic conversation continued all the way back to the house. Mel sat in her seat, rocking with the motion of the truck. She smiled. Even though the inside of the truck was loud with everyone talking, they were all smiling. She looked at Tammy, and even she was smiling. The moment felt *normal*, and she liked the feeling. She missed her mom, but it was nice to have Karen and Butch with them.

Karen saw her looking and raised her eyebrows. Mel just smiled and gave a slight nod. Her mother-in-law smiled back and went back to an intimate conversation with Little Bit, Ruckus was entertaining Tammy, Grandma made it clear she and Ruckus were not going to be friends. Nevertheless, the ride was pleasant, and Mel looked forward to supper.

Sleep never really did come. I lay in the bed and dozed, but that isn't sleep. Getting up, I pulled on a pair of jeans and a t-shirt and went out to the kitchen. I'd found a one-gallon Igloo jug and filled it with tea, leaving the empty pitcher on the counter. Everything was already loaded, and I took a look around the house before grabbing my rifle and armor on my way out the door.

Dalton was already at the old man's place when I pulled up. I walked into the open garage door, pausing to remember Ivan the Asshole for just a moment before heading into the house. There was a pile of gear where the Russian used to sit. The guys were sitting at the kitchen table drinking coffee when I came in.

Sarge nodded at the coffee pot sitting on the counter, "Grab a cup, Morgan."

I did and sat down with them. It was strange seeing the old man in regular clothes again. Since arriving here, all he's worn was the military OCP camo BDUs. Seeing him in jeans and a gingham shirt instantly took me back to waking up in his house with him standing over me.

"Wow," I said. "Throwback Thursday."

"What?" Sarge asked.

I pointed at him with my cup, "Seeing you in normal clothes again. Haven't seen that since leaving your place on the river."

He looked down at himself. "I thought I'd never wear that uniform again. Now, like it was back then, it feels normal, and this feels weird."

Taking a sip, I asked, "You got the stuff to make coffee on the road?"

"Oh yeah. I'm not going out on something like this without coffee," he pointed to a thermos sitting beside the pot and added, "we'll have some for the road too."

Dalton held his cup up, "Gotta have fuel."

"Amen," Sarge replied.

"Well, we ready?" I asked.

Dalton rose to his feet, "I'm gonna go load our gear," and placed his cup in the sink.

"Let me top off the thermos, and we'll hit the road," Sarge said as he got up as well.

I followed Dalton out to the garage and grabbed a ruck from the floor, and carried it out to the truck. There was some radio equipment as well as rifles. Dalton dropped a ruck into the back of the truck, and I heard him say, "Oh my."

Dalton picked up the grenade launcher as I carried the gear over. In a perfect example of a thick Russian accent, he held the small weapon up and said, "This very nice weapon. In my village, such weapon is most prized and worth four goats and one woman."

I laughed as I dropped the ruck in the truck. "You are not right, my friend. Not at all."

Maintaining his accent, he asked, "You want for to trade? I make for you very nice price. I trade for you my gypsy. She almost virgin. Very nice, I try myself, yes?"

It made me burst out laughing, and he joined me. Sarge came out of the house carrying his thermos. "What the hell are you two schoolgirls giggling about?"

"Just this crazy-ass Cossack," I replied. Then looked at Dalton, "You know everyone thinks you're a Russian spy or some shit."

"It's good to keep them guessing," he replied absentmindedly as he looked at the launcher.

"Looks like we're ready to go," Sarge said.

"Why are you bringing that M1?" I asked as Dalton walked back into the garage.

"If we find them and Dalton wants to try and go into their camp, I want to try and establish an overwatch. This will give us some precision fire capability."

As we chatted about it, Dalton came walking out of the garage. He had a red towel draped over his head, obscuring his face. He walked with his hands together as though he was praying. Sarge noticed him and said, "What kind of fuckery is this?"

Dalton walked up, his head slightly bowed, and looked up. "I've come for to make blessing on American war party." He held out a balled-up fist, palm up, and continued. "I have here," he opened his hand to reveal a small pile of hair, "the pubage hair of virgin gypsy." Lifting his hand to his face, he blew the hair out of his hand. Then, still slightly bent at the waist, he raised his hand to his head, touched his fingers to his forehead, and snapped it out like some sort of a salute.

I immediately burst out into laughter, and to my surprise, Sarge was also doubled over laughing. Dalton couldn't hold it back, and he, too, began a deep belly laugh. Sarge was holding onto the side of the truck, laughing. He pointed at Dalton and said, "I've met some seriously fucked up people in my time. But you are by far the most disturbed son-of-a-bitch I've ever encountered, Gulliver."

Through his laugh, Dalton replied, "Thank you, it's nice to know one's work is appreciated."

"Alright, let's load up. I'll navigate," Sarge said as he opened the door, still shaking his head.

"Road trip! Road Trip!" Dalton chanted as he got in.

I started up the truck, and we headed out. I stopped by the bunker where Wallner was waiting. Sarge talked out the window to him.

"You got the map, callsigns, and radio schedule," he said to Wallner.

Nodding, Wallner replied, "We're good to go. I'm going over there now. I'll be on the radio to start with."

"Alright then. I'll talk to you in a couple of hours."

"You guys be safe."

The sun was getting low, casting long shadows as we pulled out onto the county road. I saw Mario and Shelly packing up their wares in Altoona and pulled in. The few people still there gawked at the old Chevy as I pulled up beside them.

"Hey Mario, Shelly."

"Hey, guys, what's up?" Mario asked, and Shelly gave us a head nod as she carried a box of jars of honey to the side by side they drove to the market.

"Just headed out on a little recon mission. I haven't seen you in a while. Have you heard what's going on, what's coming?"

"We've heard some rumors that some of the DHS people are coming back with a chip on their shoulder."

"That's about right," Sarge replied.

"We're headed out to look for them now; try to get an idea of how long before they get here. From what we hear, they have a lot of people and several trucks and some armor with them.

"What can we do to help?" Shelly asked.

"Nothing yet," Sarge replied. "After we get a look at them, that could change. We'll get with you when we get back."

"Whatever we can do to help, count us in," Mario said.

"We'll find you when we get back, buddy," I replied. Mario slapped the side of the truck and waved as I pulled off.

The market in Umatilla was empty as we approached. The body we'd hung from the pole was gone.

"Someone took down your handiwork," Sarge said, looking at the pole.

"Left the sign, took the body," I added.

"Probably didn't want it to start stinking," Dalton stated flatly.

"I guess it sent the message," Sarge noted.

"Probably," I replied, "but it wasn't done right. He should have been tried in public and executed in public if he was proven guilty."

"Result is the same," Dalton offered.

"The result is, but the process also matters. If we want to get some sort of normal life around here, the process is more important than the result. We can't appear to be doing things in the dark, out of sight."

"I agree with you," Sarge replied, "but it will take time to get things to the point you're talking about."

"We have to keep working towards it. No matter what."

As we passed the plant, some of the engineers stood in the parking lot talking with Cecil and Audie. I honked as we passed, and they all waved. When we got into downtown Eustis, I stopped on Bay Street at the intersection with McDonald Street. We got out and looked around. We were going to wait here for the sun to set and consider the options for the upcoming fight.

Sarge pointed to the east, "We'll need to block Grove to force them onto Bay here. We can use these buildings to limit their movement and provide us the advantage of elevated firing positions."

"Blocking that road so that it doesn't look like it's blocked will be a challenge," Dalton noted.

"Not really. Roadblocks aren't uncommon now," Sarge replied, "hell, I bet we come across some ourselves."

"They've got some big vehicles that could be used to pull anything we put in the road out of the way," I said.

"They probably won't get out to do it. They know they're coming for a fight and will be ready for it. Seeing a roadblock, they'll just try to detour around it," Sarge disagreed with me. "If they have their shit together, they'll send a scouting element out ahead of them. Count on that."

"You know what we could do," Dalton cut in, "if I can get into their camp and they're willing to talk, I could feed them a little disinfo. Tell them you know they're coming and that you're preparing for them. Make them think that Grove is where you want them. That's where the kill zone will be."

Sarge nodded, "That's a good idea. You'd just have to be real careful."

While they talked about this scenario, I went to the truck and pulled out the map. Opening it on the hood, I looked at Eustis. Lakeshore Drive hugged Lake Eustis on the southern shore. There were houses on the south side of the road, and the lake was to the north with only a tiny strip of land between the road and lake. There was no way to drive on the little strip, and the houses would keep them on the road. It would be a one-way in, one way out situation. I called them over to show them what I was thinking.

"Hear me out," I started and traced my finger over the map along the lakefront road and laid out my thoughts.

Both men listened as they inspected the map. Sarge was the first to speak, "If we occupied the houses on the south side, they'd have nowhere to go but the lake. We'd just need a way to stop them in the road, right in the middle of the kill zone."

Dalton ran a finger along Bay Street on the map, "If we do it here, they have all kinds of cover." He looked at Sarge and added, "You know what a nightmare urban fighting is."

Pointing at the map, I continued, "There's a lot of massive trees along here. We've got explosives. We could rig some of the trees at either end of the ambush and initiate by dropping them on both ends of the convoy. Once they're trapped in there, we kill them"

ENGINEERING HOME

Sarge studied the map as his head slowly nodded. "This would be a little more complicated. We'll be more spread out, but putting their backs to the lake would put them in a shitty position. I want to look at this. Let's load up and ride through there."

Dalton picked up the map and folded it, so Eustis was on top. "We need to be careful of the exact same thing we're talking about. It really is a perfect ambush spot."

"Yes, we do," Sarge replied. "You be ready to put the hammer down if any shit kicks off."

We got back in the truck, and I headed for Lakeshore. The road is pretty narrow, with the lakeside of the road now choked with high grass and unrestrained weeds. The houses on the other side of the road are what you'd expect from lakefront homes. They were big and generally very nice. The yards varied from large and deep, with the house set back off the road to only a narrow strip of grass between the street and house. Further down, there was even a substantial elevation change with a retaining wall bordering the road in front of the houses.

I was nervous driving down the road with its canopy of trees hanging over the asphalt. The road was littered with branches, leaves, and weeds creeping out from the shoulder. In a couple of places, vines had grown entirely across the road. It looked as though it was completely abandoned and had been for some time.

"I like this," Sarge proclaimed. "This is where we'll kill them bastards."

"We should look for some sandbags. We could fortify fighting positions in the houses. They'd be completely invisible from the outside," Dalton offered.

"Hard points, good idea," Sarge replied.

Driving west along the lake, we had a prime view of the sun setting behind it. The sky was pink, fading into a dull yellow closer to the horizon. The cool air washed in over us without a windshield in the old truck. It was one of those moments that reset my mind when the reality of our lives faded completely for a moment.

Approaching one of those elaborate community entries constructed of block, stucco, and exotic river stone that didn't exist in the state with the name Etowah in tall brass letters, I pulled off the road on the lakeside under a stand of giant oaks. The sun was below the horizon now, but there was still enough light to see, and I wanted to wait for darkness to continue. So, getting out, we slung our rifles and kept an eye out as we stood on the side of the lake. The evening was quiet, and I could hear the gentle lapping of the water against the cypress trees in knee-deep water.

Sarge looked back up the road. "I like this better, you agree, Dalton?"

Dalton nodded, "Me too. I think this is a much better option for us. If we did this on Bay Street, they would have a way out one way or another. Here, we can box them in on three sides. It'll be a slaughter fest."

"Y'all get your NODs out," Sarge said as he took his helmet out of the truck. Unfortunately, we didn't have any other mounts for the devices and would have to wear them at night. Not that I minded, I sure as hell didn't want to have to wear that shitty skull crusher.

I put on my helmet and turned the device on. Then, after adjusting the focus, I got in the truck, checked to make sure it was good and started the engine. Dalton sat in the back seat with his helmet on and a plate carrier, which was unusual for him.

"You wearing armor on this trip?" I asked him, looking over my shoulder.

"Vehicle ops or a static defensive position are the only time I'll wear it."

"Amen to that," Sarge agreed as he climbed in.

Dalton's head started to jig front to back, and he began to sing, "On the road again. Just can't wait to get on the road again…."

I laughed. "Wish we had some damn music!"

"Turn the radio on!" Dalton shouted as I pulled out onto the road.

"Alright dipshits, time to go work," Sarge admonished.

"Yas sah, boss," I shouted in a horrible southern accent. "I's a good driver, boss!"

Sarge shook his head and feigned looking to the heavens, "Why? What'd I ever do? Just take me now!"

In a deep baritone, Dalton replied, "You know what you did."

Sarge visibly shuttered and slowly turned to look back. "As a matter of fact, I do. And I'll do it again." The old man turned in his seat, "As a matter of fact, I might just do it to you."

I laughed, "Woah, Woah! You two need to keep your sexual relationship to yourselves. I don't need to see that shit!"

Sarge turned back in his seat, facing forward. "I had to get stuck in a truck with two idjits," the old man lamented.

Since turning onto Lakeshore, we hadn't seen a soul, and it stayed that way down to highway 441. I slowed as we came to the intersection. Just before the highway, on the right, was a small trailer park. I watched it intently, shifting my eye, could only see out of one, back and forth between the trailers crowded close together and approaching intersection.

"Morgan, you're driving. That's all you do. Dalton an I are watching everything else. You watch the road and only the road. Do your job, and we'll do ours," Sarge scolded me.

"It's hard not to look around. I'm expecting muzzle flashes at any moment."

"You can't do it all, son. Each of us has a job, and we each need to concentrate on our job and trust that the others are doing the same. You wreck this truck because you're trying to watch the side of the road, and we're all fucked."

"What he said," Dalton echoed in his baritone.

"Roger that," I replied.

"Slow down," Sarge ordered. "Take any curves slowly. If there's a blind corner, stop, and we'll get out on foot and have a look. I'm not fucking with you, Morgan. We just need to do this perfectly. There's no room for error right now. I do not want to walk back home."

Letting off the gas, I replied, "Neither do I."

The highway is a wide six-lane affair with a median. The intersection was open, and we could see a fair distance both ways. Dalton called clear left, and Sarge followed suit with the right immediately after. I accelerated lightly through the turn, and we were on the big slab headed west.

West of Eustis is Tavares. It's a small town founded in 1880 and the seat of Lake County. It was a place I didn't much like going to in the Before. The only reason I ever went there was for traffic court. That fact notwithstanding, it was a nice little town and home of a large seaplane port. I thought about those planes, if they were still there or if someone took off in one and flew until they couldn't and set it down on a lake somewhere. I'd never know, but I liked letting my imagination run with the idea.

Driving through the area in the dark of night with no streetlights was a little different. I was seeing it in the green glow of a PVS-14. Night vision is an amazing piece of technology. Literally turning night into day and having them when your adversary does not is one of the most powerful advantages a fighter can possess.

In our new world, night meant dark instead of the world of artificial illumination we used to live in. Before, dark was something we chose to tolerate when we wanted. It could be vanquished in a fraction of a second with the flip of a switch. That was no longer so. Dark was now the unknown and could harbor hidden danger.

It was that cloak of darkness that could be used for nefarious purposes as well. And that is what I worried about as we passed by Tavares and approached the far side of Lake Eustis came up on the right. This was a choke point, the same sort of place we were looking to use for an ambush in the near future.

"I ain't seen a soul," I said as I tried to relax the tension from my shoulders.

Sarge continued to gaze out the window. "It's been about a year since this shit started. I would imagine there's a lot fewer people around now."

From the back seat, Dalton added, "But the ones that are still around are going to be far more dangerous."

"Keep your eyes open, boys," Sarge said.

Driving on the road today was a bit hazardous. They were littered with debris, from Mother Nature's attempts to reclaim the land to abandoned cars and the myriad of abandoned junk left on the road. It was kind of interesting to see what people abandoned, like the small pushcart with bicycle wheels sitting in the middle of the road ahead of me. One of the wheels had fallen off, and someone simply abandoned it where it happened.

Night vision works by amplifying ambient light. Any light source is magnified, and through the device, it's hard to miss even a cigarette cherry. In the current world where there was no artificial illumination, any source of light in the night meant humans.

As Lake Eustis passed by us on the right, I caught a small flash of light. It was confirmed when I saw it again, and this time, it moved. "Got a light ahead on the right," I said as I eased the truck towards the inside median.

Aric laid on the bed beside Fed. She sat with her back against the headboard, a couple of pillows wedged behind her for support. Aric rested his hand on her belly, a huge smile on his face.

"What are they doing there? Wrastling?" He asked.

Fred smiled, and a hand on her belly as well. "They're active right now."

"They just had supper," he chuckled. "I can't believe there's two of them." He looked at Fred, "We're going to have two kids."

"Two babies," she smiled, watching his hand be pushed from within. Her smile faded slightly, and she looked at Aric. "I'm scared, though."

He looked at her, putting his hand on her face. "Me too, baby. But we'll do it together. We'll get through it. If we weren't here, I'd be terrified. But we have a doctor and a nurse. Erin is really nice, and she made me feel a lot better after talking to her the other night."

"She's over at Danny's tonight. I think she's moving here. But that's not really why I'm scared. I'm worried about the world they will grow up in. What kind of life will they live?"

Aric laid his head down on her belly. "I have to be honest. I like this life better. In comparison, the daily parts of life are a little harder than they used to be. The pace of life is so much better now. All the bullshit of our previous life is gone. All that crap that doesn't matter doesn't actually need to be done to live. Dropping all those chains that we just accepted as normal was such a relief."

"I know. But there aren't hospitals. What if we have a problem with one of the babies? What if I can't breastfeed?"

Aric sat up and looked her in the eye and then down at her chest. Then, he smiled, "Looks like you have the equipment to feed them to me."

"I'm being serious, Aric."

He laid back down in her belly. "More babies are born outside of hospitals than are in them globally. And hospitals are a relatively new invention. If we needed hospitals to have babies, there wouldn't be any people. So birth is a natural thing. It's going to happen one way or another. And while there is some risk," he sat up and looked at her again, "evolution has seen to the process. And we have help, and I know, know it in my core, that our babies will be born healthy and will live long happy lives."

Fred hugged him. "I love you, Aric. So much."

He put an arm around her. "I love you too, Fred. More than you will ever know. You saved me, the people here, saved me. I owe you all my life, and I, for one, could not be happier."

"What do you think? Boys? Girls? One of each?" Aric asked.

Fred smiled and ran a hand over her belly. "I hope it's one of each."

"Me too," he replied, putting his hand on hers.

Thad, Danny and Dad sat a table on the porch. Supper was over and they chatted about projects needing attention.

"We need to get a milking shed built for those cows," Thad pointed out. "Fred is going to have them babies and we need to make sure we can milk them cows if the babies need it."

"Not to mention just having the milk," Danny added.

"We need some lumber," Dad said. "If we had that, I could get started on it. I can build about anything."

"I've got plenty of screws and nails, that sort of thing. Battery powered tools too," Danny said and looked at Dad, "we could knock that out in no time."

"Where could we get the lumber?" Thad asked.

Danny leaned back on the bench, "I've been thinking about that. There's a lot of downed trees from that hurricane we had earlier this year. I've got chainsaws, if we could build something like an Alaskan sawmill, we could just mill the lumber ourselves."

"Don't you guys have some Army engineers around here?" Dad asked.

Thad nodded, "We do. At the plant."

"I bet they could help us figure this out. I mean, between them and us, we should be able to sort something out," Dad replied.

"Let's stop by there on our way to the ranch tomorrow and talk to them," Danny said. "There's also the plant, there's all kinds of machinery in there that I'm sure we can come up with something to make this happen."

Danny suddenly slapped the table, startling everyone, "I can't believe I didn't think about this!"

"What?" Thad asked.

"There's a sawmill over off highway 439. It's a small operation but they all the machinery for milling wood. Saws, planers, you name it, they have it all."

Thad scratched his head, "That's a great idea, but there's no power there."

"No, there's not. But what if we went over there and pulled the machinery out and brought it here? Then we could mill lumber any time we needed it."

Danny could see Thad was unsure of that. "It would be a whole lotta work to pull that equipment out and bring it here. What if we just took a generator over there and ran it in place. Be a whole lot faster."

"That's a better idea," Dad offered, "if you have a generator that will run it all."

"We do," Thad answered, "we have a large military generator, runs on diesel at the plant. It'll run that sawmill, no problem."

"Is everything still there?" Dad asked.

Danny shrugged, "It should be. I can't see anyone pulling stuff out there with no power anywhere to run it with. But we need to go look at it."

Thad looked back over his shoulder, "It's not quite dark yet. We could run over there right now. How far is it?"

"You go the same way like you're going to the ranch. Instead of turning into the ranch, you keep going a couple of miles, and there's 439. Turn right and run down nine or ten miles and it's on the left," Danny answered. "It'd be better just to do it tomorrow since we'll be over there anyway. We won't waste fuel that way either."

"That's a better idea," Dad replied.

"We'll need to find a way to move the logs to the mill," Danny considered. "That will be the hardest part of this."

"We need a log trailer."

Danny thought for a minute. "I might know where one is. We have the fuel, and they run on diesel. So we could pull it with the duce-and-half."

"Sounds like a plan to me," Dad said, taking a drink of coffee.

Thad smiled, "I like this. It'll be a fun project."

Mel left the girls on the porch with Karen to walk the neighborhood with Erin and Travis to look at houses. They were walking towards the bunker down the dirt road past the burned remnants of Tyler and Brandy's home. Travis pointed at it and asked what had happened.

"Tyler and Brandy used to live there," Mel stopped in the road and looked at the black scar on the land. "They died in the fire. They were Jace and Edie's parents. They got the kids out, but they couldn't get out."

"Oh, that's awful," Erin said.

"It was. They were nice people. But the kids are happy and doing well here."

They kept walking, passing Mel and Morgan's place, then his parents, and came to a gate in the fence on the left. "What's back there?" Travis asked.

"It's another house, and it's a nice little place," Mel answered.

Travis started for the gate, and the ladies followed him. They walked up the pine needle-strewn dirt drive that cut through a thick stand of the very trees littering the drive. Then, finally, on the second bend in the trail, the house came into view. It was a manufactured home, double-wide, with a screened porch along the entire front of the structure.

Travis stopped in the trail and looked around. There was a shop building sitting to the left of the house. It was a large metal building with a rollup door on the front and an entry door. The entire yard was fenced and cross-fenced. "I like this," he said, looking around.

Erin started walking towards the house, "I want to go see the inside."

"I'll come with you," Mel said as she followed Erin.

Travis looked at the metal building, "I'm gonna check out the shop."

Erin and Mel went up on the porch. Aside from a layer of dust on everything, the place, from the outside at least, was in good shape. Erin looked around, saying, "This is cute."

Mel moved to the front door, opening it, "Let's go inside."

The house's interior was dimly lit as the sun was close to the horizon. Mel pulled a flashlight from her pocket and clicked it on. They used the light to inspect the house, going room by room. They talked about the place, more about the contents and the decorating taste of the previous occupants, as they went room by room.

"Can they get the power back on here?" Erin asked.

"I think so. We have power, so this one should too."

"If the power works, then the well should work too, shouldn't it? So we'd have water?"

"That's a Morgan thing, but I'm sure they can get it running."

Erin looked around, "Where is he?"

"Probably still in the shop, I bet."

"I really like this. It's not too big," Erin said as they walked back into the living room. "And I love that," she added, pointing to a beautiful wood-burning stove sitting in the corner of the living room. It sat on tile, and the wall behind it was also covered with tile. The stove had an enamel finish with a glass door. "It's going to get cold soon, and this would be nice."

"Remember, we have power."

"Yeah, but if the power goes out or the AC doesn't work, this will still let us heat the house."

"That's true. We have a fireplace in ours, and it's really nice."

Erin turned towards the door, "Let's go find Travis."

They found him in the shop. He held a small flashlight in his mouth as he rummaged around in a box. "What are you looking at?" Erin asked as she came through the door.

Travis looked up, taking the light from his mouth. "Just looking at all the stuff in here. This place is packed with a lot of perfect tools and other stuff."

The shop was large, thirty feet by sixty. In the middle of it was a two-post car lift. A long workbench occupied part of the left wall. There was a freestanding drill press, a welder, table saw, radial arm saw, and many other tools. A large air compressor sat in the back corner, and steel pipe was run to various locations in the shop.

"I like this place," he said.

Erin looked at him like he was speaking Japanese to her, "You haven't even been inside yet!"

"Do you like it? The house?" he asked.

"I do. It's nice. There's a big wood stove in the living room."

"If you like it, I'm good with it."

"No," Erin objected, "you need to come in and look at it."

"You want to look around in here?" Travis asked, looking around.

"No, there's nothing in here that matters to me."

"But I have to look at the house?" Travis lifted a hand to his face and pinched his chin, "hmmm."

"You'll be living in the house! I won't be living out here!"

Mel was shaking her head, "Men."

He smiled and stepped over, taking her hand, "Just teasing you. Come on, let's go look at it."

After Travis toured the house, it was decided it would be the one if everything was okay with it. Travis looked at Mel, "The power is on here, in the neighborhood, right?"

She nodded, "It is. They turned all the breakers off to the houses that no one lives in."

"So, all we should have to do is turn on the breakers then," Travis observed as he headed for the laundry room at the back of the house. He opened the breaker panel and checked to make sure all the breakers were off, including the main for the panel. Seeing all were off, he passed back through the house headed for the front door.

"What are you doing?" Erin asked as he passed.

"I'm going to turn the power on. Let's see what works," he replied as he went out the door.

He walked around the side of the house and found the electric meter and main breaker, which was off. He flipped off the breaker for the well and AC before flipping the main breaker for the house. It closed with a positive snap. There was no indication the power was on as all breakers were off. Travis walked around the house and went back inside.

Standing in front of the panel, he shouted, "Here we go!"

He started flipping the breakers in the panel one at a time. As he did, the lights in the house began to come on, and Mel and Erin both shouted with excitement when the living room lights came on. He continued flipping breakers and could hear Erin and Mel going through the house, checking the lights.

"Looks like it all works," Erin told Travis as he came out of the laundry room.

"That's good. I'm going to turn on the breaker for the well."

He went back and flipped the two-pole breaker for the well pump and jumped when the mop sink in the corner started to spit and cough. He waited until it calmed down and a steady stream of water poured from it before shutting it off. "Hot damn," he muttered to himself as he walked out.

Mel came out of the hallway bathroom, announcing, "It works in here!"

"Master bath too," Erin said, coming into the living room.

"I think this will work," Travis said, looking around. Then, looking at Erin, he asked, "You like it?"

"I think this will be better than where we are. We'll have some actual privacy here."

"Dave is a nice guy, and the people over there are all pretty nice as well. But I would like some privacy. It'd be nice to be able to be alone," Travis replied.

"I don't want this to come off wrong," Erin started, "but it will also be nice not having someone tell me what to do all the time too. I don't mind working and helping out. It just feels weird, ya know, having to do what Dave says."

"We'll be trading Dave for Morgan," Travis countered, then looked at Mel, "or Sarge, whoever is in charge around here."

"We don't work that way. We're all adults, and we all know what needs to be done, and we just do it. We discuss things, of course, and everyone just jumps in. No one is really told what to do, and you just do it. Morgan handles some things and Sarge others. But they aren't out there telling people what to do on a daily basis. Sure, they may ask for help with something, but that's as close as we get to being told what to do."

Erin looked at Travis, "I like Dave and Janet and everyone over there, but I think this will be better for us here."

"I do, too," Travis agreed.

"Are you going to stay the night here then?" Mel asked.

"Help me look for clean sheets."

They looked but didn't find any. All the closets were empty of linens of any kind. "I guess it makes sense," Mel said, "with no way to do laundry, people probably used all the clean ones they had before thinking about what to do. But I have some that will fit the bed. I can go get them and bring them to you."

"I'll go with you and get them, so you don't have to come back," Erin replied.

"I'm going to stay here and clean a few things up. It's not bad, but it's been closed up for a long time," Travis said.

"I think this will be a lot of fun living over here. You guys are a lot more laid back than Dave is," Erin said as they walked back to the house.

"What's the point of the world ending if you still have to follow someone's rules?"

Erin laughed, "I know, right?"

Mel got Erin some clean sheets and handed them to her. "That should get you guys through the night."

"Thank you. We haven't been *alone* since we got to the ranch."

"Oh, nice. Some alone time is always nice," Mel replied with a wink. "Remember, breakfast is in the morning at Danny's house."

"We'll be there. You guys eat so well."

"It isn't much, but we do what we can."

"I'll see you tomorrow," Erin said as she headed out the door.

Mel went back over to Danny's to round up the kids. She found them in the living room gathered around the table with the puzzle on it. Karen and Butch were with them, Little Bit was sitting in Butch's lap, and even Tammy was sitting with them. Mel thought about the girl for a moment, how close she was sitting with everyone like she was family. She smiled, looking at the girl.

"Alright girls, time to go," Mel announced.

"Ah, come on, Mom, can't we stay a little longer?" Little Bit protested.

"We have to get up early in the morning. Let's go."

"Please, Mel, can we just stay a little longer?" Tammy's request surprised Mel. Before she could reply, Butch spoke up.

"You girls want to take one of these puzzles to our house and stay the night with us?"

They all began to shout excitedly, "Yes, please, please! We want to!"

"Can I come too?" Tammy asked.

Dad patted her back, "Oh course, honey. You're more than welcome."

Tammy smiled shyly, "Thank you."

"Alright," Mom said, "pick out a puzzle, and we'll take it with us."

Mel walked into the kitchen. "Kay, do we have anything like a snack they could take with them?"

Kay looked around, "Well, we have some leftover biscuits. They could take those and a jar of honey. Would that work?"

"Perfect," Mel smiled.

She packed up the baked goods and honey and took it over to Karen. "Here, take these with you. A little snack for them later."

"Oh, snacks? We have snacks?" Taylor asked.

"Some biscuits and honey."

"Oh yeah! I love biscuits and honey!" Little Bit shouted.

"The honey is so good," Tammy moaned. "It's been so long since I had anything sweet."

The girls picked out a puzzle, and Mom and Dad got them herded up and headed to the door. Goodbyes were said, and they all left. "What are you going to do with a night all to yourself?" Mom asked.

Mel laughed, "I have absolutely no idea. I haven't had a night to myself in a year. I wish Morgan were here," she cut her eyes over to her mother-in-law, "that would make it better."

Mom smiled, "We're here now, and we want to spend time with the girls, as much as we can. There will be plenty more nights to come."

Mel put her arm around her, "Thank you. I'm so glad you're here now. Morgan used to worry about you guys all the time. It really weighed on him."

"We knew you guys had your hands full. But we had no idea he wasn't here when it happened," Karen put a hand on Mel's arm. "I can only imagine how scared you were. We knew, though, if anyone was ready for this, you guys were."

"It was tough at first. I thought I'd never see him again. Even though I knew he would do whatever it took to get home. It's one thing to think about, it's another thing when you know how far away he was. I didn't think he'd be able to do it." Mel stopped as the gaggle of giggling kids ran past them. "He walked over two hundred miles. I couldn't imagine doing that."

"You could and would. Just like he did."

"I don't know. I know Morgan. He doesn't hesitate to make decisions when there's a crisis. He said he slept in his truck the first night and started walking the next morning. He didn't hesitate. He recognized the situation immediately and got to work. And everything he did before that he had in place. It saved our lives. It kept us going until the magical day he walked up. He just walked up the road."

"His dad always thought he was a little crazy with the prepping stuff. Not that you guys ever got way out there. Just did a few things and put some things back in case. And he was right."

Mel laughed, "He's almost always right, Karen. Not that I'll ever tell him that." The two women shared a laugh as they stepped up on the porch.

With supper over, a large group left Danny's headed home. Jamie, Ian, Thad, Mary, Doc, Jess, and Ted filled the dirt track like a herd of cattle. They chatted and laughed as they walked. Mike and Crystal followed them at a discrete distance, holding hands.

"What do you think?" Mike asked.

"It's a lot different here. I love my uncle, but you guys have way more fun," Crystal observed.

"We like to keep it light. We have to do enough bad stuff, and it's nice to be able to let go and relax."

"Miss Kay is a fantastic cook too! Dinner was so good."

"We're lucky on that end. With the connections to the Army, we get a little stuff from them. We have the garden that everyone works in, and that adds to the meals."

"We tried a garden," Crystal replied as she swung their arms back and forth. "But it didn't work out. Nothing grew. There were bugs and all kinds of problems. So how do you guys keep the bugs out?"

"By hand. Everyone kind of watches the garden. A lot of people use it as a stress release, taking time in the garden to relax," Mike nodded his head in the direction of Thad and Mary, who were holding hands. "Thad, there is the real gardener around here. Him and Mary spend a lot of time in there."

"Well, it's an impressive garden for sure. It's so nicely maintained. No weeds or bugs. It's really nice."

"They keep making it bigger too. Now that we have the cows, Thad takes a wheelbarrow over to the pasture, picks up the cow patties, and brings them back. He does stuff with it, makes like a tea from some of it, composts the rest and uses it as fertilizer, and it's had a big impact on production."

Crystal stopped, stretching her arm out and pulling Mike to a stop as well. "What?" he asked as he turned to face her.

She pulled him to her and wrapped her arms around his waist. "I really like it here," she purred. "And I really like you. I want to move in with you here."

"Really?" Mike beamed and leaned in to kiss her. Instead, she pushed a finger to his lips, interrupting his effort.

"But," she started.

"But, what?" Mike asked, worry spreading across his face.

"You have to go ask my uncle for permission. It's the right thing to do, and he will respect it."

Relief washed over him, "Oh, is that all! I was worried for a minute. No problem, I can do that!"

"One thing," she interrupted again. "You need to be serious when you do it. No fooling around."

Mike smiled. In his best Austin Powers voice, he replied, "I can serious, baby." Crystal stepped back. Her head cocked to the side and hands on her hips. It was a universal message that any man with any sense understands, and Mike indeed did. He reached out for her, "Babe, I promise, I will be serious, and I'll do it the right way."

"Promise?"

He held his hand up, "Pinky promise."

Crystal studied him for a moment before reaching out with her pinky and grabbing his. "You promised."

He grabbed her and wrapped her in his arms, and kissed her deeply. The moment was interrupted by a whistle and catcalls from the group in front of them.

"Get a room!" Ted shouted.

"Awe, they're so cute!" Ian shouted, then feigned wiping his eyes, "they grow up so fast!" And fell against Jamie's shoulder.

Jamie patted his head, "It's okay. You knew this day was coming."

Crystal was blushing, and Mike spun on his heels. "Hey! Don't you people have somewhere to be?"

Thad looked around at the group, "No, not really. We got all night to mess with you."

"Oh, come on now," Mary cut in. "Let's give them some space."

"Thank you, Mary," Mike exaggerated the reply. "At least someone around here has some manners."

"You're just lucky the old man ain't here tonight," Ted shouted. "You think we're bad!" He began to laugh manically.

Crystal took a step forward, "Your day is coming too, Ted!"

Ted's laughter ceased immediately. "What?"

"Oh yeah, I see you and Janet together. Your day is coming."

Ted took a step forward. Then, pounding his chest, he shouts, "Never! I am Spartacus!"

"Yeah, well, he died!" Ian shouted.

"Says you! They never found the body!" Ted shouted back.

Everyone was laughing, and the group started back down the road. Crystal was laughing and put her arm around Mike as they moved out behind them. "You guys are so much more fun,"

CHAPTER 10

The light turned out to be someone in a small marina just past the county boat ramp. It was very dim, impossible to see without the aid of night vision. Finding people near the lake isn't a surprise as transition zones such as this contain the most resources. As we came abreast of where the light was, it quickly blinked out.

Sarge was turned sideways in his seat, his back to me, looking out the window. "Whoever's down there don't want no attention."

"Good," I sighed, "I don't want any of theirs."

After passing the little marina, Sarge spun back around in his seat. "How the hell you figure that old boy still has batteries for a damn flashlight?"

"Could be solar," I replied.

"Or one of the shitty little hand-crank jobs that had a radio as well," Dalton added.

"I guess those would still work," Sarge considered. "Sure, wasn't much light, though."

"When there is no light, a little is a lot," I offered.

We continued down the road, not seeing a soul or even signs of people. I was starting to relax as I considered what Sarge said earlier about there being fewer people after this last year. He was probably right. In the Before, estimates of the loss of life after an EMP could be as much as ninety percent of the country. It was often claimed that loss of life could happen in as little as three months, but I thought that was a bit overzealous. People are resilient and would probably last much longer. With that said, there would surely be a tremendous loss of the population after a year of such hardships as those we now face.

This mission had given me quite a bit of anxiety. I knew it needed to be done, and as I considered what we were doing, I settled on the source of my concern. It wasn't that I was afraid of what we were doing. We've done a lot of crazy shit at this point, and much of it is far more dangerous than this. It was the distance. I was far from home at the moment. Far from Mel and my girls and it made me nervous.

In the Before, an hour car ride was no big deal and demanded hardly any thought at all besides, *do I have enough gas.* Even that could be handled on the way. It's not like you had to make sure you had the car full before you left. There was plenty of fuel on the way in most cases, and all you had to do was pull into any of the numerous stations, swipe a plastic card, and fill up. You didn't even need to go in, and the transaction didn't involve *real* money, just the card.

Now, however, such a ride of only an hour or so was fraught with peril that one had to envision to mitigate the consequences of trouble encountered on the way. And the trouble you had to look out for was much different as well. Even now, a flat tire was still a concern, but it could be dealt with quickly. Running out of fuel was a big concern as no stations were lining the road with their brilliantly lit canopies offering safety and resupply. Ambushes were the most significant concern now.

We were reminded of the threat ambushes represented as we approached the bridge over the Dead River. A natural chokepoint, it was the perfect place to set up the roadblock that straddled the bridge ahead of us.

"Slow down, Morg," Sarge instructed as he sat up in his seat and leaned forward, straining to see as much as he could of the pile of junk ahead of us.

The roadblock was constructed of cars, barrels, wood, an old fridge, whatever its builders could get their hands on and drag to the top of the bridge. It may have been built before the gas ran out for most people and probably was as there was no way anyone was pushing cars up the steep approach.

"You see anything?" Sarge asked.

I'd taken my foot off the accelerator and was letting the Suburban coast. It was slowing as I scanned the top of the bridge, looking for any source of light. People sometimes have the wrong idea about night vision. Hollywood has a lot to do with movies giving the devices science-fiction level abilities. Like thermal optics being able to see through walls. It was nonsense, but most people had never even seen one of these devices in real life, let alone actually used one.

If your camo was on point in the daytime, it was just as effective at night. More so, if a person was well camouflaged and remained still, they could easily hide from observation by NVGs. With the bridge's peak above us, we looked at it against the sky. While the sun was down, we faced west and had a perfect, silhouetted view of the fortification.

"I don't see shit," I muttered.

"Me neither," Sarge replied. "Let's just sit here a minute and see if anything moves. If there's anyone up there, they might get nervous or jump the gun if we just sit here."

"Alright."

Dalton opened his door, "I'm gonna step out and take a piss. I'll watch our six."

"Roger that," Sarge replied quietly as he focused on the bridge.

I never took my eyes off the bridge, watching both the west and east-bound sides for movement. After fifteen minutes, neither of us had seen a thing. "Alright, let's try and move up a little. Go really slow."

I leaned out my window and called to Dalton, "You coming?"

He came out from behind the truck and walked up to my window. "I'm going to stay on foot until we get up there and clear that barricade. You stay in the left lane, and I'll hug the wall on the right."

"Roger that," I replied, giving the truck a little gas, and we started to roll.

"Not too fast," Sarge directed.

"I'm not gonna," I was concentrating so hard on what we were doing I didn't even get annoyed at such obvious, repetitive instruction from the old man.

As we drew closer and closer to the barricade, my pulse increased. I found myself sliding down in my seat to put as much of me behind the Cummins as possible. I was expecting a muzzle flash from the top of the bridge at any moment. Instead, at about thirty feet from the hazard, Sarge ordered a stop and told me to stay with the truck as he stepped out.

"Dalton, on me," Sarge said, training the muzzle of his weapon on the obstacle before him.

Dalton quickly moved around the truck and came up behind him. He unslung his rifle and shifted it to his left hand. Then, gripping the old man's shoulder with his right, he squeezed it, and Sarge began to move forward. I'd taken my rifle from where it rested against the bench seat, muzzle down on the floorboard, and brought it up as well. It was then I realized we were all looking in the same direction, and I put the truck in park and stepped out. Standing in the open door, I turned and faced the direction we'd come from. Someone needed to be watching our backs.

From time to time, I'd steal a glance back over my shoulder and, on one look, saw the two men move behind the barricade where a path had been left by its builders for just such purpose it looked. The bridge was divided east and west by concrete barriers, and there was even a small gap of a couple of feet between the two. You couldn't simply walk over to the eastbound lanes. After several minutes of my pulse pounding in my ears, I heard them crunching the debris on the road and looked back.

"Clear," Dalton announced as he approached.

"This has been abandoned for a long time," Sarge stated as he walked up.

"It is now," Dalton replied, "but there was some serious shooting that went on here."

"Yeah, there's a lot of brass lying up there. Every caliber you can imagine."

"How the hell are we going to get through that shit?" I asked.

"It's not as bad as it looks," Dalton replied, "we can get the left side cleared out pretty easy."

Sarge unslung his rifle, "Morg, you pull security, and me and Dalton will get us a path busted through this."

I moved up to the peak of the bridge and stood at the end of the barricade to see both approaches. Sarge and Dalton moved the old fridges, drums, and other crap piled up. It made more noise than I liked, but it had to get done. When they'd moved all the small shit out of the way, there was only one car that needed to be moved.

"Morgan, you have a strap or a chain or anything in the truck?" Dalton asked.

"I nodded, yeah. I put a tow strap in the truck just for this."

I ran down to the truck and grabbed the strap. Dalton took the strap and started towards the car. "Pull up here, and I'll hook it up."

Climbing in the truck, I pulled up until Dalton waved for me to stop. He connected the strap to the car and then to the Suburban. He started motioning me to back up, and I applied tension to the strap, then eased on the gas. The big Cummins growled, and the front of the car began to slide. Once it was moving, it was easy to keep it moving, and I pulled it down the slope and off to the side. When Dalton waved for me to stop, I pulled up a little to get the tension off, and Dalton quickly unhooked the vehicles. With the barricade now dealt with, we got back on the road.

"That wasn't that bad," Sarge said as we passed through the pile of junk.

"Wonder how many more we'll come across," Dalton wondered.

"Let's hope they're all like this one. Unmanned," I replied.

Leaving Tavares behind us, Leesburg lay before us. Leesburg is a much bigger town, despite Tavares being the county seat. We came into the business district that ran on both sides of the highway. We passed a Home Depot that had obviously been looted to the walls. Next was the Lake Square Mall. Through the NVGs, we could see the parking lot was littered with debris. There were burned cars, it looked like someone set one on fire, and it ran through the closely parked rows.

However, there were no people. Other than the small light, we'd not seen a soul. While that was a relief, it also worried me. I know there are people around. Where are they? The more I thought about it, though, the more sense it made. It was dark now, and most people didn't have any source of light by this point aside from possibly torches.

All the batteries were likely gone by now, and few people kept solar or hand crank options. The old hurricane lanterns would be nice to have, but I doubt anyone had enough fuel stored to still be burning those after a year. Not to mention running out of wicks as well. Candles would undoubtedly be used up by now. So that left people in the dark, and sunset would bring a natural end to most people's day.

The farther we went, the more I relaxed. It felt as though we were the last people on Earth, and there just weren't any people. We made it to Highway 44 in short order, and I turned to head into Leesburg. If we were going to see people, this is where we would. The highway ran through a congested area with a prominent University of Florida hospital, schools, and other municipal buildings.

"Let's keep an eye open through here. This is going to get a little congested. Buildings will be close to the road through here," I stated.

"Roger that," Dalton replied without turning around.

We were passing the hospital when we saw the first person. Dalton called from the rear, "Got contact on our four o'clock. I don't see a weapon, but he's running."

"Keep an eye on him," Sarge replied as he intently scanned the side of the road.

"He's waving his arms."

Sarge snorted, "Probably wants us to stop."

"Hate his fucking luck," I replied. There was no way I was stopping for anyone.

We rolled through the rest of Leesburg without seeing another soul. The drive was easy enough. I'd slow down at times, and once or twice we stopped to check things out, to look and listen, but we never saw anyone. Never saw any lights that would indicate there were people. It was eerie. By nine o'clock, we were on highway 27 south of Leesburg paralleling the Florida Turnpike, a vast slab of concrete and asphalt that ran from I-75 near Ocala to Miami.

I'd been keeping my eyes on the road, watching for hazards, and there was a lot when I thought I noticed something on the horizon. There was a definite glow on the horizon.

"You see that up there?" I asked.

"What?" Sarge quickly inquired.

"Up there," I pointed even though I knew he wasn't looking at me, "on the horizon, does that look like a glow to you?"

Sarge studied it and adjusted the gain on his optic. "There is definitely some light up there, and from the looks of it, it's a big light. You seeing this Dalton?"

Dalton's head came up between us. He looked out the glassless opening, craning his neck to see. "Sure looks like it. It looks like it covers a big area."

"Fires," Sarge announced. "I bet we've found them. With as many folks as they're supposed to have, there'd be a lot of fires in their camp. I bet that's what we're seeing."

"Very well could be," Dalton agreed.

I let off the gas to slow down a bit. "We need to be careful. I don't want to get too close in this thing."

Sarge started looking around, "We need to find a place to lay up and scope it out."

"Let's try and get closer," Dalton said.

We continued to drive for some time. I was going slow, maybe thirty miles an hour. We kept our eyes on the dim glow in the sky as it grew in intensity little by little. At every hill on the road, and there many as this is near the highest point in the state and very hilly, we would stop the truck, and Sarge and Dalton would walk to the crest and look over to make sure we didn't drive into a surprise. This process continued for some time until they saw fires from the top of one.

Coming back to the truck, Sarge said, "Alright. We can see them now. But there isn't shit for cover around them. We need to get off this road and find another approach."

"The Turnpike is just over there," I replied, pointing to the east. "There's probably a fence, but we could cut through it. It's lower than this, and we could use it to get closer before pulling off and finding a hide."

"Let's do it," Sarge replied as they climbed back into the truck.

I turned the truck to the eastern shoulder and drove until we found a gate that was still below the crest of the hill. Unfortunately, the gate was locked when we got out to inspect it. But it wasn't a big issue as the fence was only four strands of barbed wire.

"Let's just cut the wire here. Then, we'll use something to pull them back up and make it look whole again," Sarge instructed.

We cut the strands and pulled the truck through. Once inside, we used some paracord to pull the strands back into place and tied them off. It would take a close inspection even to notice it. A narrow strip of land was sandwiched between the two highways. We discussed the situation and decided the best thing to do was to do a recon of the strip and see if we could get close enough to the spot where the caravan had set up camp.

"Stay with the truck," Morg, Sarge told me. "We don't want to lose it."

"No, we don't," I replied.

We did a quick comms check. Part of the equipment Sarge had pried out of the Army were encrypted Harris radios. They were big and clunky but seemed very robust. They came with Comtac headsets that we mounted to our helmets, making us look like government contractors or tactitard larpers. But they were really nice and worked well. Not only did they pipe the audio of the radio into our ears, but they were also noise protection as well. When turned on, they amplified ambient sound, making them a real asset for me personally as my tinnitus was so bad my ears rang constantly. If a weapon was fired, the units produced the opposite frequency to cancel out the sound essentially.

Once we were sure we could communicate, they got ready to move out. They checked one another's kit to make sure there was nothing that would make a lot of noise or was about to fall off. As they prepared to step off, Dalton looked at me and said, "Find a place close to the truck and hide. Keep your eyes and ears open. You don't want to be sitting in it. Anyone sees it they'll come to have a look."

"Roger that," I replied as I looked around.

I ended up finding a large Sabal Palm with fronds hanging down almost to the ground. I pushed my way into them and took a seat under the bowed fronds. I pulled out my canteen and started to listen. At night sound travels farther than it does during the day, and through the amplified headset, I could hear the occasional sound of a twig snap or the brushing of foliage as they moved. It made me nervous until I pulled the cups from my ears and listened, nothing. Popping them back over my ears, I could still barely hear it. No way anyone down the road and on the other side was going to hear anything.

Danny sat on the back porch with Karl, Chad, and Imri after everyone else left. He was peppering them with questions after finding out they'd made their way from California to Florida after the balloon went up.

"What was it like?" Danny asked.

"Well, we didn't hang around long," Karl started. "As soon as we realized what was going on, we got the hell out of there."

"And you guys drove that Jeep all the way here?"

"Yeah, it was mine," Imri replied. "I'd accidentally acquired it. Someone owed me some money, and they couldn't pay. So we settled on the Jeep."

"How did you get fuel for it?"

The three men explained how they had developed a system, purchasing the parts needed the first day when stores were still open but operating on a cash-only basis. It was a fuel transfer pump and hoses sufficient to reach the bottom of underground storage tanks. The SOP they developed was to pull into a station. One of them would pull security while the other two filled the Jeep and all their fuel cans. Jeeps have notoriously small fuel tanks, which necessitated carrying several fuel cans to keep them moving.

"With the cans, we have," Chad said, "it gives us about a six-hundred-mile range before fuel gets critical."

"Did you ever have problems finding fuel?"

"Not initially and for several months after. But the longer things have gone, the harder it's getting," Karl replied.

"We've had a couple of long walks," Imir laughed.

"Yeah, long walks carrying fuel cans, the pump, hoses, and the damn battery from the Jeep! It sucked!" Chad added.

"What was it like out there? You run into much trouble?"

"Some," Karl replied. "But nothing too crazy."

"We moved mainly at night," Imri added. "We have a couple of sets of NODs and used them to move exclusively at night in the beginning. Then, as we got farther into this and there were just fewer and fewer people, we started moving in the day as well."

"You noticed the decline in people? I mean, like it was such an obvious difference you couldn't miss it?"

"Oh, for sure," Karl replied, nodding. "It's a huge difference. It's kind of strange. In the beginning, people were crowded in cities. So naturally, they thought that's where help would be and went there only to find there wasn't any."

"Not to mention the cities and towns that basically barricaded themselves and wouldn't allow anyone in and in some cases to even pass through them. So it made us have to detour around some of them," Chad offered.

"What route did you guys take?"

"Basically I-10," Imri replied.

"Yeah, Arizona, New Mexico, and West Texas suck ass. That's where we ended up taking some walks because we ran out of fuel," Chad grunted.

"What was it like? You pass through Houston?"

"No, no," Karl sat back, waving his hands. "We avoided the big cities at all costs. Instead, we'd go around them, drive off-road, whatever it took."

Imri's face was drawn, and he said, "We never saw Houston. We smelled it, though."

"Yeah, you could always smell a city depending on which way the wind was. Sometimes you get hit with it on the far side. It was awful. Just the smell of death," Chad replied and wiped a hand over his face.

"We're all vets here. We've all been in combat," Karl explained. "I've smelled cities in Iraq that weren't as bad as what we encountered."

"And the fires," Imri interjected. "So many fires."

"What? You mean cities?" Danny asked.

Imri nodded, "Yes. There were massive columns of smoke billowing from some of them early on. You could see it for miles and miles."

"I imagine most of the bigger cities are smoking ruins now. Or at least major sections of them are," Karl replied.

"Wow. I had no idea about any of that," Danny replied. "What about like New Orleans and all the industrial plants around Lake Charles?"

"New Orleans is gone," Chad replied.

"Gone?"

"Flooded. It was completely flooded. We snuck close to it one night to look. It looked like Katrina hit, and there was no recovery. Fire ripped through there too," Karl said.

"Lake Charles, all those refineries and whatnot, they all burned. Not sure what started it, but with the power going out, there are all kinds of reasons they could catch on fire," Imri added.

Danny considered all this. "This country is never coming back," he finally said.

"The United States of America is dead. At least, the previous version. There's still a chance we could build something better from the ashes," Karl mused.

"It was getting pretty bad there towards the end," Danny agreed. "Just don't know what it'll look like on the other side."

Imri pointed at Danny's hand, "What happened there?"

Danny looked down at the disfigured appendage. "Mortar attack. We were handing out food and supplies in town when the Russians launched a mortar attack on us. My wife, Bobbie, was killed."

Karl sat back on the bench, "Very sorry to hear that, Danny. But Russians?"

Danny nodded, "There was a bunch around here. They came in from Cuba and moved up the state. Morgan and the old man found them and reported it to the Army. After hearing what was here, the Air Force launched a couple of bombers and hit them. We went in after the bombing and finished them off. They were pretty fucked up after those big ass bombs fell on them."

"You killed them all?" Karl asked.

"No. We captured two. A Colonel and some other guy. They were just picked up a few days ago. They sent a Chinook down from Eglin, dropped off some stuff for us, and took them out of here."

Imri leaned into the table, slapping his palms down, "See, this is what I don't get. If the military is still functioning, that means the government is still functioning. So where the hell are they?"

"They're not really functioning," Danny replied. "The military and DHS have been fighting one another. So that's who's coming here now."

"I know you guys said that. I just assumed it was some rogue element that went off the reservation."

"No, we hit one of their camps. It was a nice camp. They had nice tents, showers, food, medical, all of it." Danny replied. "But some of the stuff that was happening inside wasn't good. So it had to end, and we were the only ones around to do it."

"And the Army helped?" Karl asked.

Danny nodded. "They said they were helping us because we were trying to affect change. So they made Morgan the Sheriff; he didn't do that himself."

Chad looked at Karl and said, "We were wondering about that. We've seen the same sort of thing in other places. Where someone has the balls and will stand up and proclaim themselves the leader in one fashion or another, but it usually wasn't good for anyone around them."

"We were unsure if that was the case here or not," Karl added. "At least initially. After we were here for a few days, we saw this was different. That you guys weren't out just for yourselves. You're doing a lot for the community here." Karl paused and pointed at Danny, "And that is what sets you guys apart from everyone else we've seen try the same thing."

"In a couple of places, the people were trying to do what you're doing here," Imri interjected. "But they either ended up acting like little tyrants, or some other larger group would come in and take over. So we haven't seen it work anywhere."

"We're trying to, here," Danny replied. We just want to try and restore everyday life, not like what we had before, you know, but something more comfortable. To make sure people can eat. Get the power back on to make life easier. Little things, really."

Karl was nodding as Danny spoke. "And that's why we're going to help you."

It felt like they were gone forever as I sat under the fronds of the tree. It was so quiet, not a breath of wind, and nothing moved. I strained to listen to the still air. I could swear that I could hear faint voices from time to time, but I was never able to determine if it was real or just in my jittery head. Eventually, I heard movement again in the direction the guys had gone, and it wasn't long before I began to decern movement.

I was relieved when they finally came into view, moving slowly and cautiously. I stood up and emerged from the palm when they were almost to the truck.

"Well?" I asked.

"It's far from perfect," Sarge said. "We won't be able to see much up there, but there's a building over there we can get on the roof of and watch."

"We're gonna be pretty exposed on a damn roof," I replied.

"There's trees in front of it that will obscure us. Movement will be what gives away. As long as you stay still, we shouldn't have any trouble with it," the old man went on to detail the plan he and Dalton came up with.

Sarge would go with Dalton and take up a position on the roof with the M1A. He'd use the scope on the rifle and a pair of binoculars to keep an eye on him. I would stay and pull security on the truck and make our scheduled check-ins on the radio with the TOC back at home. Sarge gave me a notepad with the radio checks' frequencies, times, and codes.

"We'll use the portable radios to stay in touch with one another, Morg," Sarge finished with.

"So, Dalton won't have a radio on him?" I asked.

Dalton shook his head in reply, "Too risky. If I got caught with it, it'd be tough to explain my way out of."

"I don't like you being out there like that,' I replied.

"Me neither, but it's the best we can do. I'll be alright. If they're too hostile, I'll get out fast."

Sarge looked at his watch. "Alright, our first radio check is in about fifteen minutes. So let's get that one out of the way, and we'll move out."

"I'm gonna strip out of this kit. I'll take my Glock and blades with me, that's it," Dalton told us.

Sarge took the pad and explained the radio check process. It was simple enough. Back at the TOC, one of the soldiers that have been with us for some time, Heath Whittle, would be on the radio. Heath was a Ham radio operator in the Before, and Sarge said he was very good with the radios. Either he or Wallner would be there for our check-in.

"What time does your watch have?" Sarge asked, looking at his own.

"8:45," I replied.

He nodded, "Ok, good." Then, looking over at Dalton, he asked, "You ready?"

Dalton nodded to the affirmative, and with a thumbs up, they headed off into the darkness again, leaving me with the truck. I grabbed my ruck and took it over to the palm with me. I pulled out my poncho and put it on the ground. I could feel the moisture from the ground the last time and didn't want my ass getting all itchy sitting on it. Laying it down, I took a seat and pulled an MRE out as well. I might as well have a snack while I sat here twiddling my thumbs.

Dalton followed Sarge to the building. They went inside, found the roof access ladder, and climbed up. On the roof, Sarge took his pack off and opened it up. He removed a small olive-green rectangle and unfolded two sets of legs on its bottom.

He and Dalton set the small Claymore mine up facing the opening. They connected a non-electric detonator to a short piece of detcord with a blasting cap crimped to it and inserted it into the well on the mine. Dalton set the tripwire, a very thin piece of black braided line, over the opening close to the side with the ladder and connected it to the detonator.

"That should do it," Sarge announced.

Dalton looked across the roof. "It's awful close."

"It is, but it's far enough. Plus, with the angle it's set at, we're not directly behind it. I've set these closer than this before without any real problems," Sarge replied, "Come on, let's go watch these clowns for a while. We've got a while before the sun comes up."

They went to the edge of the roof and set up the rifle. There was a short parapet wall around the roof that provided cover in addition to the trees in front of the building. While the trees helped screen them from observation, they also screened their objective from them.

The caravan had stopped at the Lake Ridge Winery. It was occupying the open field in front of the facility. The rows of grapes that were once well-manicured and tended were now mostly dead, looking like rows of tangled barbed wire from where they sat. Getting their first real look at the group, the sheer size of it took them.

"Damn, that's a lot of people," Sarge muttered, looking through the rifle scope.

Dalton had the binoculars up to his eyes. "Yes, it is. There's women, kids, old people. Some of everything."

"I see a lot of men. A lot of guns too."

Dalton scanned each of the fires he could see from his position. "I wish we had a spotting scope."

Sarge pulled his ruck open and took a large optic. It had a neoprene case around it, and he handed it to Dalton. "Here, lay this up there on the top of the wall and use it. I've got a small tripod, but the top of the wall will be steadier."

"Oh yeah, this is perfect," he replied as he unzipped the section of the case covering the objective lens.

Dalton pulled a hank of paracord from his pack and tied it to a ring on the scope, then tied the other end to his ruck before placing the scope on the top of the wall and settling in behind the huge optic. He spent a few seconds adjusting the focus to get it as clear as he could. The big lens gave him a much better view of the gypsy camp across the road, and that's just what it looked like.

"See if you can get some kind of a count on them," Sarge said from behind the rifle.

Dalton took a notepad and a pen from his pocket. "I'll try," he replied.

Dalton scanned each fire, taking notes on the many people gathered around each. He noted the number of people, sex, age and identified any weapons he saw. And there were plenty of weapons. Carbines and Ak patterns were the most prevalent rifles, but there were others. Although nearly everything was present, lever actions, bolt actions, shotguns, and numerous holstered pistols were also abundant.

As they were conducting their surveillance, Sarge asked a question.

"Serious talk, Gulliver."

"Ok," Dalton replied without looking away from the optic his eye was glued to.

Sarge adjusted the rifle before continuing. "Everyone is curious about you. Where you're from, background, that kind of shit."

"Not much to tell. I grew up in the North Georgia mountains. Childhood was rough as it was for many. I got into martial arts and found something I was really good at. Something that gave me confidence. Then I found blades, and that really changes things."

"I figured you were pretty well trained. Seeing how you handle anything with a blade makes that obvious. You ever go in the service?"

"No, didn't ever do it. I probably missed my calling, honestly. I went into law enforcement and was in corrections where I ran gang investigations and the like."

Sarge looked away from the rifle scope, "I knew you had some kind of training."

"I got some from the state. But most of my real training, I sought out myself. I was into the primitive survival thing for a long time, and I used to teach that. I also teach basic firearm skills as well as some advanced skills."

"How did you end up down here?"

"I was on a personal protection detail down south. The guy was a real asshole, and when things went to shit, I left them. He figured since he'd contracted me before it all happened that I would stay there and be his personal salvation. So I just left one night."

"He wanted you to stay around, huh?"

"Oh yeah, he thought I was going to go out and knock off the neighbors for him and take their food and shit." Dalton lifted his head from the optic and looked at the old man, "He had more than enough money to buy anything he wanted. He could have been completely prepared but chose not to. There wasn't enough food in his house to feed a man for a week. It's crazy."

"You didn't put a round in his grape?"

"Nah, why let him off easy?" Dalton replied and turned back to the optic.

Sarge snorted, "I guess a guy like that, that's used to having whatever they want when they want it, would have a pretty damn hard time living through something like this."

"I'm pretty sure he didn't make it a week. Just my opinion. Hopefully, he died miserably and painfully in the street somewhere."

The old man had prepared a code sheet for this operation for us. This one was far different from what he made me for the walk home. A couple of days before we launched, he called me over to his place and we sat at the kitchen table littered with papers. The papers were covered in sets of three letters and many, many rows of numbers.

"Morg, this is going to be a little different. While I highly doubt that these assholes have radios. The likelihood of them still having batteries is pretty damn slim. Regardless, we're going to encode everything."

Knowing we would be talking about radios, I'd brought the one I'd taken from Aaron and set it on the table. "Well, they do have some."

Sarge looked at the radio, "What in the hell is that?"

"I took it off Aaron. It's dead. He said he stole it from them before he left."

Sarge seized the radio, "How long have you had this? Why didn't you say something? He's been transmitting from here?"

"Calm your ass down. I got it from him like the first night he was here. He was scared to death, thinking we would assume he was part of them. I don't think he is. Besides, it's a commercial UHF radio. It's not going to reach all the way back to them. But," I reached out and took the radio, removing the battery, "we do know what frequency they are operating on."

Sarge took the radio back and looked at the back of it. "It's in the commercial band for sure." He looked up at me, and this will be a big help to us." He set the radio aside and tapped the papers on the table. "But we're here to talk about this."

He went on to explain what was laid out in front of him. For this operation, we would use what are called trigrams. Trigrams are a series of three letters that represent a word or phrase. It was first created by the NSA and added another layer of security to communications. The list was long, and I was surprised at just how complex it was.

There were two lists, an encode list, and a decode list. Each was in alphabetical order, either by word or phrase to encode or the three-letter groups for decoding. He then pulled out several small slips of paper. They looked like receipts with rows of numbers in groups of five.

"Now, this is where things get a little more complicated," Sarge continued. "Done correctly, this is a completely unbreakable code. Not even the NSA can break this code. It's probably overkill, but I think we need to be really careful on this mission."

He went on to explain the process for preparing a transmission. The first step is to create your message using the trigram. Then, pick the words and phrases you need and write the corresponding three-letter code for each. Once the message was encoded into the trigram, it was time to encrypt it with the one-time pad, or OTP.

He explained the process. Using the pad, you would identify the correct number for each letter. Some of these were two-digit combinations. You started with the second group of numbers on the first row. The first group was not used for the code. Instead, it was used to identify which pad was to be used.

The corresponding number for each letter, or pair of numbers, was written under the numbers on the OTP. For example, if the figure for a letter was two digits, you utilized two of the OTP digits, leaving no spaces. You would also skip the break between the groups of five on the OTP, essentially treating it as a single row of numbers.

Once your trigram was converted and written under the OTP numbers, you would then add or subtract the numbers, which would be identified in the initial line of the message. For example, if you were trying to subtract nine from two, you simply turned the two into twelve, resulting in a value of three. The ten was added merely for the math end, and it wasn't utilized.

The message would then be transmitted, the values derived from the simple math conducted on the two sets of numbers. The receiving station would have a matching OTP and would then do the reverse to decrypt the OTP and the list of trigrams to decode the message.

"It's not the fastest process in the world," Sarge concluded. "But it is one-hundred-percent secure."

I studied what we'd covered and looked up, "This is pretty easy. I get it."

"Good, you're going to be the one preparing and sending these messages back to Wallner."

"I'm assuming we're going to set the radios to dual monitor two frequencies? So I can communicate with both you and Wallner?"

"Correct. You just have to make sure you select the correct frequency before you transmit."

"You know, I'm worried about the distance we're going to from here. Comms might be a little sketchy."

"Wallner is putting up an antenna here, a tall one. We'll need to get an antenna for us. I want an HF and VHF antenna. You're a radio operator, right?" I nodded, and he added, "Good, you build a couple of antennas for us. I'm working on the PACE plan and SOI for us now."

"PACE? Speak English."

He shook his head, "I fucking hate civilians. We will also have a primary frequency, alternate, contingency, and emergency. SOI stands for signals operating instructions. It lays out call signs, the PACE, as well as some authentication."

Sarge went on to explain the SOI to me and the PACE plan. As well as the authentication codes we'd use in each transmission. The authentication code is the result of using a ten-letter word with no repeating letters. A number is assigned to each letter. A message is authenticated by giving two numbers that correspond to that letter. As long as the word is changed with each SOI, there is no way to compromise the authentication process.

We also had a numerical challenge consisting of single-digit numbers, for instance, seven. The way it worked is as follows.

Boomtown, boomtown, Ranger, authenticate three.
Ranger, authenticate four.

The total comes up to seven. Oddly enough, most people choose seven when asked this question, and for that reason, we would never use it.

Sarge decided it would be best to build the SOI together, and we spent about half an hour putting it together. When we finished, Sarge asked, "You got this?"

I nodded, "Yep, it makes sense. I really like it."

"Can you build antennas for these frequencies?"

"Sure, I'll get them put together."

I'd gone home to the shop and constructed a dipole antenna for the HF side of things, tuned to the frequency we would use. Then, I cut four pieces of number fourteen stranded wire nineteen inches long for the VHF side. Fortunately, I still have a couple of split pole BNC connectors, which make antenna construction easy.

Three of these were connected to the negative side of the split connector, with one connected to the positive. The bottom three would be separated by anything at hand, sticks, or whatever to create what looked like a pyramid with one wire running out of the top. Finally, the coax would connect to the adapter in the center, and the entire array would be hoisted into the air and connected to the radio. By increasing the height, we could achieve longer transmission distances.

A dipole antenna is pretty straightforward. Cut to a specific length depending on the frequency you intend to use. It is center fed, and one end is positive, and the other is negative. Because of the distance we would cover, I built it to create a NVIS antenna that allows for shorter-range HF comms.

I needed another piece of kit for this. First, I had to get a line up into a tree high enough to ensure comms. I took my last roll of bank line and an eight-ounce surf sinker for this. I tied the line to the sinker and poked around until I found a small stuff sack, probably from tent stakes or the like. I fed one end of the line down into the bag allowing it to coil up until I had about one hundred feet of line in the sack.

I checked the time; it was almost check-in time with the TOC. Climbing out from under the tree, I took the stuff sack with the line and weight from ruck. Just behind the palm tree was a tall pine tree. I prepared the throw bag and launched the weight into the canopy of the longleaf pine. I got lucky, and it found its way over a limb and dropped back to the ground. Since I had two antennas that I needed to put up, I tied the end of a long hank of 550 cord to the bank line. I quickly cut three long palmetto stems, lopping the fronds off and keeping the stem.

The bottom of the three legs of the VHF antenna had small round plastic insulators. I used the holes to stab the end of two stems into each hole. When I was done, the lower half of the antenna formed a triangle. There was also an insulator on the vertical element, and I secured the 550 cord to that and hoisted the array into the air. Once it was up, I connected the coax to the Harris PRC 152. These are the fancy DOD radios that I have found to be a real pain in the ass!

The dipole antenna was deployed in the same tree from a different limb. I tossed the weight on a large limb on the tree's opposite side, connected a coax to it, and hoisted it up. For HF, we will use the Yaesu 857 and the accompanying YT-100 tuner. I tied the two ends of the dipole about six feet off the ground, and it was ready to go. I brought a sealed lead acid battery to power it and had my small folding solar panel to keep it charged up.

Our primary frequency was in the VHF range and would be my initial attempt at communicating with ranch.

I was still smiling at the old man's choice of codewords. "Cheers, Cheers, Norm."

Have you lima Charlie.

Part of this procedure required authentication to ensure I was talking to the right person. It was straightforward, a ten-letter word with no repeating characters. These were assigned a number from zero to ten. For this mission, the word was *AFTERSHOCK*. A was zero; K obviously was nine.

"Authenticate Roger Charlie."

I authenticate four, eight.

"Message to follow. 8 1 7 9 7 2 7 9 8 3, break, 7 4 8 2 8 0 8 1 8 4, break, 8 3 8 9 8 9 8 9. Norm out."

Receive all.

I sat back and stifled a laugh, thinking about the old sitcom, shit, sitcoms in general, for that matter. I wish I had more of that kind of mindless entertainment on DVD. Not to mention a DVD player I could connect to the TV to watch them on. Unfortunately, the few videos we have on the iPad are wearing thin at this point. Not that there was a lot of time to sit and watch a movie. But I sure did wish I had that iPad with me under this damn palm tree!

Then I remembered another piece of kit I brought with me and dug it out. I had a small Uniden scanner, the CB75XLT. While this is a very basic scanner, it is a very handy piece of kit. I took the small single earpiece I brought for it, plugged it into the device, and pushed the small speaker into my ear. Then, turning it on, I set it to *search* and let it do its thing.

"Well, Gulliver," Sarge sat back and wiped his eyes. "I think it's the best call to wait until daylight. You should get some sleep."

Dalton's eye was still glued to the spotting scope, "I'm good, thanks. Enjoying the show."

Sarge kicked his ruck against the wall, "Well, I'm gonna get some damn sleep."

"I'll wake you up when the sun comes up."

Sarge pulled his hat down over his eyes, "I won't need you to wake me up."

It was getting hard to stay awake. I should have brought coffee. I did have a bottle of tea with me, but it was long gone. So, to stay awake, I was eating the M&M's from the MRE one at a time. Eating isn't the right word, more like I was letting them melt completely in my mouth. It takes a while to let them melt one at a time, and it was helping keep me alert. Periodically I would get up and walk around to stretch my legs. It felt good, but I didn't move far or much before getting back under my tree and going back to the candies.

The Bearcat was still on and scrolling through the bands. In normal times it picks up all kinds of transmissions. And there's way more of them than you would think. We are immersed in RF signals at all times. But in this new world, the scanner was utterly silent. It never even broke squelch until it did.

I was kind of dozy when a voice came over the scanner loud and clear. I sat bolt upright and quickly locked the frequency on the device.

Hey Chief.
Yeah.
Xerxes wants to see you.

As I listened, I pulled out my notebook and jotted down the time of the call and call signs used. It wasn't much information, but it was information. I'd pass this info when we all got back together.

Dalton took the spotting scope down, placed it on his ruck, and leaned against the wall. The fires across the street had all burned out some time ago. He'd watched as the various members of the group fell asleep and passed out in a couple of cases. The booze surprised him. That there still was booze to be had after a year. Not that there was much, it was only a small cluster of people drinking around one fire.

Dalton rubbed his eyes, leaned his head back, and rested. He checked his watch, and it was nearly four AM; he had a little time. The soft glow of morning would soon start to paint the sky. No need for an alarm of any kind. That and the fact the old man was snoring only a few feet from him.

Sarge was right, as it turned out. Dalton didn't have to wake him up. At slightly past five, the old man sat up and looked around. He looked at Dalton and said, "Told ya," before reaching for his thermos and pouring himself a cup of coffee, and passing the bottle to Dalton. "Here, wake yourself up."

Dalton took it, removed a titanium cup from his ruck, and poured a dose of the black elixir for himself. He saluted the old man with the cup, "Thanks. I need this."

Sarge got to his feet and walked over to look over the wall. The camp was quiet, with only a dull orange glow remaining where a couple of larger fires had burned down. "Anything worth mentioning?"

Dalton shook his head, "No, they're all pretty much lying right where they were when you stretched out."

"Morgan call in anything?" Dalton shook his head. Sarge sipped his coffee. "You sure you're up to this?"

"Sure, nothing to it but to do it. They're certainly not going to be expecting me to be part of the group they're going to hit. I'm pretty good at talking myself into and out of about anything."

Sarge let out a breath, "To be honest, I'm a little nervous about this. I don't like sending you in there with no backup, no real overwatch, and no way to get you out of there if it goes south."

"It won't. Trust me. This will go fine."

"Well, get your shit together, I reckon."

Dalton got his gear in order and slung his pack. Then, drawing his pistol, he press-checked it to make sure it was ready should it come to that. Once he was ready, he looked at the old man, "Cheery oh! Old chap."

"Knock 'em dead."

Dalton carefully removed the tripwire for the claymore and stepped onto the ladder. "I'll be back sometime tonight."

"Don't stretch your dick out for no reason down there."

Dalton smiled broadly, "Nevah!"

Sarge keyed his radio, "Norm, Swamprat. He's on the move."

Hearing the radio crackle, I got to my feet. "Roger that." Stepping out from under the tree and stretched my legs. I hadn't been particularly nervous sitting here under the tree. The ride was a little nerve-racking. But once I got here and had time to relax a little, I was fine. Now, I was getting nervous. My stomach was starting to twitch, and I hated that feeling.

To make matters worse, there was nothing I could do. I couldn't see anything from where I was. All I could do was sit and wait. If I was over on the roof, at least I could watch. More importantly, I could ask the old man why he transmitted like that in the open. It made me nervous.

Dalton moved silently through the thin strip of woods to the north. After about half a mile, he walked out to the edge of the trees and took a knee. He spent several minutes looking and listening. He took the time to rub dirt on his hands, face, and clothes. Camouflage isn't always what we think of. Then, not hearing or seeing anything, he moved out onto the road, turned south, and started walking.

CHAPTER 11

Dalton couldn't see the camp from the road. There was a large hill that rose gently on the left side. The convoy was camped on the top of the hill, and he wouldn't be able to see it until he was practically in front of it. He was casually watching the sides of the road looking for potential sentries and was surprised he didn't see any. They were either very good, or their security was practically nonexistent.

He started to wonder about this crew when the sign for the Lake Ridge Winery came into view. The tops of some of the trucks were just visible over the crest of the hill. He was thinking of what to do. How to get into this camp. He'd always thought there would be some guards posted that would intercept him, and he could use the opportunity to talk his way in. But he hasn't been approached by anyone, which caused a bit of a conundrum.

He kept walking, not turning his head to look towards the camp. He stared straight ahead while taking in as much as he could. As he passed the sign, he caught movement out of the corner of his eye.

"Hey man," a voice called out.

Dalton visibly jumped as he spun around, a feigned response. A long-haired man sat against the base of the sign. He was slowly getting to his feet using an old pump shotgun to assist himself.

Dalton said, doing his best to act surprised, "Woah, you scared me!" And looked around.

"Sorry, man, just wasn't expecting anyone. We don't see too many people just walking down the road these days. Where you headed?"

Dalton shrugged. "No real plan. Just kind of wandering."

"You hungry? You look hungry."

"I hate to impose."

"You're not imposing, man," the scruffy man replied with a grimy smile. "We've got a lot of people up there, and there's plenty. Come on."

"I don't want to piss anyone up there off, you know, another mouth to feed."

The man slapped his back, "No worries, man. You're safe here. No one will fuck with us. Come on up, get something to eat."

Dalton followed the man up the driveway. The camp came into view as they walked. The occupants were starting to come to life, and the sounds of camp waking up began to fill the air. People coughing, children crying and fussing, the sound of an ax splitting wood. Finally, coming into the camp proper, the man guided Dalton over to a Hummer covered in a tacky Mad Max paint scheme.

"Hey Chief," the man called out. A large man with distinct Native American features turned around.

"Yo," he replied.

"Hey, this guy was wandering down the road, and he's hungry. Think we can get him something to eat?"

The big man turned around. "Sure, come on," he waved.

"Chief will get you sorted out. Relax, man, you're not alone now."

Dalton followed Chief through the camp. "Come on," Chief said. "I'll give you a tour." Chief pointed out areas of camp as they moved. "The kitchen is back over here. They usually do a pretty good job depending on what we find." Finally, he turned and looked at Dalton, "You're in luck. We got a cow yesterday."

"Damn, how many people do you have here?"

"About a hundred."

"You can set up your camp anywhere you want. There's water over in the kitchen. If you need anything," Chief pointed at an old truck with tables set up around it, "that's kind of a store of sorts. It's barter, so I hope you have something to trade."

"I don't really need anything."

Chief stopped and pointed at a couple of trucks. "That area is off-limits."

Dalton looked over at the three MRAPs. Several men were either sitting in chairs or standing around a couple of large tents. "That the head shed?" Dalton asked.

"It is."

Dalton pointed at the trucks, "Where did you guys come up with those from? This like some military unit?"

Chief's eyes narrowed, "Does this look like a military unit to you?"

"I've heard of units that went out on their own when they realized the government was done. I've seen another one, with trucks like these not too far away from here."

"Oh yeah? Where?"

"Little town east of here, Eustis."

Chief turned to face him, "Really? What did they have?"

"A couple of those, Hummers and some other regular trucks, an old Suburban." Dalton looked around. "You mind if I hit the kitchen over there and see if I can get some grub?"

"Sure, go ahead. I'll find you in a bit."

Dalton found his way over to the kitchen that was made up of a couple of canopies and a tent. At best, it was a ramshackle affair with some folding tables and camp chairs scattered about. Several people were in the kitchen at work getting cooking fires started. Over one of the fires, a large kettle was placed. Dalton casually walked past it and glanced in. It was full of water with debris floating in it.

"I wouldn't drink that yet. Needs to boil first," a woman with a thick southern accent said.

"Looks like it."

"You knew?" She asked.

Dalton nodded, "Yes, ma'am. Walking down the road this morning and was invited in."

"Well, it'll be a bit before food is ready."

"No problem, I'll check back later."

Being a student of history and *primitive* cultures around the world, Dalton paid particular attention to certain things. In the modern world, so much is taken for granted. Daily life's labor and physical effort have been eradicated in most cases. Tasks such as hauling water, firewood, food, and the acquisition of anything else daily life requires have been eliminated. At least for the *developed* world.

When the necessity of these burdens returns, it quickly becomes clear just what is essential. Dalton observed the numerous containers in use in the camp. Everything from Jerry cans to two-liter bottles. Canteens, fancy water bottles favored by many in the Before, were undoubtedly present. However, it was ubiquitous clear plastic water bottles that were omnipresent. They seemed to be everywhere, with even the children carrying them.

The kitchen was another place where the types of containers caught his eye. It's typical for a village to possess at least one and, if prosperous, several large metal kettles. They could be aluminum, stainless steel, cast iron, or even cheap pot metal. But they will be metal containers of significant size.

These containers are used for everything from purifying water to boiling the laundry. This camp did not have what Dalton considered a *large* pot. The kettle sitting on the fire at the moment wasn't more than three gallons. And while that seems large, most commercial kitchens contained pots of significantly larger volume. It made cooking for large groups much easier.

Instead, what this camp had were numerous smaller pots. Ones you would be accustomed to seeing in any home kitchen. Dalton had dropped his ruck on the ground and sat with back against the tire of a flatbed truck. The truck was antique, more rust than anything. But the location provided a clear view of the kitchen. And he was very interested in just how they kept all these people fed.

Watching the kitchen crew prepare the morning meal crushed any appetite Dalton possessed. Several plants were being prepared for the pot, some he knew to be less than safe to consume. They were even chopping grass into fine pieces. Of course, humans are not designed to eat grass. But it was the *livestock* that really did it for him. He watched as the woman with the thick southern accent pulled a pair of welding gloves on before throwing a sheet off a large cage.

The cage was full of cats, both adult, and kittens. Picking up a small club, she opened the top of the cage, keeping it closed as much as possible, and reached in to seize one of the terrified animals. It hissed and went rigid as cats will do. It tried to claw her, to bite as it spit. Another woman quickly shut the top of the cage as the first began to beat the cat in the head with the club until it eventually went limp. Once it had, she laid it on a table and delivered two more forceful blows to the animal's head, cracking the skull and spilling the contents of the skull over the table. He'd seen enough.

Dalton wandered the camp making mental notes of the people. What he found was not what he was expecting. While many people were occupying the camp, few appeared to be in fighting shape, and even fewer were armed, at least not openly armed. There were many armed people around, however. And it appeared there was some sort of division or separation of the people in the camp.

Most of the armed individuals were clustered around a couple of specific fires. There were always several of these armed folks wandering around the camp. They were the security force for whoever was running things. Dalton walked past the *off-limits* area when I voice called out to him.

"Hey, big man!" A voice called out.

Dalton looked over and saw Chief waving him over. "Come over here."

He walked up to the cluster of camp chairs arranged around the fire that several men occupied. Dalton walked up and greeted them with a nod as they looked him up and down.

"What's your name?" One of the seated men asked.

"Dalton."

The man leaned back in his chair, locking his hands behind his head. "Chief here says you came through Eustis. That true?"

"Yeah, I was there for a few days, but I didn't really care for it."

"Why not?"

"There's a guy there calling himself a Sheriff. Kind of runs the town, and I'm not too fond of being told what to do."

The man studied Dalton for a minute. Then, standing up, he said, "Charles Tabor," and held his hand out. Dalton shook his hand, and Tabor pointed to an empty chair, saying, "Have a seat, Dalton."

Karl and his guys were standing in front of their Jeep as everyone was loading up to head out for the day's training. Dad, Danny, and Thad were talking about the sawmill and told the guys they were going to take a detour and check it out on their way to the ranch. Mel herded the girls into the MRAP as Mom waved goodbye from the porch.

Jamie was behind the wheel of the big truck as Mel took a seat and leaned forward, asking, "You going by Gina's to pick them up?"

As Jamie released the airbrake on the truck, she replied, "Yes, ma'am!"

Dad, Danny, and Thad got into the little red truck and took off before the others were ready. As Thad pulled out onto the county road, he said, "I hope that thing is still functional."

"I bet it will be," Danny replied. "Not like anyone has been using it or could even do anything with it."

"Be a good little job too. Having the mill," Dad offered.

"We're about to find out," Thad replied.

They drove past the ranch and turned onto County Road 439. About six miles later, they were turning into the gate of the sawmill. A sign hung out front, B. G. Sawmill. The gate swung open, and the drive was littered with leaves and other debris. It was obvious there hadn't been any vehicles coming through in some time.

"Looks good so far," Thad said as he stopped at the gate. "Butch, hop out and look at the driveway. Just want to make sure there aren't any surprises in the road there."

Dad opened his door, "Good idea."

He walked out in front of the truck and looked at the dirt two-track. As he moved down the path, Thad followed. The route was clear, and they were standing in front of the mill in a moment. It consisted of several large machines under a high tin roof. There were still logs on some of the machine's boards on others. It was as if they had just shut down for lunch.

"Look at this," Danny said. "It's all here. So if we can just get that generator over here, this will probably run just fine."

"If we can find that log trailer with the grapple, we'll be able to move timber in here pretty easy," Dad observed.

Danny pointed to a large pile of logs, "There's a lot of logs already here. We could cut a lot of boards with what's here."

"We need to look at the motors and see what voltage they are," Thad said as he wiped the dust from a nameplate.

Danny looked over his shoulder as he did, "What's it say?"

"480 volts."

"Perfect," Danny replied. "That's what the generator at the plant is. It'll work."

Thad wiped more dust off the motor, "We'll go to the plant this afternoon and talk with the engineers. See when we can get it over here."

"Don't forget," Dad interrupted, "Morgan is an electrician too."

"Yeah," Danny agreed, "but he isn't here right now."

"He'll be back. After hearing everything he's done since all this shit started, I have no doubt he'll be back."

Thad chuckled, shaking his head, "He is a mess."

The front legs of Terry's chair were off the floor as he leaned against a console in the small control room of the plant. Audie was explaining what he needed to and what he intended to do. Terry sat and listened as he stared at the ceiling, his hands cupped behind his head. After Audie laid out his plan, Terry's chair slammed to the floor.

"This sounds like a great idea. It'll be fun, and it'll help with providing food for the community."

"Exactly," Audie replied, "and it'll be a whole lot of fun."

Terry leaped to his feet. "Let's take a walk."

The two men walked through the plant, stopping to examine various pieces of machinery. Audie pulled a role of surveyor's tape from his pocket and would wrap a piece around each part they decided would be a candidate for their upcoming project.

"I need a truck," Audie stated as he wrapped a piece of flagging around a long auger drive.

"You'll have to talk to Morgan about that. We have the boom truck that will help with some of the stuff you need to get."

"For sure, but a pickup would be a lot better."

Terry turned and started to walk away, "Let's start pulling the parts we'll need. I'm sure Morgan or someone will stop by at some point today."

"Let's get some tools," Audie replied as he turned to follow.

Karl laid on the ground beside Mel. The Minimi chattered in her hand as she fired short bursts. Karl looked downrange at the target those rounds were chewing up. He smiled and looked over at her, patted her shoulder, and ran a finger across his throat, the signal to a ceasefire. Mel let off the trigger and pushed the ear protection up on her head.

"Mel, you don't need to shoot anymore. You've got this," he laughed, "you're just wasting ammo at this point. You can't possibly get better."

Mel looked downrange at the target at others around her continued to fire. She smiled as she admired her work. "I like it. I'd like to shoot some more."

Karl got to his knees, "I know it's fun. There's nothing like full auto to wake you up in the morning. If you still want to work on something, we can go over the loading and malfunction drills."

Mel rose to one knee. "We've done that already. I think I have it down."

Karl patted her back once again, "You do. You're as ready as I think I can make you."

While Mel had the little belt-fed machinegun down, others were still on the line. Mel removed the belt from the weapon and picked it up by the carrying handle, and walked over to the Hummer where others who had also achieved an acceptable level of proficiency were also hanging out. Placing the weapon on the hood, she turned and leaned against the bumper beside Dad.

"You handle that thing pretty good," he said.

Mel smiled, "I've always liked shooting. Morgan used to teach me." Her smile faded, "I was a little slow coming around to this new reality. But that's over now, and I'm not sitting on the sidelines anymore."

Dad puts his arm around her shoulder. "You know, after all this went down, the way things changed as they did, I never worried about you and Morgan. He was preparing for this his whole life. I always thought it was kind of silly." He paused to look at her, "We used to talk about it, often."

"He never went overboard with it," Mel replied. "We never really sacrificed anything for all the stuff he did. He used to say, we have to live for today while we prepare for tomorrow."

"Because you'll need those good memories when the time comes," Dad finished.

Mel smiled, "Told you too, huh?"

Dad laughed, "As I said, we talked about it often."

Mel wandered over to the tree where Erin was sitting with Little Bit. Ruckus was on the tree, Little Bit was running around the base, and the little limb rat played a game of hide and seek. Erin was laughing at her when Mel dropped down to sit beside her.

Erin looked at her, then back to the thunderous firing line. "Taking a break?"

Mel leaned back to rest on her hands. "No, Karl said I was doing good and just wasting ammo at this point."

Erin shook her head, "You're nuts. You know that, don't you?"

Mel shrugged, "I just want to be capable. If some asshole needs killed, I don't want to have to rely on someone else to do the killing."

"Not me. I don't want any part of it. I mean, shooting is fun, kinda. But I just don't think I could do it."

Mel looked over at her friend, "Erin, I know for a fact that if it came down to you or them, it's going to be them. You have it in you, you just don't want to, and neither do I. But I'll be ready in case it happens."

"You're probably right."

"How are you liking the new house?"

Erin's eyes rolled back, and she looked up into the sky. "It's sooo nice! Just to be alone with Travis, just the two of us. It'd been so long. It's really nice. The weirdest part is the quiet. You know, we lived with a bunch of people in that house, and it was never really quiet. That house is silent, and Travis isn't exactly a big talker," she laughed.

Mel put her arm around Erin's shoulder, "Well, you're welcome at my house any time."

"I just don't want to be a bother."

Mel laughed, "believe me, girl, having you come over to hang out with me would never be a bother."

Erin kind of looked over at Mel, "Well, I'm not trying to be a bitch or anything, but Morgan is a little intimidating. I mean, he never smiles or anything. Seems intense all the time."

Now Mel's head rocked back as she laughed, "You just don't know him. Yes, he is busy all the time and has a lot on his mind. But he loves to laugh, and he's pretty funny. You'll see. And personally, I think he's pretty cute too. But I'm biased." She said, winking at Erin. They both chuckled.

"Just giving you my first impression, you know. Not an accusation or anything."

"Don't worry. He's happy that you guys are there. Having Travis here adds another guy to help with things. Having you here gives us a nurse. Plus, you're my kind of bitch," Mel replied with a smile.

"Who you are calling a bitch, bitch?" Erin replied, and the two laughed some more.

As the two women chatted, Karl asked Ted and Thad to step off the line for a sidebar conversation. Then, seeing the men group up, Dad walked over to them as well.

Karl started the conversation. "I know Morgan and Linus aren't here to discuss this with them, but I think we should issue these weapons out along with ammo to the people we're training here. What do you guys think?"

Ted didn't hesitate to respond, "Good idea. Of course, it was going to happen at some point anyway."

"I know Morgan and Sarge would agree, and Thad said that having some trained people spread around would be good for us," Ted finished.

"Good," Karl replied, "I just think it's the right thing to do."

"Plus, we won't have to haul them back and forth for training," Thad noted.

Karl turned to look at the line of trainees. "How do you think they're coming along?" He asked Ted.

"I'm surprised with how quick they're picking it all up. Granted, we haven't got to any SUT stuff, but they are doing very well on the simple movements we've been working on."

"What's SUT?" Dad asked.

"Small unit tactics," Karl replied.

"Ah, fire and maneuver," Dad acknowledged. Then he posed a question. "If you're going to let these folks take these weapons home, shouldn't they be taught how to disassemble and clean them? The training you guys have given on the use and handling has been great, but no one has covered that. Not yet, at least."

Karl nodded, "That's where I was going, Butch. Let's shut the line down and get them broke up into groups and get everyone trained on it." He looked up into the sky, "It's midafternoon, plenty of time to teach this task."

"I'll go break them up," Ted replied.

"Have you guys heard from Morgan?" Karl asked.

Ted nodded. "I know they made their check-in. They've found the group and are conducting surveillance on them." I have a radio, and if anything critical comes into the TOC, I'll know about it."

Dad laughed, "I know I've been out of the Army for a while now. But what the hell is a TOC?"

"Tactical Operations Center," Ted replied, adding, "Don't worry, Butch, you'll catch on."

"Well, the Army was a lot different back then. You guys do shit a hell of a lot different than we did."

Thad smiled that broad smile of his, "And we do things way different than the Army today!"

Karl made a face, "I can see that," and chuckled.

The rest of that afternoon was spent with the trainees broke up into groups based on their issued weapons. Mike, Ted, and Karl's guys gave detailed instructions on the disassembly and reassembly of the various weapons. First, the students were cross-trained in every weapon in the arsenal. Then they were instructed on how to clean and maintain their weapons. It was quickly realized that more cleaning kits were needed, and Mike made a note to look through their armory to see how many more could be had.

"You serious?" Bubba asked Karl when he was told to take his rifle home with him.

"It ain't gonna do you any good stored in the armory. Everyone is taking their assigned weapon with them." Karl took a notepad from his pocket and asked for the Ak, which Bubba handed over. He recorded the serial number and handed it back.

"Why'd you do that?" Bubba asked.

"I'm retired Army, Bubba. This is the way it's always been done. Not to mention it only makes sense to know who has what weapon."

"But," Bubba started, "this is my rifle now?"

"Yes, it is. You are now officially part of the defense force."

Dad, Danny, and Thad were leaning on the Hummer, talking about stopping by the plant on their way home to discuss getting the generator.

"I'm excited to get it and see if that equipment will run," Thad said.

"Me too. It'll be nice to have access to lumber," Danny added.

"Shit," Dad started, "I'd just like *something* to do," adding a laugh.

Danny lifted his rifle off the truck, "I think we're going to have something to do soon."

"Not the kind of *something* I'm looking for. I've been there and done that already."

There was no smile on Thad's face this time, "I sure don't want it." Instead, he looked at the Ak he'd traded his coach gun for, "I like guns and damn sure think we need them. But I don't want to have to use them. I like to think of them as more of a deterrent. If everyone has them, you gotta think twice about what you're doing or saying."

Dad nodded, "An armed society is a polite society. That's just a fact."

Thad looked across the field, "Looks like this is winding down. You guys want to go to the plant?"

"Yeah, let's go. I'll go tell Ted we're heading out."

At the plant, they found Audie, Terry, and Baker standing in the open roll-up door in front of the huge pile of corn. As soon as they pulled up, Audie started smiling.

"Just the boys I wanted to see!" He shouted as they got out of the truck.

"You're just the people we're looking for as well!" Danny replied.

"What can we do for you?" Baker asked.

"We need that generator you have," Thad answered.

Audie looked at Terry, and the two shared a smile. "How about a trade?" Terry asked.

"What do you need?"

Audie nodded at the little red pickup. "I need that for a little while."

Thad looked over his shoulder at the truck. "That's a fair deal."

"What the hell are you going to do with a three-phase 480-volt generator?" Terry asked.

"We're going to try and get a sawmill running. We checked it out this morning, and that generator will run it," Danny said.

"Well, the plant is running fine right now. So you can have it, but if we have a problem here, we may be calling you guys to bring it back," Baker said.

"That's fine," Danny said, "the plant is far more important than a sawmill. But getting some lumber to build a couple of things would be huge."

"I haven't seen the generator," Dad said, "but is it a typical military unit? On a trailer?"

"Oh yeah, it can be towed," Scott replied.

"Audie, why don't you ride home with us, and you can take the truck back home," Thad offered.

"That's a good idea," Danny said, "and you can stay for supper."

Audie patted his belly, "Now you're talking!"

As they were shooting the shit, the convoy passed by on their way home. Horns honked, and everyone waved. The group chatted a little about their respective projects for a while as they walked through the plant. Audie pointed out the equipment he intended to use for the mill. The conversation proved fruitful because everyone had a different perspective, and a couple of new ideas were tossed into the mix.

"I like the idea of a large round water trough, Butch," Audie said.

"Cut a hole in the bottom, and that screw auger you've got will be able to push the meal into a hopper of some kind," Dad replied.

"That'd be easy. I already know how I'll mount the wheels and the motor to turn the top one."

"This has been fun and all," Danny said as he stretched, "but I'm starving."

"You ready to go, Audie?" Thad asked.

"Yeah, let's go!"

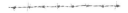

Our radio check-ins were set twelve hours apart. The planning that goes into these kinds of missions on the military side is pretty impressive. The codes we're using are very interesting. But they are only one part of the SOI or Signals Operating Instructions. I didn't realize it when I was walking home, and Sarge gave me that notebook that it was an SOI. But this, this was much more.

The following check-in was coming up, so I took out the notebook and verified the message to be sent. I hadn't heard anything from Sarge, and we were keeping off the radios as a precaution. If there was trouble, he would let me know. That left me sitting under the palm tree trying to stay awake, and that task was getting more and more difficult. To aid in staying alert, I would get up periodically and walk around a little. I never left the sight of the truck, just enough to get some blood flowing and get my brain in gear.

I used these little walks to check the antennas and do a minimal security check. I kept my ears open at all times, though my hearing was a little reduced because of the earbud for the scanner that I was wearing. The scanner also helped with staying alert. I was jarred awake a couple of times when the scanner picked up the group's radio traffic. It was never anything of much interest, but I filled out the report Sarge taught each time I heard it.

The SALUTE report is a standard military method of reporting activity. It's more suited for visual information, but it worked for this as well. The way the report works is as follows:

S- Size, number of individuals, vehicles

1. Activity, what are they doing

L- Location, pretty obvious
U- Uniform, what are they wearing
T- Time, self-explanatory
E- Equipment includes weapons, radios, and anything else that gives insight into the group's capabilities.

A shorter version called a SALT report also uses the same procedure as the SALUTE. It's used to update a preliminary report. I asked Sarge why we were doing these.

"Seems kind of silly to be playing soldier to me," I said to the old man.

"Let's be serious for a minute, Morgan. There's a reason we do things a certain way. Uniformity. If we use one standard for things, everyone does it the same way. Everyone will learn to do this, this way."

"Ok, I get that. Makes sense." With a confused shake of my head, I asked, "Why are we starting this kind of thing now?"

"I should have got on all this sooner. That's on me. Honestly, I didn't think DOD would be around any longer. But they are and will be. DOD is the only functioning branch of the United States. They're it. And like it or not, we're part of it. So some changes are coming soon, for the better."

"Like what?" I'd asked.

"We'll get to that later. But, right now, you need to get these things down, so pay attention."

I was still curious to see what he had up his sleeve. I learned a long time ago that the old man would tell you what he wanted you to know when he wanted you to know it. So, making my way back to the palm tree, I turned on the radio and prepared to send my message.

"Norm, Norm, Cheers." The reply didn't come immediately this time, and I had to make the call a few times. Eventually, I did get a response.

Norm, have you Lima Charlie.

"Authenticate Foxtrot Kilo."

Authenticate one, nine.

"Roger that, message to follow."

I gave a message that said we're still here, and there is still nothing going on. Wallner acknowledged the message, and that was it. Back to trying to stay awake. Dalton would be out until sometime late tonight probably. He made it in and would have to figure out how to get out of there at some point.

I was considering the situation when the radio broke squelch on the team channel.

Norm, Gulliver inbound.

I was shocked by that. It was early afternoon. I assumed he'd wait until after dark to get out.

"Roger, standing by to stand by."

Sarge watched Dalton through the spotting scope as he walked down the driveway with another man that was only a little short of Dalton's towering height and obviously of Native American descent. He switched to the rifle and kept the crosshair on the man as the two made their way to the road. He was ready to drop the big Indian at any moment, but it proved unnecessary. When they got to the road, the two shook hands, and Dalton turned and started walking south, and the other man turned and walked back up the driveway.

Dalton walked a couple of miles down the road until he came to the bottom of a hill that provided him complete cover from the camp and crossed the road and walked into the thin screen of trees before turning back north. He moved with purpose but stopped at random intervals to conduct listening halts.

He did this out of habit even though he knew it wasn't necessary after his time in the camp. The group used the appearance of force as their only form of security. The only visible security, like patrols, was focused inward. There was no real outward security, save the occasional sentry. It was as if they were more concerned about their own people being a threat than any outside one.

Sarge stayed on the roof but took the tripwire to the Claymore down and prepared the gear to move. He kept looking to the south for Dalton as he worked. He wanted an AAR, After Action Report, and he wanted it now. I decided to get out from under the tree and get my blood flowing. I was dreading the drive home. As tired as I was, the possibility of falling asleep was substantial. Maybe one of them would drive.

I was squeezing MRE cheese onto a cracker when the radio sounded, *Moving to you.*

I gave a terse *roger* in reply and focused on my snack. I always thought the best thing in the MRE was the cheese and crackers. Even though the crackers would have made a good video challenge like the kids were always doing before. Trying to eat those things with nothing to drink was nye impossible!

I was sitting on the hood of the Suburban when I heard them. They were moving steady but cautiously. When they made it to the truck, the old man dropped his ruck and looked at the antennas I had set up.

"Damn, good job, Morg."

Dalton dropped his ruck and went straight to the case of MREs. He quickly picked one out and tore into it. Then, instead of using the heater, and ate it cold. And instead of opening it, he cut one corner off and squeezed it into his mouth like a big square bag of toothpaste. Sarge started asking him questions immediately.

Taking a drink from his canteen, Sarge said, "Alright, Gulliver, out with it."

Dalton took a notepad from his pocket, leaned back against the truck, took a deep breath, and began.

"They've got somewhere right around one hundred, maybe one ten in there. The majority are non-combatants. I counted thirty-seven that were visibly armed. Their security is shit, as in nonexistent." He took another squeeze from the pouch. "Nearly all of their security, if you can call it that, is focused inwards. I saw a couple of sentries, but that was it."

"So, they aren't too worried about being attacked but are worried about internal threats. That's interesting," Sarge said, thinking aloud.

"The people in there are just normal folks. Good people, really. The conditions they're living in are rough, to say the least. They offered me food, but I'm not a fan of cat."

"Cat?" I asked, unsure I heard him correctly.

He nodded as he squeezed the last remnants from the pouch. "Yeah, cats. They treat them like livestock. Have a big cage full of them. I watched the cook woman put on welding gloves, reach in and grab one, and club it to death. Fucking eating cats."

"Holy shit. I mean, we used to joke about it. I never actually thought anyone did." I was feeling queasy. But then, I knew if I were hungry enough, I'd eat anything I could kill.

Sarge shook his head, "Desperate people is all. You see Tabor in there?"

"Oh yeah. Boy, does he have a hard on for you, Leftenant" Dalton laughed.

"He has that effect on people," I added with a smile.

Dalton pointed at me, "He wants your ass worse than him, and that's saying something! He really hates you," he nodded at Sarge, then at me, "but you're on a whole different level. Kept talking about taking that star and keeping it as a trophy."

Sarge snorted, "Now who has that effect?"

"We should have just lined them up and shot their asses," I replied.

"See," Sarge snapped, pointing at me, "that's why he wants to kill your ass. You're just a mean son-of-bitch."

Now I laughed, "Whatever, Kettle."

"I think we're coming at this all wrong," Dalton interrupted.

"How so?" Sarge asked.

"The people with them aren't really *with them*. They're there out of convenience. Safety in numbers and all that. I didn't see anyone chained up or anything, but some of them, I think, are not there by choice. So if we conduct the ambush we have planned, a lot of innocent people are going to get killed for no reason."

Sarge was rubbing his chin, "I was already thinking that."

Dalton tore an MRE cookie open, "I think a simple decapitation strike on them would be enough."

Sarge nodded and pointed at him, "That's just what we need to do," he nodded.

"I don't know," I said, "that's going to get a little complicated."

"How so?" Sarge asked.

"How are we going to do that? I mean, we start shooting at those assholes with all those people around, and some of them will get killed anyway."

"I have an idea on that," Dalton said as he shook the cookie crumbs from the pouch.

Sarge watched him chew for a minute, hell, less than a minute, before he got irritated. "Well, you gonna share your brilliant plan?"

Dalton took a pull from his canteen before he laid it out. "Well,

Morgan has a point about knowing who is where in their convoy. I know which trucks him and his security people ride in. That parts pretty easy. The hard part is going to be knowing when they get on the move."

Sarge nodded, "I think I see where you're going with this."

Dalton nodded at me, "How many batteries do you have for that radio?"

"Three," Sarge answered for me.

"That's enough."

"You're not planning what I think you are? Are you?" I asked.

"The only way to know when they'll move and where they'll go is to keep an eye on them," Dalton answered.

"You want us to leave you here to what, follow them?"

Dalton tore another MRE pouch open, "You know another way?"

I pointed at the pouch, "You know there are only two cases of those, right?"

"That's why I'm eating so much, can't carry two cases in my ruck."

"Enough supper talk, knuckleheads," Sarge barked, "Back to the business at hand. We need to write up a new SOI for Dalton. You take the PRC-152 and the batteries. We'll set up a call schedule," he stopped and thought for a moment. "I'm also going to send some of Wallner's boys out as a QRF," he squinted at Dalton, "just in case you get your big ass in a bind."

"No worries, Leftenant!" Dalton said in a deep voice, "I shall endeavor to persevere!"

I stretched, "I'm gonna take a nap while you two tactitards plan out your secret squirrel shit. I haven't slept at all."

Sarge didn't hesitate, "Might as well, you're as useless as a cock flavored lollipop at a lesbian convention." Damn, the old man was fast.

I just stood there blinking as Dalton doubled over in hee haw laughter. All I could come up with was, "Da fuck?"

"You're playing pee-wee ball in the big league," Sarge sniped as he took a step towards me and put a hand on my shoulder. "Don't worry, Son. Yer balls'll drop one of these days."

"You're driving home," I replied and opened the back door of the truck and laid out on the seat, sticking my feet out the opposite window.

Sarge watched this and looked at Dalton, who'd finally recovered from his hysterics, "Da fuck?" And I laughed.

As was the custom, Kay was standing on the porch when the crew from the ranch pulled up. She always did this when anyone returned from a day away from home. Only now, Mom was standing there with her. The two women had become fast friends and spent a lot of time together. It was funny to hear the two talk about the other as the compliments were nearly identical. *She's such a dear. It's like I've known her my whole life. She's such a good cook. And she likes things neat and clean.* I'd heard these and more from both of them with only minor variations between them. It was kinda spooky.

Little Bit jumped from the big truck, Ruckus clinging to her back for all she was worth, and ran up the stairs, wrapping her arms around Mom's legs.

"Grand Ma!"

Mom rubbed her hair and smiled at her. "Hey, Little Bit, you hungry?"

Little Bit's body went limp, as children will do when attempting to be dramatic. "I'm starving!"

"Lucky for you, supper is ready," Kay said with a smile.

Ruckus had maintained her spot on Little Bit's back until this moment. As Mom opened her mouth to say something, the little limb rat appeared on her shoulder. Seeing the rodent, Mom's attitude changed immediately. With one hand on Little Bit's head, she peeled her leg from the little girl's grasp while saying, "No, no, no, no!"

Little Bit laughed, "Grand Ma, Ruckus is sweet," she grabbed the limb rat from her shoulder, holding her close to her face, "you're a good little squirrel, ain't ya?" But, of course, being a limb rat, Ruckus's reply was to stand in her hand, put a front paw on her nose and look around, which got everyone who could see to laugh.

The laughter brought the other kids out, and the giggling and squealing began. Kay quickly herded the kids into the house, ordering them to wash up for supper. Mel and the girls walked up, and all greeted Mom. The girls were chattering, and they followed the kids into the house to wash up as well.

Mom looked at the machinegun hanging from a sling over Mel's shoulder. "Are you shooting that thing?" She asked.

Mel nudged the menacing weapon and smiled. "Yes, I do."

Mom's face twisted, "Why not just use something smaller? Isn't it heavy? And loud?"

"I like the weight. It makes me feel good. And it is loud, deafening," she looked at the weapon again. "But it has a very high rate of fire." Again, she looked at Mom, "Means it shoots a lot of bullets, real fast."

"I wouldn't want to do that."

"I don't want to either, Karen. But if I have to, I know I can."

Thad and the guys walked up to the porch. Audie sniffed the air. "Sure smells good!"

"Miss Kay and Miss Karen do a great job at supper time," Thad said. Then looked at Mom, "Where's Mary?"

"She's down at Fred's. I think those babies are getting close. Someone needs to be with her all the time."

"You fellas go on in and get supper. I'm going down to Fred's and see Mary."

Dad and Danny took Audie into the house and introduced him to Mom and Kay. The two women quickly fretted over him. Mom took him out to the porch and sat him down. Kay came out with a cup of coffee and set it in front of him. No sooner had he picked up the coffee than a plate appeared as well. Audie looked around, "You ladies are efficient!" He raised the cup, "Thank you."

Mom patted his shoulder, "You just let us know if you need anything."

Supper went as it generally did. People gathered at tables and talked while they ate. Thad had returned with Fred and Aric to Kay's admonishment.

"Fred, you shouldn't be out of the house!"

Fred put her hand on the older woman's arm. "Kay, I'm pregnant, not dying," she said with a smile. "I need to get up and move around."

"Well, you get on the porch and sit down. I'll bring you a plate."

Aric made his way to the table where Karl and his crew were sitting. He'd quickly fell in with them after their arrival. The men blended well, and it was someone new to talk to.

Setting his plate on the table, Aric said, "Hey, boys. How's the training going."

Imri was chewing a mouthful and pointed at him with his spoon. "You know, I'm stunned how quickly they've picked up this."

Chad quickly agreed. "He's right. I've trained a lot of people in my day, and these people are either really smart or really motivated."

"Or both," Karl added.

As everyone chatted, Mel went to the table where Mom and Kay sat. "Can you two watch the girls for me? I'm going to walk down to the bunker."

"Why are you going down there?" Mom asked.

"Looking for news about Morgan?" Kay asked softly.

Mel nodded, "Yes. I mean, I know he's fine. It's just; I get really worried about him when he's away."

"Of course, we'll watch the girls," Kay said. "Go see what you can find out."

Taking her flashlight from her hip pocket, Mel walked out the screen door and around the house. She looked up into the clear sky, obscured only by the trees over her head. The Minimi bouncing against her roused her from her cosmic gaze. She adjusted the weapon and then shouted, "Fuck!" She'd just realized she had the weapon but no ammo for it. All the ammo was in the MRAP. Not that she needed it or even would. It was just the fact she was carrying a weapon with no ammo. She wasn't worried, more annoyed. Besides, she still had her Glock on her hip. She made a mental note to remedy the situation.

The entrance to the bunker was dimly lit. Mel could see the glow as she approached. Concentrating on the glow, she was startled when she heard a voice, "Hey Mel." She stopped short and instinctively reached for the Minimi. A light clicked on, "Whoa, Mel," Red said as he illuminated his face. He was sitting on top of the bunker.

Mel looked up, "Sorry, Red."

Red was smiling, "Don't apologize. Your reaction was priceless."

Mel looked down at the weapon, "It was just a natural reaction."

The smile faded from Red's face, "Sadly, Mel, it's the right one today."

"Yeah, but I think we're fixing that."

Red nodded, "I believe you're right. You here to check on the radio?"

"I just want to see if they've heard from them, is all."

"We have, go on in."

Mel went into the bunker and found Wallner sitting at a small folding table with a couple of radios sitting on it. Wallner was sitting with his feet up on another chair. Looking up, he smiled and said, "Hey Mel! What a surprise."

"Hey, Wallner. How've you been?"

Rocking his chair forward, he stood up, "I'm good. I guess you're wondering about Morgan?"

"I know they had some call-in schedule, and I just wanted to see if they have been making them."

"You don't have to worry. They've made them all. The last one came in just a little while ago."

"What'd it say?"

He shrugged his shoulders, "Basic, still here, still watching."

"That's good. Just nice to know he's ok."

Just as she finished the statement, the radio broke squelch. *Cheers, Cheers, Swamprat.*

Wallner's eyebrows went up, and he picked up the microphone. "Have you Lima Charlie."

We're RTB. Cancel tomorrow's work.

"Roger that," Wallner replied, giving Mel a confused look.

She held her hand out, and he handed the microphone over. Then, keying it, she said, "Hey Morgan."

It took me a minute to wrestle the mic from the old man. "Hey, babe."

Sarge snatched the mic from me. *Keep the chatter down. You'll see him soon enough.*

I was incredulous. "What the hell was all that? You just said that in the open! And not for the first time!"

"We know they don't have any comms equipment now. So ain't no one listening to us."

I grabbed the notebook with the SOI. "What was all this shit? I've been sending those fucked up codes!"

"If you paid attention, you'd realize we didn't know whether or not they had comms. Now we do so; there's no need to use codes."

I sat quietly for a minute, rocking my feet that were still stuck out the window. Then, sitting up, I climbed over into the passenger seat, knocking the old man's hat off as I did.

"You damn idjit," he cussed, grabbing at that nasty wore-out hat, "what the hell are you doing?"

He was driving with his NODs on, and I could see him looking at me like some sort of crooked cyborg. "Just getting up here to keep your old ass company."

Snugging his hat back on his head, he replied, "I thought your pansy-ass needed a nap."

I removed my PVS-14 from the pouch on my plate carrier and attached it to my helmet as I replied, "It's way more fun to fuck with you." Turning the device on, I looked over and adjusted the focus. "Why are you wearing that stupid skull crusher? You have a damn helmet."

"I've worn those uncomfortable sum bitches long enough."

We rode in silence for a few minutes as the old man raced down the road. He was driving a hell of a lot faster than I did on our way out. After staring out the window for a while, I asked, "You really think it's smart to leave him alone out there. I mean, if he gets his ass in a sling, it'll take us hours to get to him."

Sarge glanced over at me, "Not to damage your delicate feelings, Morg. But I wouldn't want to leave *you* out there alone. I would Mikey and Ted, they're retards, and everyone knows retards are hard to kill. And I damn sure would Dalton. He's pretty feral and dangerous as fuck. I think he'll do ok."

"He doesn't even have military training. He's never served. It would have been better to send the guys out. At least there would be some support amongst them."

"He's gonna have support. Soon as we get back, I'm sending Karl and his crew out. That's three more men, not to mention their Jeep. He won't be able to keep up with them if they start moving. But according to the intel he gained inside, they don't intend to move for a day or two. We'll get Karl and his boys on the road tonight. Get your notepad out and prepare a message. I'll give it to you."

"Why the hell are we going to use codes now? You already shit the bed on that one."

"It's different to make a call saying we're coming home. It's entirely different to send out tactical information over an open net. We don't really know who all is out there that may be listening."

I was surprised by the statement. "Like who?"

Sarge shook his head in the way he does when he's annoyed, "Clean the shit outta yer ears! I just told you, *we don't fucking know!*" Then, he looked at me, "Where's your notepad?"

I got it out, flipped my NODs up, and turned on the red headlamp hanging around my neck, "Proceed, oh grumpy one."

"Get Karl's people loaded up. Food, fuel, water, and ammo. Tell them to draw explosives. Doc can get it for them. They need the Goose too."

I copied as he spoke, then looked at it. Do you have any idea how long this will take to get ready?"

"Yeah. So, enough of the chin waggin', get to encoding!"

It took a little while to get the message prepared. I couldn't send what he wanted verbatim. There were no trigrams for some of the words, so I improvised. During the time it took to prepare, the old man was flying down the road. It wasn't very late, but it was dark, and the lack of a windshield in the truck kept blowing the pages of the notebook around.

"Would you slow down a little? It's not a damn race," I complained, trying to keep my place in the trigram list. Suddenly the truck's breaks locked up, and the Suburban practically stood on its nose. I had to grab the dash as shit slid off my lap. "What the fuck?" I shouted as I looked up.

We were stopped at the bridge with the barricade we'd cleared on our way out. I looked up and immediately knew why we were stopped. "That's not good," I muttered.

"No, it's not."

The barricade had been rebuilt. Most of the junk we'd moved was now back in place, along with a lot of other shit. We sat looking around as the Cummins rattled, adding an eerie soundtrack.

"What do you want to do?" I asked.

"I don't want to drive over it."

"There's another way, but we'll have to backtrack a long way. Highway 44 takes the other side of the lake. We have the time, and it's better than getting into a gunfight out here." Then I had an idea. "Hang on," I said as I started to climb over the seat again. This time the old man didn't bitch. I worked my way to the back of the truck, grabbed the 320 and the belt of ammo Mike gave me, and climbed back up front.

Sarge looked at it and asked, "Where the hell did you get that?"

"Mikey gave it to me. I thought we might need the extra firepower."

Sarge grabbed the belt of shells for the weapon and looked them over. "Gimme that thing."

I handed him the launcher, and he loaded a shell into it. Leaning out the driver's window, he fired the round up into the air. The flare burst into a bright white light high above the bridge. We could see the dancing shadows of the roadblock the illumination created. I grabbed my binos and looked at the barricade.

"See anyone?" Sarge asked.

I didn't answer right away as I scanned the pile of junk blocking our path. It looked as inanimate as it had when we passed through the first time. But then I spotted movement, not just a dancing shadow, but a lateral, deliberate movement. "Yeah, there's someone up there."

Sarge opened the launcher, tossed the spent shell out the window, and loaded another one. "Well, let's make sure they know we're not fucking around." He leaned out the window again, not bothering to flip the rear sight up, and fired an HE round at the haphazard fortification before us. The forty-millimeter projectile slammed into a fridge sitting on the roof of a car and detonated.

I was impressed by the blast, "Damn!"

The old man wasn't waiting for any return response and quickly loaded another round and fired it into another section of the barricade. It detonated, blasting junk and debris over the side rail of the bridge and into the river. Unlike the first hit, this one was followed by a howl of anguish from some poor bastard. As he reloaded the weapon, whoever was up there began to offer some ineffective fire back at us. I grabbed my rifle, flipped my NODs down, and shouldered it. Hitting the PEQ-5 IR laser switch, I started sending steady but controlled rounds at the blockade.

Sarge reloaded the launcher and fired another round. This one landed short. It was a smoke round and began emitting a large cloud of white smoke. He quickly reloaded the weapon and shoved it into my lap. "Fire this one up there. Just point it at the barricade; it'll land where it needs to."

He slammed the truck into reverse with his hands free and floored the gas. The Cummins rattled like a jar of marbles as the truck started to gain speed. I quickly fired the smoke round right through the glassless windshield, this one landing shorter than the first, but we achieved the desired result as the two rounds completely obscured the top of the bridge. Dropping the weapon into the floorboard, I shouldered my rifle and began shooting again.

Sarge reached over and put his hand on my weapon, "That's enough, Morg. Just wasting ammo at this point." We were still backing out at an alarming speed. I lowered the rifle, and he said, "Hang on!"

I instinctively reached for the dash as he jerked the wheel around, and the truck felt as if it was going to roll over in the middle of the J-turn he was executing. As the front of the truck lined up with the road, he pulled it into drive, and we were quickly leaving the bridge in the rearview. I looked back through the truck's rear, but all I could see was smoke.

"I don't see anyone," I said as I swiveled back around in my seat.

"Good, I don't know who was up there. But the fact they repaired the roadblock says a lot about them. This sucks, though. I wanted to send that message from the top of the bridge. Now we'll have to stop and probably set up a quick antenna to get this message out."

"Better than trying to shoot it out with whoever was up there. It didn't sound like they had any real weapons, sure weren't shooting much."

"No, they didn't. I heard a shotgun go off a couple of times. They were probably hoping to hit us and take what we had."

"They had no way of knowing we would come back the same way," I concluded.

"Sure, they did. Most people do. I knew better but thought we could get away with it." He looked over at me, "You never take the same route back that you take out, and you really should never use the same route twice, in a perfect world."

"It's not like we're fighting a real military here."

"We don't know who the hell is out there. We kicked the shit out of those Russians at the auto auction, but you can bet your ass we didn't get them all. If they had any Spetz with them, and you can bet your ass they did, they could be running around out here. They do the same thing our Green Berets do, form up guerilla forces."

"What?" I asked, finding it hard to believe.

"I'm not saying that's who it was. Just that it's a possibility."

I turned in my seat to face him. "Then why in the hell are you just now bringing this up?"

"We haven't seen any yet. You do your job and let me do mine. Besides, there's some changes coming pretty quick that we need to talk about."

"Like what?"

"You gonna navigate or run your cock sucker?"

"I can do both; I can multitask. You can obviously run your face hole while you drive, so what the fuck is going on?"

Sarge explained that the government of the United States no longer existed. All the continuity plans went out the window after the President was captured. The Department of Defense charged him with treason for inviting the Chinese and Russians into the country. They weren't there for humanitarian aid. They were there to essentially divide the country and keep the President in place as a puppet figurehead. Once he was eliminated as well as those loyal to him, our traditional allies were quick to come to our aid. He told me of the thousands of American refugees in Canada and Mexico. The ones that crossed the southern border had suffered harshly at the hands of the cartels, and thousands of them were sold off to human trafficking rings.

With the collapse of the drug market in the US, the cartels turned to selling their previous customers to the highest bidders. While we'd managed to push the Chinese off the west coast, they'd simply moved south and were now in Mexico. Americans were rounded up and placed in internments camps where Chinese PLA officers processed them. Those that had any sort of connection to the government or military were shipped to China, as well as countless women.

I sat stunned for a while, only giving him instructions on where to turn. "That's fucked up. I wish we could do something about it."

"We're getting there," Sarge replied and continued laying out the New American Order as it was being called.

The Department of Defense had moved all operations to Cheyanne Mountain. It'd taken most of the year to get the bulk of our forward-deployed forces back, most, not all. But there were enough now that they were starting to implement a plan to restore the nation.

"The Russians have to be completely dealt with, though," Sarge stated, surprising me.

"I thought they were dealt with," I replied, slightly shocked. "We destroyed them in the airstrike."

"We destroyed *those* Russians. There's plenty more of them. There's a lot of them in Orlando. What we did to them at the auto auction only stopped their movement this way. There's plenty more of them to be dealt with yet." He looked over at me, more of a gesture in the dark, and said, "which is why the Army is sending out conscription units. Military service is now mandatory."

"Holy shit! Really?" I was surprised when he said there were units tasked with conscription missions. They traveled through the country and rounded up able body individuals who were then put into a training pipeline.

"What are we supposed to do? Current estimates are seventy-five percent of the country is dead. Warlords roam the countryside doing the same thing, forcing people to fight for them. But, at least in the Army, they are treated better, and there is a legal framework for what they're doing."

"I guess that's true. We're going to need bodies to rebuild the country. But power will be the biggest issue. I just don't see how that's going to happen quickly."

"It's not, but they're already at work on it."

Sarge detailed how South Korea, Japan, and Taiwan produced the transformers needed to restore the American power grid. The engineers to perform this work were also coming from these countries and the Saudis, which he said was a shock, England and Australia. Aid was also pouring in from numerous nations.

"After we kicked the Chinese asses, we signed a treaty with them," Sarge said with a sigh. "Only reason they did was because we still have a vast nuclear arsenal, and they realized quickly we would actually use it. The strike on the Chinese crippled their navy. They'd sent everything they had, thought this was the best chance to turn us into a Chinese province. When they saw we were serious about this shit and sunk three-quarters of their navy, they backed off."

"Sounds like they didn't have a choice."

"They didn't. And the Russians didn't really have a navy anyway. So the poor bastards that were deployed here are now abandoned. The Russian government is content to play in the Baltics now, which they are doing. The Poles, Brits, French, Germans, and some others have stacked so much armor at the Fulda Gap; I'm surprised it isn't sinking into the Earth."

"I'm surprised the Chicoms didn't move on Taiwan," I noted.

"Oh, they wanted to. But after a terminal x-ray and the announcement that Taiwan is a strategic partner of the US now, they know they must keep their hands off. So instead, they're fucking with India, and that's getting pretty hot."

"Thanks for the update on international politics there, Cronkite, but what does any of this mean to us? Are we going to have to deal with more Russians?"

He let out another long sigh. "We're in a unique place in Florida, and because we have been so effective at dealing with the Russians and other issues, getting power back on and all, we're going to be utilized as a logistical hub. And yes, we will be dealing with more Russians."

"Why, we're hell and gone from any ports? That doesn't make sense."

He explained that Tampa would be uninhabitable for hundreds of years. Jacksonville is still operational. There's an airbase there as well as the port. Supplies are flowing into it. Virginia, Texas, and Louisiana ports are all operational. The Texas and Louisiana ports are responsible for everything west of the Mississippi to the Rockies and north to Canada. Savannah, Charleston, and Boston are all operational again as well, and that's where the bulk of the aid is coming in. Long Beach is handling the west coast, but raids out of Mexico are causing issues there. Hampton Roads and Baltimore were slag heaps.

"How the hell are they moving all this shit, and why haven't we seen anything here yet?"

"This is all just now getting going. First, we have to find a location here that's rather large and get it set up to begin receiving material and personnel. But there's a major push to restore the railroads."

"Personnel?" That worried me.

"I don't think we're going to see much in the way of people. But we will certainly see some—specialists of various disciplines. We've been asked to make a survey of the Central Florida area. There's some Giger Counters coming in on the first load. They want to know how much of Tampa is irradiated. But we have to look at everything from I-10 south. Excluding the panhandle."

"South? How far south?"

He looked over at me, "Till our feet get wet."

"There's no fucking way we can do that! We don't have the people, fuel, vehicles. I mean, the logistics to do that alone will be huge."

"It's coming. A lot of it, lots of everything is coming."

"When?" I asked, still shocked at hearing all this.

"Within the next couple of days."

I turned that over in my mind for a minute. "Wait, they aren't sending their conscription teams here, are they?"

"You don't have to worry, Morg. They won't roll up your girls. The brass agrees that we've already done more than our fair share. Far more than anyone else from what they told me. We, correction, you, will be the civil authority for a new district in Florida." He paused and hung his head for a moment, "and I will be the military governor."

"Are you fucking with me? Why the hell would they do that? No one even knows who the fuck I am?"

"Oh yes, they do too. I've been submitting reports up the food chain since they first brought the SINGARs gear. Everything we've done here has been reported to them. Your name is well known. As is mine," he shook his head, "fuck, I hate my life."

"What does this mean? What the hell do they think I can do here?"

"Morgan, what you--," I quickly cut him off.

"We. Whatever comes next better be *we* because I haven't done shit here on my own."

He nodded, "What *we* have done is far more than in most of the country. There are other areas where people came together and worked hard to keep their communities alive. But it's the anomaly, not the norm. So, anyone who has shown any sort of leadership initiative is in the same position you are."

"We are," I reminded him.

"Yeah, we are."

I looked down at the notepad in my lap, "Are we gonna just wait to get home to get this message out or what?"

"Hell no! Send it!"

I tried a couple of times to get it out without success, and we decided to pull over and throw a quick antenna up to transmit the message. We pulled over on Highway 44, and Sarge pulled security while I got the VHF antenna up. After contacting Wallner and going through all the James Bond shit, I sent the message.

As soon as Wallner confirmed receipt of the message, Sarge started pulling the antenna down. "Let's get this shit loaded and get on the road!" Sarge barked.

I tossed my ruck in the truck as Sarge climbed into the passenger seat and called out, "You're driving!"

"Fine by me, we're almost home anyway."

Mel was walking back towards the house when she heard an ATV behind her and looked over her shoulder to see headlights bouncing towards her. Stepping off the side of the road, she waited. Red came flying up and skidded to a stop. "Hop on, Mel just got another radio call!"

As she got on behind him, she asked, "Is everything ok?"

"They didn't say there was any trouble, but they are asking for Karl's people to load up and prepare to leave. Hang on!"

They raced down the road towards Danny's house. Erin came running out to the road, hearing the ATV. Seeing Mel, she held her hands up in the universal, *what's going on*. Mel smiled and waved for her to follow. Then, sliding sideways through the gate and skidding to a stop in front of the screen door on the back porch, they succeeded in scaring the shit out of everyone. As Mel hopped off, Red called out to Karl.

"Karl! You and you guys need to kit up ASAP!"

Karl, Imri, and Chad didn't hesitate and jumped from their seats. Several people asked what was going on as near panic was setting in. Finally, Thad rose to his feet, "What in the hell is going on?" His voice boomed over the chaos unfolding around him.

"I don't know. We just got a message saying they needed to draw some gear and be ready to leave," Red asked.

"Did it say anything else?" Ted asked. He was on his feet as well, weapon slung.

Red shook his head, "No, just said for them to be ready. Get kitted up."

Karl stepped casually off the porch. "Do you have a copy of the message?"

Red pulled it from his pocket, "Here."

Karl rubbed his chin as he read. "Calm down, everyone—nothing here to worry about. We're not going anywhere right away. From the looks of this, we're waiting for them to get back." He looked up and smiled, handing the note to Imri. "Relax, everyone." Then he looked at Imri, "Start getting it loaded up."

The girls were visibly upset, and Mel went up to sit with them on the porch. "Sit down, girls. Everything is fine."

Little Bit didn't look convinced. On the verge of tears, she asked, "Where's Daddy?"

Mel sat down beside her, putting her arm around her, "He's Ok. I just talked to him a few minutes ago."

"Really?" Taylor asked, obviously not believing what Mel said.

Mel smiled, "Yes, really. I just talked to him. They're not far and will be home soon."

Audie never moved from where he was sitting. He continued to eat his supper without any noticeable change in his actions. Chewing a bite, he looked around the porch, "You sure are an excitable lot."

Danny laughed, "You're new around here."

Audie looked around again. "This kind of thing happen regular?"

"Let's just say it's not totally uncommon," Mike added as he and Ted walked off the porch, following Karl's crew as they headed around the house.

As I turned onto our road, Sarge told me to drop him off at his place. When we pulled up, there was a lot of activity. The guys were running around carrying various pieces of gear or personal kit. Sarge quickly hopped out, barking orders as he did. All I wanted to do was go home, but I got out for a minute.

"You got fuel?" Sarge asked.

"Getting it now!" Chad called back.

Mikey came out of the garage with the Goose over his shoulder and a large, tall ammo can in the other hand. "Where do you want it, Karl?"

"Put it in the trailer!"

"We need another PK!" Imri shouted.

"There's two in my room, Imri. Go grab one!" Sarge shouted back. "Karl," he called, "Come over here so we can go over this."

Karl walked over and leaned over the hood. "Alright, Top, what's scoop?"

"You're going to go out and hook up with Dalton." He slid a piece of paper to him, "Here's your SOI."

"Gulliver?" Karl laughed, "Pretty fitting."

Sarge pointed at the map, "Here's the route you'll take out. I highlighted it. We just came back on it, and there weren't any issues." He then pointed at the original route we'd taken out, "Stay away from this one. There's a barricade on the top of this bridge. We went through it on our way out without trouble. But on the way back, it'd been repaired. We took a little fire from it."

Karl's eyebrows went up, "You were shot at?"

"Only a little and completely ineffective. Couple rounds from a 320 quieted them down, but we rerouted to the alternate."

Karl nodded, "We've got a 203 and the Goose. I don't think we'll have any trouble."

"Now look, Karl. You're not to engage these assholes. I just need you guys to track them, not be seen, and let us know when they're headed this way."

"Simple enough."

"Once we know which way they're going, we'll coordinate an ambush. According to Dalton, most of the people there are noncombatants. We don't want to inflict casualties on them if we can avoid it. We have an unconfirmed count of forty-ish."

"If they're traveling in a convoy, all we really need to know are what trucks they're in. Hit those, and it's done," Karl stated flatly.

"That's it in a nutshell."

Karl looked at Imri, "You got everything?"

"I think so. This isn't a big deal. We should be good."

"Hey Mikey," Sarge called out. "Get them that camo net!" Looking at Karl, he said, "Might come in handy."

Karl nodded. That it will."

"Before you boys head out," Sarge looked around, "let me get a pot of coffee on for you."

"If you have any you can spare, I have the gear to make it on the road," Imri said as he and Mike put the camo net in the trailer of the Jeep.

The old man nodded, "I do; I'll fix you some up and make you a fresh pot."

"Looks like you boys have this shit under control. I'm gonna go find some supper," I said. I walked back over to the truck, opened the door, and paused, "You guys be careful!"

"Nothing to this, Morg," Imri replied with a broad smile. "Walk in the park. Go see your beautiful wife and get some food."

"Thanks, brother," I replied with a wave.

I drove the Suburban back to the house. It was dark, which meant everyone was still at Danny's, so I walked over there. I could hear those familiar voices as I crossed the yard. A dim glow was coming from Aaron's tent, and I stopped beside it.

"You in there, Aaron?"

The fabric rustled, and that all too familiar tearing sound of a tent zipper followed, with his head quickly appearing. "Hey, Morgan. When did you get back?" He asked as he climbed out.

"A few minutes ago. Why are you out here? Did you get supper?"

"I'd just got in my tent right before you pulled up. I heard the Cummins and was getting out of my sleeping bag. I ate, then there was a Chinese fire drill, people running everywhere, I felt like I was in the way and left."

"Much ado about nothing, my friend. We're just sending some guys out to surveil that group, is all."

"Isn't that what you were doing?"

"Kind of. We just did a quick recon to find them and try to get some intel on them."

He rubbed his arms as he was standing there in a pair of shorts and no shirt. "I assume you found them then?"

"We did." Seeing he was chilled, I said, "Why don't you put on a shirt or something. I'd like to talk to you a little about them."

"Sure," he replied hesitantly, "but I don't really know much about them."

"You know more than we do, buddy."

He ducked into his tent and came out with a hoodie, and pulled it on. "What do you want to know?"

"We kind of have the idea that most of the people with them don't really want to be there. Not like they're being held there, just a safety in numbers thing."

"I'd agree with that," he quickly nodded, then his tone darkened, "but some are being held against their will. That's certain."

"Kind of got that idea as well. We also saw your buddy Chief."

Aaron pointed at me, "He's the one you have to look out for. Tabor runs the show, but Chief is the muscle."

"We'll get them sorted out soon enough."

With his hands jammed into the pocket of his hoodie, he asked, "Why are you guys doing all this? I mean, why go looking for a fight? Most people don't want to deal with that sort of thing today."

"Because someone must, and we have the capability. Do you want to wander through a wasteland for the rest of your life? Or would you rather someone, anyone, do something to try and improve life? This country was fucked up when The Day finally arrived, and we have the opportunity of a second chance."

Sheepishly, he replied, "Well, yeah. Everyone wants life to be better."

"You know the official figures for the number of people that have died in all this?"

He shook his head. "Nearly seventy-five percent. It leaves less than seventy million people in this country if that's true. If we ever want to try and restore the country, it will take everyone single one of us to get it done."

He stood with his head down, shrouded by the hood. Finally, he looked up and brushed the hood from his head. He studied me for a bit. "I want to help, Morgan. I agree with what you just said, and you're right."

I gripped his shoulder, "That's good to hear. Some big changes are coming soon. Things are about to change."

Shrugging his shoulders, Aaron replied, "Got nowhere else to go. Guess I'll just stay here and help where I can."

I pointed at the tent, "You want something better than that to stay in?"

"I'm comfortable for now. Maybe later."

"Alright, man," I nodded at Danny's place and added, "I'm going to go get some supper."

"You should. It's good," he replied as he knelt to get back in the tent.

As I walked around the house to the back porch, I saw Mel sitting with Mom and Dad while the girls sat at another table. The kids were busy with Ruckus, and I opened the screen door, causing everyone to look up.

"Morgan!" Mel practically shouted as she got up.

I smiled, "Hey Babe, what's for supper? I'm starving."

She ran up and threw her arms around me. Hugging me tightly, she said, "I'm so glad you're home."

Hugging her back, I said, "So am I, Baby, so am I."

"Go sit down, and I'll get you a plate."

I kissed her, "Thanks, Babe."

I sat down at the table with Mom and Dad. Thad and Mary quickly joined us. Everyone said they were glad we were back and how they'd all worried. Naturally, they all wanted to know what we found out, and I gave them a rundown. I kept to our little recon mission and didn't bother saying anything about the news the old man laid on me. He was going to have to do that.

I'd waited on Mel to get back with my plate before I got into it. Miss Kay was quickly at my side, smiling as she usually does. "So glad you boys made it back."

"We're all good, Kay. He's at his place getting the guys ready to head out."

Her smile widened, if that was possible, "Oh, I knew you'd get back alright. Just glad you're all back now."

"Well, we're not all back. We left Dalton out there. That's why Karl's crew is going out tonight. To link up with him."

"You guys have any trouble?" Dad asked.

As I was eating, I shook my head, "Staying awake was the only problem I had."

"Did you see them?" Mel asked.

"I didn't directly see them. Sarge could from the roof of the building he was on. Dalton obviously did. I stayed with the truck, pulled security, and operated the radio. As I said, the hardest part was staying awake."

"You guys figure out where to ambush them?" Thad asked.

"That plan is fluid at the moment. We're sending the guys out to shadow them. There's a lot of civilians with them. Way more innocent folks there than ones we need to worry about. So, just hitting the convoy in an ambush would probably get a lot of people killed that don't deserve it."

Dad grunted, "That makes this task a hell of a lot more difficult."

"Are there children?" Mary asked.

I nodded as I took a bite of a biscuit, "There are. Many."

"I didn't even think about kids," Mel said as she considered the ramifications of the fact. "We can't just be shooting into trucks or whatever that might have kids in them."

"That's why we're sending the guys out to keep an eye on them. We'll need to conduct as precision of a strike as we can."

The girls came over to our table, with each of them telling me they were glad I was back and hugging me. To my surprise, even Tammy hugged me.

"Mom, we're going home to play Monopoly," Taylor said.

"I'm gonna win!" Little Bit shouted.

"You have to put Ruckus in her cage," Lee Ann said. "Last time, she jumped on the board and ruined it."

"She has to go to sleep soon anyway," Little Bit responded, petting the little critter.

"Ok, girls. We'll be home shortly," Mel replied.

The noisy rabble left the porch and headed home. We stayed talking for close to an hour when we heard a truck coming down the road. "Here comes the old man," I said.

Kay stood at the end of the table as we chatted and quickly headed to the kitchen. "Let me get him his supper and some coffee," she said as she hurried off.

"This should be good," Thad laughed.

As soon as he came through the door, we all heard him. "Hello, Kay! Smells delicious in here!"

"Go on out to the Porch, Linus. I'll bring you a plate and some coffee right out."

He came out on the porch, looked at everyone, and announced, "Who died? Y'all act like you're at a wake." He took a seat at the table beside Dad. "Hey Butch, how are you doing?"

"I'm good ole buddy. How was the trip?"

Sarge nodded at me, "I guess you've already heard it all."

"Everything worth telling, I reckon," I replied.

Kay came in and set a plate in front of Sarge along with a cup of coffee. "Not much to tell, really. Just a little sneak and peak." He took a sip of his coffee and looked at Dad, "You know how boring recon can be."

"I did it a little different," Dad replied. "Throwing grenades from my Loach was how I performed recon."

Sarge laughed. "Yeah, I guess that is a little different than what we were up to."

He immediately set to his supper, and everyone gave him some time to eat without interruption. I damn sure knew how hungry he was. After he'd gotten most of it down and was on his second cup, he started answering questions.

"How long they gonna be out?" Thad asked.

Sarge shrugged, "Hard to tell. It depends on what those assholes do."

"How are you going to do this without hurting any of the children?" Mary asked.

"That's gonna be the hard part, Mary." Sarge looked around the table, making eye contact with everyone. "The last thing I want to do is hurt any of the kids or civilians of any kind. That's why we're upping the ante here and sending more men out. They will watch these guys, and we'll work with them to figure out how we'll do it."

Kay was sitting beside Sarge with her hands folded on the table in front of her. Sarge reached out and put his hand on hers, "Don't worry, Kay. We'll be alright."

We heard another vehicle coming, and in short order, a raucous crowd came through the door of the house. Mike had Crystal with him and Ted. Doc was with Jess and Ian and Jamie there as well. They came out to the porch noisily. They were very obviously in a good mood.

"What the hell's wrong with you, idjits? Giggling like schoolgirls," Sarge barked.

Mike stood up straight and held his arms out to his side, "What's not to be happy about? Life is good."

"You been keepin' yer head up yer ass too long at a time."

"Oh, come on, Boss. We've got some fun shit going on," Ted replied.

"Except you sent the wrong guys," Mike pouted, and Crystal patted him on the back. "Should have sent us."

"No, he didn't," Doc interrupted, "we didn't need to go on this."

"I agree with Ronnie," Jess added. Then she looked at me, "How was this trip home?" She asked with a smile.

"Shorter," I replied with my own smile.

"It's a lot faster when you drive, huh?"

"Oh, we got jokes?" I quipped, "Not getting shot helps a lot too."

Her smile disappeared, "Not funny."

Laughing, I asked, "Too soon?"

She furrowed her brow, "Way too soon."

I laughed at her and slapped the table, "It's never too soon!"

Doc had remained silent until I slapped the table. He leaned over to Jess, wrapped an arm around her, and said, "It's never too soon," and kissed her cheek. She nudged him but didn't say anything.

You two done flirting?" Sarge asked, getting a laugh out of Doc.

"I don't know about the rest of you, but I'm beat, and I'm gonna go home to my soft bed," I said.

Mel quickly got up from her seat, "Sounds like a great idea."

"I think we'll head home too," Dad said as he got up from the table, "come on, Momma."

We all said our goodbyes. I'd completely forgotten about Audie. I saw him when I arrived but never spoke to him. He was sitting at a table by himself, still eating. He raised a spoon at me, "See ya later, Morgan."

"Damn, I never got a chance to talk to you. So what are you doing here?"

"I'm borrowing Thad's little truck. Need it to run around and scavenge parts for the mill."

"You staying the night here?"

He looked around, "Never thought about it. But if the offer is open, sure."

"I'll get you fixed up," Danny quickly replied. "You can even get a hot shower."

A broad smile cut across his face, "Hot shower, you say? Now! I'm definitely staying!"

"Need anything I can help with?" I asked.

"Nah, we'll be hard at work on the mill tomorrow. The engineers are already pulling some of the equipment we need out of the plant."

"Sounds like it's in capable hands then. Just let me know if you need anything," I replied and waved as I stepped off the porch.

Mel and I held hands as we walked back to the house with Mom and Dad. Mom looked over and asked, "You glad to be home?"

"Oh yeah. It was only one night, but I don't really like being away anymore. Home is comfortable, familiar, and stable. Out there, it's not comfortable, definitely unstable, and feels like you're in a different country."

"You guys have so much going on," Mom interrupted. "It's kind of dizzying."

"We haven't done much of anything in a long time," Dad added. "A typical day was digging graves and going fishing or me going out into the swamps on the river looking for food. Every day was work."

"You ain't seen nothing yet," I half moaned.

"What do you mean?" Mel asked.

"You'll see soon enough. From the sounds of it, things are about to get a whole lot busier out here."

Dad laughed, "I don't see how it can."

"You'll see," is all I replied.

We told Mom and Dad goodnight, hugging Mom, and Dad and I doing what was once our usual greeting or farewell. Kind of hard to explain. It was just something we'd always done, and it made me smile.

"Glad you guys are here," I said.

He slapped me on the back, "See you tomorrow."

"Goodnight," Mel said as we turned to go into the house.

Mel leaned into me as we stepped up on the porch. The dogs were all there, looking like a K-9 mass casualty event. "What's this news you were talking about?" She asked as I opened the door.

The kids were spread out around a large ottoman in the living room. The board was all set up, and they were already at it. The girls looked up when we came in, all smiles.

"Who's winning?" I asked, knowing they had just started.

"No one yet," Tammy said and rubbed her hands together, "but it's starting to get good!"

"No training tomorrow," I said, "but don't stay up too late."

"We won't," came a chorus of replies.

We left the girls to compete at capitalism and went to our room. I wanted a shower, and Mel wanted to know more about *the news*.

I sat on the bed to take my boots off. "I really don't want to talk about it tonight."

She stood in front of me, hands on her hips. She wasn't taking that. "I don't care. Spill it."

I let out a moan and fell back on the bed. "Okay, okay."

I gave her the Cliff Notes version of what was going on. She sat down on the bed beside me and listened intently as I talked. When I finished, she started to rattle off questions. I covered my face with my hands.

"This is why I didn't want to get into it. I really don't know more than I just told you."

She wasn't about to yield, though. "This sounds kind of like a big deal, Morgan. I want to know more. We need to know more."

Sitting up, I pulled my shirt off. "You're right. We do. But we were kind of busy and didn't get to talk."

"Busy doing what? You guys said your trip was uneventful. It sounds like lots of time to talk to me."

Tossing my shirt at the hamper, I replied, "You are correct. It was uneventful in today's world. What was eventful about it was having to clear a roadblock on our way out only to find it manned and rebuilt on our way back."

She looked surprised, "What happened? Was there a fight?"

Standing up, I pulled my pants off, "Wouldn't call it a fight. We just launched a couple forty-millimeter rounds into it and detoured around. Just took longer."

"Why didn't you tell me?"

I shrugged, "What was I going to tell? Nothing happened."

As soon as the words left my mouth, I knew I'd fucked up. I didn't know how, just that I had. Women, most women, have a universal *I'm pissed now* stance they take to let you know. Arms crossed over the chest, and the hip cocked to one side. And that's just how she was looking at me now.

"So, you only tell me about this kind of thing, if what, if you get killed!" She practically screamed the last part.

"Hey, calm down," I nodded at the bedroom door, "the girls are out there."

She took a couple of steps towards me and jabbed a finger in my chest, "I don't care how *uneventful* your little adventures are. From now on," she started to poke me in the chest as she said each word that followed, "you will tell me everything, fucker." Her eyes narrowed, and she added, "Got it?" Then she smiled and blew me a kiss.

I wrapped my arms around her, "You're right. I will. Promise."

She shoved me away, "Damn, you stink. Go take a shower."

"Slow the hell down, Karl!" Chad barked.

"You scared Woodchuck? You can say you're scared," Karl replied, not taking his eyes off the road. All three men in the truck wore NODs. One of the things Sarge was curious about was how they acquired some of the more advanced equipment the men had.

"I'm not scared. I'm also not suicidal!"

Imri tapped Chad on the shoulder from his position in the back seat. "Really? Not even a little bit?"

"I'm not scared, asshole," Chad replied.

"No, I meant suicidal." Imri held his thumb and index finger about a half-inch apart, "not even just a little bit?" Chad didn't reply, just shook his head. To which Imri added, "Come on, man! Give me some hope!"

"Maybe our suicidal navigator can get us to where we're going," Karl sniped. "Can you wait that long, Chadster?"

Chad looked at the map and mumbled a reply, "I don't know. Jumping out of this thing is sounding better and better. You're going to take a right at the next light."

"Imri, see if you can get Gulliver on the radio," Karl said.

"Gulliver, Gulliver, Fire Star."

Imri had to press the headset to his head to hear the whispered reply.

Fire Star, have you five by five.

"Roger that. We're about twenty mikes out. Has your position changed?"

Negative. Nothing further to report. Gulliver, out.

"He's sitting there waiting on us," Imri shouted up to Karl.

"Good, let's get this show on the road!" Karl banged on the roof of the Jeep. "It's been far too boring for far too long!"

Sarge had prepared a detailed map for Karl, and he knew when he should start slowing down and did so as they passed by Lake Harris. Being the old Green Beret he was, Karl even crossed over the median to drive on the opposite side of the road to lower the risk of contact. Humans are creatures of habit, and even when the societal restraints that governed their behavior fall away, many of them choose to continue to follow them. If for no reason other than habit. Something as simple as driving on the wrong side of the road could keep you out of an ambush.

It was fully dark now, and Karl drove slowly and deliberately. He was watching the roadside for a marker left by the old man. It was simple, just a five-gallon bucket with a hole knocked in the bottom and pushed over a tree limb just inside the screen of trees on the side of the road. The old man had made the hold to ensure no one took the damn bucket. The developing world understands the value of containers. Americans had only recently taken this to heart, and an item like a bucket wouldn't be left lying. That is unless it was useless.

"There it is," Chad pointed.

"Got it," Karl replied as he pulled off the paved road and drove through the grass to the ancient trail that led into the woods. The track was nearly impossible to spot from the road. But once you were on it, it was apparent. If not a little overgrown. It didn't take long to find the building Dalton was perched on. He met them on the ground and showed them where to hide the jeep.

"Chadster, you and Imri get this thing covered up with the camo net," Karl instructed as he got out of the Jeep. Then turned his attention to Dalton.

"How's it going?"

Dalton spun on his heels and started walking. "Follow me."

Once on the roof, Dalton laid out the scene before them. It was dark, and both men were looking through the NVGs, but the range cards Dalton had drawn up explained what they couldn't see in the dark. The area was relatively well lit from the numerous campfires still burning, making getting Karl up to date much easier.

"So, where's the shit bags we're supposed to smoke?" Karl asked.

Dalton pointed to the range map, "They're sitting right back here."

Karl nodded, "In the middle of the camp. Smart, I guess, surrounding yourself with civilians in case you're attacked."

"It's certainly one method," Dalton replied as he pulled his NODs off and sat back against the wall.

While Karl continued observing, Chad and Imri came up on the roof. Imri nearly shit himself when his head cleared the ladder access, and he found himself staring straight into a Claymore.

"Holy fuck!" He nearly shouted as he quickly ducked, banging the crown of his head on the metal access for the roof.

Karl turned to see Imri emerging from the hole, rubbing his head. "Imri, you know if that was real, you would'a never heard it."

Crossing the roof in a crouch, he replied, "Yeah, still scary to drag your nose over one as you come through a hole!" He dropped down against the wall and handed Dalton a small parcel he'd carried.

"What's this?" Dalton asked as he unwrapped the small cloth.

"Miss Kay wanted to make sure you had supper."

A smile spread across his face, "That's one fine woman."

"You have any idea how long these ass hats are going to sit here?" Karl asked.

Taking a bite of a biscuit with some form of meat in it, Dalton replied, "Nope. That's why you're here. We're just going to have to wait and watch."

"What a shit hole," Chad commented. He was peaking over the edge of the parapet wall to get a look at the camp. "I've seen better-looking camps in Iraq."

Dalton replied in a perfect aristocratic British accent, "They aren't the most disciplined lot, Guvna, more of a loud rabble. Wouldn't you say, Nigel?"

Chad never looked away, "Who the fuck is, Nigel?"

"Oh, come on, Chad. Little British humor never hurt anyone," Karl commented.

"No such thing."

"As what?" Karl asked.

"No such thing as British humor. They're so tight they squeak when they walk."

"Why, my good man. What a simply dreadful thing to say of the Queen's subjects," Dalton countered. The statement was dripping with the accent.

"Fuck the Queen," Chad muttered.

Dalton feigned shock and covered his mouth, "Proper fuck?"

CHAPTER 12

The next morning the living room looked like a mass casualty event had taken place. Little bodies were everywhere, and a now jam-packed Monopoly board sat on the ottoman. Yellow, blue, and green bills were scattered about. I tipped toed past them and into the kitchen, even keeping my mouth shut when I stepped on a little red hotel. Limping into the kitchen, I pulled the fridge open as quietly as I could, grabbed the tea jug and cup from the cabinet, and headed for the porch. I didn't want to risk waking them up coming back in for more.

Opening the door, I just shook my head. The dogs, like the kids, were sprawled out everywhere on the porch. Not nearly as concerned about waking them up, I nudged Meat Head's ass out of the way to get to a chair and sat down with a, *finally!*

It was quiet, in that place where the rising sun changes the color of the sky but isn't yet high enough to illuminate the horizon. I sat rocking, enjoying my tea. I was lost in thought and solitude when one of the dogs farted. And it wasn't the typical silent yet lethal dog fart. More like a gassy mule's pressure relief valve finally gave way. It lasted for a long time, and Drake never even flinched while the noxious event took place! Just like those silent farts, this was unspeakably bad. Like it had a physical presence all its own.

Getting up and grabbing my cup and jug, I said, "For fuck sake!" So much for my peaceful morning.

Going back inside, the Gremlins were still sleeping, and I slipped into the bedroom to get dressed. I tried to be as quiet as possible but woke Mel up anyway. She didn't roll over or even show her face.

"Why do you get up so early? You got cows to milk or something?"

"I just do. Not really my choice."

She pulled the blanket up over her shoulder and tightened the drawstring on her hoodie to close it as tight as possible. It made me smile at her. For as long as I could remember, she slept in one, a hoodie. She cracked me up at night to see her get ready for bed. It was also a pretty handy indicator if you paid attention. Hoodie meant sleep. No hoodie, well, that had another meaning. No hoodie nights were always better.

Once I was dressed, I put the plate carrier on, grabbed my rifle, and slung it before filling a Nalgene bottle with tea and heading out the door. I doubted anyone was awake at this hour. But I was going to go for a walk at least. I found Barry, one of the Guardsmen on duty at the bunker. In the opening, dim light filtered out around him, and he was sitting in a camp chair.

"What's up, Morgan?" He asked.

I pulled another chair over and sat down. "Nothing really. I usually spend the mornings sitting on the porch drinking some tea. Unfortunately, this morning the dogs conducted a biological strike, so here I am!"

He laughed and slapped his knee. "Drake, huh?"

"How'd you know?" I asked with a laugh.

"Dude, they come down here all the time, usually about supper time. They know there's gonna be someone here with food. So, they always come down. And he, hands down, has the worst farts!"

"I know, the smartest of the bunch, and you can't stand to have him around!"

Barry looked down the road, "At least they didn't follow you."

"Hear anything from the guys overnight?"

"They checked in. Made it to Dalton, and are just waiting now."

"We'll see how long it takes them to make their move. The place they're in won't support them for long. Nothing really around it. They'll have to head out to find resources soon."

"You think you'll be able to stop them before they get here?"

"With a certainty. They'll never make it here. We have to change our plans a bit, too many civilians with them. We need to take out the trash without killing a bunch of people that don't deserve it."

Barry just shrugged, "If they decided to run with that crowd, they can't be innocent."

I rolled my head to the side to see him, "True, but if we just start tarring people with the brush of guilt by association, where's that leave us?"

"Fewer people to be worried about."

I snorted, "It would be easier just to nuke the entire lot. But they've got kids with them as well. Not everyone there is an evil prick. Some of those people are there simply not to be alone. Safety in numbers and all that shit."

"I guess you're right."

We were bullshitting about nothing really when I heard a noise coming from the direction of the old man's place. Looking over my shoulder, I said, "Guess I'll go see what he's up to already."

"Have fun with that grumpy old bastard."

Standing up, I replied, "Oh, he ain't that bad."

"Yeah, but he's been out of the Army for a while now. Really could lay off the shit."

I laughed out loud, "You think the Army did that to him? Shit, I bet he ended up in the Army because it was the *only* place he fit in. You know, break glass in case of war?"

Barry shook his head, "Sure as hell wish no one broke that damn glass."

As I started to walk away, "Oh, you just wait for what's coming. You think he's a pain in the ass now!"

Barry looked visibly disturbed, "Like what? What's coming?" When I didn't answer him, he stood up. "Morgan! Like what?"

"You'll see!" I shouted over my shoulder.

The garage door was open, and both war wagons sat in the driveway. Light spilled out onto the two little vehicles, and I could hear Sarge's voice. Stepping into the garage, I found Sarge and the guys sitting on stools at the workbench.

Sarge leaped to his feet, "What in the holy hell is going?" He did an excellent job of looking panicked.

"You done?" I asked.

He walked up to me, "What's happened?"

"Sit your old ass down and drink your coffee. Just because I don't come down here in the morning doesn't mean I'm not up. I need to meditate before dealing with your old ass."

Mike laughed, "I need to medicate before dealing with him!"

Sarge glared at him, "You'll need a hell of a lot more meds if you keep it up."

"So, no training today. What's the plan?" I asked.

"We need to go look at a couple of places that we can set up an HQ in. There's going to be a lot of shit showing up here soon, bodies too. So we need a place to billet them and a warehouse," Sarge replied.

"That's what we were talking about," Ted added.

I pulled up another stool and sat down, "I have a couple of ideas about that."

"Enlighten us, oh great one," Sarge retorted.

"Do you have any idea how many people they may be sending?"

He shook his head. "No, and it will probably be constantly changing with people coming in and out."

"The high school in town has a kitchen, and all the classrooms can be converted to either offices if that's even needed, or barracks. It's close to the OJ plant, and there's plenty of storage capacity there and already manned."

"Has the power been turned back on there yet?"

I shook my head. "No. But it probably wouldn't take long to survey the place and heat up whatever sections we wanted to use."

"We'll need a kitchen for certain. Is there anything else?"

"There's the Umatilla Baptist Church. But I don't know what facilities they have there."

The old man sipped his coffee and thought for a minute. "I think the school would be best. With what I'm being told is coming this way, we'll be able to provide at least one meal a day to folks in town. Maybe not every day, but most. Not to mention the troops coming in will need the kitchen as well. Get with Baker, tell her we need the high school powered up, and the kitchen inspected."

"You should take Miss Kay to inspect the kitchen," I added quickly. "If anyone knows school kitchens, it's her."

"That's a damn good idea that I will certainly take credit for," Sarge replied with a shit-eating grin.

"I'm staying here," Mike interjected. "I'm not moving to town, and I'm not getting rolled up into any units deployed here." The fact he said it seriously, not even a hint of sarcasm, let us all know he was serious.

"I'm not either," Ted added.

"Boys, we're not going anywhere. I am or will be the final military authority here. I'm being given the authority to do whatever it takes in our efforts to restore the country. We'll be busy, but this team," he wagged his finger back and forth at us, "stays together, period."

Just then, Crystal came out of the house. She was radiant and smiling. "Hey, Morgan. Breakfast is ready, boys." She pivoted and returned to the house.

Mike leaped to his feet, "Come on, Morg, have some breakfast." He smiled, and I could see he was genuinely enamored with her. "She's a great cook."

"Why not," I said as I stood up.

"It's not Kay's cookin'," Sarge added, "but it ain't half bad."

"*Whatever,* old man. You know you like her cooking!" Mike countered.

Crystal had the table set for four when we came into the kitchen. "Have a seat, boys. I'll get you a plate."

"Aren't you joining us?" I asked.

As she scooped eggs onto a plate, she replied, "I kind of nibble as I cook. Go on, sit down."

I took a seat and poured myself a cup of coffee while the old man gave me the stink eye. But he let it go. I guess coffee was probably on the manifest of the incoming shipments. While we ate, we talked about what we needed to do.

I needed to go by the market and talk to Kelly, the guy that made shoes, to see if he had any for kids and go over the list Vincent gave us for what he and his people needed. We needed to look at the high school and go over it. Obviously, the ongoing operation shadowing the DHS fucktards, meant we needed to be ready to move on a moment's notice.

"Thad, Dad, and Danny are going to go to the plant and get that generator and take it to the sawmill. If we can get that running, we can get a milking barn built for the cows," I said.

As we talked, Doc and Jess came into the house. Greetings were exchanged around, and they declined breakfast, saying they were headed to Danny's and would eat there.

"When are you planning on going up to Juniper?" Doc asked.

We were just talking about that. I need to round up a few things first. Probably tomorrow," I replied.

Doc grabbed a coffee cup from the cupboard and poured himself a cup. "Ok. That'll work. I need to go to town and get with Chris Yates, the other medic and see if he can go with us."

Jess and Crystal stood off to the side chatting. My mind wandered from the discussion at hand as I looked at Jess. The image of her when I first saw her at the rest area in Perry popped into my head. Then the days after and all that happened-- how she'd made herself such a part of this family. That was how I thought of it, my family. Now she stood in the kitchen of a house with electricity and running water. A carbine slung across her back.

No one ever went anywhere without a gun. Today, it was as natural as putting your shoes on. In the Before, people that took responsibility for their personal security were demonized or laughed at. Yet none of those that disparaged those responsible individuals were actually anti-gun. Rather, they chose to outsource their responsibility to someone else across town and hoped they would arrive in time when they needed them. The logic of that never made sense to me. This dream of a utopia where you didn't need to protect yourself was just that, a dream.

The System was the problem. When the artificial systems we created came crashing down, Nature stepped into that void. Survival of the fittest was the ultimate arbiter of logic. If you were capable of logical thinking, you quickly concluded that if you didn't have a means to defend yourself, you wouldn't live long. That having the ability to project force over a distance was the best life insurance on the planet. And that meant a gun until something better came along.

I had a slight smile on my face when Jess looked over and saw me. "What are you grinning at?" She asked.

"Just taking a stroll down memory lane is all."

She walked over to the table and put an arm around me. "I told you I could take care of myself and wouldn't be a problem for you."

I laughed, "I wouldn't put it quite that way," I put my arm around her waist, "but I'm glad you're here." I paused and looked around the kitchen, "That goes for all of you. I couldn't imagine what life would be without all of you."

"You need a hanky? You done snot nosing, or do we all need to hold hands and sing kumbaya?" Sarge asked.

Crystal walked over and put her arm around Mike, "I think it's sweet. Not to mention, I think the same thing from time to time."

I smiled at him across the table, "You're nothing if not predictable. You grumpy old fuck." This got a laugh out of the guys. "I'm taking the little buggy today, so I can get all this running around done."

"Knock yourself out there, Dear Abby."

Looking at Doc, I said, "I'll get with you this evening." He replied by raising his cup at me. Then, looking at Crystal, I said, "Thank you for breakfast. It was delicious."

"You're welcome, Morgan. It was nice having everyone here this morning."

I went out and got into the buggy, and headed back to the house. I was going to see if Mel wanted to go with me today for the running around I needed to do. The house was alive when I got there, everyone was up, and the Monopoly game was back underway.

"Who's winning?" I asked as I came in.

"I am!" Tammy beamed. "I've never actually finished a Monopoly game before!" She was obviously having fun with the game.

I walked over to the board and observed it for a minute. "Yikes, look at all the houses and hotels! Some expensive real estate there."

Tammy rubbed her hands together. "Yes, it is."

"What are you doing today?" Lee Ann asked.

"I have to run to town and do a few things."

"Can we go?"

"I'm driving one of the little buggies, and there isn't room."

"Ah, come on, Dad!" Little Bit shouted.

"Let me talk to Mom," I said and headed for the kitchen, where I heard Mel messing around.

She was bent over rummaging around in the cabinet under the sink. I walked over and slapped her ass hard. I really should have thought that through. Because naturally, she hit her head.

She came out from the cabinet, rubbing her head with a look on her face that would've turned me to ash if it was possible. But I was already on the defense.

"I'm sorry, babe! I didn't even think about it, and it was just a natural response to seeing your ass poked out there."

Still rubbing her head, she smiled, and it scared me. "That's alright. I know you didn't think about it. No harm, no foul."

I cocked my head to the side, "You're not mad?"

Done rubbing the hurt away, she said," No, I know you didn't mean it," and came up on her toes to kiss me. Now I was really nervous. She'd get even when she wanted to. This was sure to cost me.

"Ok," I replied nervously. "Well, I came home to see if you wanted to go with me. I have to go to town and take care of a couple things. Thought you might want to go."

"That'd be nice," she smiled back. "Are the girls going with us?"

"I have one of the old man's buggies, and it's not really big enough for all of them."

Mel walked over, opened the front door, and looked at the little vehicle. Then, shutting the door, she came back to the kitchen, "They'll fit. Little Bit could sit on my lap if we have to." She stepped over and put her arms around my neck, "It'd be nice to go out as a family. All of us together for a normal kind of day."

I put my arms around her waist and kissed her. "Baby, if that's what you want, then absolutely."

"It is," and she kissed me back. "I want to go to Danny's so they can have breakfast first and see if we can maybe pack a lunch. I'm sure we could find a place to have a picnic."

"I know just the place," I replied.

"Girls!" Mel called out. "Get dressed. We're going to get breakfast and then go to town."

Cries of, *yah,* was the reply. That and a stampede of feet as the girls all ran to get ready. I was refilling the Nalgene bottle when Mel asked what I needed to do. I told her about needing to find shoes for kids. How we needed to check out the high school and go by the OJ plant.

"Who are the shoes for?" She asked.

I told her about Vincent and his people. How I'd got a list of what they needed and that we would probably be going to see them tomorrow. She wrapped her arms around me again.

"See, that's why you are the man you are."

"What do you mean?"

"You're always trying to help others."

I shrugged it off. "It's what you should do. It's just what's right." She kissed me again and headed for the bedroom.

"This will be fun. A relaxing day with the girls," she said over her shoulder.

While they all finished getting ready, I went out to the shop and put together some tools for connecting the power. I was certain I would be the one doing the electrical side of things.

Once everyone was ready, I was pleased to see both Lee Ann and Taylor had their weapons with them. I was even more impressed when they both performed a condition check on their firearms when they went outside. Again, muzzle discipline was on point, and the girls conducted the task like a pro.

"Good job, girls. You did that perfectly. Safely. I'm proud of you both," I said, giving them both a gentle squeeze on the back of their necks.

"Can I have a gun, Morgan?" Tammy asked.

The question caught me off guard. "Well, Tammy, you can. But first, you have to have some training. We have to be sure you can safely handle one before carrying one. Have you ever shot a gun before?"

She shook her head and looked dejected. "No."

I put a hand on her shoulder, "That's not a no, kiddo. And we'll get you trained up quickly. We'll start today."

She looked surprised at the reply, "Really? You mean it?"

"Absolutely. You need to know how to defend yourself, and we will teach you to do so."

She crashed into me, wrapping her arms around hips. "Thank you, Morgan." She stayed there a little longer than I was comfortable with, and I rubbed her head.

"It's ok, kiddo. You're part of the family now." She looked up at me, and I could see her eyes tearing up. "What's the matter, sweetie?"

She looked at the girls and Mel, then back at me and asked, "Can I call you Dad?"

I was stunned into silence. I didn't know what to do. Thankfully Mel, who was now also tearing up, came to my rescue. She knelt beside Tammy and patted her back. "Sweetie, you can call us whatever you want. Morgan is right; you are part of our family now and forever."

Tammy threw one arm around Mel, squeezing me tight with the other, "Thank you, Mom."

I was trying my best not to cry along with the two of them. Unfortunately, they were both full-on crying now. Fortunately, I was saved by Little Bit, who always seemed to have superb timing.

"Yay! We have another sister!" And the girls moved in to join the group hug.

"Alright," I shouted, "everyone get in!"

Tammy gave me one last smile as she ran off with the other girls, and they started climbing into the buggy. Mel put her arm around my waist as we watched, "Didn't see that coming," she said as she wiped tears from her face.

"Me neither," I replied, kissing the top of her head. "Come on, let's go."

We went down to Danny's, where the kids quickly ate breakfast. I sat with Mom and Dad while Mel and Kay put together a picnic lunch. As soon as Mel mentioned it to her, Kay got all in a tizzy about it. Thad and Mary arrived, and Thad sat down at the table with us. He was all smiles.

"I can't wait to get that generator," he said as he slid his colossal self into the picnic table.

"Me too," Dad replied, taking a sip of coffee. "It'll make for a hell of a project."

"We get that mill running and some lumber cut, we can start building the milking barn. Having milk will be really nice," Thad replied.

"What are you doing today?" I asked Mom.

She smiled, "Just going to piddle around with Kay. It's very relaxing here."

That brought a smile to my face. "You have no idea how happy it makes me to hear you say that."

She looked at Dad. "We really thought we'd never see anything like this again. We thought the days of plenty were gone. Not that there's an overabundance here, but there is enough. Everyone is fed and has shoes and clothes. Being here is such a relief."

Dad looked into the bottom of his cup, "Yep. I thought I'd die without ever seeing another cup of coffee." He looked back up. "This really is a little slice of heaven here."

"We all do what we can," I replied.

Thad reached across the table, putting his big hand on my shoulder. "It's all because of you, Morgan. I remember that day we met on the side of the road. You didn't need to offer me any help, but you did. I'd been shot at, warned away, and treated like a monster. But not you. You just walked up and introduced yourself."

"Yeah, well, Jess didn't want to take you on," I said with a laugh.

He laughed that deep baritone laugh. "And you didn't want to take her on!"

"Which is why I didn't have a problem with you. I already had her to deal with, and I figured I'd need the help."

"Everything happens for a reason," he replied as he released my shoulder.

"Yes, it does. You going straight to the plant?"

"Yes, sir!"

"You going to?" I asked Dad.

"Wouldn't miss this for the world."

"We're going be headed out too. I'll follow you guys up to the plant, and I need to talk to Baker real quick. Then I follow you guys out to the mill in case you need any help."

"That'd be good. I don't do electricity. Anything you can't see, hear or smell that can kill you is something I want no part of," Thad pointed out.

I laughed, "Well, you can hear it, see it and smell it. But it's generally a terrible day when you do."

Thad pointed at me, "That's exactly what I mean!"

"I'm with Thad. I don't do electricity," Dad added.

"Girls, you finished with breakfast?" Mel called out.

The girls all carried their plates into the kitchen, where Kay took them. "You all look excited!" Kay said. "You looking forward to your picnic?"

"Picnic?" Taylor asked.

"Yes," Mel replied, "we're going to have a little picnic today."

There was a flurry of excitement as the girls all dashed out of the house.

"I'd say they were excited about it," Kay observed with a laugh.

"I think they are," Mel replied. "Thank you for putting this together for me."

"Oh, it was nothing, Mel. You have a good day with your girls."

"And my man," Mel said with a wink.

"And your man," Key replied with a sly smile.

Danny came downstairs, and we all went out and got into our vehicles. Thad, Dad, and Danny would take the Hummer so they could pull the generator, and we would follow them. Once everyone was loaded up, we headed out with the girls carrying on in the back of the buggy.

Little Bit sat on Mel's lap facing to the rear so she could join in the fun. Mel's Minimi was propped muzzle down between her legs. It was an interesting juxtaposition of a mother and a young daughter with a belt-fed machinegun. And I liked it.

As I drove, I called Baker on the radio and told her we were on our way. She replied that the generator was ready to go, and they'd even made us some cables to use to hook it up. The trip to the plant didn't take long. The day was bright and clear, and the temps were pleasant, in the upper 80's. It was a lovely day for a drive.

Once we got to the plant, I told Baker about our plan for the high school and that we needed to inspect it. She said they would get over there and look at it and start energizing the circuits and check the place out. Turning power back on presented issues on occasion, they would need to take their time going over the place. I told her I would meet them there after going to the mill. Thad and Danny could hardly control themselves and were in a hurry to get moving, so we quickly left.

Pulling into the sawmill, I told the girls to stay close by but to stay away from the machinery.

"We're going to be turning the power on here, and this stuff could just start up, so stay away from it."

"Can we play on the pile of logs?" Tammy asked.

"Sure," Mel replied. "Just be careful."

Thad pulled the generator around to where the power came in and dropped it. I walked over with Mel, opened the panel, and started taking the cover off.

"What can I do to help?" She asked.

"Nothing at the moment, but I'll need your help, so stay close by."

Dad and Danny were stretching out the cables the engineers made for us. I turned all the breakers off and disconnected the old power from the main lugs. To get them out of the way, I nodded at the meter base and told Mel to open it up so we could pull the short piece of cable out that ran between them. She impressed me, asking for the Allen wrench needed to loosen the lugs and getting right to work on it.

Once we had the old power out, I ran the new cables into the panel using the precut knockouts at the bottom to get them in and tighten the lugs. While I was doing the power, Dad and the guys were going through the machinery to ensure there were no obvious hazards when we started testing things.

Stepping back, I looked at the panel. "Well, that should do it."

"It's ready?" Mel asked.

I nodded just as Thad and Dad came around the corner. "Looks like everything is clear in there. Nothing on any of the saws or anything," Dad said.

"The moment of truth," I said to Thad. "Fire it up, and let's see what she does."

With a massive grin on his face, Thad hit the starter for the generator. It turned over once and fired, belching a cloud of black smoke into the air. There were a couple of shouts as it settled into a steady idle.

"Now, the moment of truth," I said and flipped the main breaker on.

Since all the breakers were off, nothing happened, of course. Then I flipped the first breaker. The label indicated it was for the big saw. The breaker stayed on, and I told Dad to go hit the start button. We all watched the big blade as he walked over, looking at us apprehensively, he pressed the green start button, and the saw whirred to life. Now, there were real shouts and cheers.

We went through the various machines one at a time. The process was simple, turn on the breaker then turn on the machine. I was stunned everything worked. We had to clean a couple of birds nests out as we went along, but other than that, everything started right up. Once we knew all the machines worked, I went back through them to test the controls. Each one had a green start and a red stop button. A couple of them even had safety switches that needed to be tested as well as emergency stop buttons.

"I can't believe it all works," I said, truly surprised.

"Isn't it great?" Thad mused. "We can make any lumber we need now."

"We just need to get that trailer with the grapple on it," Dad observed.

"I know where it is," Danny said. "Let's ride over and look for it."

"You need to take this with you," I said, pointing at the generator that now sat silent.

"Oh yeah," Danny replied, "we can't leave this here. If Baker and them can get the power on out here, it won't be an issue. But for now, we'll just take it back with us."

"I don't know if they'll be able to. The power plant isn't very big, and we're miles from there now. May just have to use this every time."

"Are there any oil filters or anything for the generator?" Danny asked. "It probably needs to be serviced."

"Not a bad idea," Dad replied.

"I doubt it. But the old man is working on something with the Army. Maybe we can get some stuff from them to change the oil. The Hummer and some of the other vehicles could use it too," I added.

"Let's get it hooked back up and go look for that trailer," Danny said.

"I'll leave you boys to it then," I said. "We have to go inspect the school."

Scott and Terry really got into the construction of the grist mill with Audie, and the three men clicked well. Audie was one of those perpetually happy men. A smile on his face and genuine positive nature set everyone around him at ease. He was also intelligent and could engineer his way out of nearly any problem. He was a natural fit for the engineers.

The three men had put Thad's little red truck to work, running all over Eustis and Umatilla, looking for parts the plant couldn't provide, which wasn't all that much. The biggest thing they needed was the vessel the grist stones would be mounted in.

The grain is fed into the top stone through a hole in the center when operating. The way the stones are cut forces the meal out around the outer edge of the stones, so there needs to be something there to catch the

ENGINEERING HOME

newly ground product. This was solved with a large, galvanized water trough that was about six feet in diameter.

This freshly ground meal needs to dry. This would be accomplished with a six-inch diameter screw conveyor that would pick up the meal as it collected in the bottom of the trough and carry it to where the finished meal would be dumped into bins. The lack of any kind of bags to package the meal in was a major issue that would have to be addressed later.

Another screw conveyor was installed with a hopper on the end mounted to the ground. This would be used to shovel the grain into, and the screw would carry it up to a mezzanine level above the grist wheels, where it would dump into another hopper on the screw that fed the grain into the top of the mill. This resulted in a mill that one or two men could operate with ease.

The idea was to use the big plastic tubs oranges were transported to the plant in. One of these would be placed on a pallet jack, and a tractor with a bucket would be used to fill the bin. The bin would then be pulled over to the mill and shoveled by hand into the hopper. The same kind of bin would catch the finished product.

The three men sat on buckets looking the project over. It was complete and ready to be tested, but Audie was concerned.

"That galvanized trough is nice, but it's got a flat bottom. So the meal will have to be pushed with a shovel or something into the outlet for the lower auger," he said.

Terry sat scratching his beard. "I was thinking about that. There really isn't a good way to do it."

"What about attaching something like a vibrating motor or something?" Scott asked.

"I've got it," Audie said. The other two men looked at him expectingly. "The shaft the stones are mounted on runs all the way through them. So we could make a simple four-spoke collar for it and mount sweeps to them that are angled to push it to the hole."

Audie took a piece of soapstone from his shirt pocket and began to draw on the floor. "It'd be like this."

"Oh, I see. That's perfect," Terry said, nodding his head.

"Won't take long to make that either," Scott added.

"I know where a collar is that will work; I'll go get it. You guys want to find some steel to make the spokes and arms to mount the sweeps to?"

Terry stood up and stepped over the sketch. "I know where there's some pieces of stainless we can use for the sweeps. There's also some conveyor belt back there. Let's cut a four-inch strip and mount it to the bottom of each sweep, so we're not having metal on metal."

Audie smiled and wagged a finger at Terry, "That's a great idea. That's how that needs to be done. Alright, I'll get the collar while you guys get the other stuff."

With four men conducting the surveillance of the group, they were able to keep shifts to two hours. It was pretty tedious, just sitting and waiting for the camp to move out. Chad was on duty when one of the MRAPs came over the hill in front of the winery and down the driveway towards the highway. He took a pair of binos out and glassed the truck. Then, without looking away, he said, "We've got movement."

Dalton was lying under an oak tree with his boonie hat pulled down over his eyes. He pushed the hat up and sat up, rubbing his eyes. As he stretched, he asked, "What is it?"

Karl was already on his feet and watching the truck as it pulled onto the blacktop and turned north. "One MRAP headed north."

"Probably going to recon the route," Imri interjected. "Or to scout for a new spot."

Dalton was on his feet now and took out his small pair of Steiner Predator 10x50 binoculars. While the others watched the truck fade from view, he started scanning the camp.

"Camp's pretty busy," he observed.

Everyone turned their attention to the camp. "Oh yeah," Chad agreed. "Definitely going to break camp soon."

"They're within striking distance of Umatilla," Karl noted, still looking through his optic. "They could roll out from here and drive straight there. Be there in less than an hour."

"We need to send a message back to base and let them know there may be a recon element moving on them," Dalton said.

Chad set his binos down, "I'll prep a message."

"Is that scanner still running?" Karl asked.

Dalton picked it up and looked at the little screen. "Yes. It's set to close call. If they transmit on VHF, it'll pick them up."

"Good," Karl said with a nod. "If they have radios, now is when they'll use them."

Chad read the message he'd prepared, "One MRAP departing headed north. Potential recon moving to town. Recommend LP/Ops be established on high-speed avenues of approach. Need to add anything?"

"I think that will do," Karl said. "Encode it and send it."

ENGINEERING HOME

Sarge and the guys were busy cleaning an assortment of weapons on the house's driveway when Red came flying up on a four-wheeler. The old man had a broom handle in one with a t-shirt wrapped around the end of it, using it to push down the bore of the Gustav recoilless rifle.

When Red skidded to a stop, he paused and asked, "What's up your ass?"

Red pulled a piece of paper from a pocket as he walked over. "Just got this over the radio."

Sarge took the paper and read it. He rubbed his chin in thought when Ted asked, "What is it?"

"One of the MRAPs left the camp. Could be a recon element coming to town to take a look."

"You want to meet them? Give them a little surprise?" Mike asked.

"I want to get eyes on them, for sure. But I don't want to engage them or for them to even know we saw them. Might prevent them from coming."

"Isn't that the point?" Doc asked.

"No, the point is to kill them all at one time."

"Then we need to set up an LP/OP," Ted said.

"Yes, we do," Sarge singsonged in response. "You two get your shit together and go into town. Find a place where you can see Lake Shore and Highway 19. See if they show up." He paused and looked at Mike, "But do not engage them. For any reason."

Mike held his hands up, "Alright, alright, I'll have to wait to kill them."

"Yes, you will; now get your shit packed up, take the other buggy and get your lazy ass out of here."

In a thick southern drawl, Mike replied, "I'm not lazy, sarge. I'm just so tired all the time."

Sarge's boot shot out towards Mike. He deftly dodged it, saying, "Damn, either I'm getting faster, or you're just getting older and slower, and I don't think I'm getting faster, so…."

"Keep it up, shit head. I know where you lay your head at night. You'll wake up one of these nights, and I'll be standing over you."

Mike shivered, "That just gave me the heebie-jeebies! Just the thought of waking up to your face, coffeeless no less, scares the shit out of me."

"Keep it, keep it up," Sarge mumbled and looked at Ted, "Would you please take charge of your retarded ward for me?"

"I got him," Ted replied and walked over to Mike, putting his hands on his shoulder and saying, "Come on, Mikey, I've got a new jar of paste."

In a cartoon character voice, Mike replied, "Paste? I love paste!"

"You really should stop fucking with him before he fuckin' kills your ass," Ted replied.

"Shit, he lives for it, and you know it," Mikey laughed back at Ted.

Ted gave him the stink eye and replied, "I'll grab my kit and meet you at the wagon."

As the guys loaded their gear into the war wagon, the old man walked up with a notebook. "Here's the codes for today. Trigrams and OTP. If it's an emergency, you can transmit in the clear. Where are you thinking of posting up?"

Ted took the notebook and put it in his pocket. "Probably right there at Bay and Lakeshore."

"Do a radio check with the guys at the bunker before you head out," Sarge replied. "Find a good hiding spot and stay out of trouble." Sarge looked at Mikey, "I mean it. You two be safe."

"We will, boss," Mike replied seriously.

The old man nodded. "Alright, get your asses moving."

"I'll drive," Ted said as he climbed into the war wagon.

They stopped by the bunker and performed a quick radio check to ensure everything functioned. Once the radio was confirmed, the guys waved at Wallner and Red as they took off. The ride into town went quickly, and Ted pushed the war wagon as time was of the essence. His speed drew curious looks from some as they shot past them.

At the corner of Bay and Lakeshore in Eustis is a big yellow two-story building on the northwest corner. It even had a roll-up door on Bay Street. Some of the windows were busted out, which made getting in easy. Mike used the chain to hoist the door up, and Ted pulled in through the now open door. The first thing they did was clear the structure to ensure they were alone.

Once the building was cleared, they set up their LP/OP position in the southeast corner of its second floor. From the ceiling, Ted hung a large woven sniper's veil. It was positioned to be in front of them, between them and the window. This would hide any movements they make. All other windows on that side of the building were also covered with cardboard, scrap lumber, and even some newspaper. Again, this was just to prevent an incidental exposure from one of the other windows.

The corner was perfect as there was one window overlooking Bay and another over Lakeshore. This way, they could keep an eye on the entire area. Once the space was prepped, they settled into the long and tedious job of observation. Mike dropped his pack on the floor and laid down, resting his head on it.

"You take the first watch," Mikey said as he stretched out.

"Imagine that," Ted replied as he set up a tripod and attached a spotting scope.

I met Baker and Eric at the high school. The girls were all excited to be there. It was a kind of throwback to how things used to be and an opportunity for them to do things in the building they would never have been able to before. They quickly disappeared into the large campus, with Mel admonishing them to be careful and not break anything.

"So, what's going on with this place?" Baker asked.

"Has the old man talked to about what's coming?" I asked.

She shook her head, "No, what's up?"

"I'll have him come give you guys a full brief. But the gist of it is that DOD is sending some troops down here along with a bunch of supplies and possibly vehicles."

"Really?" Eric asked, excitement in his voice.

"*Really?*" Baker asked with far less excitement.

I nodded. "Looks that way. The old man is being made the Military governor for the state."

"No shit?" Baker asked. I nodded again. "What units are they sending, and who will be in charge of them?"

I shrugged, "No idea. I just know they are coming." Baker's face soured. "What's wrong?"

"Well, I like the idea of things moving forward, getting things put back together. But I am not excited at the thought of some shitty little officer coming and trying to order us around."

I held a hand up to stop her. "That's not going to happen. Mike and Ted already made it clear that they felt the same. The old man told them they didn't need to worry. He'd look out for our people, and no one would be shanghaied into another convention unit."

Baker let a long breath she didn't even know she was holding. "Oh, thank God." She leaned over and patted her chest. "I was so worried about that. I mean, I love the Army. But I love this *New Army* even better."

"Can't say I blame you," Mel offered. Then she looked at me and said, "Tell her the rest."

"The rest what?" Baker asked.

"It's nothing," I replied, not wanting to talk about it.

"Sarge will be the military governor, and Morgan will be the civilian governor," Mel replied with a smile.

"What?" Baker asked in amazement, then looked at me with a sly smile. "And what do you think about that, Sheriff? I mean, Governor?"

"Don't even start, Baker," I replied.

She laughed, "Alright. We'll talk about it later. First, let's go find the main electrical room. We've already energized the primary over to the school. All the transformers held none blew up."

"Alright, let's get the kitchen heated up. The old man should be bringing Kay up here to look at it."

We went into the building and located the main electrical room quickly, and started sorting out how to restore power to the facility. This also didn't take long because everything was very well labeled. In no time, we had the lights in the electrical room and all the breakers held after being energized.

We were standing in the electrical room when my radio crackled. *Morgan, you guys here?* Sarge's voice called.

"Yeah, we'll meet you at the kitchen," I replied.

Roger.

We met the old man and Kay in the kitchen. She was talking to Sarge as we came in.

"The real question is, does the gas still work?" Kay wondered as she looked things over.

"The power does," I replied as I walked in. "Let's hope the gas does."

"Good job, Baker," Sarge said as we came in and added, "Hey Mel. How's it going? Those girls excited to be out of the house?"

"Oh yeah. We're going to have a picnic later."

"He smiled, "That's nice."

"Hello, Baker!" Kay called out. "I never get to see you! How are you doing?"

"We're good, Miss Kay. How's the kitchen look?"

Kay turned back to the very messy kitchen. "Well, it's obviously been looted, but other than that, it's not in bad shape."

As the inspection continued, it was discovered that none of the appliances in the kitchen were gas, they were all electric.

"That's a bonus," Baker observed, "everything in here works. Look at the size of that mixer!"

She was looking at a gigantic Hobart commercial mixer. It was the kind of thing you would see in an institutional or commercial bakery. You could make a lot of bread at one time in the thing.

"That'll mix up a batch of biscuits," Sarge commented.

As Mel, Kay, and Baker walked through the kitchen checking things out, I asked Sarge about the guys.

"One of the MRAPs left the camp. Probably a recon element headed to town or to look for a new camp. I sent Mike and Ted out to Eustis to set up an LP/OP. They're setting up at the corner of Bay and Lakeshore so they can see both of the potential routes these assholes might take coming in."

"Shit. I hope they're not coming to town."

"Doesn't matter," he replied with a shrug. "They aren't going to do anything with just one anyway. I hope they do come to town. They won't see much, and it'll make them bolder, and that will lead to them making mistakes and us killing the shit out of them."

"I hope you're right."

The ladies finished their kitchen inspection, finding it fit for service. "Everything looks good. We can start cooking in here as soon as we have something to cook," Kay announced.

"So what's all this Governor shit?" Baker asked.

The old man shot me a glare before answering. "I'm guessing he's already told you."

"Not really. Said you would."

He glared at me again, "It ain't just me. He's the civilian Governor."

"He told me that. And you're the military Governor. What else? Something about personnel and vehicles coming?"

"Yes. That's why we're looking at the school. We need a place to billet them and someplace to store the material they're bringing with them. There's going to be a lot of stuff coming and several people. We will be tasked with some new missions that will take a lot of coordination to pull off. The best part is we will now start receiving regular supply drops from the DOD. So we'll be able to provide at least one hot meal a day for the folks in town."

"Wow," Baker replied, stunned at the revelation. "That's a lot to take in."

"We're going to be getting pretty busy."

As Sarge spoke, the girls came tearing into the kitchen with a cacophony of screams and laughter. At least they were having fun. They swarmed around Mel, begging to go on the promised picnic.

"Quiet down, girls," Mel admonished them. "We'll be done soon."

Sarge smiled at them. "Always full of energy. Don't know how they do it."

"It's called youth, Linus," Mel replied. She always called him Linus, and he never complained. But I know deep down he really wanted to, and it always brought a smile to my face.

Instead, he just smiled back at her. "Indeed it is, Mel, indeed it is."

"When is all this coming?" Baker asked.

"Soon. Very soon," Sarge replied.

"Well, if we're done here, I think it's time for a picnic," Mel said, getting a round of cheers from the girls.

I looked at the kids, and they were pretty excited. "Yeah, guess we'll go have us a little picnic. You girls run out and get in the buggy. We'll be out in a bit." The girls headed for the parking lot and I turned to Sarge. "I need to go check on shoes for the folks up in Juniper. We need to make a run up there soon."

"I know," Sarge sounded frustrated. "Just too much shit all going on at the same time."

"A-fucking-men," I replied. "I'll see you guys back at the ranch this evening."

We left the school. I was sitting at the intersection of West Ocala and Central Ave, also known as nineteen, thinking when Mel asked what was wrong.

"Oh, nothing. Just thinking about running over to the juice plant real quick to check on the mill."

"We have time. Let's do it."

I turned south and headed for the plant. I drove around to where the corn was unloaded and told the girls to wait in the buggy while Mel and I walked in. She came up beside me, taking my hand. We wandered into the vast building and looked around. The mound of corn was impressive. It would make tons, literally, of cornmeal.

We found the engineers with Audie and Cecil standing around their Rube Goldberg grist mill. I called out to them as we approached. "We making meal yet?"

Cecil looked over his shoulder, and a smile quickly spread across his face. "Hey Morgan, Mel, how are you today?"

"We're good, Cecil," Mel replied. "How's your day going?"

"Fair ta middlin."

"We're about to fire it up, Morgan. You arrived just in time," Audie announced.

"No shit? You guys are done with it already?"

"Yes, sir. Ready to see the first run?"

"Let's do it," I replied.

Audie moved around and started the various motors that ran the wheels and conveyors. I was surprised how quiet it all was once it was running. There was a large plastic tote filled with corn sitting on a pallet jack. Audie started shoveling the corn into a hopper. A screw conveyor carried the grain up and dropped it into a shaft that took it down into the stones. In short order, there was cornmeal falling out the sides of the stones. A cheer erupted from all there.

"Look at that," Cecil said as he stepped over to the mill and collected some of the meal into his hand. He pushed it around his palm with a thumb, "That's a good grind. Not bad for not even having to adjust them."

"I set the stones with a feeler gauge," Audie explained.

"Would you look at that," Terry said as he did the same as Cecil did. It wasn't long before everyone had some meal in their hands. As if cornmeal was just discovered. It may not have been a new discovery, but it was a rediscovery.

"What's the plan for distributing this to the people?" I asked.

"We're kind of in a tight spot on that end," Audie replied. "For now, we're just going to fill tubs like this one with the finished meal. Then, we can take the meal into town and give it to people in whatever container they can bring to us."

"I guess that will work," I replied. "We got the high school powered up earlier. The kitchen is fully functional. It needs a little cleaning up, but it's all there, and it looks like it all works. We'll be able to turn out at least one hot meal a day for folks in town."

"That's great," Scott said. "Not like there's too many folks left around here."

"If they're here, we'll try and feed them," I replied to him. "We're going to run. It looks like you guys have plenty to do."

Audie tossed a shovel load into the hopper and looked up. "We'll be here, got plenty to get ground up."

As Mel and I walked back to the buggy, she said, "That's amazing. And look at all this corn. There's so much."

"And this was just our first effort. Imagine what we will be able to produce moving forward."

She grabbed my arm, resting her head on my shoulder, and said, "It's really nice to see things improving, finally."

"Yes, it is, babe. Let's run to Altoona real quick. I need to talk to someone there before we head out to have our picnic."

"Where do you want to go?"

"I was thinking Grasshopper Lake."

She looked up, a broad smile spread across her face, "That would be great! They can swim if they want."

As we climbed into the buggy, I replied, "That's what I was thinking."

We made a quick run to Altoona, and I found Kelly there at his table. He had numerous pairs of carpet shoes laid out. "Hey Kelly," I called out as I was getting out of the buggy.

"Hey there, Morgan. Nice ride."

"Yeah, it's alright. I need to talk shoes."

"It's better than no vehicle," he shot back with a smile. "What can I do for you?"

I took out my notepad and marked down the shoe sizes Vincent had given me for the kids. Although the adults would get boots, we had over a hundred pairs. "I need shoes for kids. Here's the sizes."

Kelly took the paper and looked at it. As he read down the list, he would reach out on the table, pick up a pair, and set them aside. "I'll need to make a few pairs of these that I don't have. I can have it ready tomorrow if you like."

"That'd be perfect, buddy."

"Whatcha trading?"

"How about ten pounds of cornmeal?"

"Cornmeal? Where the hell we getting cornmeal from?"

"We planted a field up near Eustis, and it's been harvested, and I just left the mill that's grinding it all."

Kelly looked shocked, "We have a grist mill?"

"We do. It took some tinkering to get it working, but the engineers got it up and running with the help of Cecil and Audie."

"Who the hell are they?" Kelly asked before waving it off, "Doesn't matter. I just can't believe we have corn and a mill, that will have cornmeal. It's just crazy."

"We've been working on things for some time, my friend. Not only that, but soon, we will be turning out at least one hot meal a day at the high school here shortly."

"We don't hear shit out here. It's a total information blackout." Kelly replied.

"There's some substantial changes coming soon. Things are about to get a little better."

"They can't get much worse."

I laughed, "Never say that, man. Or Murphy will be like, *really? Hold my beer.*" Kelly laughed, and I bid him farewell and got back in the buggy with Mel and headed for Grasshopper Lake for some much-needed relaxation.

The girls were singing some song as I drove. With the wind whistling by, I couldn't really hear them, but it was awful nonetheless. But it was nice just to be out doing normal things. We passed by the ranch, waving around the burned-out hulks of the armor we'd destroyed there. It was a warm sunny day, and I was looking forward to it.

I hadn't even turned the buggy off before the girls were out and running to the water. They ran in with no regard for their clothes and just started splashing and playing. Mel opened the bipod on her Minimi and set it on the buggy's hood, and I climbed up on the bumper and sat down.

Mel climbed up beside me, and I leaned against her. "We need to do this kind of thing more," she said.

I patted her knee, "You are absolutely correct. We do need to find ways to relax and enjoy ourselves." I put my arm around her and patted her hip, "The fact we kind of have the time to do this shows things are improving, I think anyway."

"You should go get in with them. I'll lay the food out."

"I was thinking that myself," I replied and hopped off the buggy and kicked off my boots, and took my socks off as well. I removed the plate carrier and my t-shirt and took off at a dead run towards the water. The girls were all grouped up, looking at some curiosity they'd found. I splashed into the water, and they looked up. Then, seeing me headed straight for them, they all screamed, but it was too late, and I was on them. Throwing my arms out wide, I wrapped all four of them up, and we went crashing into the water.

It was bedlam. Splashing, screaming, and laughter filled the air, and it was the most beautiful melody I'd ever heard. I had the upper hand for a minute, but the girls recovered quickly and soon had one on each arm and leg, and I drug them around in the water. Then there were turns for piggyback rides, picking them up and throwing them into the water. And splashing, lots of splashing.

After about half an hour of water wrestling, I was worn out and told the girls it was time to eat. "Come on, you monkeys, let's eat. You can play more after."

We all hung out around the front of the buggy as we drip-dried. Little Bit was stuffing some biscuit in her mouth when she asked, "Mom, you going to get in the water?"

"No, sweetie. I'm not swimming today."

"Why not?" Taylor asked, "You never swim. It's not like you have anything else to do."

"Yeah, come on, Mom," Tammy said, causing Mel and I to share a look. It would certainly take some time to get used to it.

"Leave Mom alone, girls. If she doesn't want to swim, she doesn't have to," I stated. But I looked at Little Bit while talking, bounced my eyebrows, and winked at her, getting a huge smile and giggle out of her.

The girls inhaled their lunch and were quickly back in the water. I helped Mel clean up from the meal, and we walked down to the water holding hands. "You sure you don't want to get in? The water feels great," I asked.

"I would, but I don't have anything to wear. I didn't know we were coming here."

"Get in with what you have on. Everyone else did."

"No, I'll wait. Next time."

"Next time my ass!" I shouted as I scooped her up in my arms and started walking into the water. Mel protested loudly, but the girls squealed in delight.

"Throw her in! Throw her in!" Little Bit shouted.

"Yah! Mom's getting in!" Lee Ann shouted.

I was about waist deep when I stopped and looked at Mel, "Might want to hold your breath."

"Don't you…." I didn't hear the rest of the hollow threat because I threw her into the water.

She went under and came back up, wiping her face with her hands as she shouted, "It's so cold!"

"You get used to it, Mom!" Little Bit shouted.

CHAPTER 13

"MRAP is returning," Dalton called out.

"Get a message out, Chadster, find out if they saw it in town," Karl said as he took out his field glasses.

"Probably just scouted their next campsite," Imri observed.

"Might be," Karl replied. "I wish we could see into their camp to know what they were doing."

"Might be a good idea to be ready to move on short notice," Dalton added.

"We're pretty tight now," Karl replied. "Won't take us long to get it buttoned up and ready to move. We'll have to wait until they are completely out of that camp and down the road before we follow them."

"That's what I'm worried about," Chad chimed in as he prepared the message to send, "that they see us following them."

"One thing at a time, boys," Karl replied.

Mike was on watch with Ted trying to nap when the radio crackled.

Ponderosa, Ponderosa, Rogue 1.

He heard Wallner's voice come back over the radio, *Rogue 1, Ponderosa, have you lima Charlie.*

Prepare to receive traffic.

Send your traffic.

Mike took out his notepad and began copying the message. It wasn't very long, and he was soon at work decoding it.

With the message sent, Chad signed off, *Rogue 1 out.*

ENGINEERING HOME

Ted pushed his boonie hat up on his head, "What's that all about?"

"Working on it. Give me a sec."

After a minute or so, Mike read the message. "MRAP has returned to camp. Was it seen in town?"

"My guess is they were looking for a place to move camp to."

"Guess we don't need to hang out here," Mike observed.

"Naw, let's load up. I want to go by the ranch and see Janet before we go back."

"Why don't you two just move in together like Cyrstal and me?"

"She doesn't want to leave her dad, and I don't want to move out there."

"I can see that. Kind of sucks, though."

Ted laughed, "Ya think? Just a whole fucking lot! Call it in that we're coming back."

"Roger that." Mike keyed the radio mic and spoke slowly and deliberately.

"Ponderosa, Ponderosa, Stinkeye."

Stinkeye, Ponderosa, have you lima Charlie.

"Stinkeye is RTB."

Copy, Ponderosa out.

Thad and Dad walked around the log trailer, inspecting the hydraulic lines and other necessary components. Danny was up on the crane checking it out.

"No fuel in it," he called down.

"Everything looks to be in working order, though," Dad replied.

Thad was at the front of the trailer and patted the hitch, "We're going to need a bigger truck to tow this with."

"That Duece back at home should pull it just fine," Dad offered.

"Let's take the generator back and get the truck and come back for this. We'll bring some fuel and try to start it before we even move it," Danny said.

"Sounds like a plan," Dad said as he headed for the truck.

They made a quick run home and pulled up to switch trucks at the old man's place. Sarge came out of the house with Kay when he heard the Hummer pull up.

"What's the word?" He asked.

"The sawmill is up and running," Thad replied.

"And we found a log trailer with a grapple. So now we can move logs around," Danny added.

"So, we're in the lumber business?"

"Looks that way," Dad replied. "We just need to take the Duece to go get it."

"You taking the Hummer back out?" Sarge asked.

"No, just the truck. We'll get the trailer brought back here and make sure it works. It will be easier here with tools and whatnot if we need to repair it," Dad replied.

"I'm going to get some fuel for it real quick," Danny said, "I'll be right back."

"You boys want some lunch? We've got biscuits, and a delicious soup Kay made," Sarge asked.

"I could stand a bite; how about you, Butch?" Danny replied.

Dad patted his belly, "I think I could stand it."

"You men come on in and have a seat. I'll fix you up a plate."

They all went in, and Kay and Sarge filled them in on the inspection of the school. They chatted about what was coming their way soon and the delivery that was headed their way, and how it would change things in their small community.

"Sounds like they're expecting a lot out of us," Thad noted.

"They are," Sarge replied, then sipped his coffee. "But if we're ever to get this country back on its feet, it'll take a lot from all of us to it."

"They really expect us to try and survey the entire state?" Danny had returned in time to catch that part of the discussion.

"Looks that way. But they're bringing in more bodies, vehicles, and tons of supplies. We're going to establish an actual clinic in town. We're getting a lot of medical stuff. Rumors are going around that the Russians are using some biological agents. Something with Malaria."

"I've had Malaria. That shit is no fun," Dad added.

"I thought we took care of the Russians," Thad said.

"We took care of those Russians. There's still a bunch of them around. Cubans too. Funny thing about the Cubans, though, lots of them are reported to have deserted and joined the Cuban community in South Florida. I guess even 1800's America is still better than modern Havanna."

"When's this delivery supposed to arrive?" Dad asked.

"They're coming overland, and from the sounds of it, it's a pretty big convoy. We should see them day after tomorrow if they don't run into any trouble. They're bringing another tanker of diesel and one of stabilized gas as well. We're getting some Hummers and a couple of Bradleys too. Loads of ammo, food, all kinds of shit."

"Miss Kay, that was delicious," Thad said, "thank you." The rest of the men joined him in thanking her.

"Oh, it was no bother at all," Kay replied as she picked up bowls and carried them to the sink.

"Thad, old buddy, where is that beautiful bride of yours?" Sarge asked.

"She's down at Fred's. She spends most of her time down there. Keeping an eye on momma."

"That's a good thing. We're due a couple of babies any time now," Kay added from the sink.

Dad stood up, "Let me grab some coffee for the road; we have a trailer to get here before dark."

Kay walked over and handed Dad a thermos. "Here, Butch, I fixed this for you. I knew you'd want some to take with you."

He took the bottle, turning it over and looking at it. "I carried one of these every day for years." Then, looking back up at Kay, he added, "Thank you."

They quickly departed in the Duece headed back to where the trailer was waiting. There was a lot of talk about what they would do with the equipment once they had it and verified it worked. As well as discussion of it not working and possible issues that will need to be dealt with. However, in no time, they were at the trailer, and Danny was climbing up on the machine to fuel it.

Holding out a hand, Danny asked, "Pass that can up, Thad."

Danny poured the first five gallons in and asked for the next one. While he was fueling, Dad checked the motor oil and hydraulic tank to make sure they were good. Once it was fueled and the fluids checked, it was time to start it.

"Butch," Danny called, "you want to try and start it? You've got more experience with equipment than I do."

"Sure," Dad replied as he climbed up into the cab.

After a brief pause that raised the pulse of Danny and Thad, the engine started to turn over with a cloud of black smoke billowing out of the exhaust stack. Then, just when it sounded like it was going to start, the sound changed, and it was obvious the battery was dying.

"Shit!" Dad shouted. Poking his head out, he called out, "Battery is dead!"

"I thought about that. Hang on a second," Danny replied as he jogged over to the Duece. He returned with a can of starting fluid and a set of jumper cables. "Thad, get that battery out of the bed of the truck!"

Thad grabbed the battery and set it on the fender of the crane. Danny was already up on the machine opening the battery compartment and waiting for Thad to connect his end. Soon as the batteries were connected, Danny called out to Dad, and he hit the starter again. This time, as soon as it started to turn over, Danny gave the air intake a squirt of ether.

The engine whined, and black smoke boiled from the smokestack. Then the ether made it to the engine, and it started. The engine was very rough, but it settled down as soon as the ether burned off. All of them cheered at the success.

"I'm going to pull the truck around!" Thad shouted. "Danny, can you back me up?"

Thankfully the trailer had a pintel hitch because it was the only option they had. Dad stayed in the cab as they hooked up the trailer. Once it was connected, Dad called for them to back away. He was going to try the boom and see if it worked.

As soon as they were out of the way, Dad grabbed the levers and pulled back on the boom lift control. It rose slowly, and the controls were a little sloppy, but it worked. Next, he tried the swing to the left and right, and the controls responded.

"Controls are a little sloppy, and she's kind of ragged, but it works!" Dad called down before shutting it down and climbing off.

"Let's get it back to the mill then," Danny said. "It runs, and it works, so we don't need to take it back home."

"That's a good idea," Dad agreed.

"Let's get moving then," Thad added as he climbed into the driver's seat.

We stayed at the lake for several hours, letting the girls play in the water. Mel and I sat and talked, being careful not to talk about the goings-on and the current situation. We both were seeking some normalcy, and it was terrific. My plate carrier was hanging on the buggy just behind me with my radio in a pouch on it. It was on, and the whole time we sat there, I prayed it wouldn't go off.

And it didn't. Mel called the girls out of the water, and we all kind of sat around talking while they dried off a little. I wasn't worried about the seats getting wet, just freezing them on the way home. It was a beautiful warm day, and it didn't take long for them to stop dripping and be mostly dry.

"Dad, do you have anything to drink?" Little Bit asked.

"I have a Camel Bak in my ruck. I'll get it."

"It's empty," Taylor announced. "We drank it on the way here."

"No problem, give me a minute, and I'll refill it."

Little Bit looked around, "From where?"

Grabbing my pack, I took out the Sweetwater filter and headed to the water's edge. "From right here."

Setting the pack down, I assembled the pump and started filling the bladder. Mel came over with a canteen that the kids had already emptied, and I filled it. Mel took the canteen back to the buggy, and the kids passed it around. Once the bladder was full, I put the pump away and tossed the ruck back into the buggy.

"You carry that thing with you everywhere?" Taylor asked.

"What? The filter? Yes, I do."

"I guess it's a good idea since there's no bottled water anymore."

I grabbed the canteen and shook it, "This is bottled water."

"You know what I mean," she replied with a smile.

"You guys ready?" I asked.

A chorus of cheers erupted as they all clamored to get back in the buggy. We quickly bounced down the sugar sand trail that ran to the blacktop and headed home. The girls were in a good mood, and so were we. Any time the girls get a chance to burn off energy is good.

And I should have known it wouldn't last. Because just then, my radio crackled to life.

Stumpknocker, Sherrif.

"What's that?" Mel asked.

"The old man, let's see what's up," clicking the mic, I returned the call, "Send it."

Just got word from Rogue 1, convoy on the move. You need to RTB ASAP.

"Already on our way. Twenty mikes."

"Is that the people we're looking for?" Mel asked.

"It is."

Mel picked up the Minimi and opened the feed tray cover. Then, seeing the rounds securely seated, she slammed it shut. "I'm ready for them."

There was a bit of chaos when we made it back to the house. I drove straight to Sarge's place. There were several people there. Many of our group and even some of the Guardsmen. It was a hive of activity.

Mel told the girls to walk home and change their clothes as we got out. They didn't argue and were more than happy to go to the house. I watched as they walked away. Lee Ann's H&K bounced off her hip as she and Tammy grabbed at one another, giggling. It made me smile. While the submachinegun was out of place, seeing her act like a kid again warmed my heart. It provided hope, and we all needed hope.

"What's the word?" I asked as I stepped into the garage.

"All we know is they're moving. The boys have to stop to make a radio call to put up an antenna. We're just waiting on them to call in."

"So we don't know where they are right now?" I asked.

Sarge shook his head, "No."

"Are we going to be leaving soon?" Mel asked.

"I don't know when that will happen, Mel," Sarge replied.

"Then I'm going home to change clothes. After that, I'll be back."

As she turned to walk out, I slapped her ass, "I'll be here."

People began to gather at the old man's garage. Before long, Ian and Jamie were there, along with Doc and Jess. Then Mike and Ted showed back up.

"Where the hell you two dipshits been?" Sarge asked.

"Ran by the ranch to see Janice for a minute," Ted replied.

"We ain't got time for you to be playing sucky face with your girlfriend," Sarge barked back.

"Anything new?" Mike asked.

"Whole outfit is on the road now."

"Oh shit. You want us to go back?"

"Naw, not yet, Mikey. Get some chow or rest or something."

Mike cocked his head to the side, "You feeling alright?"

"Not now, Junior. Now fuck off."

"Come on, let's get our gear," Ted said.

We all hung out there for a while talking, but we all decided to move to Danny's and have dinner when nothing was happening. So we strolled down the road in a big group. There was joking and laughing, even if it was a little tense. We ran into Arron on the road, and he came up beside me.

"What's going on?" He asked.

"Looks like your friends are on the move."

"They coming this way?"

I nodded, "Looks that way. We have some people following them right now."

"Well, I hope they leave you guys alone." He replied as he stared at the ground. "Is there anything I can do around here? You know, to help out? I feel like a burden, and I'm bored."

"I can use your help," Thad said. "I've got a barn to build over there," He added, pointing to the pasture where the cows were grazing. But, he said, "The pay isn't great, but the benefits are pretty good."

Aaron brightened up at the offer, "I'm a decent carpenter. I'd love to help with that."

"We're going to get started tomorrow. We have to mill the lumber first, and then we can make the barn."

Aaron looked confused, "You guys have a sawmill?"

Thad smiled, "We do now."

Kay and Mom were busy in the kitchen when we arrived. Most walked around the house to the back porch and took seats at the table. Mel peeled off and went to the house to get the girls, and they soon joined us. I had to smile when I saw Little Bit sitting at the table doing the Jello neck bead bob. She was worn out from a day of swimming.

ENGINEERING HOME

The porch was loud with conversations, and the atmosphere was relaxed when I heard my radio crackle to life.

Stumpknocker, Stumpknocker, Rogue 1, how copy?

I quickly looked at Sarge as he rose from the table and headed for the door. I followed him as he answered.

"Go for Stumpknocker."

We believe these guys do not have any radios. They haven't reacted to any of our traffic. Going to transmit in the open to save time.

"Roger that, SITREP?"

The circus came to town. Stopped in Tavares at the boat ramp just past the bridge. Looks like they're setting up camp again.

"Copy. Maintain visual and update hourly."

Copy Rogue 1 out.

Several others joined us as Sarge spoke. When the radio chatter was over, I asked, "Should we move on them?"

"Not yet," Sarge replied. "We're going to wait and see what they do. I really want to limit civilian casualties."

"I just don't want to be surprised by them."

"We won't be. With Karl and Gulliver out there, we'll know what they're up to long before they could make it here."

As we talked, a scream erupted from the house. We all spun to see what was going on. Kay was shouting and waving a radio. "Fred's in labor! Fred's in labor! We need Ronnie and Erin to go down there right now!" Kay was almost running across the porch.

A cheer erupted from the porch as people started to move. Mel ran off with Erin, Jess, and Doc, with Kay bringing up the rear. Unfortunately, in a lack of proper planning, there were no vehicles at Danny's, and they ended up having to use ATVs to get to Fred's. Aric was on the front porch holding a radio in a death grip.

"She's in the bedroom," he told Doc as he and Erin bounded up the stairs.

Doc and Erin made it to the bedroom to see Fred reclined on the bed, her forehead soaked in sweat and Mary holding her hand.

"I don't know what to do," Mary said with a pained look on her face.

Doc smiled, "You don't have to do anything, really. This is going to take its course. We're just here to help." He looked at Fred, "How far apart are the contractions?"

"I don't know."

"Should we be timing them?" Mary asked.

Just then, a contraction hit Fred, and she let out a scream of pain. Doc checked his watch told Fred to relax. "I'm going to check your dilation to see how far along you are."

Fred was in a nightgown, and Doc put a pair of gloves on. "I know this will seem a little personal, but I have to."

Fred nodded, "Do what you have to," and licked sweat off her lip.

Mel found Aric still on the porch. He was soaked in sweat as well and pacing the porch. "Aric, we need towels and something to place the after birth in."

Aric's face went pale, "Wa, what?"

"Do you have a dishpan or something like that? Where are the towels?"

"There's extra towels in the hall closet across from the bathroom."

"I'll get those. You find us a container," Mel replied just as Fred let out another scream of pain.

"Is she alright?" He asked, looking in the direction the pained howls were coming from.

Mel patted his arm, "She's fine, Aric. It's just part of the process. Now, get me a container."

"Right, right," he replied as he stumbled away.

Mel grabbed an armload of towels and carried them into the bedroom. "Here's some towels. Aric is getting a pan or something for the after birth."

"Ok, good call," Doc said.

"Her pulse is elevated as well as blood pressure," Erin said as she peeled a blood pressure cuff from Fred's arm."

"To be expected," Doc replied.

Thad arrived at the house and poked his head into the bedroom, making sure not to look at the partially exposed Fred. "Anything you need?"

"No, we've got it under control," Doc replied and looked at Fred. "You're about ten centimeters, Fred. It's going to be time to start pushing here soon. I'll tell you when."

"We need blankets for the babies," Erin instructed.

Panting heavily, Fred replied, "They're…in….the…..spare bedroom."

"I'll get them," Mary said as she dipped out of the bedroom and around Thad.

When she returned she was holding a couple of small baby blankets and stood beside Thad. He put his arm around her and pulled her in tight.

"This is scary," Mary said.

Thad gave her a squeeze, "It's natural. Happens every day."

Mary's eyes were glued to Fred. "I know. It's just; seeing it makes it real and scares me."

Thad smiled and looked down at her, "Why does it scare you?"

With tears in her eyes, Mary looked up and said, "Because I'm going to have to do it."

For a moment, it didn't register, just what Mary had said. Thad stood there smiling, looking at his lovely wife as tears streamed down her face. All he could muster for a reply was, "Huh?"

Mary whispered her reply, "I think I'm pregnant."

Thad's eyes went wide, "You're pregnant?" He nearly shouted.

Suddenly the room was silent, and all eyes were on Mary. Kay was first to react, busting into tears and rushing to hug Mary. "Oh, Mary! You sweet thing! You're going to be a momma too! This is unbelievable!"

"Yeah, unbelievable," Thad muttered.

Mary's eyes were glued to Thad, and she wasn't sure just what he was thinking. "Are you ok?" She asked.

Thad snapped out of his trance and scooped Mary up in his arms, picking her up and swinging her around. "Yes! Yes, I'm alright! I'm going to be a daddy again! I love you, Mary!"

The room filled with laughter, cheers, tears, and some sobs. That is until the next contraction hit Fred.

"Alright, everyone, one baby at a time here!" Doc shouted.

I was sitting at a table with Sarge, the guys, and Jamie and Ian when the radio came to life.

I'm going to be a daddy!

We all looked at one another. "That's Thad," I said.

Sarge keyed his radio, "Can you repeat that, Thad?"

I'm going to be a daddy! Mary is pregnant!

It was bitter-sweet news to me. Sweet because I was happy for my friend. Bitter because it was another potential for disaster. Babies being born is joyous. But it presents the opportunity for something bad to happen to the baby and the momma. Plus, knowing Thad lost little Tony, I was sure this baby would bring memories of his son back to him.

"Well, how many more babies are we going to have around here?" I asked and scanned the faces at the table. They were all smiles.

When I got to Jamie, she said, "Don't even look at me. No way, no fucking how." We all erupted into laughter.

Then the radio broke squelch again, and *We have a beautiful baby boy!*

There were shouts and cheers. Little Bit came running over and slammed into my side. "I want to go see my babies!" Ruckus jumped from her shoulder onto the table and started picking up a few crumbs from dinner.

I roughed her hair, "Not yet, kiddo. There's only one so far, and it'll be a little bit before you can go see them. Tomorrow."

"But I want to see them now, please?" She begged.

"Not yet. Now go back over there with your sisters."

Dejected, she replied, "Ok," and scooped up her limb rat.

"Another baby," I said.

"It's good news!" Mom replied. "It's exciting to see so much," she searched for the right word, "normalcy."

"I guess so," I replied.

Just then, the radio crackled again. It was Jess, "The second baby is breech."

Sarge quickly replied, "Do you guys need anything?"

"No, Ronnie and Erin are working on it. Uh, they think they can fix it. I sure hope…." The radio went dead.

"This is what I was worried about," I said.

"That's not good," Mom added.

"Ronnie is a great doc. He's delivered babies in combat zones. I'm positive he handle it," Sarge said.

The crackled once again, *Stumpknocker actual, Stumpknocker actual, Rhino one six, how copy?*

I looked at Sarge, concerned, "Who the fuck is that?"

Made in the USA
Columbia, SC
04 July 2024